T0369309

THE REMNANTS OF PAGAROTH

THE RESURRECTION

BOOK ONE
of the Trunket Saga

J.T. SPEARS

iUniverse

THE REMNANTS OF PAGAROTH
THE RESURRECTION

iUniverse books may be ordered through booksellers or by contacting:

iUniverse
1663 Liberty Drive
Bloomington, IN 47403
www.iuniverse.com
844-349-9409

ISBN: 978-1-6632-6196-0 (sc)
ISBN: 978-1-6632-6195-3 (e)

Library of Congress Control Number: 2024907162

Print information available on the last page.

iUniverse rev. date: 06/21/2024

CHAPTER
ONE

JHAVON WAS NEVER in a hurry to get home after a long day at the shop––no matter the weather. He enjoyed walking past the warm houses with candles in their windows sills. Every now and then he'd steal a glance at certain families having dinner at their tables. However, there were some he avoided altogether, and walked by with his eyes to the ground. The dark silent ones, whose inner bitterness reflected his own misery. Miserable homes, he thought of them. Poor, rickety, shabby old things. The only ones that appeared to stare at him as he walked by....

He approached his own with dreary despair. A small cottage with dark windows. It sat behind a short wooden fence.

He could hear the excited dog whimpering and scratching at the door before he had a chance to lift the latch. It jumped on his lap when he stepped inside. "Alright now. Alright now," he said to the dog, patting and ruffling its brown fur. He reached up to yank on a chain attached to an oil lamp against the wall. Dry flint scraped the rough metal inside, drawing sparks, lighting the oil-soaked wick. A soft glow swelled from within the lamp and filled the room. The dog barked once, as if to thank him.

The soft light revealed nothing too special in the cottage. Just a few wooden chairs, and a squeak from a startled mouse that scurried off to find another shadow to hide. There was a table set against the wall to his right, where he a found a half-eaten loaf and a small block of cheese sitting in a crowd of crumbs. He broke off a tiny piece and held it in his palm while the dog took it with a sideways chomp! He took a bite of his own, then filled a mug with water from a nearby tub and sat himself on a straw mattress in the corner.

"Anything exciting happen when I was gone?" he asked his furry companion. The dog rocked a curious brow and wagged its tail. Its snout inched ever so close to the bread in Jhavon's hand. "All you ever think about is your own belly." He offered it the last bit of cheese.

After a meager supper, he stretched himself out on the bed, staring up at the dark wood in the ceiling.

He had no siblings to keep his company. Just his dog.... As an infant, he was told that his father died before he was born. His mother passed while giving birth to him. And for most of his life, his uncle, Fhelghor, saw to his care and upbringing. Well...at least he tries; as well as any dirt-poor drunk and gambler could....

Rag's Port, a harbor city just six leagues east of Ragath's river, was a rich city indeed. The revenue it received from exports kept its citizens, like Mr. Ghran, donned in fine threads and jewelry. A trunket was known for his cunning and improvisions. There was always a way for a trunket to survive in the world. So in a city like Rag's Port, poverty was somewhat frowned upon. The rich parents of children often spoke down on the poor in their presence, who in turn would tease and taunt their less fortunate counterparts with cruel words.

Jhavon had finished his basic education while his uncle was still able. He could add, subtract, and divide. His reading wasn't too awful, either. His uncle had paid for his apprenticeship as a watch-maker with the little money (he claims) that Jhavon's mother had left for him. And even that (he claims) wasn't enough to fit the entire bill. So he went into his own pockets and forked out the rest of the money to Mr. Laan, Jhavon's trade master.... So he claims.

Jhavon didn't have any real friends. Just silly boys who constantly made him the butt of their jokes. He wore ragged clothes that had different color patches that covered different holes. He owned just one pair of shoes that curled up at the front; and he saw the cobbler just once a year to replace the soles....

"What is it boy?" he asked, noticing the dog spring up on its haunches to growl at the door.

There came the rusty sound of the door's latch being raised. Jhavon sighed and laid back down. "Be still, boy," he said "It's nothing."

When the door opened, a smelly trunket stumbled inside. He wore a long coat and kept a bent posture that made him look hunched. "Dat you, Jhavon?"

"Aye," Jhavon replied from the dark corner. The pungent smell of stale mead was already beginning to fill the small room. "Just me, is all."

The dog barked.

"Quiet dat damned mutt, will you."

"Hush, boy." Jhavon massaged the dog's neck, calming it down a bit.

Fhelghor slurred and babbled off some incoherent words. He all but crushed his hat when he took it off his bald head and sat it on the table atop the bread crumbs. "Dat mutt didn't snatch the loaf I left for you, did he?"

"No, uncle. All's there when I came in."

"Well..." Fhelghor began, but then his mind trailed off to something else. He grunted again, as if the thought of something funny popped into his head....

Because of a trunket's large hands, it was impossible to fit into any shirt (or coat) by pushing the arms through the sleeves. So for this, all of their upper garments came open at the sides, and fastened with either buttons or fancy zips....

Fhelghor sat on his own straw mattress at the other end of the room and tossed his coat aside. He reached for something in the dark corner. There was a strike a match, then a candle glowed to life and cast a wavering light on his haggard face. He reached over to the candle, pipe in mouth. The flame seemed to bend toward him, as if summoned by some enchanting spell as he sucked and puffed out two clouds of stroke.

Both uncle and nephew hardly said more than a few words to each other. The days and nights often went by between them in silence. It seemed each was a consumer of time—the only commodity they could actually afford. One was yet to purchase a future of promise; while the other had long bought and squandered his away....

The following morning, Jhavon awoke to the chimes of the town's tower bells. He went about his tasks in the same monotonous order: wash himself and draw a cup of baleyroot's tea. By the time he stepped out of the cottage, Fhelghor was still fast asleep; his paddle-like hand tucked under his head; warm drool still oozing through his lips, and his pipe tipped over––spilling its ashy contents on the dry straw.

The sun always seemed to kiss the horizon in the Land of Trunkets, and the waking town of Rag's Port was not a slothful one in the least. The street vendors already had their fruits and goods on display. The young children were already skipping off to school with their books and bagged lunches. The racks in the bakery shops were already filled with fresh pastry. And the tall masts of three ships could already be seen docking in the distant harbor down town.

Young apprentices, like Jhavon, were already in their workshops. The hammering from a nearby blacksmith sang rhythmically with the morning's peal. And so did the clatter of nails and the sawing of wood.

"Hey, Trunsly!"

Jhavon turned just in time to see the yellow-haired trunket boy catching up behind him. He was older, perhaps in his late teens; he wore a sly grin of mischief that Jhavon often mistook for friendship. He was the carpenter's apprentice, who'd once sold a new watch to Mr. Laan for a price that was too cheap for the miserly watch-maker to refuse. Since then, he called out to Jhavon as he walked past the carpenter's shop each morning. It was a welcoming hail. The only one he ever received. However, this was the first time the boy had ever approached him.

"Aye, Khile," Jhavon said, with a nervous smile.

"Oh, thank Mox I found you just in time," Khile said. "The rest of these sloths are too lazy to do anything else. I need you to help me lift this box of supplies for the shop that just came in. I won't take too much of your time. I swear it."

Jhavon sighed as he eyed the big clock on the wall of the town's tower. He had more than a few minutes to spare, and Mr. Laan's shop was just a short block away. "Sure thing, Khile," he said. "Where is it?"

"Oh, it's just over here, around this bend." Khile was already hurrying down the street, towing Jhavon close behind. "Cone along now, it won't take too long." He took him around the corner to a shed filled with bales of hay.

"Where's the box?"

Khile cringed at the sudden outburst. "Not so loud, Trunsly," he said, taking a nervous glance over his shoulder. He allowed the moment to slip by before he felt satisfied they hadn't raised any alarms. He hurried into the shed and went about lifting the bales to reveal a long wooden crate hidden beneath. "Come on, Trunsly."

Jhavon grabbed one end of the crate while Khile began to lift at the other.

"Thieves, aye!" A gruff voice exploded behind Jhavon all of a sudden.

Startled, the poor trunket dropped the crate and spun around to face their accuser (who must've been close by to hear them in the shed). "No sir, we aren't thieves. Just hauling these supplies over to the woodshop."

At the mention of the wood shop, Khile dropped his end of the crate and bolted out of the shed.

"Woodshop?" the trunket asked. He had a fat mean face, and a head that sunk into his neck. "Boy, this here's no wood supplies. This here's you stealing on my property. You and that other boy. Come! I'm going to take you down to the warder's court. He'll know what to do with you."

"No, sir," Jhavon pleaded as the trunket grabbed him by the collar. "We weren't stealing. Those are woodshop supplies. I swear it. Just have a look and see."

"You must think I'm some fool, boy. I won't fall for any of your petty tricks. Why would woodshop supplies be hiding under my straw? Em...? I thought so. Come! Off to the Warder's you go!"

Jhavon was too weak to resist the trunket as he dragged him away from the shed. He pleaded his innocence once more, but his words fell on deaf ears.

He was relieved when he saw Khile coming back from around the shed. Perhaps he could convince the stubborn trunket that the crate was indeed for his wood shop. However, what he didn't see was the long metal pipe concealed behind Khile's back as he snuck up behind the trunket and bashed it across the back of his head with a good whack!

The trunket's head jerked forward. A shocked expression fell on his face and his eyes crossed over. He loosened his grip on Jhavon as he fell backward on the damp grass where he remained still as a rock.

Khile stood panting nearby, the metal pipe appearing like a brittle stick in his big hand. He looked surprised at what he's just done, staring down at the trunket's body. He could tell he was dead, just by the way his vacant eyes gazed up into the sky. He dropped his weapon, as if suddenly coming out of some deep trance, and ran off again to leave Jhavon behind. This time, he would not be returning.

As innocent and naive as young Jhavon was, it did finally dawn on him that Khile had indeed coaxed him into stealing the trunket's crate (and whatever it contained). But he would make it all right with him. He would revive him.

Then they'll both go down to the wood shop and march Khile off the warder's court together.

He knelt down next to the trunket and propped his head in the crook of his arm. "Sir," he said, shaking him gently. "Wake up, sir."

But the trunket didn't even bat his eyes that gazed up through space and eternity. Jhavon felt something warm and moist in the back of the trunket's head. It was blood! His heart froze just then. A whimpering gasp slipped throu his lips––

"What in Ragath's name is going on here, boy!?" An old trunket shouted, coming up towards them. He took one look at the pipe, the stolen crate on the ground, Jhavon's bloody hand. "Murder!" He yelled through quivering lips.

"No, no, sir..." Jhavon said, backing away from the dead trunket. "Wasn't me. I swear it."

"Murder! Murder! Fhelghor's boy just committed murder!"

A window suddenly popped open...its shutters flapping up against the wall of a house nearby. But he couldn't tell from where.

Someone screamed.

"Fhelghor's boy committed murder! Robbery! Murder!"

The old trunket began to approach Jhavon. "Come here, boy!"

Thinking of nothing else, Jhavon fled. He bolted through the street as fast as his little legs would allow.

"Murder! Stop him! Stop the boy!"

CHAPTER
TWO

HE WAS TIMING the bumps of the moving wagon, peeking through the flax that covered the cargo tray each time it rode over a stone.

Back in Rag's Part, he had managed to slip into the wagon as the farmer bargined with a local vendor over the price of fresh pumpkins he'd just hauled in from the countryside. An hour later, he was leagues away from town....

The wagon's wheel went over a large rock this time, bringing up the left side of the cargo tray. He took the opportunity and jumped out, laying still in the tall grass that hid his body.

The farmer, startled by the sudden rustling, spun around and eyed the empty field for robbers....

Jhavon waited until the wagon was out of sight (and earshot) before standing up in the grass. He knew he couldn't go back home. Anyone guilty of murder in Ragath were hanged in the town's square on the same day they were caught. And if there were any bounties on his head, Fhelghor would be the first to sell him out.

The fact that he would never see his home again didn't bother him much. His uncle Fhelghor, was as much of a parent to him as his dog was. There were no courts in Ragath. Just a handful of Warders assigned to certain districts who acted as Judges. There weren't any trials to be held. They voted either "aye" or "nay" on whether to punish the accused. And with a live witness to testify against him, the Warder would certainly vote "aye" to his execution....

He waddled westward through the tall grass, using his big hands to part the yielding blades. Unable to see the ground, he was wary of snakes––or even worst, whok holes. The field seemed to go on for leagues, but he didn't care. He'd rather be itchy and tired, than clean and rested with a noose tied around his neck.

He paused when he heard a shrieking sound rip through the air in the distance. He searched the cloudy sky, though he already had a good idea where it came from. Only twice before had he ever heard it. But he only saw it once. "A mox hound!" He dove into the grass, forgetting all about snakes and whoks. That awful shriek sounded again. A long high pitch, like grinding metal. Then came the dull flap of the giant wings.

He covered his head as the flapping sound grew louder. He thought he felt the beast snort its hot breath on the back of his neck. The warm odorous wind flattened the grass in the field. With tiger-like paws, the hound swooped down, ripping the back of his tunic before rising up into the air again.

It wouldn't miss on its next attempt!

Jhavon scrambled to his feet and dashed through the field, ignoring the thin blades that cut into his hands and face. Out of sheer panic––and a need for more speed perhaps––he raised his legs higher as he ran, as though trying to hurdle the grass that slowed him down. He could hear the beast closing in; feel its hot rotten breath pushing the grass forward. A huge shadow suddenly loomed over him, with wings as wide as a boat, spread and poised like a hawk swooping down on a rat.

The force of the beast's snout crashing into his back caused him to lose his footing, but he didn't fall, because his body was already sailing through the air. The field fell from under his feet as the mox hound took him higher and higher. The majestic sight of Ragath's Peak was like fine needles poking through the clouds across the horizon––but Jhavon didn't care to appreciate such rare beauty at that point. He struggled frantically, slapping and punching against the sweaty snout.

He pulled at the piece of tunic that was pinned between the mox hound's teeth. The inferior fabric ripped, and his body lurched down. Up ahead, the Ragath's River was quickly approaching. The beast couldn't possibly know what the young trunket was trying to attempt.

With two fat fingers placed in the new hole, Jhavon pulled the old cloth apart. It ripped all the way down, stopping at the thick stitching that ran along the collar. His body lurched down again, and he hung painfully by his neck. He couldn't breath!

Ragath's River gleamed brilliantly below. Its still surface reflecting the path of their flight in mirrored perfection.

Losing air fast, Jhavon tried again and reached up to the back of his neck where the tunic's collar stretched. He hooked two fingers between the space and pulled with his last dying strength until the last stitching finally broke! His naked body fell through the air. He could hear the hound's angry shriek as he splashed into the cold river.

—●—

He broke the surface with a loud gasp, blinking water from his eyes as he tried to locate the river bank. He judged the closer one on his right to be no more than a hundred yards, so he just cupped his big hands and swam in that direction.

The hound circled from above, avoiding the water as if it was the lake-of-fire itself.... It's said that a mox hound's fur can become very heavy when wet, preventing them from flying. If it dove behind Jhavon in the river, it wouldn't be able to get back out. It'll drawn. Rivers and lakes were like quicksand to these creatures. So for now, all it could do was shriek down at the trunket below.

As Jhavon's feet finally made contact with the river's rocky bottom, he waddled quickly to the shore and sped into the forest where the trees were all red, even the gnarled trunks and branches. A forest called: The Red Forest.

The midday sun beamed through the red leaves and cast the entire forest in a soft crimson glow. He couldn't help but feel he was running through a living womb as he went deeper into the woods. He took comfort in the midst of the scarlet cluster. No longer could he hear the terrifying shrieks of the hound. Maybe it had lost him and given up.... When he thought of this, he slowed down, allowing himself to recover from the exhaustion of the swim. He tried to peer through the red leaves, up into the blue sky, but he saw nothing.

He listened intently for the sound of flapping wings, whether off in the distance or nearby. But all remained silent, save for the rustling of the red leaves and the sound of his own ragged breathing. He leaned up against one of the trees, convinced that the danger had passed. It amazed him how much his body ached. Side-stitches started into his ribs with each breath. His mouth and throat had gone dry, throwing him into a coughing fit.

He was wet, cold, and naked. But at least I escaped the hound, he thought, as he kicked off his wet shoes. Not many could say they have. With powerful eyes, and a strong nose––inherited from the Eternal Mox himself––the mox hound was one of the best hunters and trackers in Ragath. From the air, it could follow a trunket's scent for many leagues. And with the Eternal's eyes, it has the ability to zoom in on its prey, and see through the darkness of night.

The mox hounds were all imported from the Land of Mox, and they were employed all throughout the different realms. They're mainly used for tracking, and are highly dependable because they're easily trained. And unlike dogs, they need not a fugitive's clothing to pick up on a scent. A trunket's (huge) palm print would do. The same went for any kind of body fluids. There's nothing that a mox hound couldn't track.

They'd probably brought the hound to the crate he was holding at the shed. It more than likely picked his scent from there. And if that was indeed the case, then it must surely have picked up Khile's scent on the murderous pipe. Surely, the hound must've led then to Khile first. Surely, Khile had confessed to killing the trunket and cleared Jhavon's name.

But who was he kidding? That slimy Khile must've put everything on him to save his own skin. Why else would the hound fly this way to catch him?

The sudden snap of a rotten twig disturbed his restless thoughts. He sprang up with a start and spun in the direction of the sound. It was then the piercing shriek stung his ears.

He screamed in pain under the assault. He could see the hound approaching on his left between two trees. Its long body brushing up against the large red trunks.

He stumbled back, tripping over a dent in the ground. He was too exhausted to flee, and the hound was just a few feet away. Great horns, bigger and thicker than any goat or ram's, came out of its head and curled into a pair of sixes. Though it had no mane, it resembled a lion, having two coin-shaped eyes like an owl. The huge wings were folded on its back, atop the flow of its thick golden-brown fur.

Sharp claws came out of its puffy paws and stabbed into the decaying leaves on the ground. A long pink tongue slid out of its mouth and licked at its own chops, while a black bushy tail swept back and forth as it got closer.

Jhavon scrambled up to his feet again. He was sure the mox hound had no intentions of taking him back to Rag's Port after all the trouble he put it through. He was sure he was about to be eaten!

The hound flapped those huge wings and stirred up dust and dead leaves in the air. Its face wrinkled with pure rage. It lunged at the little trunket, but something held it in place. It shrieked again...but this time, pain and agony thrummed throughout the high pitched sound. The wings flapped frantically, as if wanting to take off in a hurry.

It was then he noticed that the hound was sinking into the red foliage. It was now chest-deep in it. But Jhavon was still confused. Hadn't he just walked by on that same spot? It was solid ground!

As the hound sank into the red soil––more quickly it seemed––it wrestled and pawed at the earth, hoping to find any kind of solid purchase. Its large eyes, that once looked so deadly and fierce, now appeared to be pleading for his help. The trapped wings flapped out in the air, attempting to escape through the power of flight, but failed and dropped back to the beckoning earth. Its shrieks of terror now sounded like cries of despair as it struggled to keep its head above the ground. Red leaves and dirt poured into its mouth, cutting off the fearful cries before it went under and was seen no more....

Dead silence followed. And the ground that had just swallowed up the mox hound regained its firmness. Had it not been for the scattered leaves strewn about, it would appear as if nothing had ever been there at all.

To test the ground (as well as his sanity) Jhavon found a rock as big as his own hand and lobbed it on the spot where the hound had just been swallowed up. The heavy rock landed with a dull thud and rolled to a stop on the solid ground.

The sound of a chirping bird reached his ears just then. More followed, and soon, the entire Red Forest came alive!

It was only then he realized he hadn't noticed the absence of the birds before. As though they'd been watching the deadly confrontation in silence.... Nor was there any doubt they'd witnessed the whole thing––

"What good business do a naked trunket have with an abomination...eh...?"

"Startled, and frightened out of his wits, he spun around and found the eldest of men standing behind him. Well over six feet tall, he was probably the tallest man that Jhavon had ever seen.

It was the closest he'd ever been to a human. The man's face was old! Rough, and gnarled, like all the tree barks around them. Long white hair spilled over his shoulders on the large black cloak that had obviously seen better days.

The old man suddenly bent over with the ease and grace of someone still in their youth. His face now inches away from Jhavon; the drawn, sunken eyes, the color of mercury. "Well?" he asked in a harsh tone.

Jhavon took a timid step backward. The large hands instinctively covering his nakedness. He'd heard the most horrid tales of these savage humans: wielders of magic and casters of evil spells. And this one, appeared to be the most evil of them all!

"Well?" the old man asked again. "Aren't you going to speak? I can always pull the abomination back out of the ground, you know. Maybe she could give me better answers. How would you like that, trunket? Eh? Do you want me to bring back the hound?"

A tremulous Jhavon shook his head. "N-no..no, sir."

"Ah...." The man said with some satisfaction. He straightened himself back up again, towering over the trunket. "So, the trunket can speak.... I'd almost forgotten what your kind was like. It has been so long. I remember those hands well enough, though. Ah...it's coming back to me now. Those hands. The strange armor. Those dreadful weapons––" He paused here, giving Jhavon a wary stare. His white, bushy eyebrows, knit into a thoughtful frown. "Can't quite remember you being so small, though. You can't be no more than three feet tall. But tell me...how much are you in years, trunket?"

"Just twelve, sir."

"Twelve!?" He said this so loud, it made Jhavon cringe. "Mox hounds hunting boys? Like criminals? Hmmm.... You don't look like a criminal. How'd you come to be here then? Trunkets are forbidden from entering the Red Forest. Did you know that, boy?"

"No, sir," Jhavon replied. "I didn't know that. See, it was the hound that——"

"And what about the hound, boy?" The old man was suddenly interested in the naked trunket's strange dilemma. "Tell me."

"Aye, sir.... It was the hound, sir. The hound brought me here. Flew me all the way from Rag's Port."

"Rag's Port?" the old man asked. "You mean, Ragath?"

"Well...sort of, sir. It's the port in Ragath. So it's called Rag's Port."

"And they keep those abominable hounds in Ragath?" He stroked his long white beard as he said this.

"Aye, sir. In Rag's Port...the warders breed them up from babies, and train them. Well...the warder...he sent the hound after me because he thought I killed someone."

"You?"

"Aye, sir."

"You couldn't kill anything. I can see that from here. You haven't hurt so much as a fly in all of your twelve measly years. I can see it from here... right through your spirit."

"Well...that's what they thought, sir. I tried to tell'em. But no one believed me. So I left that place——escaped, so I wouldn't get hanged."

"Hmm...." The old man stood and thought for a while. "You can't go back to this...Rag's Port, you say? Or anywhere else in Ragath?"

"No sir," Jhavon said. His voice tremored with sadness. "I can never go back home. Or else the hounds would find me and take me back to the warder's to be hanged."

"And your mother and father? What's to become of them? They must surely be worried about you?"

"Both dead, sir."

Just by the looks of the trunket's skinny frame and wearisome eyes, the old man could tell he wasn't being well taken care of. The boy was used to living in hardship. Whoever he was living with had seen to that. He was truly alone in the world. In a world that hated his kind. "So where to now, boy?" he asked. "Now that you can never go back home, where will you go?"

Jhavon appeared as if the thought hadn't occurred to him till now. He shrugged. "I don't know, sir. I don't have to faintest idea. Maybe I'll just stay in this here forest."

The old man sighed and looked around at the trees with their crimson leaves. He weighed the odds of the trunket's survival in his mind. There were very few trunkets outside of Ragath. Nothing that he could think of would ever land in the boy's favor. He wouldn't survive on his own. Probably end up as a eunuch slave to some golem in Danwhar.

He made up his mind as he walked past the trunket, his bare feet stomping over the same spot where the earth had just swallowed up the mox hound. "Come with me, boy."

CHAPTER
THREE

NOW DRAPED IN the long black cloak, Jhavon struggled to keep up with the old man's steady strides. The garment was so big, it smothered his little body and drug more than four feet behind him on the ground. But at least he wasn't naked anymore. And he felt so warm that not even his bare toes were affected by the cold grass.

It seemed they'd left the mox hound in her grave on an entirely different world. The magnificent birds could be heard all around; many swooped down over their heads, showing off their brilliant feathers.

Flowers of all kinds wobbled in the wind on flimsy stalks. Each exuding smells, it seemed, according to color... like lavender is so supposed to smell like this...or pink with purple streaks are meant to smell like that, and so on. Rad grass grew from the earth to expose the fields of brown mushrooms, where spotted deer nibbled delicately at their plump round caps....

They traveled for the better half of the day––westward, it appears, because the old man kept the sun ahead of them. But as the sky grew faint, they came to rest near the bank of the Ghi River.

"You must be hungry, boy," the old man said, staring down at the trunket, all wrapped up in his cloak that appeared to have swallowed him up.

"Aye," said Jhavon, coming up to the old man's side. "Very much so."

Smooth stone and rocks now covered the bank, and the river had narrowed significantly since Jhavon had last seen it. On the other side, the Red Forest still stood in all its majestic splendor. Each tree competed with the other for the warmth and freshness of the clear open sky.

Jhavon looked on with great curiosity when the old man suddenly moved closer to the river and stooped down where the water kissed the land. "What are we to do now, sir?" he asked, worried that he might've disturbed him somehow. He studied the man's face in earnest: the white hair and beard that hid most of his lower jaw. He had a thin face, with many lines running along his cheeks and forehead. His eyes were puffy and dark around the sockets as if he'd just been awakened from a deep sleep.

"I'm about to catch us some fish, boy."

Jhavon gave him another curious look, then stared dubiously around the bank. "But, sir," he began. "How can you catch fish without any poles and lines?"

"Poles and lines?"

"Aye, sir. A pole to tie the line; and...oh...a hook, sir. And bait...you need bait for the hook. A worm is good bait."

"And this is how trunkets catch fish?"

"Aye, sir." Jhavon replied proudly. "A trunket can catch any fish."

"But I'm no trunket, boy," the man said. "Besides...I have my own methods...." And with that, he went right back to staring into the surface of the water.

As the moments went by in silence, Jhavon heard the sudden flickering of water from somewhere in the river, but had looked up too late to see what it actually was. Only the faint ripples remained on the surface. But then... from the shallow part of the river, came the long body of a large salmon, swimming through the water until it came sliding right up on the slippery rocks of the river bank.... He stood, frozen and amazed, upon witnessing the bizarre scene––

"Don't just stand there, boy!" the man shouted. "Go get the thing before it changes its mind!"

Snapping out of his stupor, Jhavon dashed across the few yards on the rocky bank and jumped on the fish as it flapped about like a mad bull.

"Is that one enough? Or do you think we need another?"

"No, sir," he said. The fish was as big as his own body. "This one will do quite enough. Enough for three or four––"

"Trunkets, you mean."

Jhavon paused (his fat hands holding the big fish down) and considered what the old man had just said. "No," he managed to say, after a moment's thought. "I think you're right, sir. We might need one more...."

———•———

The day had eventually faded into the night, and even the Red Forest (with all of its enchanting wonders) would take to the shadows like everything else. A small crackling fire blazed and danced between the old man and the trunket.

The skeletal remains of eaten fish lay in the flames, burnt and charred like scorched twigs.

Still wrapped up in the large cloak, Jhavon sat quietly near the fire, listening to the nightly sounds of the forest, while the dwindling flames sent small specks of glowing embers up into the air. The old man was sitting nearby—eyes closed, rubbing thoughtfully at his white beard. Long pointy nails jutted out from the tips of his fingers. Every so often, he would give an occasional grunt, or shake his head disdainfully as he held some secret debate in his mind.

Jhavon would often pause to look up at him, intrigued by the man's own private thoughts. The human was the most strange and mysterious man he'd ever known. But come to think of it...he was the only human that Jhavon had ever known. Of course he'd seen humans many times before. Rag's Port always had them roaming about her docks and taverns. They were loud and boisterous creatures, with an insatiable appetite for trunket mead.... Mr. Laan always said that humans were nothing but tall trunkets with small hands. But never had Jhavon seen a man as old, withdrawn, and magical, as this one....

Though he'd eaten a small portion of his fish, his belly was more stuffed than he could ever remember. The old man however, after having eaten his entirely, took to eating what the trunket had left untouched. And yet, he still regretted that he hadn't caught two more.... How could any human do such things...? The little trunket was more than anxious to find out.

"Sir..." his voice had grown soft and weak from sitting in silence for so long. He was barely heard above the din of the crackling fire.

"What is it, boy?" the man said. One of his silver eyes peeked open and reflected like metallic chrome off the campfire's dwindling light.

"How..." Jhavon began, but then paused as he searched for better words. "Why did the fish come on the land like that?"

The man's eye squinted for a moment then winked shut again as he continued to stroke at his long beard. "Because I asked then to."

"But how, sir? I don't remember ever hearing you say anything to them. And even if you did, how can the fish hear you under all of that water?"

"There're methods to these things, boy. Methods that a young trunket would not easily understand."

Jhavon found himself confused again. It was the same answer the old man had given him when he asked about the camp-fire that seemed to light itself. 'I have my own method', was all the old man had said. He never explained anything....

The next morning, Jhavon was stirred from his sleep by something cold and wet rubbing against his cheek. He turned and opened his eyes just in time to see a long pink tongue as it gave his forehead a sloppy lick.

With a frightful gasp, he swatted at the beast and scrambled up to his feet. He rubbed at his face, trying to clear the smudgy vision of sleep from his eyes, then gazed at the thing that had nearly startled him to death in the dawn's dim light. A horse! No.... A young colt. A brown one...with a crooked white line running down the length of its snout. It stomped an impatient hoof into the ground and jerked its head upward with a loud snort.

"Well boy...?" the man said, coming up from behind.

Jhavon spun around and saw him mounted on his own horse. A light-gray beast. Fully grown. Spotted with brown and black blotches here and there.

"Don't tell me that you don't have any horses in Ragath."

"We have horses, sir. But this one's so––"

"But nothing, boy. Don't you know how to ride one?"

"Just a little, sir."

"Well mount the thing, so we can get going. The day's not going to wait for us you know."

"Aye," said Jhavon. He moved with caution toward the young colt, then rubbed a comforting hand along its neck and back. The same way he was taught, as all trunkets do, when mounting a horse for the first time.

The colt didn't have a saddle, nor any bridle or reins of any kind. It was still wild, having never been ridden before.

Only when Jhavon felt satisfied enough that the colt wouldn't bray and buck under his weight, did he finally hop onto its back.

The colt neighed and shied to its left, threatening to rear up on its hind legs. But Jhavon held steady, patting and rubbing gently along the animal's neck until it began to relax and he felt safe enough to ease his grip on the thick black mane.

"Well, come on then," the old man said, with a hint of approval sewn between his words. He turned his own horse around and kicked it into a slow gait through the forest.

Jhavon steered the colt past the spot where they'd camped the night before. He noticed that only a clear space remained; just dirt and leaves, as though a camp-fire hadn't blazed there at all....

As the sun made its slow trek across the sky, and the morning's dew began to dry, the two rode on. The sound of rushing water from the river nearby gradually reduced itself to a trickling pour as Ragath's River finally came to an end in a small creek.

As they spent more time together, Jhavon felt he was beginning to understand the old man a little better. Though they hardly spoke, he imagined the man might be something from out the many tales he'd heard of treelings, rykes, and so many other mythical things. He figured the old man was probably some guardian of the woods––though he dared not ask.

"Sir," he began, after a long thought. "Where do these horses come from? I mean...how did you find them?"

"I didn't find them, boy," the man said. Four gutted fish hung from two vines along his horse's neck. "They found us.... Same as the fish."

"Where are we going?"

"To Pagaroth."

Jhavon knew all too much about Pagaroth. The land of shamans, protected by the Ghi River, encircled by the impenetrable peaks of the Eternal.... It was said that Pagaroth had erected those mountains to protect his offspring during the war of the gods. "And why Pagaroth, sir?" he asked. "What's in Pagaroth?"

"Because it's the only safe place that I know where to send you."

"Sir...."

"Aye."

"What's an abomination?"

"Why do you ask that?"

"Because I heard you call the mox hound an abomination. We never call mox hounds abominations."

"Well, that's what they are, boy."

"And why is that, sir?"

"Because it's unnatural. Made and mixed with different other things. These lands are filled with them."

"Mox hounds?"

"Not just mox hounds. There are many others. Things that weren't meant to be."

"You mean...the mox hound wasn't meant to be?"

"Aye. Among many others, far worst than mox hounds."

"What could possibly be worst than a mox hound?"

"Pray that you never find out, boy."

"What about this forest? Do abominations live here?"

"No abomination can ever live in the Red Forest.... The goddess, Laap, saw to that."

"Was it Laap, who made the trees red?"

"That she did, boy."

"And why's that, sir?"

"To mock your god, Ragath.... It is his waters that flow into her lands. So she turned the trees into the color he hates most."

"And shat about the abominations? Why are they forbidden from living in the Red Forest?"

"Because they have no soul. But not only that...the goddess saw them as a curse on the land. And because they were Llok's own creation, she couldn't just rid them into extinction, either. So with the help of Pagaroth, she cast a clever spell in the earth (without Llok knowing), making it thirst for the blood of all the creatures that aren't pure."

"So the mox hound is not a pure creature?"

"Very few things are truly pure in this world, boy. And Laap's spell wasn't perfect. You don't have to be an abomination to spend your last days in the Red Forest. As it turned out, there're much worse things. As many unfortunate folks have found out for themselves...."

For three whole days and nights, the two made their way through the forest until they finally came into the Land of Laap.

At first sight, the green trees and sprawling fields that covered the land appeared unnatural to Jhavon's eyes. For leagues, this land rose upon rolling hills. Tall rocky mountains stood to the east with their jagged, snow-capped peaks. Rich farmlands stretched out in the distance with their old barns and mills appearing to be nothing more than discarded toys.

The old man steered them clear of the villages, preferring to stick to the wooded areas instead. Something Jhavon thought strange, but didn't bother to ask. He spent most of his days in sheer boredom while the old man pondered on private things to himself. On nights when it rained, there was always a cave (or rocky formation of some sort) that was available to accommodate them and their two horses. The old man never hunted, because their food always came to them, either by land or air. Berries, apples, and pears grew from the strangest of places and seemingly always in the way of the path. All the young trunket had to do was reach down from his mount and pick the fruit right from the stem....

They soon came to the Ghi River, just days after coming out of the Red Forest. On the other side laid the land known as Pagaroth, at the heart and center of Hagaraak. There, they were met by one of the strangest looking creatures that

Jhavon had ever seen. It conducted a small ferry boat that took passengers back and forth across the river. A hunched figure it was... wearing a black hooded cloak that hid most of its pale, damp face, that looked as if it sweated slime. There were no fingers, or feet, that Jhavon could make out, except for a shy tentacle that would peek out of its sleeve every so often. Though he only saw it move just a few inches to make room for them as they boarded the ferry, it moved as if it slid on wheels or floated on air. The writhing tentacles that hid beneath its bulgeous garment made slick, slithering sounds on the ferry's deck.

The creature didn't speak, though it seemed to communicate with the old man, who held out two golden pebbles in his palm that was quickly whisked away by one of its sticky tentacles.

Only then, was the ferry pushed away from the shore. Though not by any poles, rods, or oars of any kind. But from a sudden shift in the river's current that seemed to contradict its natural flow....

"What kind of creature was that?" Jhavon asked, once they mounted their horses and left the ferry on the other side of the river.

Unlike the pure blue skies of Laap, the billowing clouds that covered Pagaroth were so thick, clustered, and gloomy, they left no room for the sun to shine through. Within them, quick flashes of lightning streaked, followed closely by the sonorous thrum of thunder.

"Mannix, is one of the remnants of the Eternal Baas," the old man replied. "Only they can command the water of the rivers and seas. But this one's also a sorcerer, skilled in the art of magic."

"What's a sorcerer?"

"You'll soon find out, boy. These lands are filled with them."

A bright flash illuminated a portion of the sky just then. The deafening sound of thunder roared, causing the trunket to cringe while looking up at the sky. "Think a storm's brewing, sir," he said. "Maybe we should find shelter."

"Hasn't been a storm in Pagaroth for thousands of years. Hasn't rained a single drop since then, either."

Jhavon frowned, for he thought this strange. Because as far as his eyes could see, the land of Pagaroth was covered in green grass and tall leafy trees. And contrary to what the old man had just said, to looking up at the dark, billowing clouds above, it looked as if it rained in Pagaroth everyday. "But how, sir? With all the clouds and––"

"The clouds mean nothing," the man cut in, grimly. "Your ancestor, Ragath, brought changes to the natural world once he figured out how to do it. He cursed the sky over Pagaroth, and forbade the sun from warming the land, forever. Only through the richness of the land––and the Ghi River––do things still survive. Both Pagaroth and Baas saw to that."

"But those are just stories, sir. Tales told over the years. Like the rashweeds that grow everyday in Ragath. No matter how many times you pull them out, they'll always grow back."

"I don't believe in stories, boy." The old man kicked his mount into a steady gait....

For the nights that followed, it became apparent to Jhavon that the old man might've been right about the skies over Pagaroth after all. The constant flash of lightning and the incessant drumming of thunder seemed to dominate everything else that was to be seen and heard in the land. They encountered folks who greeted them with wary stares as they rode by.... The people were as unfriendly and reclusive as the looming clouds that darkened the sky and cast their land in perpetual gloom.

Never before, in all his short years, had such a place rubbed off so negatively on the young trunket....

It came to the eleventh day of their journey when the two eventually came over the crest of a grassy hill that overlooked the expanse of a great castle. Huge stone and rock (imported from the giants' dominion in Gargaath) formed her walls like pieces of a dismantled puzzle that was ingeniously pieced back together. Her countless windows were as clear as crystal glass. So tall––from her foundation to her steepled roofs––she stood at least 100 feet. Her massive gates stood no less than 30 feet. The high walls stretched so far out in the distance, her rooks appeared to be leagues apart.

"Go down there, boy," said the old man, tossing a small pouch at the trunket. "Give that to the one named Shurlan, and tell him that you are to be admitted into his school."

The pouched looked so tiny in the trunket's big hands. He wondered what it contained that was so important for this...Shurlan...to have, but he dared not ask the man, who never seemed to be in the mood to answer his questions. "Aye, sir..." was all he said. "Only Shurlan will have this pouch. And I will tell him to admit me into his school––" but then he paused, and a thoughtful frown disturbed the curious look on his face. "Uhmmm...what kind of school is this school, sir?"

"You'll soon find out, boy. Now get going."

"Aye, sir," Jhavon replied, then kicked his colt into a careful trot down the steep hill. He soon stopped when he noticed the old man wasn't following close behind. He turned around to find him still mounted on the hill-top. "Aren't you coming, sir...?" His timid voice just barely above a whisper.

"No..., I have other things to tend to. Here is as far as I go, none further. Get going now, and be well.... Go on...."

"Aye, sir," replied the trunket, swallowing a sorrowful lump. He'd grown quite attached to the man, despite his harsh tone and manner. He wondered why he couldn't at least accompany him down to the gate, but (like so many times before) he dared not ask. He simply turned back around and headed down the hill.

As he got closer to the gate, his heart swelled when he heard the thumping hooves bearing down on the ground behind him. Surely, it must be the old man! He probably changed his mind and decided to come along after all!

But when Jhavon spun around, all he saw was the spotted gray, bare-backed and unmounted.

He stopped, allowing the horse to catch up while he scanned the hilltop...but the old man was nowhere in sight. With a doleful sigh, he kicked at the colt again and trotted the two horses toward the castle's gate.

CHAPTER
FOUR

THE KINGDOM OF Pagaroth, like those of Laap, Llok, Ragath, and Mox, had endured the test of time from when the Eternals still lived and the lands were joined as one. It was here, where a great battle took place between the mighty trunkets of old and the remnants of Pagaroth. It's these very same walls (of this fortress of a castle) that stand now, so seemingly endless in length. So formidable. So impenetrable. And yet...it had once fallen to the sons of Ragath, gifted with the knowledge of commanding the ground-fires to erupt from the depths of the earth.

Aye...these walls had once fallen!

Blown apart from beneath!

Those same stones; once set in place by the giants of Gargaath, sent scattering up through the air like dead leaves in the wind.

From the empty sky, the Eternal Ragath opened up his portals and unleashed his hordes of abominations and creatures from other realms. Fire-breathing beasts, and beings possessing strange magic. Hellish creatures, more hideous and dreadful than the fabled demons of Danwhar, whose skin and hide were as impervious to sword and arrow as the trunkets' armor.... It was they, sent by Ragath to slaughter the descendants of Pagaroth at these very gates.

Aye...as well as those mighty trunkets of old, to whom the kingdom of Pagaroth had once fallen....

A knock came from the door and roused Shurlan from a deep sleep. He rose slow and muddled, stirring in his large chair as the knocking persisted.

"Come," he said, coughing the frog from his dry throat. There was an opened scroll on a granite desk in front of him. The flame of a half-burnt candle appeared smudgy in his blurry vision.

The door eased open with a long creak as a man, donned in a fine purple tunic, entered the room. He had long black hair with gray strands in most places; same as his beard that was trimmed low. "There's someone at the main gates who wishes to speak with you," he said, coming around the desk.

"And what is this man's purpose for coming here, Jhekath?" Shurlan asked.

"We don't know. He wouldn't tell us. He only wishes to speak to you. And..." he paused, as if bracing himself for Shurlan's anticipated reaction. "He's no man. He's a trunket."

"A trunket?" Shurlan said, with a curious frown. "Trunkets haven't roamed these lands in ages. Are you sure?"

"Aye. It is a trunket. Hands bigger than my head; much shorter than this desk. And he appears to be just a boy at that."

"Demanding to speak only with me?"

"Aye."

Shurlan leaned back in his chair for a moment's private thought.... A trunket boy, was what Jhekath had said. Being a lykine, remnant of the Eternal Llok, Shurlan had inherited all of his ancestor's lanky features. He was quite slim, standing well over eight feet tall. To accommodate for his unusual size, all of his chairs were specially built. His long limbs were like twigs, and his hands were so thin that the sleeves of his silky green robe hung several inches from his wrists. He had bright green eyes that shone like emeralds on his narrow face that hid behind a long white beard, and a head full of flowing white hair. "Let's go see what this is all about then." When he rose from his chair, he towered over Jhekath by two feet. "A trunket, all alone in this kingdom, is one thing. But a trunket boy, coming into this kingdom and wanting to speak to me, is quite another."

"My thoughts were just the same. It's the only reason why I didn't send the boy away...."

The two walked purposely through the castle's great corridors, then outside, ignoring the curious stares of all those they walked by. He could hear the whispers and murmurs of the people...the "great" Shurlan, rarely seen outside the confines of his own study, was now hurrying though the courtyard toward the main gates.

———————•———————

Though seated on his colt, the young trunket couldn't help but feel overwhelmed by the enormity of the castle's great walls. Each of its stone blocks were larger than him in both weight and height. The wall stood as tall as any one of the giant morgahs in Vlak's Forest. He got the strangest feeling whenever he stared up at the rook high above, as if the prominent slab would suddenly tip over and crush him.

At the main gate, he appeared as a tiny mouse, sniffing at the bottom crease of a door six feet tall. The wood smelled old. Older than any lump of rotting log in the forest....

The gate shuddered open with a crack so loud that it startled the horses. The crank of sorrowful groans soon followed as huge rusty chains turned gears that caused the main gates to open outward. The horses both shied away to avoid being struck as the gates opened just wide enough to allow the tallest of men to come stalking through.

But this was no ordinary man!

Jhavon knew this much, as he studied the creature that approached him. Humans are never that tall; nor should they be as slim as this creature was. A lykine maybe...or a treeling. But not a man.

"I was told that you wanted to speak with me," Shurlan said, giving the trunket and his horses a wary look, before sweeping his eyes across the rim of the surrounding hills. He felt kind of silly, half-expecting some great trunket army to come rolling over the dark slopes.

"Are you him, sir...? Shurlan, I mean.... Are you Shurlan?" The trunket shivered visibly under the looming figure, whose green silky robe flopped in the wind like a lazy flag.

"I am Shurlan. But who might you be? And how is it that you're here at our gates? And——" he paused, regarding the other riderless horse that wasn't fitted with a saddle. "And where's the other trunket that came with you?"

"There's no other trunket, except me, sir. But an old man once had this horse.... My name's Jhavon, and I——"

"So where's this old man now, Jhavon?"

Jhavon swallowed nervous lump before he replied. "He's not here, sir. But he says that I must speak to you."

"He did?"

"Aye, sir."

"And why so, Jhavon?"

Jhavon shrugged. "I don't know, sir."

"Then what message did this...old man...say you should give to me?"

Jhavon raised a clenched fist and opened it slowly, revealing a small pouch in his palm. "It belonged to the old man, sir. He said that only you should have it."

Shurlan reached out with his long fingers and took the pouch, squeezing and feeling on the hard object inside. He poured the content out in his palm and gave a shocking gasp when he saw what it was. "Where did you get this, boy?!" His voice took on a grim tone.

"The old man, sir. He told me that only you should have it."

Shurlan gazed down at the blue gem in his palm. It was a shard from Ragath's sapphire. Just one of the thousands of pieces that had been broken and shattered by the Eternal goddess, Laap. "Tell me, boy. What did this old man look like?" His eyes roamed across the hills again, more carefully this time.

"Very old, sir," the trunket began. But then he hesitated, unsure of how to describe his old companion correctly. "He could easily be 80, or 90, or maybe even 100 years old. Long white hair. Silver eyes...like shiny––"

"White hair and silver eyes, you say?"

"I should think, sir. Aye. Silver eyes...like shiny metal."

"And what else, boy?"

"He gave me this cloak," Jhavon tugged at the black cloak, still wrapped protectively around his body. "Because I lost my clothes, trying to escape the mox hound in the Red Forest, Well...the old man killed the hound. Buried it in the ground.... Or...or maybe the forest did."

"The Red Forest, you say?"

"Aye, sir."

"And what business do trunkets have in the Red Forest?"

"None at all, sir. I think. But it was the hound——"

"The mox hound?"

"Aye, sir," Jhavon replied, after a moment of hesitation. But then he went on to describe the events of the past eleven days. And as he came to the end of all his accounts, Shurlan regarded him with less suspicion than he had before. He was quite certain that he knew the true owner of that black cloak. And not to mention the piece of sapphire he still held in his palm.

"And you say that these horses came from the Red Forest?" Shurlan asked, walking over to the spotted gray, passing a delicate hand along its smooth back.

"Aye.... The old man couldn't have gotten them from anywhere else. He told me that it was they who found us. Same as the fish, sir.... And he said that I am to attend your school."

Shurlan gave a low grunt as he became very amused by the trunket's tale.... His old master hadn't changed one bit. "So tell me, boy. What can you do?"

"Do...sir?" Jhavon became confused.

"Aye....For you to attend my school, you must be able to do something. Anything?"

"Well...I can fix a watch. Or a clock. Any watch or clock for that matter. It doesn't make the slightest difference what kind it is. If it ticks, then I can fix it."

"A watchmaker?"

"No, sir. Not a watchmaker. I only learned to fix them so far. My old teacher, Mr. Laan's the watchmaker."

"Then what else can you do, boy?"

"Uhmm...nothing else, sir."

Shurlan eyed the young trunket, seated on his wild colt, donned in nothing but his old master's cloak, in a land where trunkets hadn't set foot on in centuries––perhaps for many millennia. It was obvious that he'd been unwillingly cast from his own land. The boy was destined to be a watchmaker, perhaps the best in Ragath. But destiny––as the old lykine had witnessed so many tines before––can, and do sometimes change.... The trunkets had came close to ruling the entire world at one time. Not through magic, or sorcerery. But with science. The Eternal Ragath himself, given enough time, had came into possession of great power. But Ragath's gone now. And the trunkets, with their clever tools and machinery, are all that's left remaining of him. As are the remnants of all the other Eternals, but at least they still possessed some kind of magic. And even they, as the centuries went by, had become rare and scattered, compared to the days of old.

What harm can one soft-hearted trunket bring to the land of Pagaroth?

"Come boy," said Shurlan. "Let's not keep these gates open any longer.... And bring these fine horses with you."

CHAPTER
FIVE

THE SUN DID little to shine through the dense clouds that covered the sky over Pagaroth, except cast the land in a shade of the darkest gray. As the day wore on and the night slowly crept in, complete blackness would fall and another everything in sight. There aren't any bright twinkling stars and full moons to see here.... Better if one didn't have any eyes at all, perhaps. Or birthed in the deepest cavern in the earth.... Only through the aid of lit torch, can one venture (with much caution) outside the comfort and safety of their own home....

In the castle's gardens...between the rows of neatly trimmed shrubs and hedges, Shurlan stood. Behind him, light shone through the castle's many windows to cast his long dreary shadow on the ground's lawn. Quick flashes of lightning sparked within the enveloping clouds to illuminate the land for the briefest of moments.

"What else can harbor a lykine's thoughts for all eternity, other than times long gone?"

A strange voice. Coming from nowhere, yet sounding from many places. A voice spun from the wind, instead of the mouth. Each syllable, each word, bouncing, swirling, gripping, then slipping through time. Echoing, then fading from his ears.

"Even after all these years, Morella," Shurlan said, staring across the black horizon. "He still refuse to set foot on this land. His own land."

"At least not for too long," Morella replied. Her words thrummed like two plucked strings.

A playful wind tugged at Shurlan's fingers where he held his old master's cloak. He loosened his grip and allowed the enchanted garment to slip from his hand. The cloak floated in mid air, then made a swift glide over his head, slowly circling around him like a black ghost. "How is it, that a trunket boy––of all creatures––can bring such a man back to Pagaroth?" It appeared as if the cloak had asked the question while it hovered above the ground in front of him.

"The boy's life was in danger," Shurlan said. "But I don't think that had much to do with anything. It was the boy's pure heart."

The cloak spun quickly around, fanning out in the air. But then it straightened up suddenly and folded itself in two.... A pale hand materialized beneath the fold as a woman, dressed in a long white gown, shimmered into existence from a thin mist of wispy smoke. An Elemental! A remnant of the Eternal Mox, made from the wind and the very clouds that formed her shape––never appearing completely solid. Her face was just a swirling mist. Her gown, nothing more than thin smoke. When she moved, she managed to keep that ghost-like image of hers intact, allowing only thin trails of vapor to fade behind her.

"I know all about this trunket, Shurlan," she said, gliding across the lawn to replace the old man's cloak (seemingly without notice) back into his hand. "But what do it mean?"

"I must assume that you were with us at the gate then." Shurlan's tone carried a hint of contempt for Morella's eavesdropping.

"I was."

"Then you heard all what the trunket had said. And you what he possessed."

"A shard from Ragath's stone.... But maybe the pouch was protected with magic."

"It was not. I would've sensed it."

Morella rose up from the ground, head tilted up to the black sky in prayer....

Bright lightning streaked behind the clouds, but then froze, as if trapped in time. On the ground, the castle and the surrounding gardens remained illuminated. The captured light revealed suspended bats in mid flight, and snooping moles on the grass that were stuck in motion.

The Elemental's trick of stopping time was the only way that light could be captured long enough to wash the black from Pagaroth's skies. However, it kept everyone (and everything) else frozen in time as well.

"And like I said before, Shurlan," she said, as she floated back down. "What do all this mean? No living mortal can ever set foot in the Red Forest. Nor can he touch that which is empowered by an Eternal, much less carry it around as if it was his own."

"It means the trunket is no mere mortal. He was born in the lands that surround Ragath's Peak. And no one's ventured that far into that cursed land in ages. Who knows what kind of pure bloodlines still exist there."

"A trunket of old blood, Shurlan?" Morella sounded concerned. "Wouldn't it be dangerous to have him here? What if––"

"What, Morella...! There's nothing here for him to do. He has no enemies here. No cause. No purpose. His dreadful kin haven't walked the earth for thousands of years.... Days long gone, as you say. We have nothing to fear from this one. His heart is pure. He came to us, wrapped up in my master's cloak."

"So you want him to remain here in Pagaroth?"

"I have no other choice, Morella. It is not my wish, but that of my Master's. He wouldn't have sent him to us if he thought it would put us in the way of harm."

Morella sighed. "For our sake, I hope that Rahjule is still sound of mind, Shurlan."

"That's no concern of yours."

"Well...I guess it's farewell for now then."

The Elemental waved Shurlan a solemn goodbye. Like blown smoke, her form slowly drifted away and down between the neat rows of hedges until all signs of her had vanished.

At the bat of an eye, the lightning flashed and darkness immediately followed as the movement of time commenced and nature continued at its normal speed.

As Shurlan watched the last trails of Morella whisk behind a circular shrub, he clenched tightly to the old man's cloak. "You're never truly away, are you?" he seemed to ask it, regarding the lifeless material in the window's light. He allowed the cloak to slip from his grasp and fall to the ground.

The grass squirmed to life just then, and grew until its short blades covered the enchanted cloak and pulled it into the earth....

Back in the warm confines of his study, Shurlan walked along the rows of shelves, where an endless amount of scrolls (records of both the ancient and modern times) were kept. Just a fraction of his magic was used to send a candle floating down a dark aisle to light his way. The countless parchments constantly drifted in and out of light and shadow. He caused it to stop before rounding a corner, lowering it close to the floor while the mellow flame swayed from side to side. He found the two voluminous scrolls he sought and pulled them out from the bottom shelf.

Once seated back at his old desk, he prepared the ancient records, using a subtle spell to carefully unroll them so as not to ruin the brittle parchment. Both were written in the old language, perhaps 4,000 years ago, but not much older. Their author, an unknown oracle, predicting the return of the Eternal, Ragath. It asserted that the Eternals, Pagaroth and Laap, hadn't truly perished like the others, who'd become undone when Ragath removed their essence from the world. Instead, they'd been sent to the netherworld, where they must dwell amongst the lost souls of the goddess for all eternity. However, as for the Eternal Ragath, such was not the case.

According to popular theory, the portal god must've surely used one of his own portals to escape the netherworld the instant he found himself there. He would then spend the next few eons trying to find his way back to earth, traveling through the countless other worlds and dimensions until eventually discovering the right gate to Hagar.... Ragath's return, according to prophecy, is an inevitable one. And in the absence of the powerful Eternals to resist him, the world would easily fall into his hands....

The second scroll foretold the many signs that would mark the Eternal's return. Most were inaccurate and misleading, and therefore discarded as crazed ramblings all throughout the millennia. All, except one...which Shurlan was now vigilantly searching for.

Many hours would go by before the last of the two scrolls stopped rolling. It rose higher in the air and stretched itself out at full length before the dying candle's dwindling light while Shurlan read the ancient script. "There will come a time, when Ragath will find a world very similar to our own. And in this world, all the other Eternals will still exist and there will be peace all throughout those lands. With much greater knowledge than he'd ever possessed before, he would destroy the Eternals of this world, including his own self. And when this happens, the force of the power that created us all will be caused to form another. But this new creation will not be another Eternal, for this new creation will be of flesh and blood. And this one will come into the dark realm of our world, bearing relics from the lost Eternals Laap and Pagaroth. And from this day, be warned, the return of Ragath is surely near."

The scroll rolled itself back up and floated down gently onto Shurlan's desk.

With a heavy sigh, the ancient lykine leaned back in his chair and pondered on what the passage meant. Out of sheer necessity, the creation is always forced to cause some kind of intervention to come into existance. It was why the Eternals were created. However, creation cannot destroy itself.... Rousing himself from this muse, he got up and walked over to the far end of the wall. He stooped down and pulled out a loose brick, exposing a hidden compartment. He reached in for the small golden box that sat there, and when he opened it, a brilliant blue light filled the entire room.

Inside this special box, was a huge chunk of Pagaroth's sapphire that had been pieced back together throughout the ages; though it was only less than half of its original size. The rest of it was still lost to the world.

Shurlan took Jhavon's pouch and dumped the tiny shard into his palm. It immediately took on the radiance of the larger sapphire in the box. He felt a bit surprised that the shard was indeed kin to this powerful gem (for all purposes, he secretly hoped that it wasn't), but when considering the bearer, there shouldn't have been any doubt.

Solely on its own, the shard rose from his palm and floated into the box, where it refitted itself into its broken slot.

If the prophecy proves true and Ragath do return, Shurlan thought, as he closed the box and slid it back into the wall. May the gods help us all...!

CHAPTER SIX

AT THE SLIGHTEST hint of dawn, Jhavon was stirred by the chimes of bells resonating all throughout the small kingdom. For a brief moment, he thought he was back in Rag's Port, and his encounter with the mox hound was a bad dream. But the solid walls in his small quarters, and the soft mattress upon which he laid, served to remind him of his sudden good fortune.

And good fortune it was indeed, considering the old cabin that he once shared with his dog and uncle. Other than the days he spent traveling with the old man, he couldn't remember ever eating such fine cooked food for supper. The maids and servants had all called him "sir" as they tended to his needs. And as if to ensure the previous night's performance wasn't just a fluke, he was awarded with the same royal treatment when the servants arrived at his door with breakfast later that morning....

The tunic and other undergarments that were provided for him, however, were more suitable for lykines and humans. Without the fastening buttons stitched to the side of the clothing, he couldn't wear any of the undershirts. And as for the tunic, he was forced to cut off the sleeves for his hands to fit through just so he could put it on.

When Jhekaath came into the room, he gave the oddly dressed trunket a curious look, but then he noticed the big hands (as if for the first time) and grunted knowingly. "I'll see to it that our tailors do more to suit your needs at once, Jhavon," he said.

"Just the sides, sir," the trunket replied, holding up the white undershirt. A fat finger drew an imaginary line from the armpit, all the way down. "Buttons should be placed along here once the cut is made on both sides."

"Hmmm…" Jhekaath said, nodding thoughtfully. "And this is how all the trunkets' garments are made?"

"Aye, sir. Mostly so. But there're other designs, made by special tailors who could make every stitch and seam unnoticeable. Quite fancy, but confusing and difficult to get into. They're worn by the wealthy. But most trunkets in Rag's Port prefer the simpler design. Just a few buttons along the sides will do."

"I see…. I'll make sure to inform our tailors of your requirements. Otherwise, they might be tempted to get too fancy with your tunics and jerkins."

"Thank you, sir," Jhavon said, failing to catch the man's humorous attempt.

An odd moment of silence snuck in between them, causing the young trunket to cast a nervous eye to the ground.

Jhekaath took the opportunity to look at what was left of his breakfast, and was surprised to see he'd only taken three or four tiny bits out of the baked bread. And though a knife was provided for him, the cheese wasn't sliced but had just a few bite-marks in it as well—as if a little mouse had been nibbling on it. And other than the jar of milk, which had only been drunk just a quarter of the way, the trunket had barely eaten anything at all.

"Didn't you like your morning meal?" he asked. "We can give you something else if—"

"Oh no, sir," Jhavon said, politely. "Breakfast was just fine. Just a bit too much, is all."

Jhekaath frowned. "Too much?"

"Quite, sir."

He did remember hearing, or reading, something about the trunket's meager diet. They ate very little. Probably due to their small size, he thought. "Very well then," he said. "Come along with me. I'll show you to the grounds. The servants will be here shortly to clean up."

Being clothed in the old man's robe for so long, Jhavon had grown accustomed to the warmth of the enchanted garment. Without it, he was immediately reminded of the cold the instant he stepped outside. Even with a caps drapped over his shoulders, he shivered as the strong icy wind kicked up.

Beneath the gloom of the cursed Pagaroth sky, the citizens of this small kingdom carried on as if nothing unnatural were placed above them. The horses still hauled their lumbering wagons filled with food-stock and supplies. Officials, donned in their courtly robes, spoke quietly amongst themselves as they headed toward the castle. Tall wizards roamed the gardens, where the flowers were so beautiful, it appeared as if they'd been plucked from the Red Forest. And beyond the gardens, the giant wall stood like a man-made mountain stretching all around.

"The Eternal Pagaroth built those very walls," Jhekaath said, after they'd walked some ways, and seeing how it held the young trunket's fascination. "Before the war, he built this castle with rocks that he toted from the land of giants."

The trunkets aren't much believers in the doings of the other Eternals (nor their remnants). Their scientific minds caused them to look toward nature for life's secrets, other than attributing all that was unknown to the gods. Even their own Eternal, Ragath, was merely a thing of fable and tradition, passed down by their ancestors. "But this isn't like any other kingdom that I know," Jhavon said. "It's quite small. Coming through the countryside, I only saw a few villages with less than a handful of cottages there. Where are your merchants and tradesmen? How do you collect your taxes?"

"We don't," Jhekaath said. "Pagaroth is a cursed land. And as you've already observed for yourself, there aren't much people who live in this realm. Most of them have long fled to the foreign lands of Danwhar, Laap, or Llok. Just a few choose to remain, because Pagaroth once promised us that the land will never cease from growing crop. Food is in rich abundance here. Our soil is more richer than any other land in Hagaraak."

"And yet, sir," Jhavon said, still not fully convinced of the so-called cursed land. Pagaroth's castle seemed so out of place in such a dark world. "Without the sun, how can the land grow anything?"

"Because this is the land of Pagaroth. Our god make things grow. Not the sun."

"And what is this castle then? It functions as if its the heart of the entire kingdom."

"This is a school now. Pagaroth's School of Merit. Nothing more. The wizards, the witches, the lykines, and all those who possess other gifts from all across Hagaraak, come her to better their crafts. One of the best schools by the way."

That's when Jhavon remembered what the old man had told him. He did mention something about a school once. However, he didn't think he meant the entire castle to be a school. It was all beginning to make sense to him now. The court officials he once saw, could just as easily have been the school's instructors. There weren't any knights to be seen anywhere, and yet, there remained that mountainous wall and gate, and guards.... He'd hate to see what they kept out at night.

"Ah," Jhekaath said, pointing toward a stable. "There're the stables. We can go in and check on your horses if you like."

Jhavon's eyes brightened at the mention of his young colt, which served as a reminder that he actually did own something in this cold and dark world. "Aye!" he said, with growing excitement. "I would like that very much...."

When they arrived at the stall where the colt was kept, they were surprised to see that it wasn't there. Nor could they find the spotted gray that had been placed right next to it. Just two empty stalls with mounds of straw covering the ground.

"They were probably taken out for a little run," Jhekaath said. He led the trunket down the corridor, past all the other horses in their barred stalls, before coming out into the big field behind the stables. And once there, they saw the two horses putting up a great struggle as five handlers tried to bring them under control. Long ropes were fastened around their necks while they neighed, kicked, and reared up on their hind legs, pulling the handlers this way and that way.

"These are the most wildest beasts I've ever seen!" one of the handlers said, as Jhekaath and Jhavon came close enough for him to notice. His whole face was splattered with mud, and his hollow cheeks puffed from heavy breathing. He kept a tight grip on the rope as the spotted gray reared up again, threatening to pull him off balance. He was forced to sink his feet in the mud to regain his footing. "Been going crazy all night...ever since the boy left them.... Made the other horses nervous and all riled up." He then turned to Jhavon. "How'd you ride these two in here all the way from Ragath, boy?"

"They aren't from Ragath, sir," Jhavon said, moving in cautiously to the colt's side. "They're from the Red Forest. And only me and the old man know how to ride them."

"Get out of the way, boy!" shouted another handler, upon noticing Jhavon was getting too close.

Jhekaath stood off to the side, preferring to observe the spectacle at a save enough distance.

The colt reared, bringing up two front hooves dangerously close to Jhavon's head. The trunket timed the beast's wild movement, and as the colt landed, he grabbed hold of the rope and placed a gentle hand along the side of its neck. "Let go of the rope, sir," he told the bewildered handler as the colt's wild tantrums began to subside.

For a brief moment, the muddy handler hesitated, then looked over at Jhekaath.

"I saw the boy riding the colt just the day before," Jhekaath said, with a mild shrug. "I think he has things well under his control now."

Slowly, the handler eased his grip on the rope that had rubbed the skin on his palms raw.

The young trunket was now stroking along the colt's mane. He then untied the rope from around its neck. "Release that other one, sir," he said to the handler holding the spotted gray. "I think its alright now."

The bemused handlers all turned from the boy and his young colt toward Jhekaath, who smiled and nodded his assent. The instant they released the spotted gray, it moved over to where Jhavon stood.

"It's the sky, sir." the trunket said, passing a warm hand along the gray's snout. "It frightens them."

"Nonsense, boy," said one of the handlers, swatting a glob of mud from the sleeve of his shirt. "The others get on just fine. They're just wild horses, is all."

"These horses are not like the others. Your horses are the beasts of Pagaroth; born under a black sky. But these two are from the Red Forest, where the skies are the bluest of blue. The land there's pure and untouched, and all the animals drink from the River of Ragath.... You may treat and ride the beasts of Pagaroth. But you will never ride these."

The handlers all broke into laughter just then. One of them came up to Jhavon. "What was it you say? Some kind of curse, boy?"

Jhavon shook his head. "I don't know any curses, sir. Just these horses."

"And I know horses too, boy. There isn't one that cannot be broken; not one that I cannot ride. Whether they be from Llok, Mox, or Danwhar, they all come under these dark clouds to be broken."

"That may be true with those from other lands. Bit I assure you, these horses will never be ridden by anyone other than the old man and myself. And they're not wild. They're beasts of the Red Forest. If you've ever been to the Red Forest and see what live there, and what cannot, then you'll understand better than I can tell you that you'll never be able to mount any of my horses."

"Hmph!" The handler gave a derisive snort.

The others just stared at Jhavon and his two horses that began stamping their hooves into the mud, as if daring them to challenge the boy. "We shall see..." one of them said, before turning around and heading back toward the stables.

———•———

"They're the most finest horses that I've ever seen, Jhavon," Jhekaath said, when they returned to the stables and placed the two horses back into their stalls. He admired the spotted gray, and adored the young colt. "Tell me, Jhavon... of this Red Forest. I haven't heard much about it, except that its forbidden, and no man has ever set foot in it and returned to tell the tale. But you're claiming to have done just that. So you must tell me. What's in this Red Forest?"

"Things you've never seen, sir," Jhavon began. But after a moment's thought he changed his mind. "Well...that's not entirely true. You have seen these things before, but not as they are in the Red Forest. The beasts are all the same. But in that forest, they live differently. The birds know things, and they sing as though they wish to speak. The land itself would swallow up anything that don't belong there.... This I've seen with my own eyes when the mox hound followed me into those woods. The earth became like water as soon as the beast set foot on it!"

"Then how is it that you were not swallowed up as well?"

"Well...I...I don't know, sir. I didn't think to ask the old man about it. The thought never occurred to me till now."

"Well, maybe the Red Forest took a liking to you, Jhavon."

"It sure looked that way. Or I must be lucky...."

The two left the stables and made their way back to the castle, but not before Jhekaath informed all the trainers and handlers that they were not to touch the young colt and the spotted gray in any way. And from then on, it would be Jhavon's sole responsibility to go down to the stables each morning to care for his own horses.... This bit of news seemed to disappoint some of the handlers, especially the two who were so bent on breaking them in.

On the days that followed, Jhavon would wake each morning and hurry down to the stables to tend to his horses. Bags of feed were always provided, and whatever else that was needed for their care.

The handling came natural to the young trunket, who always took them out into the field (without their reins and bridals). They seemed to anticipate his every move before hand and follow his every command.... That was something that not even the most experienced trainer could get a normal horse to do. However, it also made a weird spectacle to see the pint-sized trunket, who could barely mount his own colt, handle the two horses so well and with such ease. It appeared as if he was speaking directly into their minds....

One day, while riding the colt, he noticed one of the handlers coming out of the stables to scan the entire field, as if searching for someone in the distance. When he spotted Jhavon, he whistled loudly across the two hundred yards and waved him to come back inside....

"There's a young lad wishing to see you, Jhavon," the hardler said, as Jhavon neared the stables.

The trunket dismounted his colt and peered around the stable's wide door. Far down the front end of the corridor, he saw a young boy standing next his stall. The boy was donned in a long purple gown, and wore a pointy black hat that hid most of his forehead.

For as young as he appeared, the boy still stood a whole foot taller than Jhavon. As he got closer, he noticed him staring down at his enormous hands with wild confusion etched all over his face––maybe even fear. He must've surely been subjected to the far fetched tales of evil trunket lords and demons as an infant. "Are you the trunket, Jhavon Trunsly?" he asked, adding courage and depth to his thin voice.

"Aye," Jhavon replied, as he led his colt into the stall. "And who might you be?"

"My name is Shurwath, from the Land of Laap. I was ordered be our Dean, Ms. Morella, to fetch you at once."

"A Dean...? And what is a Dean, Shurwath?"

"The one who oversees this school.... Come along now. She's waiting, and I've already missed half of Ms. Wicket's class."

Shurwath, whom Jhavon soon found out to be a young wizard, led him through the grounds and into the castle. Two large doors stood propped open that allowed both student and teacher to come and go as they pleased.

In Rag's Port, the trunkets weren't novices when it came to carpentry and building. So Jhavon had seen his fair share of beautiful cottages, and even more beautiful interior designs. One of the most grand displays of the trunkets' talent, was Ragath's Temple that stood in the middle of town——said to be one of the finest temples in all of Ragath.

But what Jhavon saw in Pagaroth's school was entirely different, and on a much grander scale. It seemed like the walls went up 100 feet just to carve a great arch into the ceiling that stretched the entire length of the hall. Intricate carvings and sculptures of both wood and stone stood everywhere to be seen in all splendor and magnificence. So life-like, they appeared trapped, as if wanting to move——but couldn't! Great statues of marble and brass told their own tales of times long forgotten, when heroes and gods roamed the earth....

As he followed the young wizard through the hall, he felt as if those carved and polished eyes followed him in return. Their hard faces like expressions of loathe and damnation for the evil deeds of his ancestors.

Many students walked by, most dressed in purple gowns——like Shurwath——towering high above the trunket, fixing him with their own curious stares——

"Head back to your class now, Shurwath," a strange echoing voice said, apparently from out of thin air. "I'll see to Mr. Trunsly from here."

"Aye, Ms. Morella," Shurwath said, preparing to take his leave. "I hope to see you again some time, Jhavon. Farewell for now."

A bewildered Jhavon was still looking about——at each passing student, to see whose lips had spoken so oddly.

However, not wanting to be rude by delaying Shurwath any longer, he abandoned the mysterious task to address his new friend. "And you too, Shurwath," he said, as the young wizard was already well on his way down the hall. "Farewell for now."

"Mr. Trunsly."

Jhavon spun around and gazed at a door across the hall that appeared to have just spoken. "A-Aye?" he said to the door.

A little girl giggled at him as she walked by.

The door eased itself open to reveal an empty desk, stacked bookshelves, and scrolls in a small room.

"You may enter," this enchanted voice said.

He hesitated for a moment, but then stepped inside.

The door closed itself shut.

There came a mist, like thin smoke, that rose up from the floor. It all gathered into one mass behind the desk, swirling and churning until a face had finally took form.

Surprised, Jhavon took a step back. "Spirits cannot walk the lands," he said, but more out of assertion than amazement.

"And if that's so Mr. Trunsly," Morella said. "Then what does that tell you about me?"

"I-I don't know."

"If Ragath sent all the spirits from this world, then I surely can't be a spirit. Or can I?"

"Surely you cannot be a spirit," Jhavon replied. "So you must be something else."

"And that I am, Mr. Trunsly. Not a spirit, but something else. I am Morella, dean of this school."

Jhavon paused, obviously at a lost for words as he stared into the elemental's swirling mass.

"I was told by our principal, Mr. Shurlan, that you are to be admitted into our school of merit."

"A-aye, Ms. Morella," the young trunket replied. "That's what the old man said I must tell Shurlan."

"Did he?" Morella asked, with feigned wonderment. She pictured the boy and her old master, walking through the Red Forest together.

"Aye, Ms. Morella. That he did."

"Well now, Mr. Trunsly. How do you like Pagaroth so far?"

"Since I can't return home, I should think that I like Pagaroth just fine."

"That's very good, Mr. Trunsly," Morella said. "Most of our students come to Pagaroth for one thing only. Do you know what that is?"

"No, Ms. Morella."

"To enhance their skill to its full potential.... Do you have a skill, Mr. Trunsly?"

"I-I don't know."

"Well...what did you do while living in Rag's Port?"

"I fixed watches for Mr. Laan at his shop."

"So you are good at fixing things?"

"I don't know, Ms. Morella. I've only learned how to fix watches, but nothing else."

"Hmm..." Morella said, thoughtfully. "So you don't know what you can actually do. But you have a skill at fixing watches."

"Aye, Ms. Morella. I should think this is so."

"You must excuse me for a little while, Mr. Trunsly." Morella said, her cloudy form already beginning to dissolve. "I'll return very shortly." She vanished from sight just then, leaving Jhavon all alone in the small room....

When she returned, her ghostly image was like thin smoke leaking through a crack in the wall and collecting itself again behind the desk. "Your instructor should be here soon, Mr. Trunsly. And I must inform you that before you are officially admitted into this school, we must first discover what hidden talents you possess."

"Aye..." was all the trunket could say, even though he hadn't the slightest idea of what Morella actually meant.

The door opened up all by itself once more, nearly bumping into the side of Jhavon's head this time.

A man dressed in a long brown tunic walked in. He had curly red hair that matched his eyebrows, and a chin as sharp as a table's corner.

"Ah...there you are, Aaron," Morella said.

"I came as fast as I could," Aaron said. He kept a cordial expression, even when noticing the little trunket sitting right next to him. Most of Pagaroth had already heard of the young trunket boy who had somehow managed to rouse Shurlan's interest––so much so that he was instantly admitted into the school. And then there were the stories of magical horses that he single-handedly captured in the Red Forest.

"This here's Jhavon Trunsly, from Rag's Port," Morella said. "Jhavon's not yet sure of his main skill, so we must help him find it."

"Aye ma'am," said Aaron. He was certain he could find the trunket's skill without much trouble. He already knew (as everyone else did) that Jhavon was some kind of controller of beasts, and that he'd flown to the Red Forest on a mox hound.... "I'm pretty sure we can find the trunket's skill easy enough."

"Thank you, Aaron," said Morella. "You are now both excused."

Jhavon's meeting with Morella was so abrupt, he wasn't quite sure of whether he should follow Aaron out of the room....

The two walked down a long corridor until they came to the southern wing of the school and headed outside through a back door. A small cottage stood directly ahead, where low trimmed hedges boardered the castle's gardens to the right.

He thought it was strange when he noticed the cottage didn't have any windows, and the flat metal roof made it look like a shoe box on a cobbler's shelf.... When Aaron opened the door, and the two stepped inside, an eerie feeling came over the young trunket as he immediately found himself staring down at the dirt-caked ground. More alarming, was when he looked up toward the ceiling and saw that it was at least 100 feet high. The cottage, that at once looked big enough to house just two humans, now appeared as if a small section of Vlak's Forest could fit inside of it.

There were sharp rocks all around; some as large as the mythical moss-covered boulders in Ragath. Along the logged walls, were all sorts of pointy things made from metal and wood. And the same jagged contraption was piled high––way off in the distance, too high to climb, and too cluttered to walk through. Within this mega heap of junk and disorder, Jhavon thought he he recognized the giant axle of a wagon here, a rusty wheel there, and a solid iron block (that might've been the head of a giant hammer) somewhere else....

"I think the cottage grew a little," Jhavon said, still staring up and around the place in wild wonderment.

"It didn't grow," Aaron replied. "On the contrary, we've shrunken down to the smallest size."

"Shrunk——" the trunket began to ask, but then paused and gave the new environment a second eye all around. He would soon discover that the large rocks surrounding them were nothing more than giant clumps of dirt; the same dirt that made up the ground. "But how...? What magic can anyone possess that make things shrink? And why didn't all those piled up things shrink as well?"

"Shurlan's magic," Aaron replied. "A very old lykine spell." He stooped down and pinched something off the ground. It was a tiny ant. He held it out so Jhavon could see it crawling on his palm. "Only those that live are shrunkened once they enter this cottage. Otherwise, this harmless little ant here might be the size of a horse. And I heard of your love for horses Jhavon, but I wouldn't want those claws there seizing me around the waist and having me for supper. These ants are notorious flesh eaters."

"It's just a magic cottage then?"

"That it is, Jhavon."

The cottage was nothing more than a place where old things were stored. Old toys, boxes, broken clocks, chains, and all sorts of other junk were all clustered together to form one huge impassable mountain.

"So..." Jhavon began. "What am I doing here? And what's the purpose of this magic cottage? Why make things shrink, when they're perfectly normal the way they are?"

"Here's where students come to discover their talents—if they don't already know it."

"And how am I supposed to do that?"

"By getting through to the other side."

The young trunket just gazed at the formidable contraption in the distance ahead. Even from where he stood, it had an unapproachable appearance to it, as if promising certain death to anyone foolish enough to come near it. And not only that, but it looked highly unstable as well; as if the whole thing might come crashing down at the slightest touch. "But...but how-how am I supposed get through all that, Aaron? It's impossible for a trunket to climb something so high."

"Nothing's ever impossible, Jhavon. You'll find your skill soon enough. Take me, for example...." Aaron shook the ant from his palm then raised a hand toward the heap. With a whinning groan, the metal began to bend, twist, and conform with everything else——wood, glass, and iron——all twisting and rolling into each other until a small tunnel was formed, revealing a clear path to the other side.... "I was just as blind to my gifts as you are right now, Jhavon," he said. "But then I was brought here, and told that I won't be allowed into the school until I made it through to the other side." He lowered his arm to his side and the tunnel suddenly just collapsed in on itself, sending a great cloud dust up into the air.

Jhavon covered his eyes (with those big hands) from the oncoming cloud, then turned to Aaron and said dispairingly. "But I don't have any magic. I'm just a trunket."

A frown fell across Aaron's brow as he gave the trunket a skeptical eye. "No magic?!" he cried. "But how'd you ride in on the back of that vicious mox hound?"

"I never rode in on any mox hound, Aaron. I was captured by the hound, and it flew me all the way across Ragath. I was dangling from the tip of its fangs the whole time. There was no magic involved. I fell into Ragath's River and escaped into the Red Forest from there."

"Hmmm..." Aaron said, giving his stubbled chin a thoughtful rub. The trunket's story hadn't convinced him entirely, so he eyed him with more suspicion. But then he noticed the strange buttons that lined the sides of his tunic. "What are those?" he asked, pointing down at the buttons.

"Oh, these..." Jhavon held up the side of the tunic to better show off the buttons. "These are for my hands. Once I get them through, I can button then up, like you see them now. Jhekaath had the tailor make them specially for me."

"Hmm...I see.... But how is that you survived the Red Forest? And why can't anyone, other than yourself, ride your horses?"

"I don't know, Aaron.... But those horses are indeed from the Red Forest, and no one, other than me and the old man can ride them."

"Ah..." Aaron said, as though becoming more enlightened by the trunket's explanation–his eyes beaming on his smooth face. "So you do possess some kind of magic. You just don't know what it is yet. But we'll soon find out..."

———•———

On the left side of Shurlan's shrinking cottage, Aaron had built himself a small cabin from what looked like hundreds of toothpicks sawed at both ends. There was a neat round portico that resembled a man's fingernail sitting just above the front door. The window-sills were the most oddly shaped, for they were sawed to fit the small pieces of chipped glass that had to be brought in from the outside world.

The winding walkway was made from flat stone covered in moss, so thick, that it looked like grass.

There stood a short row of coops nearby, where few chickens, geese, and ducks were kept. And from somewhere behind the cabin, the bleating of sheep and goats could be heard as well....

For the most part, Aaron's cabin was just a pint-sized ranch, sitting on acres of lumpy land that was only two square-feet in the outside world....

Jhavon was greeted by the pleasant smell of cooked food as he entered. He marvelled at the strange furniture inside: chairs and tables made from curved shavings of wood that had been glued together. The curtains were nothing but thick strands of thread tied together like stiff mats. All the candles along the walls were more than likely molten down and reshaped to better suit their tiny world.

"Brought a guest over for lunch, I see," a middle-aged woman said from the kitchen. Her long red hair was wild and unkempt. Her round chubby face was lined and wrinkled, however, it didn't so much serve as a betrayal her age as it did to testify on the behalf of her past beauty. And this fact hadn't become more evident than when her expression fell blank upon noticing the trunket's huge hands. "And one so far from his homeland at that," she said, in a tone that was equally flat and vacuous.

"Ah...aye ma'," said Aaron, walking up to his mother and planting a loud kiss on her cheek. "I see you've heard of Jhavon; the trunket from the Red Forest."

"You mean, Ragath," she said, still staring at Jhavon. "Nothing lives in the Red Forest that don't belong there."

"Ah...but from in and out of the Red Forest he did indeed come to our land, ma'. He and an invisible old man, on two enchanted horses, and a cloak so magical that the very winds must yield to its power."

"Stop telling tales, boy," she said, giving him a playful slap on his shoulder. "You imagine things like you're drunk on mead. These things about cloaks and invisible men——" she paused and shook her head. "All childish imaginings."

"Maybe you should get out more, ma'. Go down to the stables and see the horses that no one but the trunket could ride. Maybe then you'll realize that what I say is true."

"Don't need to go anywhere." She went back to stirring her pot of bubbling stew. "The winds tell me everything.... Oh! and speaking of the wind. Is that what the wind-witch snuck in here to tell you?"

"Aye," said Aaron, chewing a mouthful of bread.

"Trunkets don't have any magic," she said. "He'll never make it through that thing. Probably get himself hurt trying. Or even worst.... A damned shame what Shurlan and that wind-witch put you children through. And all for what? So you can leave here without a purpose, other than fulfilling some old lie. A damned shame. All of it."

"Morella says he has a skill," Aaron said. "He just don't know what it is yet. And it's my job to find it."

The woman gave a wary sigh and turned to get a better look at the trunket. Her steel-gray eyes bored deep into his, searching for his soul. "There's no magic in this boy at all, Aaron. No trunket ever do. They only have brains. But then again...maybe the Red Forest saw something in him that I cannot." And with that, she turned back to her pot of stew.

There came that strange feeling again (as when with the old man) when Aaron's mother said this; as though she'd broken some spell that Jhavon had succumbed to. In his mind, images of a much younger woman stood, so many years ago. Memories of past loves, from times long gone, was all that remained. He felt this same foreign, nostalgic sickness, when he was with the old man. At that time, he'd thought it might've been the combination of losing his home and the old man's grumpiness that had perhaps dampened his spirits and thrown him into a long gloomy despair. But quite the contrary happens to be the case here, because he now lived behind the safe walls of Pagaroth's castle, and Aaron's mother——though pessimistic at first——was as every bit as cheerful as Aaron was.

The trunket figured that it had to be something else about these humans that made him feel what they felt deep down——as if through words, out came certain portions of their past, secretly woven into the tone and pitch of their voices....

After lunch, and still fat from his bowl of stew, Aaron led the trunket through the cabin's back door to begin his test. But on their way past the herds of sheep and goats barred behind their pens, Jhavon noticed there wasn't any grass for them to graze on. The ground on which they walked was as dry and barren as any desert's. And yet, the cattle looked plump and well fed. And the stew (he enjoyed it so much) was meaty and filled with all kinds of vegetables.

"Aaron," he said, as the two began to put the cabin and the small ranch behind them. "How do you feed your stock?

And where did your mother get water, and so much potatoes and carrots to put in her stew?"

"It's very simple, Jhavon," Aaron replied. "As tough as all this might be for a trunket to believe...if you were to combine what me, my mother, and all of our life stock eat in one day, we still wouldn't have consumed a portion of what one man eats in one meal."

"Aye...but——"

"I'm getting to that point, Jhavon.... Small tubs of ground-up corn, vegetables, and grass (for the life stock) are provided for us on a regular bases. You'll be surprised to learn how far just two drops of water and a handful of flour from the outside can go in this shrunken little world of ours. And it's convenient, since we don't have a sky to begin with, we don't miss it much. And in here, we're saved from listening to that awful thunder all the time."

Jhavon hadn't noticed it before, but at the mentioning of the sky he realized how silent it had all been in the cabin. He looked up at the high ceiling and saw five giant lamps hanging above. Though they illuminated the entire cabin as bright as day, they appeared as distant as five alien suns....

When they got to the base of the obstacle, he found it to be much higher and daunting than he'd first thought. It was a mountain of sharp, jagged things, jotting up to at least 100 feet in the air. A mountain of thorns and rusty spikes——was what came to mind as he gazed up to the top, wondering how he could grab told of anything without slicing off a finger.

"Well..." Aaron began, looking down at him with a sly grin. "The best time to start anything, is right now."

"Aye.... But how am I supposed to get all the way up there? Where am I supposed to start?"

"You can start anywhere you like."

"But how?"

Aaron shrugged. "That's what we're here to find out, Jhavon. We're here to find your skill. You can take as long as you like: days, weeks, months... years. It doesn't matter."

"And what will you be doing?"

"I'll be watching. It's my job. Nothing more. I'm forbidden from helping you, though."

"It's impossible for me to climb this, Aaron."

"Nothing's impossible."

"Maybe if I had magic. Then I'll fly, or jump, or make the whole thing turn to sand, or maybe even make a great hole right through it––the way you did. But I'm just a trunket. How can I ever climb that thing and walk over to the other side?"

"I don't know," Aaron said, shaking his head. "You just have to develop your own method."

CHAPTER
SEVEN

FROM THE VERY beginning it was evident that Jhavon would not have completed this huge obstacle on his first day. However, it didn't stop him from trying.

For hours, he searched the base of the structure from one end of the cabin to the other, hoping to find the easiest route in which to make his climb. And to his dreary reckoning (but not disappointment) he saw none that would allow him higher than 7 feet.

Despite this first failure, he didn't leave the enchanted cabin dismayed in the least. When he returned to his room, he spent the rest of the night making plans for the next day.

At the slightest hint of dawn, he hurried down to the stables to tend to his young colt and spotted gray, then allowed them to run the field at their leisure until the time came for him to head into the cabin.... He spent this day, not exerting his efforts in vain, but on figuring out different ways that would provide him some kind of lift to the obstacle's summit.... In Rag's Port, he recalled how the builders used ropes to manipulate devices that raised them high in the air to replace a window or patch up a roof. But that was the extent of his knowledge on that particular matter. He knew what it was, but he didn't understand how

It worked. So over the next few weeks he worked tirelessly on recreating this device....

Through his experience with watches, he understood the purpose of gears. He knew that it wasn't just one gear that made the hands move, but many, made from different sizes. However...it took just one to make these other gears move. It was called the main gear; and through its steady rotation, it caused all the others to move, which in turn caused the three hands to move at different speeds....

"Tell me, Aaron," he said one day as they sat in the cabin, filling their stomachs with lamb's stew. "Where can I get a watch?"

"Oh, I don't know," Aaron replied between mouthfuls. "Old Hollan, maybe."

"Old Hollan?"

"Aye...lives in the basement...under the castle.... Cleans the halls at night.... A horder, that one.... Finds all kinds of trashy things and keeps them for only Vlak knows how long."

"So he probably has a few watches to spare then."

"He just might.... How much do you need? You know they're probably all shattered and smashed to bits."

"Doesn't matter if they work or not. And I only need about two or three.... I want them for their innards."

"Their innards?" Aaron looked surprised at this. "What in Pagaroth's name do you ever need a ticker's innards for?"

There was silence as Jhavon busied himself with a mouthful of soft lamb, before he swallowed it down with a mug of tomato juice. He then turned to Aaron and gave a casual shrug. "I have my own methods...."

Old Hollan didn't exactly live in the castle's cellar. He lived one level below it, where all the waste and sewage collected and sunk into the yielding earth. The pungent smell of piss and shit was stifling down there. And the rats mobbed in droves to feast on their treasure....

Jhavon followed Aaron's burning torch down a narrow flight of dark, winding steps. They soon came to a tunnel where the ground remained as firm and dry as if they were on the surface. Along the walls, sat little droplets of smokeless fire that floated in mid air and burned without the aid of oil nor wick....

"Halooo...Old Hollan!" Aaron hailed, as they rounded a corner.

"Must you always be so thunderous, boy," a rough voice grumbled in reply as it bounced off the walls before fading down to a faint echo. Light spilled from a room up ahead to lean against the adjacent wall like a broken plank. It was soon blocked out by a large shadow. "And who's this you bring with you? What's the meaning of this intrusion?"

"Just a kindly visit, dear Hollan," Aaron said, giving the hunched old man a cordial pat on the back. "My little friend here requires your most gracious service."

In the light of Aaron's torch, Hollan's wrinkled face looked as rough as warped leather. His gray eyebrows were thick, and long enough to nearly overlap his sunken eyes. Beneath the dark hood, his long white hair poured out, making a perfect match with his beard and mustache. His fat rosy nose crinkled up as he squinted and leaned in closer to get a better look at the trunket. His dark eyes bored into Jhavon's; so close, he could smell the old man's breath––

"A trunket!" Old Hollan lurched back with a start.

71

"Aye," Aaron replied, noting that Hollan didn't need to look down at Jhavon's hands to make such a claim.. "A young gifted one at that. It is he, who has come to seek your assistance."

Hollan's thick brows shot up into his forehead, revealing his small beady eyes for just a second. "What's a trunket doing here, in Pagaroth?"

There was a moment's hesitation as both Aaron and Jhavon wasn't sure as to who the question was actually meant for.

"It was the old man, sir," Jhavon finally answered. "He sent me to Shurlan, so I can join the school."

"Old man?" Hollan asked. "What old man? From where? And what does he know of Shurlan?" He leaned back down into Jhavon's face with surprising speed, despite the ugly bend in his back. He frowned deeply, knitting the ends of his eyebrows. "Say...young trunket," he began in a soft, conspiratorial tone. "What did this old man look like? There aren't many who can give Shurlan orders you know."

"He was old, sir." Jhavon said. He was tempted to say 'like you', but he didn't. "His hair was long and white. And his eyes looked like silver coins. And he wore a big black cloak––"

"Silver eyes, you say?" Hollan's face lit up just then. He showed off a spacey row of crooked teeth as he spoke.

"Aye, sir."

"And a big, black cloak...? Tell me, boy...did you say a big black cloak, and eyes like silver coins?"

"Aye.... The same, sir. I'm most sure of it."

"Hmmm..." Hollan straightened himself back up again. His long bony fingers reached out from the dark sleeves of his robe to stroke thoughtfully at his beard. "And you say, this here trunket's gifted, Aaron?"

"Aye, Hollan," Aaron replied.

"Well...what can you do, boy?" Hollan asked Jhavon.

"I...I don't know yet, sir." Jhavon replied.

"Trunkets can't possess magic, Aaron," Hollan said. "So how's this one gifted, as you say? He doesn't even know what he could do."

"He came from the Red Forest," Aaron said.

"The Red Forest, you say?" Hollan looked a bit surprised when he turned to Aaron.

"Aye...and he has two horses that he brought from out of the Red Forest as well. No one else can ride them––other than Jhavon...not even the best trainers and handlers in all of Pagaroth can get close enough to pet them."

"Hmmm...horses, you say?"

"Aye."

"Tell me, boy." Old Hollan turned to Jhavon. "Where did meet this old man?"

"The Red Forest, sir Hollan."

"Hmmm.... And what color are these horses, boy?"

"One's just a brown colt, sir. But the other's fully grown: a spotted gray."

Old Hollan didn't speak after that, nor did he ask anymore questions. He simply turned around with an amusing grunt and waddled back inside. "Well, come on then," he said over his shoulder. "No sense standing about in the dark any more than we have to."

As they crossed the threshold into Hollan's place, Jhavon. noticed the rank odor (that once seemed to smother every bit of air around him) was gone. It was as if an invisible barrier was preventing it from entering. The faint smell of brewed tea replaced the foul scent. Up above, just below the ceiling, two rows of small flickering flames floated in mid air. Same as the ones that lit the tunnels––just a bit smaller––like bright lemons hanging from invisible trees. Bright enough to reveal the permanence and solidity of the ancient rock that made up the ceilings and walls––and the foreseaken cobwebs that hung ballooned from their corners like old tattered sails. Yet dim enough to wash the shelves with books and scrolls (and all the cluttered spaces) in a soft blanket of amber.

Old Hollan walked through the cluttered room as if plodding through a muddy swamp, brushing things aside that stood in his way and ducking below others. Jhavon followed closely behind Aaron, mimicking his cautious steps that not always landed on empty ground.... There were old worn-out swords, and axes, and dented war hammers that hung along the walls. There were all kinds of rusty armor standing about like empty shells of knights long dead. Old helmets and discarded (armored) legs could be seen laying amongst all the junk on the ground. And for a fleeting moment, Jhavon thought that perhaps old Hollan might've been living in that old magical cabin at one point in his life––leaving most of his junk there....

"Now, boys," Hollan began, coming to the back of the room, where he found an old chair near a small table that looked surprising clean, save for a lone iron mug sitting on top of it. "What can I do for you?"

"Jhavon needs some old watches," Aaron said, as he regained his balance after nearly tripping over an old discarded boot. "Any old watch would do. Doesn't matter if they tick or not.... Right, Jhavon?"

Jhavon nodded. "Aye, sir Hollan. Any old watch would do."

Hollan groaned painfully as he sat down in the chair. He reached over the table and grabbed the mug, but then shook his head with a loud grunt when he brought it to his lips. Ha released his hold on the handle just then, but the mug didn't fall. Instead, it just stood in the air, then floated gently back down to the center of the table. He pointed at it with an accusing finger, causing a small yellow flame to rise up out of the liquid like a fleeing bubble to sit right between the mug and the table. Within seconds, thin whisps of vapor began to rise from the hot tea.

"I must presume that Ms. Morella is your sister then?" Jhavon said, after witnessing the clever trick.

With a swift flick of his hand, Hollan brushed the flame from existance, but a troubled frown fell over his brow when he leaned forward in his chair to address the trunket. "And how did you presume this much...boy?" His tone had suddenly become defensive. Grim.

An uncomfortable silence settled in the room.

Jhavon quietly scolded himself for speaking so untimely. "I...well..." he faltered, choosing his words more carefully this time. "The remnants of the Eternal Mox rule the wind," he said, then nodded over to the hot mug. "Fire is nothing more than hot air."

"Hmmm..." Hollan leaned back in his chair. His former demeanor losing some of its rigidness. "Is that what they taught you in Ragath?"

"Aye, sir. We're all taught the properties of the Eternals. And it's said that Mox once brought great fires from the skies."

"You trunkets always did have all the brains," Hollan said, bringing the hot mug back up to his lips with loud sip. Then he laughed. A muffled, chuckling sound. He turned to Aaron. "Did you know that Morella's my sister too, boy?"

Aaron shrugged, shaking his head. "Not the slightest clue, Hollan. Don't think anyone else knows, either. You don't behave like siblings to one another."

"We're not exactly siblings in that sense," Hollan said. "But we come from the same land. The Land of Mox. She's a bit older, though. I think."

"Heard she was the first daughter of Mox," Aaron said.

"Hmph!" said Hollan, with a hint of skepticism, as he took another long sip from his tea. "So, what is it about watches, boy?" he asked, changing the subject. "I think I might have some laying somewheres about."

"Ask the trunket, sir," said Aaron. "He thinks they can get him out of Shurlan's cabin."

"Hmmm...and by what methods do you propose to accomplish with these, Jhavon?" From somewhere within his black dusty robe, out came his hand, holding three shiny watches. Three separate, yet distinct ticks, came from each watch.

Aaron, who'd obviously grown accustomed to the old hermit's eccentricities, regarded the trick with feigned boredom.

Jhavon, however, was completely taken aback as he gazed at the watches in disbelief. Not only were they in working order, but they appeared brand new––and of the finest make––as if they'd just been bought from Mr. Laan's very own shop. "By...by methods of my own design, sir Hollan," he said, swallowing a nervous lump. "I haven't quite figured it out yet. But I will, once I get things moving along."

"You trunkets were always experimenters of things," Hollan said. The three watches drifted from his hands and floated over toward Jhavon. "Always tinkering and tinkering. I'd hate to see what you would have done if you ever possessed magic."

———●———

He hated taking such fine watches apart; but he couldn't see any other way to make the lift that would take him to the top of the obstacle. He even saved the outer casings, and promised himself to rebuild them in the future when it was all said and done——and he was finally admitted into Pagaroth's school. And though such a future seemed so distant to him now, he knew it might never be attainable without the tools he acquired from Hollan's room.

Also from Hollan's room, Jhavon had managed to get his hands on a spool of thread and some needles. With the former, he wrapped around his finger until it became one big ball. And with the needles, he bent four into small hooks and sat them all aside.

The next day, after leaving the stables, Jhavon hurried down to the cabin and opened the door. "Halooo...!" he shouted inside. "Stand clear...!"

He knelt down and scanned the area, making sure the space was clear of any bite-sized cattle, or people, walking around nearby. Then he took the wrapped up thread, the hooks, and all the gears from the gutted watches, placing them gently on the ground before stepping inside and swinging the door shut....

CHAPTER
EIGHT

AARON LOOKED CONFUSED as he stared at the new junk Jhavon had brought into the cabin. The gears that came out of Hollan's watches were like big wheels (of all sizes) with jagged rims––the smallest being the size of a plate. The wrapped thread was now a big mound of thick rope, and the four bent needles were now four deadly hooks. "We're gonna have to put a good blunt on those hooks," he said, pointing at the giant needles on the ground, "they look sharp enough to snag a whale."

Though Jhavon had heard Aaron's sarcastic comment, he didn't answer right away. He was busy collecting up the gears in his hand. Most of the gears were now bigger than the trunket, and he could fit two of his fat fingers right through the holes. He stacked them up till they became just heavy enough to carry––without straining––and began hauling them away. "We'll bang them out later," he said, dragging the gears back toward Aaron's cottage. "Just help me get these things out of the way."

"I'm not supposed to be helping you with anything."

"You're not helping me. You're just cleaning up this part of the cabin."

"Hmm.... I never thought of it that way. I guess cleaning up is not the same as helping." And with that, Aaron picked up five gears (him being stronger than Jhavon) and hauled them back to the cottage.

They each grabbed two hooks and dragged them back. However, with the huge mound of thread, Aaron was forced to use his magic to float the heavy ball near the obstacle.

Jhavon immediately went to work on his plans, bounding and connecting the different gears.... From shaved wood, a board was made, where ha drilled a fist-sized hole in the middle. Here, he placed his main gear, then lodged a twig (now a sturdy rod) through its center to use as a turning shaft on the other side where more gears were to be connected and set firmly in place.

The whole contraption was beginning to look like a small engine, with just one gear on the side of the board. When turned, this one gear moved all the others. Each gear turned at different speeds, and some, in different directions with a series of mad clickety-clackety sounds....

"What is it....?" Aaron asked, on the day when Jhavon had finally finished his strange work. All the gears, save for the main gear, were hidden inside a crudely shaped wooden box. There was a wooden fork that served as a stand, propping up the contraption on the side of the main gear, lest the whole thing lean lopsided on the ground like a buggy without a horse. "Some kind of trunket invention?"

"Not quite," Jhavon replied, looking over his machine with some pride. "I don't think this was ever made by any trunket before. It's not a new invention, either. Just an improvement of something else."

"Something else? What kind of something else?"

"A pulley."

"A pulley...?" Aaron gazed with uncertainty at the thing, making a slow circle around it. "Never seen a pulley like this. It's nothing more than ropes and wheels. But this... this...thing, looks more like a coffin than any pulley I ever saw. And the rope——" He turned and pointed at the rope that was yet to be put any good use. "All this time, and you still haven't used it. So how can this be any kind of pulley?"

"I had to make some adjustments. The ropes and hooks were easy enough. But I would never have found anything as small that could serve as a wheel. So I had to find something else. That's when I thought about the gears in a watch. But then I found out that gears are such unstable things. So I had to make further adjustments until I finally came up with this...."

"But what is it meant to do?"

"Whatever pulleys can do. And a whole lot more, I think. For instance... here——" Jhavon walked him over to the front end of the pulley and placed his hand on the main gear. "How much force do you think it would take to spin that big wheel on the other side?"

Aaron studied the wheel (that was just a big gear) for a moment. "A horse, maybe," he said, remembering how much magic he had to use just to haul the thing over.

"Not in the least, Aaron.... I'd say a baby could move that gear without any problems at all, once it turn this main gear."

Aaron looked down at the small gear in disbelief. "No..." he said, shaking his head. "It's impossible."

"But I thought you said that nothing's impossible."

Aaron laughed. "That I did, Jhavon. That I did.... But I wasn't referring to babies at all when I said this."

"But I'm telling you, Aaron. If you'll just give the box a little lift, I'll show you."

Aaron frowned, but did what the trunket asked of him and caused the box to hover just a few inches off the ground.

Jhavon moved to turn the main gear, but for better effect, he used his pinky finger instead and spun it with little to no effort at all. On the other side of the box, the wheel turned. Muffled, ratting sounds, could be heard inside as all the different-sized gears worked at their own speed.

"By the great horns of Mox!!" Aaron said, genuinely astonished. "If I wasn't seeing it...I would never believe it.... But if that little gear can spin that big whell, then I'm guessing it can spin anything else as well."

"Right you are, Aaron," Jhavon replied. "I can lift us both, and perhaps four or five others, to the top of that obstacle with little ease."

———•———

Even while building his "gear box", Jhavon's mind was constantly trying to figure out how to get the heavy things to the top without the help of Aaron's magic. He already ruled out trying to hoist it up, and building another pulley didn't make much sense, either. His only option was to operate the pulley from the ground, which was a challenge in itself....

He spent the following weeks drawing up plans for the creation of some kind of scaffold or platform. A structure that might be tall enough to get him to the top.... In the horses' stables, he collected a handful of straw, and when he placed it in the cabin, they became long wooden beams.

He began his construction with a simple design: four 4x4 wooden beams, each six feet high. Two other beams crossed each other (diagonally) for strength and support. Three broad planks of shaved wood went on top and served as a platform to complete the first section of the scaffold.... The process was repeated, and a second section was built, and then another and another. Soon, he was standing 36 feet high on a stable scaffold, though nowhere near the top of the obstacle. He did, however, get a glimpse into its chaotic structure from that height.

From there, he decided to finally put the pulley to use and attached two hooks securely to the edge of the sixth platform. Just one hook was responsible for lowering and hoisting. The other held the rope that lapped over the two and wrapped itself around the wheel (the big gear). About five inches from the smaller main gear, Jhavon had some kind of mechanism built in place, which was nothing but a bent needle––hammered deep into the wood until only a protruding loop remained visible. The rope was then placed through the loop and around the main gear. This ensured him that the rope would remain secured at all times.

A board was made for him to stand on, with two ropes attached to it that would eventually twist into one as it was tossed over the hook. His main concern with the hooks, was that they might provide too much friction and make it difficult for the ropes to slide over. His other concern, if the cargo was too heavy, the hooks might straighten themselves out or be yanked from the wood when put under too much strain.

As he stood on the lift, he pulled on the rope and watched the wheel turn slowly from its propped position.

Soon, the ropes became taut while the wheel spun and lifted his platform effortlessly into the air. He stopped pulling when he reached about four feet high, bringing the lift to a slow halt. He looked up and saw the hooks still firmly in place. He jumped up and down several times––each time coming down harder on the lift––ensuring himself that the hooks remained firm. Satisfied that the lift would hold his weight, he pulled on the rope again to continue his rise on the first platform. From there, he continued his work, hoisting supplies and other building materials on the lift. After the construction of three more platforms, he attached new hooks to raise himself higher. And three more after that, raising the lift higher and higher until he found himself standing atop 18 platforms, which was just about 108 feet high in the air!

He was just about levelled with the top of the obstacle, with the 18th platform higher by just about a foot, and four feet away from the edge. However, after a whole month of planning and building, he was none too enthusiastic with this accomplishment. To his utter disappointment, he stared across the sharp jagged peaks of wood and metal, jotting up into the air as far as his eyes could see. It was like looking at a forest of dead trees, where the canopy was nothing but crooked twigs and rotten branches. He doubted if he could make it more than ten feet without falling through some deep crevice to his death....

———●———

"Others have done it, Jhavon," Aaron said, as the two walked the young colt back to the stables.

Three whole days had gone by since Jhavon had last been to Shurlan's cabin (he secretly vowed never to go back again). "They all had magic, Aaron," he said. "They flew, jumped, floated...or like you: simply walked right through it. I can't do any of these things. Trunkets don't have magic."

Neither said a word as they entered the stables and made their way past the stalls.

Easing the young colt back into its home, Jhavon flinched as the long tongue slipped out at the at the beads of sweat on his brow. He smiled, giving it an affectionate pat on the neck in return.

"Even if you had magic, Jhavon," Aaron began. "You still wouldn't have it that easy. If you're not trained in magic at birth, then it's a hard thing to find. It's only when we face our greatest adversaries, do we ever find it. And even then, it's only if you truly want it. So I'd say that magic has very little to do with it. It's all in the will."

"Is that how you found yours?"

"Aye. My mother didn't want me with the gift. I don't know why. But then we came to Pagaroth.... Up until then, I didn't have any magic at all. Not until I was thrown in this cabin and made to get over the same obstacle that you face now. It wasn't easy, Jhavon. I didn't even know what I possessed. At least you have your lift and pulley machine. Me, and the few others that I oversaw, didn't have anything."

"So why didn't you just quit?"

"Because we would never have been admitted into the school until we overcame our obstacles. And that goes for you too, Jhavon. Unless you get past this obstacle, you'll never begin your schooling––and you'll be forced to leave Pagaroth."

Jhavon's expression went from being gloomy, to a bit more apprehensive. "Leave Pagaroth...?"

"Aye."

"But...but where will I go? Who's going to––"

"That wouldn't be anyone's concern once you and your horses leave." Aaron's tone became serious.

Jhavon gave a bitter scoff at the thought of being all alone in the dark world without the old man and his cloak. He couldn't survive anywhere else. And the very thought of returning to Rag's Port, where the mox hound awaited, made him shiver....

CHAPTER
NINE

"SO, THE TRUNKET has made his first machine," Morella said, as she made a swift swirl, up and around, Jhavon's pulley. When she came to a sudden stop, the rest of her misty self was slow to catch up and form the rest of her shape.

Shurlan stood nearby, staring up at the scaffold and lift. He was both intrigued and impressed at the same time.

"I must admit, Shurlan. I haven't seen this kind before. It looks harmless enough. But this is only his first. I'm sure there'll be others. More crafty...more dangerous."

"Not from this one, Morella," Shurlan said.

"He's a trunket! They make war. They make machines that make war."

"Not this one, Morella," he said again, walking slowly around the machine, careful not to touch it. He admired the craft, and the creativity that the trunket had put into his work. Though it appeared to be nothing more than some wood shavings, thread, and watch-parts all pieced together, it was all fitted to suit a special purpose. And for all of its height and apparent flimsiness, the scaffold was still steady and well built. "What do you think gave the trunkets such power to create, Morella...? From nothing, they bring things into being and make them work as if they were alive."

"The same thing that made Ragath want to rule the world. The lust for power."

"Not entirely true, Morella," Shurlan said. "For it's the very same Ragath that once saved the world. It was why he was created...out of necessity. And maybe it was out of necessity that he decided to change things on his own... who knows? But I don't think he craved any power. Was he misguided by his own thoughts and purpose? Aye.... But not from a lust for power."

"Hmph!" was all Morella said as she made a graceful swirl between the legs of the scaffold, then up through the platforms until she reached the top.

Shurlan watched the ghostly form hover high above like a puff of smoke.

"So what will he do now, being as though he built this thing so high?" she asked. Despite the fact she was almost near the cabin's ceiling, her enchanting voice spoke softly into Shurlan's ear. "What will the trunket build next?"

High up above, the smoke faded, and she instantly reappeared at his side. He turned to her, gazing into the wavering eyes. A mischievous grin cracked on his face just then. "I honestly do not know, Morella," he said. "I was thinking along those same lines myself—"

A flicker caught his eye in the distant cottage, where Aaron lived with his mother. He thought he saw someone standing by the window. But no one stood there now.

Morella followed his gaze. "I wonder what that witch has to say about all this?"

———●———

He thought If he took his time, then getting across the obstacle would be easy enough. In fact, he'd already picked out a few places where he might begin.... The problem didn't lay in finding his way across; it was the arduous task that stood in his way. With all the sudden cliffs, crevices, and deadly ditches to overcome, getting to the other side might take months.

He'd fashioned a six-foot plank that was broad enough––and strong enough––for him to safely walk upon, and brought it up the lift with him one day. He stretched it over the wide gap at the top of the platform, creating a little bridge, then gingerly made his way across.

It didn't take long before he realized that he was actually standing on a rotting piece of wood. There were deep grooves, where termites (probably undisturbed for centuries) prospered in the billions within this giant as they ambled up and down between the long splits and cracks. He couldn't help but imagine what they might've looked like if they were at their normal size––and whether they would've favored trunket flesh instead of wood.

The rotted wood had broken off at some point. Whether at the middle, or somewhere near the end, he couldn't tell. But there were deadly splinters protruding everywhere from the jagged edge; each as sharp––and pointy––as needles, and long enough to skewer him right through. To his left, and right, sat rusty metal poles (all twisted and tangled) leaving huge gaps for his little body to fall through. He thought of changing his route, where he could move around the wood, but soon changed his mind when he found there were too many different directions to choose from. Each being a dark passage into the unknown, where his odds of getting lost (forever) were greatly heightened. And thus, after deciding that his journey had been hampered for the day, he walked back to the platform and lowered himself back dawn the lift....

——●——

The very next day, the young trunket houled four more of those six-foot boards up the platform and dragged them across his little bridge, then over the rotted wood for about 300 yards where the break was.... Here, he connected and fastened them all together with nails and rope to form one long plank. Then, with all his strength, he pushed it over the break where the vicious splinters snapped off on contact, due to the weakening of age and time. Their remaining stumps provided good support for the plank, as he soon discovered (and to his complete disappointment), that turned out to be at least two feet short.

Luckily, the other side of the wood was already on a steady decline, and had easily led Jhavon to the source of its fracture. It was an old anvil (as big as the stables on this scale) with its crushing weight pressed down on the wood that had more than likely caused it to break the way it did. It must've happened when Aaron had demonstrated his power and made that long tunnel through the obstacle before allowing it collapse on its own unstable weight.

The anvil hung dangerously on the wood, balanced by a combination of luck and the last bit of strength the rotting wood may have left. The upper end leaned against the back of what looked like an old chest.... This provided some kind of hope for the young trunket as he saw a way out to the other side. The old chest must be leaning, or is being supported by something else. If only he could get down to the other end of the wood that stood straight up in the air....

It would take him another two weeks to return. But when he did, he was equipped with the strangest of things that Aaron had ever seen. The funny-shaped hooks, and rope, he'd grown accustomed to. But not the weird device that had taken the trunket nearly two whole weeks to build.

This one operated on three different gears, and was covered, by a round-shaped wood that was as big as a plate. A hole was bored through the center where a short wooden crank was fitted. This crank could turn either backward or forward, same as the much larger pulley machine. A rope was then slid through a hole at 'the top of the device, and when the crank turned, it either slid up or down through the other side.

He showed Aaron how it worked once, hanging dangerously from the top of the 8th platform with the strange device attached to his hip. As he wound the crank backward, rope was slowly released to lower him gently to the ground. Then he wound the crank in the opposite direction and his body rose (with little effort) all the way back up to the 8th platform....

And with this device, the young trunket lowered himself down the rotted wood. A big bundle of rope hung from his shoulder as he took one cautious step onto the anvil, fearful that it might fall and bring about his end. However, he soon found the metal surface stable enough, and unaffected by the feathery weight of his tiny body.

When he came to the other end of the protruding wood, he let the rope fall from his shoulder and unwound it. Two rocks were tied to his hook for added weight, and when he slung it up the length of the wood, it might've made it to the top on his first attempt if the hook had only found purchase.... After two more tries, he finally managed to get it over. He pulled lightly, feeling the hook's point take tiny bites into the brittle wood. He pulled harder, and this time, the hook didn't budge. He yanked at it, and it still held firm. To test it further, he hung with all his weight, just dangling there till he felt safe enough that the hook wouldn't slip. Only then did he turn the crank forward and mounted slowly to the top.

The old chest, he soon found out, was not upright at all––but was actually laying on its side. The contents that was once inside had been long spilt.... The end of the broken wood extended well above his head, about 20 feet, with his hook deeply embedded at the top.

He gathered his rope and tossed the bundle behind the wood. The hook was gone, but the rope was his only means back if he needed to return to the platform.

The old chest was made from good material. The surface was smooth, but the wax that had prolonged its decay, peeled in many places where the ends were as sharp as razors. In other places, swells formed great lumps like hills of glass, causing him to slip and slide when he tried to walk over one on the bald soles of his shoes. So to save time, he avoided both....

When he reached the long edge of the chest, he noticed that it was jammed against something round, and came just about midway from where the top should've been. From there, was a giant assortment of rusty, rotted, and broken things that stretched out as far as the eye could see. The drop from the chest was about 10 feet. A jump he could easily make without his rope and hook, but he didn't have any other means getting back up....

He returned the next day with two more bundles of rope. He brought two more books along as well, one in which he hammered deep into the hard wood of the chest to lower himself down onto the metal's rusty surface. It appeared to be a wheel safe kind; the hidden spokes buried under the debris of junk. At about 20 feet wide, he had enough room to walk without ever having to worry about losing his balance.

There weren't anymore elevations that was safe enough to travel, so he guessed that the rest of his journey would be down and through the obstacle itself. He studied the area below, carefully deciding his next path, before deciding on a large splinter of wood that shot up between the spokes of the wheel. Hopping off the ledge, he lowered himself down, testing the strength of the splinter by jumping on it.

Satisfied the wood might hold, he yanked the rope out of his device and left it hanging from the hook as he walked down the steep decline of the splinter....

The rest of the way was more climbing and jumping––off short ledges––than anything else. He couldn't walk no more than a few feet without crawling, or climbing over things. It grew darker as he made his way further inside, but not too deep, lest the shadows smother the last bit of light that shone through the cracks. The vivid images of giant bats and owls swooping down with their sharp claws and hungry beaks plagued his young mind. However, the enchanted lights, thrown by the hovering fires in the ceiling above reassured him that this world was no more real than his own imagination.

In spite of his best intuition and navigation, he found himself going down, deeper into the guts of the obstacle—where the light lessened with every step he took. Though it was the smoothest, safest path for him to follow, without the light it soon became completely dark and he was forced to turn back around....

For the next few days, he pondered on a solution to this problem. The dark path was much easier than the ones he had to follow on the surface. But there was always a sudden cliff, crack, or some other problem ahead of him that he needed to see from a safe distance. He tried torches at first, but the light they emitted didn't shine far enough for him to anticipate his steps well in advance. There were still too many holes, and obstructions, hidden beyond the radiance of a torch.

There weren't any lamps in Shurlan's cabin, save for the light that shone from the ceiling. Nor did Aaron ever think of making one, for there was never any need, since the inside of his cottage was already well lit. But Jhavon didn't think that a lamp would've done him any good anyway.

To continue, he needed something that shone brighter, and further, than any torch or lamp ever could....

———•———

During the long months in the cabin, Jhavon had managed to build himself a little wagon to haul different things in. Just a small wooden box that rolled on four buttons that served as wheels.

Aaron had long since learned to leave the gifted ones to themselves while in the process of finding their skill. No matter how hard the obstacle may seem, he always turned a blind eye. Nor did he offer his assistance. However...he always paid close attention.

Jhavon was the first of his kind to enter Shurlan's cabin. It was true; the trunkets are incapable of developing any kind of magical talent. But the gifted are almost never born with magic——his self included. They had all once stood in front of the obstacle with dreary eyes and weary minds, before discovering their individual strengths.

But the trunket was different.

His gift, which had flourished right before Aaron's eyes, was one in which he'd never seen before in his short 21 years. So he found most interest in witnessing the young trunket build his machines and gadgets.

'Tis true...Jhavon might never become a sorcerer or a wizard. But he wouldn't grow to become anything less, either....

Aaron stood behind his wooden fence and waited till Jhavon came walking by with his wagon, just so he could tag along with him to the place where he did his work. There was a clear, round-shaped glass (most likely from one of Old Hollan's watches) laying in the wagon's bed. Aaron figured that the trunket must've encountered a new problem inside the obstacle. As to why Jhavon would ever need the glass, was beyond his imagination. But so were the gears, hooks, and ropes——that made up all the trunket's inventions——had once been.

He also noticed the physical changes in the trunket as well. His black hair, which hadn't been cut since he'd first arrived at Pagaroth, had grown down to his shoulders. From his many labors, muscles began to form along his arms and chest, giving him a look that was more mature. And there were changes in his attitude as well. He didn't play games as the other children of Pagaroth did. Instead, he only tended to his horses and his tedious work in the cabin. He always preferred to be alone. He was more quiet, and often looked to be lost in some deep thought....

With the shaved wood, Jhavon made something that resembled a drum with a round base that was about seven or eight inches in diameter. Because he hadn't yet fashioned it any fancy coverings, it looked more like a fat tube than anything else. Aaron wasn't quite sure of its purpose, however, because as soon as it was made, the trunket set it aside to tend to other things....

Two more days would go by before Jhavon returned to the cabin where he worked on the thick glass, filing down on the edges with a rough, flat stone. Every so often, he would pause to take measurements with his rope, gradually causing the glass to decrease in size as it became more round. It was hard, repetitive work, where the trunket was constantly filing, then measuring, filing, then measuring, until the newly shaped glass fitted perfectly into the top half of his make-shift tube.

So, the trunket's drum-thing has a purpose after all, Aaron thought to himself; he witnessed Jhavon apply a thick glob of binding paste on the inside of the wooden tube where the glass quickly became fastened. With a circular wood of equal diameter, the trunket then covered the back and attached two hinges to be used as some kind of door to open and close at will.

The little drum-thing might've resembled a big clock, but it didn't have any hands, gears, or numbers. For now, it was just an empty frame. But when Jhavon placed a small candle inside, the glass brightened and sent a faint light forward.

"You made yourself a lamp," Aaron said one day, when he fell under the impression that Jhavon had finally completed his work. "Aye...! A strange one at that."

"A different kind of lamp, is all," the trunket replied. He turned the lamp slowly, his watchful eyes following the beam as it lit the ground for up to ten yards. "This one could push the light a bit further."

Aaron nodded (enlightened) as he stared at the projected light that shaped itself like a giant egg on the ground. "I can only assume that you've decided to go through it."

"Aye...but only as long as the trek remain smooth, and I don't have to climb too much."

"Hmm...sounds like you stand a reasonable chance of making it through after all."

"As long as my luck holds."

No more than five minutes would go by, before the light grew dim and the lamp's glass became so black that the candle's flame appeared to be nothing more than a vague speck.

Jhavon swore under his breath and swung open the little door he had just attached. A thick puff of black smoke waft up in his face. "I should've thought of that," he said, fanning the smoke away. He found an old rag nearby then wiped the glass clean of the black soot.

"A few holes at the top should fix that," Aaron said.

"Aye. Small ones, though. I'm afraid they might lessen the brightness of the lamp. But that can't be helped."

Jhavon returned to the obstacle the next day with his new lamp strapped to his back. He brought along two extra ropes and hooks, just in case he needed to climb (which he highly suspected he might). The added weight slowed him down and made his gait awkward, but luckily, his test was one of endurance and not speed.

He crossed his past bridges with ease, and lowered himself down through the growing darkness.

The day before, while back in his room at the castle, he had pulled a single strand of his own hair and cut it into little pieces before coating the ends with tiny globs of sulfur.

He would use these...sulfur-stubbed...little pieces of hair as match sticks to light the candles in his lamp. In the pitch dark, the lamp's beam shot forth and fanned itself out in a wide sphere, casting a bright light for about twenty yards all around. It was much brighter than any other lamp or torch.

He shone the lamp all around, flashing the oval light that seemed to offend the unseen creatures that hid there. Way off in the distance, laid hidden traps he would've surely fell victim to had it not been for his latest invention. He averted these with ease, anticipating well in advance when and where to change direction....

He traveled for a whole week. Each time covering more ground and going deeper through the obstacle. However, he was also finding it harder to get back out. He soon found himself spending up to eighteen hours in the obstacle––nine hours, both coming and going. And not too long after that, he encountered his next problem: Time.

He also found that his lamp wasn't shining as bright, nor as far as he actually wanted it to go. So he spent a few more days trying to figure out this problem as well. But as far as time was concerned, there was very little that he could actually do. Even if he had known the full extent of Morella's time-stopping powers, it would do no good on an empty stomach whenever he ran out of supplies.

For the brightening of his lamp however, the solution came easy enough. He'd long noticed how shiny metals reflected the light of fires––especially brass and smooth silver. His only problem was in finding such a metal that was thin enough to suit his needs. The thinnest sheet of parchment would be a ten-inch slab of skin once placed in the magical cottage.

It was only after noticing the many beautiful paintings hanging about in the halls of Pagaroth's castle, did he find his answer. It laid deep within the paints that made up the knights in gleaming armor, posed upon chiselled horses in backgrounds of the most brilliant greens and blues. The only reminder of Pagaroth's once liberated skies. Days long gone that took its people, and the artists, along with it.

And yet, there were others who still remained––though not as great––who still held their brush to canvas and brought their dreams and visions to life. Though not many lived in Pagaroth. Just one, who attended Shurlan's school.

———●———

Her name was Julie Wessler, from the Land of Laap, in a place called Copper City. A very slim little witch-girl at the age of twelve, with thin white streaks flowing down the left side of her long black hair. Her face always looked pale and innocent. However, she wore the kind of frown that would make anyone appear evil and malicious. Her life was that of spells and sorcery. But painting was her true passion....

A cheerful sun, draped yellow, tossed its light over lumpy hills covered in blurry trees. White clouds dotted the blue sky. A bird, too far for the eyes to distinguish, flapped toward the distant horizon––the outstretched wings and tiny body looking like a crooked letter 'M'. The muscles of a black steed bunched and rippled under its hide as Julie's brush swept back and forth to form its tail.

"If only Pagaroth still had skies like these," she said, as the brush moved swiftly across the canvas. Her voice was thin, yet high in pitch, making her sound like a talking cat. "I think it would be the greatest land in all of Hagaraak."

"But it still is, Julie, my dear," Aaron replied, imitating the voice of an old wizard. "Pagaroth was never known for its skies. And this was so during the times of the Eternals as well. It was always known for its rich land. The blessed land that gave life to all.... And that never did change, now did it?"

"Hmph!" Julie frowned and pouted. Her dancing brush never once losing momentum. "Well...that just tells me that you've never seen Laap, or Danwhar, or even the Land of Mox for that matter."

Jhavon––standing quietly nearby––remembered the lush green land as he and the old man came out of the Red Forest, and thought that Laap was indeed beautiful.

But Aaron just waved a dismissive hand. "Danwhar's all swamp and rocks. And Mox––" He paused for a moment's thought. "Well...I've never been to Mox. But still, I'm pretty sure the land there could never compare to Pagaroth."

"Well," Julie shot back. "I've been to Mox. And I say that it is. By far."

"When compared to Laap, you mean." Aaron shot back with a wry grin.

Julie pretended not to hear the remark. She busied herself with her canvas instead. Her brush whipped then dabbed at a small patch of grass. "In a few more years I'll be able to shrink your head down to the size of a pea."

"Ah, but this is where your oversight begins, my dear Julie." Aaron stepped quickly around the little witch, then positioned his head beside the canvas. "'Cause you see...my head shrinks everyday. And much smaller than a pea, I might add." He brought his hands up to his cheeks and made a funny face that resembled a surprised chicken.

Julie laughed (a very soft, fine-tuned giggle). She aimed her brush at him. "Lhevak!" A speck of green paint splattered the tip of his nose.

Aaron jerked back with a start, nearly losing his balance as he swabbed at the slippery paint with the heel of his palm, smudging the green across the left side of his face in the process.

Julie laughed some more. She jabbed her brush forward, feigning to cast another spell, delighting in the fact that she made him flinch.

Aaron regained a bit of his old composure (though not immediately at at first). "I see that Ms. Wicket's been teaching you a few nasty tricks."

Julie shrugged. "Some tricks. But not the nasty ones. Those, I invented myself."

Jhavon took in the whole playful scene in silence; only contributing the slightest of nods and smiles, unsure of whether he should laugh or add to the conversation.

The gloomy light from outside shone through a long window with a hazy glare. Specks of dust could be seen floating off the wooden floor whenever Aaron dragged his feet—rising up through the ghostly light before drifting back down again.

The spacy roam was empty, save for the paintings, a stool where Julie sat, and the easel that held her canvas. Their voices bounced off the walls with faint echoes, giving a sense that silence was much better preferred....

Julie spun around on her stool, as if noticing Jhavon for the first time.

"This here's Jhavon," Aaron said.

"A trunket?" asked the little witch. A stick rose from somewhere on the dusty floor, floating right into her awaiting hand. A pink gem stone glowed to life at the broad end of it. "The one who comes from the Red Forest?" She walked over toward him, face beaming with interest.

"The very one," Aaron said.

"Well then...I'm pleased to meet you, Jhavon." Even at 4½ feet tall, she still towered above him by more than a foot.

"Likewise," Jhavon replied, though the word barely escaped his mouth.

Julie curtised in return. "What can you do?" she asked.

"Huh...?" Jhavon frowned, but not because he didn't understand the question. He simply didn't know what answer to provide, for he wasn't quite yet sure of what he could actually do.

"Jhavon's still in Shurlan's cottage," Aaron said, coming to the trunket's aid. "He's getting along quite fine, though. And he makes the most impressive things."

"Things...? What kind of things?"

"Just about anything," said Aaron, speaking up for the timid trunket a second time. "From clocks, to watches, to machines...things that could lift you as high as the highest roof. He can do anything––isn't that right, Jhavon?"

Totally caught off guard by Aaron's broad swank, all the speechless trunket could do was nod in silent agreement.

"But enough about us, Julie," Aaron went on. "Do you mind giving us an example of your talents, then maybe we can deal with the true purpose of being here."

Julie's lax posture became rigid as she tapped her staff on the floor. "I weave spells," she said, with as much pride as her frail body could muster.

Aaron shook his head (in disappointment) at the weak display of what they were teaching the remnants now. In his day (just seven or eight years ago) there hadn't been as much pomp and pageantry as there was actual skill. Here...the girl could hardly conjure up enough paint to cover the tip of his nose. And yet, she carried on as if she was the queen of all witches. "Jhavon's here to learn how to make a special kind of paint."

"Oh...?" she said, staring down at the young trunket. "And what kind of paint might this be?"

"Silver," Jhavon said. He pointed to a large painting leaning up against the wall. "Like the one you have there."

Both Aaron and Julie turned to the picture of an old wizard holding a staff that looked quite similar to hers, except for the green gems embedded into the wood. He was donned in a bright silver robe that gleamed in the sun's light.

"My great-grandfather?" she asked.

"Aye," Jhavon replied. "That one."

"Well...that's simple enough. The right mixture of oils and pigments might do the trick."

"Aye...I understand that much. But how do you make it shine that way? It has a very glossy finish to it, like the real thing."

"Oh——" Julie began, suppressing a modest grin. "I should've known that was what you meant. It's a painter's method. Simple enough, yet——"

"Most methods are," said Jhavon. "But only to the one whose method it belongs."

Julie's brow rose with a start. She turned back toward Aaron with a childish giggle. "Why...he speaks like Mr. Cobber."

Aaron gave an innocent shrug in reply.

"You need an egg," she said.

Jhavon looked dubious, unsure of what the witch actually meant. "An egg?"

"Aye. Not the yellow gooey part, though. Just the clear part. Unless you want to make a green, or a bright orange."

"And that's it then?" Aaron asked. "No special dyes? No added elixirs? Just one egg...from a chicken....?"

"Or a goose," Julie said. "Or a duck. Just about any egg would do. But a chicken's egg is more——" she paused, looking up at the ceiling for the right words.

"Choicer?" Jhavon offered.

"Ah...aye——" Julie replied. "A chicken's egg would be more...choicer."

CHAPTER
TEN

EVEN IN THE most well lit areas of Shurlan's cottage, the bright beam of Jhavon's lamp could be seen as it swept across the huge walls. With a few extra modifications and improvements, it out-shone its predecessor by at least sixty yards.

As anticipated, he found the silver paint coated within the lamp enhanced the candle's light more than it reflected it. And to increase the lamp's brightness even more, he added two more candles.

However, with these modifications and adjustments, came their own difficulties as well.... For one thing, the egg's clear gel, though dried, was still fuel for the candles' flame. Once subjected to the constant heat, they bubbled and burned, threatening to ignite a fire inside the lamp. So for all its shine and gloss (and to Jhavon's total regret), the egg was only good for enhancing the color of paints, but not quite suitable for what he had in mind. But Jhavon wasn't deterred in the least. For though his first experiment had failed, he'd gained some important knowledge in the process.

Since he now knew how the paint got its shine, he experimented with different oils, mixing and testing to see which can better withstand the lamp's heat. He also discovered that a particular mixture produced an even brighter, glossier color, than the egg itself.

Using the same glass, he remade the lamp's frame, making the base more round instead of flat. And to decrease any direct contact with the heat, he shortened the candles and placed them further to the back of the lamp.

As a result, what he was finally left with, was something quite different from his first lamp. Because of the new round bottom, it looked more like a tall helmet than anything else. The silver paint was so shiny, it made a crude reflection of his face; and what it did to enhance the candles' flame was unmatched....

"How far is it to the other side of the obstacle, Aaron?" he asked, one day, as the young colt and the spotted gray trotted about in the open field.

"Ohh...I'd say about six or seven leagues. No more."

Jhavon sighed as he did a quick metal calculation of the journey. Walking straight across would be three times the length of Rag's Port. With great despair, he shook his head.

"Something the matter?" Aaron asked, sensing the trunket's distress.

"Aye...I could never make it across in one day. It takes almost a whole day to go and come now. And I could tell that I'm not even close to being halfway across."

"Hmm," said Aaron, with a thoughtful nod. "I do see your point there. A most valid one at that. It did take me a whole day to walk across the thing myself. And that's without anything standing in my way. But with you––" he paused, while trying to figure it out in his head. "I'd say, with you... about three or four days."

"More like six, or eight, because I have to come back."

"Hmm...I haven't thought about that. But you don't have to worry about coming back, Jhavon. Once you make it through the obstacle, there's no need to do it all over again."

"But even if I do make it through, how am I supposed to get back without going through the obstacle all over again?"

"You'll find the answer to that question once you make it through."

Jhavon spent the next few days on preparing to make his final journey through the dark expanse of the obstacle. He would have to pack enough food and supplies, and Aaron had promised to look after his horses while he was gone. His only concern, was running out of rope while encountering some cliff or other difficulty. But by then, he figured that he would have no other choice but to turn around and start over anyway.

———•———

Not much food was required for the trunket's meager appetite, but the gallon of water that he brought along added extra weight to his already heavy load. He had to haul the lamp under his arm, which made the trek more uncomfortable, but at least he had adequate light.

The lamp's bright beam pierced through the darkness for nearly 100 yards. As he'd done many times before, he searched every corner and hole for the best possible route before moving on. However, he would soon encounter his first problem with the lamp that he had not (or should've) anticipated.

Unlike the first lamp––which used only one candle–– this one held three. So within the first hour of his journey, he began to feel the heat coming through the wood. And not long after that, the smell of roasting paint reached his nose, forcing him to blow the candles out.

He sat there for a while in the dark, waiting for the lamp to cool down. Though it was brighter, it worked for a much shorter period of time, which obviously slowed him down.

When he began again, he decided to quicken his pace, hoping to make up for the lost time. And soon enough, he was forced to blow it out again. But this time his thoughts wouldn't be shrouded in darkness, but on what looked like an old boot, sitting no more than thirty yards up ahead.

It sat in an awkward position (this boot), with the toe pointed up. A part of its sole was ripped off, so whoever had worn it last, had their toes exposed. The whole boot however, was trapped between the wide gap.

About ten yards up ahead was a long splinter he would need to get by, then avoid a jagged hole that appeared to have been punched through the wooden box by something heavy and round. He gazed at the path up ahead for a minute longer, committing every detail to memory before blowing the lamp out again.

Now in the dark, he tried to picture the terrain. Every crack, dip, and hurdle, laying themselves out on the platform in his mind. If he thought something to be amiss, he would turn the lamp back on to find whatever it was before continuing on in the dark. He counted his steps as he went, figuring every seven or eight to be a yard. With outstretched arms, he felt on the splintered wood in his path, then walked carefully around it.

For the next five to ten yards he had to deal with the horrible thoughts of falling through the upcoming hole.

And giving in to his fears, he was forced (reluctantly) to sling the hot lamp from his back and relight the soft candles inside. He made a wide sweep as he scanned the entire area in front of him, but then became confused when he couldn't find the hole. He swung the lamp around, moving it slowly, and froze in fright when he saw the gaping hole no more than five feet behind him! His footprints left a long trail in the collected dust, missing the fatal fall by mere inches!

When he made it up to the boot, he relit his lamp and shone the light across the wide gap which he figured to be at least fifty feet in diameter. Then he flashed it from left to right, hoping to find a bridge––or anything that might help him get across––but he found none. Not even a narrowing in the gap.

There was a large bale of straw on the other side, tilted at a steep angle as if it was resting on something else that was held up by another. The loose straws stuck out from everywhere and looked like a dishevelled bundle of logs.

The boot's heel was jammed up against the bale. Its massive size appearing to crush the logs under its own weight.

The scent of old rubber and moldy leather added to the musky smell in the air. Jhavon propped the lamp on the boot, making it stand so he could work with his hands free. He moved fast, mindful that the whole lamp could erupt in flames if he left it unattended for too long.

He grabbed one of his hooks and ran over to the boot's instep. With a great swing, he sent the hook and rope over the boot. It landed with a soft thud and dug itself into the weak material when he gave it a good yank. Then he hurried back to his hot lamp and blew the candles out....

Save for all the dust (that had been settling there for centuries), the surface of the boot was surprisingly smooth. With little effort, he pulled the hook from its entrapment that was as brittle as dried mud.

He tried to picture the boot in his mind. It didn't have any laces, just a stiff lifeless tongue that was curled back like a squirrel's tail.

From where he stood, the incline wasn't as steep as he'd first thought. But the smooth surface of the boot made walking in the dark very dangerous.

When the lamp cooled down to a bearable lukewarm, he sat it down and shone it toward the boot's tongue. Taking the hooked rope, he climbed over it and stood on top. He was now in the middle of the gap.... Somewhere below, the heel was jammed into the straw, and should it slip from its place, the young trunket would fall along with it––quite possibly to his death.

Above, he did a quick study of the straw that stuck out and hung over the boot. He knew how strong the things could be; strong enough to hold his weight at least. But what he didn't trust, however, was their actual length. He knew that the further one protruded from the bunch, the weaker it really was, and might slip from its place at the slightest touch.

For this reason, he aimed for the shortest one and swung his rope. The hook flew a short distance then wrapped itself around the straw where it became snagged.

Jhavon then repelled down the boot's tongue and hurried back to his smoking lamp.

———•———

He felt refreshed when he awoke the next day, despite his sore muscles and aching wrist. A small fire danced under a clay pot where he boiled water for his pagsroot tea.

What he first thought to be a bale of straw, wasn't exactly that, as he eventually found out. It was an old bent mattress instead. The flaxen covering was torn, where the contents of straw had spilled out. It was strong enough to climb (as he soon discovered, once he came to the top of the crest), and even though the rest of the way didn't appear levelled, it was all straw and flax as far as his eyes could see.

There were enough logs (straws clustered together) where he could safely walk, or perhaps hop over the few gaps in some places. Huge logs shot up in the air, and joined so close at times, he could barely squeeze his little body through.

It was a slow journey. One that had taken all night and caused him to set up camp on three ajoining logs of straw. However, as easy and safe as this giant mattress had been, he was eager to get off and continue at his normal pace. For each day spent there, meant a whole day's lost—not only of time, but of food as well....

Save for the crackling of the campfire, all was silent. In the midst of the overwhelming darkness, the fire's flame appeared to be nothing more than an oasis-like chasm, an anomaly that never belonged in this black world....

The pagsroot tea was rich and strong, but bitter. Its warmth roused new bursts of energy within. The substance entered his blood and soon cleared his mind. He quenched the fire with his first piss of the day before he packed up and moved on.

He grew accustomed to moving about in the dark. With the aid of his lamp, he committed every detail of his surroundings to memory. His mind was adapting to the strange world, where he constructed his own mental maps. He counted his steps. He depended more on his sense of touch, feeling the ends of logs with the tip of his shoe before leaping over small gaps as if they were puddles.

He travelled for the better part of the day, before spotting an object on the mattress that was so large, it exceeded the range of his lamp on both sides. And judging from the dull shine of its reflection, it appeared to be metal. The sheer size and weight of it was probably what caused the huge dent in the mattress.

He blew out the lamp and walked the rest of the way, stopping just a few yards short when he felt the mattress beginning to sink. He relit his lamp and shone the bright beam slowly up the rough surface, but to the trunket's dismay, the top was too high for him to sling his hook over. But even if it wasn't, he figured the surface might've been too smooth––and hard––for the hook to find any kind of purchase.... His only option would be to go around. However, his most difficult choice would be on deciding which way is the shortest.

———•———

Jhavon didn't know exactly how long, but he guessed it must've taken him up to nine hours before he finally reached the eastern end of the mattress. Regardless of what method he'd used in choosing which side to travel, he'd chosen the side that was covered with less flax.

In the normal world, the coarse material would appear rough, but well knitted together. However, when shrunken down to the size of an ant, Jhavon found it to be a worst hinderance than the straw itself.... For one thing, it had way too many holes and gaps. To fall through, would mean landing on the giant straw below––and he didn't even want to think about climbing his way back out of all that! And if he was really unfortunate, he could just as easily fall through a gap in the straw (after slipping through the flax) as well. A mishap that would surely lead to his death. So it was much safer to travel on the giant straw and avoid the troublesome flax at all cost.

And as for the huge metal thing that held the mattress down, it had continued far into the darkness, way beyond the trunket's vision. But such a heavy metal (for its size) could only belong in just a few places: a blacksmith's workshop, for example. Jhavon guessed it to be some big iron table. Or a door perhaps, that once protected some secret vault.

Downward, the strands of logs protruded through the flax in so many places, it made hopping from one to the other an easy feat for the trunket. With a path already set in his mind, he went: one, 2 feet below...two, a little off to the right and about 5 feet down...three, down another 7 feet to the left...and so on...until he finally reached the end of the mattress and repelled himself down.

Though it was only two feet down to the surface, the giant logs of straw still protruded through the flax at the edge of the mattress and stood in his way.

He made his first leap down and realized his mistake the instant he pushed himself off. From out the darkness, a log came up so suddenly that his legs buckled under the unexpected impact, causing him to lose his balance and fall forward on his hands and knees.

Shaken——but unharmed——he rose back up slowly to his feet and walked over to the edge of the log. He peered over, straining his eyes through the darkness, barely spotting the outline of the next log that appeared to be much further down. With knees slightly tent, and both hands gripping tightly on the rope, he shoved off. The blind jump and the felling of falling into nothing was almost overwhelming. He held his breath, as if expecting to land in a sea of water. And what should've lasted for only a second, seemed to go on forever.... But then his feet touched the log and he tensed his body against the impact.

Only then did his breath return, and he immediately leaped off into the next jump, not wanting to wait for any new doubts and apprehensions to sneak into his mind.

In this method, he took the rest of his jumps. One after the other, until he landed on a flat wooden surface. He couldn't tell exactly what it was. But whatever it was, it had to be very strong to hold the weight of the thick metal slab above. And from where he stood——shining his lamp——the surface appeared to be clear of all obstructions, far beyond the lamp's range....

After two days of non-stop skipping and jumping, walking just ten straight paces felt as unfamiliar to his legs as if he'd just grown them. To ensure that he was heading in the right direction, he kept the mattress to his left side at all times.

When he grew tired of walking, he set up camp and downed a meager helping of bread and cheese, then sipped some tea that made him sleep for only Ragath knows how long....

He rose the next day and set off again, walking completely past the mattress after two hours or so. He was tempted to round the corner as he went by (just out of curiosity) but he pressed on.

An idea had came to him the night before and he hadn't stopped thinking about it since then. The constant stopping to leap over dangerous cracks and bottomless holes, had slowed down his pace a great deal. He guessed that he was at least 40 feet below the top of the obstacle, so the ground shouldn't be too far off. And with the absence of so many things to fall through, his pace would be a whole lot faster. His only problem laid in making sure he had enough rope to get himself down––and he only had two remaining. To add, if the ground below proved to be cluttered and more impenetrable as when he first began, he would be forced to make his way back up to where he started. And depending on when and where he made this daunting discovery, the setback could cost a whole day.

His final decision came when he made it to the edge of the wood. And as if by coincidence, the lamp showed the other side to be at least 30 yards across. So out of haste, desperation, and a dire need to end the arduous journey through this dark world, he told himself that down was the only way left for him to go.

The ground itself was within the range of his lamp. The sight of giant rocks and huge clumps of dirt, gave him the sense that he'd already made it. However, the drop was straight down, with nothing in sight for him to repel against. Two ropes would be sufficient for him to get down––had there been another log, or protrusion, where he could reattach a hook and continue for the remainder of the climb. But one rope would never be long enough to cover the entire drop.

For this, he devised an ingenious plan....

After stomping the hook into the edge of the wood, he lowered himself with the cranking device. He would pause every so often to use his lamp and see just how far he had to go before the rope's end. Directly up ahead, he could see the wide expanse of the wood's surface that ran all the way down to the bottom. Jhavon guessed it was probably a closet of some kind.

When he came to the rope's end, he stuck the hook (with the second rope attached) right through it. He used his big strong hands to pull the cranking device from the end of it, leaving him to dangle freely by one arm, while he prepared to fit the end of the second rope through the device.

The weight of his own body was already beginning to pull his muscles taut. He struggled to get the second rope through, and when he finally did, he cranked with all the speed and strength he had remaining.

But the trunket would soon find the irony in his own creation, that had once been so instrumental in his progress thus far, was now beginning to work against him....

To compensate for the lifting of heavy weights, he made the device as easy to crank (and uncrank) as possible. With all different gears in place, he would be able to lift––not only himself––but three or four others as well. It wasn't designed for speed, but for strength. So no matter how fast the crank turned, the rope was only allowed to move through the device at one constant speed. A speed that wasn't even considered to be a moderate one in the least.

And this was what plagued the young trunket now. His arm became more strained by the second, while the rope slowly made its way through the device. And to make matters worst, there was no way he could've pulled it back out in time in order to reattach it to the first rope and relieve his aching muscles. Nor could he get the second rope all the way through the device before his arm gave out, in which case he would surely fall down to the surface below.

He cursed his own stupidity for the oversight of such a critical problem. A painful groan escaped his mouth as his strained muscles continued to burn. His palms grew sweaty and he could feel himself slipping. A loud cry pierced the darkness when the last bit of strength left his arm and he released his grip, falling into the black depths....

———•———

His body came to a sudden, neck snapping, stop!

He cried out in pain as the harness, which kept the cranking device strapped firmly to his waist, dug into his skin––rubbing the flesh raw just below his ribs. He allowed himself to just hang there, spinning slowly around in the black void, though grateful that he was still alive and had somehow managed to escape any serious injury.

Thanks to the stationary design of the gears that held the rope firmly in place within the device, he happened to save his own life by shortening the fall––though by how many yards, he wasn't yet quite sure....

With his good hand, he felt for the rope, grabbing hold of it to stop himself from spinning while he moved to work the crank with the other. It was jammed however, not being able to wind backward nor forward. A gear must've fell loose during the fall, thus causing the entire device to malfunction.

He let out a grievous sigh at his ill fortune. There was only one way down, but he hated the idea of abandoning the device. It was his only means back up if he could only——

He sighed again and dismissed the thought from his mind. His reason... he would rather be stuck on the ground than trapped in mid air. So his only option was to untie himself from the device and climb the rest of the way down.

After carefully bringing the lamp from around his shoulder, he relit it in the most awkward way, then shone it all around with trembling hands. He found the old closet directly ahead, and to his back was the same jungle of twisted metal and wood that made up the obstacle. Below, the ground was off by at least 20 feet; a distance he was sure he could cover, despite his sore arm and bruised ribs.

He gripped tightly on the rope while loosening the straps from around his waist. The muscles in his arms tensed when the device was set free and his body was left dangling in the air once more. He reached timidly for the rope with his injured hand, wincing in pain as he lowered himself down past the device, slowly working his way till his feet touched solid ground.

In the silent womb of the dark, he threw off his lamp and sack then sat down and thanked the gods that he was still alive. He felt the strongest urge to set up camp and rest for a while, but he was more eager to get going and put the dark world behind him, forever.

The lamp's bright beam shone through the chaotic debris of the obstacle, and to his growing apprehensions, he couldn't find a space wide enough for his body to crawl through. The pain in his side seemed to increase with each step as the coarse fabric of his jerkin rubbed against the raw flesh.

He decided to go eastward where the obstacle continued at a downward slant. He trained the lamp's light at the base as he walked past the solid metal slabs and wooden boards that wouldn't even allow the flow of water to trickle through. But he knew there had to be a break somewhere. If not, he would simply walk back in the opposite direction until he found one.

Ever mindful of preserving his candles and matches––a supply that was dwindling very quickly––he was forced to use the lamp less often and rely more on his memory to navigate the dark terrain....

His break came at the point where the east end of the gap became completely blocked off. At first glance, he feared he might have to turn back around, but then sheer curiosity caused him to go in and get a closer look. And as luck would have it, he did find a small space there; a narrow slant in the left corner of the blockage. There was also something totally odd. Two large wooden planks sitting opposite from each other. Both were poised on big logs (like the giant straw in the mattress).

In a place that was supposed to be chaotic, with debris strewn all about, this gap in the obstacle was where he found things neatly arranged. Too perfect for it to have been any coincidence. But then again, he saw with his own eyes when Aaron opened a tunnel right through it, then caused it to cave in on itself. He didn't know the extent to Aaron's power. For all the trunket knew, he could've arranged things exactly as they are now, as easy as a bird knew how to fly.

When he shone the lamp through the gap, the diagonal slant seemed to go on forever——way beyond the range of the lamp's beam. It could've led to any place, Jhavon knew. But like everything else, it must certainly come to an end at some point. And wherever that end happened to be, he would decide where to go from there.

It was perhaps the most awkward position that he'd found himself in thus far. He had to tilt his body at a forty-five degree angle, with the opposite wall pressing down on his stomach, allowing room for sideways movement only. He had to drag his lamp by the straps——as well as his sack of supplies——as he sidestepped through the narrow passage.

The air was stale inside there, and it made breathing difficult. The trunket had to force himself not to panic, fearing he might use up all the oxygen in the small space.

Out of sheer habit, he reached for the lamp, but found the space too tight for even this simple maneuver. So he pressed on in the dark, determined to keep going until he made it out, no matter how long it took.

It must've gotten to be late evening when he noticed a very faint light up ahead in the distance...like a thin slash in a hidden wall. And after some ways more, the light grew brighter. And brighter and brighter still. And not too soon after that, he recognized the dull shine to be that of natural daylight. Outside!

He moved with an exhilarated pace, but then frowned as he realized that he'd lost track of time inside the obstacle. He'd thought it was near night when he first entered the passage. But it was perhaps more closer to dawn, which meant that it was still early afternoon in Pagaroth.

Soon, the giant stones that made up the castle's walls came into view. The sound of voices––and the hammering from somewhere else––came into earshot as well. And not too long after that, he found himself standing at the threshold between the obstacle in Shurlan's cottage and the outside world.

A gigantic shadow loomed over him just then. And before he knew what was happening, a loud bark sounded and a giant nose came sniffing at him!

He stumbled back in sheer terror, tripping over his own lamp, fearing he was about to be eaten by the giant dog. The smell of its foul breath filled the entire passage.

"Move boy! Move! Get out of the way!" It was Aaron; his voice sounding more deep, now that he was a 90 foot giant. "Jhavon! Jhavon, is that you?"

There came a thump––then a painful yelp from the dog.... The shadow retreated and the light returned.

"Jhavon! Come, Jhavon. It's safe now!"

IT BLENDED PERFECTLY in the pitch darkness of Pagaroth's night. Only momentarily––whenever the lightning flashed behind the clouds––was this black shawl of a creature exposed as it sidewinded its way over the land.

One diligent enough, with the quickest eye perhaps, may glimpse the creature––if only for half of a second's time. With good sense, a trail can be followed…aye…even through this stygian hue, until the next flash of lightning. However, the illusion may be long executed by then when both sky and cloud conceal the creature's path. And the one who sees will become the one who saw, doubting his wits and eyes altogether. "Its nothing…" he'll say, for that's what it probably was––just a shade of black the lightning failed to scare off….

Not even the guards, high in their towers, could sight this slick phantom with dreary eyes and sleepy heads. And with their arrows aimed at their own feet, they were as effective as caged dogs guarding a treasured tomb.

Like smoke from the blackest flame, it flowed over the garden's lawn with less noise than the dawn's stealthy mist. Up along the castle's great walls it went, avoiding the reckless light of a mounted torch, before slipping through the crack of a nearby window.

It was here where it poured itself, like black ink through water, out onto the polished floor in some room. It slid under the tables and chairs then headed towards the back where the long shelves of books and scrolls stood. Between the narrow aisles, it formed into a black cloud of bubbling sap before finally becoming a solid man.

Well...not exactly a man.... Its smooth skin still retained its midnight hue, and appeared slick and glossy under the candles' light. There was a head, but no face––save for a pair of red beady eyes.

Long black fingers traced over the spines of books, quickly flipping through the pages. It crept on smoky feet, so the weight of its own body went unnoticed on the loose floor boards.

It slinked down to a bottom shelf and rummaged through a stack of scrolls, pausing when one of great distinction caught its eye. It raised the parchment to regard the golden handles and intricate carvings etched with delicate precision on the ancient knobs. So ancient, they might've been done by the hands of Ragath himself. The golden handles, dug up by none other than the Eternal Pagaroth––a gift, from one god to the other.

It unrolled the scroll to get a glimpse of the ancient text. In its careless haste, the brittle parchment tore almost completely in half, parting the sacred words of a language long gone.... A low groan rattled inside of its throat that might've been a fearful gasp if it ever had a mouth.

It rose off the floor, carefully rolling the scroll back into place before locking the little gold clamps that kept it shut. It moved to leave, but then froze in its tracks, all senses poised––alerted to some other presense in the room! The black shiny head looked from side to side, irritated by all the book shelves that blocked its view. But then it jumped suddenly, as if startled! The shocked expression of a thief when caught. And before he had the chance to look up at the ceiling, the wide mouth of a python came clamping down on its head!

The scroll fell to the floor with a loud thud as the creature tussled with the snake, whose thick girthy body had already expertly coiled itself around him.... The creature became trapped, and its own life was now in danger as it felt the beginnings of the python's deadly squeeze.

The snake unclenched its mouth from its victim's head to stare at the thief. And not long after that, its scaly face morphed into that of Shurlan's. The old lykine's head still moved from side to side on the snake's body while it held tine thief firmly within his clutches. His emerald-green eyes bored into that of the creature's.

"How dare you come in here like this?" Shurlan said. A forked tongue flickered from out of his mouth, almost licking the creature's glossy face. His voice slurred, sounding slithery. "Abomination! What are you doing here? Speak... Ohlar...before I crush you!"

Ohlar shook his head then puffed himself into a cloud of black smoke, leaving the snake's coiled body to drop on the floor like dead rope. Nor did he waste any time in recovering the scroll while maintaining his cloudy form––

"Morella!!!" Shurlan called out as he got to his feet. His voice was so loud that it shook the entire room, and even the smoky demon became stunned when the nearest window burst open at that instant with a violent gust.

Morella swept into the room and blew Ohlar off his smoky feet. Loose pages flew up in the air and all the candles were blown out as the two kicked up strong winds in the wake of their struggle.

"What's the meaning of this intrusion, Ohlar?" Morella's warped voice could be heard within the wrestling clouds. Her white misty form blended with that of the demon's, creating a swirling fog of gray.

Shurlan followed the windy battle that appeared like a violent storm raging along the walls and ceiling in his study. Book-shelves were toppled, hurling scores of books and scrolls on the floor. His own hair tugged in the wind, and the sleek fabric of his green robed pressed on his body as if he was standing on the tallest peak of Pagaroth's Hill.

"Answer me, Ohar!"

"None of your concern, Morella," Ohlar replied, his voice sounding just as warped and enchanting as Morella's. "This is beyond any of your understanding." The black smoke became solid and Ohlar's body dropped to the floor. He made a dash for the window again.

Morella gathered her own mist and shot herself toward the fleeing demon like a burst of steam.

Still stalking the battle, Shurlan kept a keen eye on the hand that held the scroll. He wiped at his own hair that whipped across his face and obscured his vision, then formed his right arm into that of a giant spike-crab's claw from the Sea of Baas. Long and deadly pearl-colored spikes covered the segmented arm and blue claw where the teeth were as sharp as needles.

As he reached back, the four segments formed a spiky crest. Then it zipped forward at the blink of an eye, bringing the vicious claw to chomp down on Ohlar's hand with an ear-popping snap!

An agonizing wail soon followed as the thief's severed had puffed into a cloud of harmless black smoke.

The scroll went tumbling through the air and out the window.

The thief followed, with Morella close behind him.

The claw-armed Shurlan jumped out after them, changing himself into a big gray owl as he fell through the sky. With sharp nocturnal vision, he spotted the falling scroll and dove down, clutching it between his talons before it had a chance to hit the ground....

Leaving Morella to chase after the intruder (only she could catch up to him now) he flew back into his study and landed gracefully on his feet as he changed back to his normal self. In the dim light, he examined the sought-after scroll, noting (with some anger) the torn section of the brittle parchment.

Morella's mist came drifting back into the room some minutes later. All the windows swung themselves shut behind her.

"Ragath's notes," Shurlan said, as she eased up beside him. He didn't bother inquiring after the thief. For shadows were just that. Powerful creatures of the dark. Abominations! Birthed by the sons of Mox and the daughters of Laap. A thing of sky and flesh. He doubted that she was able to capture him.

"After all these years?" Morella asked. "But who would ever want such a thing?"

"Whoever wants to see his return," Shurlan replied. "But this——" he held up the scroll by its golden handle. "Wouldn't do anyone the slightest of good. Without the power of the Eternal, it means nothing. Mere childish scribblings."

Shurlan parted his long fingers and caused the scroll to hover in mid air. And at that same moment, the bookshelves all stood themselves up. All the books, scrolls, papers, and other debris that were scattered all around––rose up into the air and floated back through the aisles where they found their original places. Ragath's scroll soon followed, where it nestled itself back between the other parchments on the bottom shelf. Then everything was just as it were before, save for all the dust that had resettled on the furniture in the room.

"It was just a warning to us," he said. "Or it could be that Ohlar was just searching for treasure. And according to prophecy, there's nothing in this room that can prompt his return."

Morella shook her head. She wasn't convinced. "It came too sudden, Shurlan," she said. "And he said it was beyond our understanding."

"Aye.... And beyond his as well! There's nothing here, Morella. Just old books and scrolls collected over the eons. No mortal, or son of Mox, can help Ragath now. Those days are forever gone. We're all that's left of those ancient times. Remnants...."

Shurlan moved to walk out of the room, but then paused (struck by a sudden thought) and turned back around. He wore a blank expression as he faced her. "If he is to return Morella, it wouldn't be in this manner. Stealing secrets that he himself created?" He cocked an inquisitive brow.

Morella couldn't find a suitable reply. However, she couldn't help but feel that Shurlan was hiding something from her.

"Inform the guards to be on high alert for the next few days," he said. "Put extra torches along the castle's walls, if it makes you feel any better." And with that, he left the room.

———●———

There exists a land across the Sea of Baas, that's said to be more enchanting than the Red Forest. More mysterious than the Land of Llok. Where the wooded areas span far greater than Vlak's Forest. Where the creatures are more strange and deadly than anything that exists in the Land of Mox. A world much larger than Hagaraak, yet it possessed just one river that ran all throughout the land for thousands of leagues. A river, known as the River of Life, that feed Morgah's Lake. That separate the lykes from the barbarians, and the barbarians from the dreadful rykes in the Land of Rykaath––where the river's mouth stretched ten leagues wide.

At a certain point, the River of Life will eventually turn into the Great Falls, and drool millions of gallons from an astonishing height of three and a half leagues, as though falling from the Morgah's Peak. The thunderous roar of water smashing upon the rocks below can be heard all the way past Rykaath, into the Land of Barbarians.

'Tis here, where the shadowy demon, Ohlar, had fled–– some twelve thousand leagues across the Sea of Baas. His gray smoky form whisked under the Great Falls, where the water became a smooth clear sheet upon protruding rock that parted the tame flow like a drawn curtain.

'Tis here, he slipped unnoticed to all, behind this great waterfall where a narrow ledge ran a great ways along the rock where the Eternal Vlak is said to have once hid from Morgah. And despite the thunderous noise outside, once behind the luquidy drape, things became quite peaceful and calm––and surprisingly dry! Just a faint drone could be heard coming from outside, as if all sound was forbidden to past this clear curtain that flowed from high above.

Thin gray smoke trailed the path in Ohlar's stealthy wake. All the way along the curve that stretched for one and a half leagues, then into the mouth of a cave that suddenly appeared in the rock.

He flew through the long dark tunnels, slipping past the countless stalagmites and stalactites that jutted out from the ground and ceiling like crocodiles' teeth, before reaching the first of many torches that would light the rest of the way to his destination where he rounded one final bend to enter the well lit cavern and solidified himself....

Compared to the rest of the cave, the cavern's floor was evenly levelled. Surprisingly smooth as well, with shiny walls that reflected the dozens of melon-sized balls of light that was just floating about in the air. And quite similar to Shurlan's study it was...furnished with cute little tables and chairs, and shelves upon shelves of ancient books and scrolls....

An old man, donned in a long black hooded robe, rose up from where he sat (near one of the shelves). A ball of glowing light rose up beside him, illuminating the top portion of the bookshelf behind his head. Another descended from the cavern's ceiling and settled near Ohlar's face to betray the defeat concealed within his red beady eyes.

The man regarded the demon carefully under the warm light. A faint twitch jerked his white eyebrows when he noticed the severed hand where nothing but a small puff of black smoke remained. "So you've failed," he said. His sharp voice was like cracked glass and made fading echoes off the cavern's shiny walls. "Hmph...! I see that Shurlan hasn't allowed the passing eons to dull his wits——" he paused there, eyeing the demon more intently while making an inquisitive frown. "Or was it another?"

"Aye, Zhorghan," Ohlar replied. "I would've had the scroll if Morella hadn't interfered when she did. I could've——"

"Escaped with your treasure?" Zhorghan asked, not caring for Ohlar's excuses.

The demon looked away in disdain. The physical pain in his hand was long gone. However, the resentment of such a loss was still fresh in his mind. Due to the fact that he was not a direct descendant of Mox (like Morella), he was made of flesh, blood, and bone. "I hand't counted on Morella."

"Hmm...the very daughter of Mox," Zhorghan mused, while walking over to an old desk nearby. The ball of glowing light followed closely behind. "She's everywhere, that one. Wherever she wishes to be, she can. Aye...the Eternal blessed her with an astonishing gift indeed."

"The wind witch."

"Aye. That's what they called her...once. Just a notch before my time, I guess. Long before Ragath brought chaos to the world. And the goddess Laap hadn't yet existed. Both you and her roamed these lands...did you not? But had it not been for the sons of Mox, mixing about with the remnants of Llok——or vise versa, I suppose——you might've been more...complete...."

"It was the way of the world in those times," the demon said, moving closer to the shelf where Zhorgan once stood.

"Before Laap came to be, none of the Eternals knew that they were creating abominations."

"Or as Laap chose fit to call," Zhorgan said. "For all the world could've known, you might be just as normal as the rest of us."

"But that's not how the rest of the world saw it."

"Hmm.... So...tell me, Ohlar. How did it feel when the goddess condemned you and your kind as abominations, unfit to live on the earth, even though you lived on the same earth much longer than she did?"

Ohlar shrugged, as if the question had no meaning at all. "Many died during the Years of The Hunt. Most went into hiding. But some of us fought back."

"The Forbidden Wars?"

"Aye.... Laap went against Llok's decree; which forbids any of his creation from becoming undone, whether it be abomination or not. It was the only thing that gave any of us a fighting chance. The goddess was strictly forbidden by the rest of the Eternals from erasing us. But they had no control over their own remnants, who were already convinced that we should be wiped off the face of the earth. And that proved more difficult than any one of them could've imagined––as you see me standing before you right now, in a time when all the Eternals and most of their remnants no longer exists.... But I fell nothing for those times now, Zhorghan. Those days are long forgotten. I still live in the world. And that is all."

"Hmm...." Zhorghan leaned back in his chair and steepled his fingers with a reverent sigh. "Well...back to more important matters then. The scrolls that contain Ragath's most inner thoughts––I'm guessing––is a lost cause now. Being as though you've...been interferred with... by Morella?"

The demon wasn't lost on Zhorghan's mocking tone, but he ignored it all the same. It was only through a mutual interest that brought the two together, where one couldn't succeed without the other's help. Not that Ohlar was more powerful than the mighty wizard––where he can easily kill him. But it was Zhorghan, who was bearing his patience and suppressing the strong urge to end the abomination's miserable life, lest he himself fail in accomplishing his task. However, the demon knew this all too well, and he played upon the wizard's arrogance very wisely. "I think it's just as well," he said. "I'm sure the castle will be heavily guarded for quite some time."

"Ragath's scrolls aren't that important to us anyway. We'll just have to keep searching the outer world for––"

"But all's not lost, Zhorghan!"

The wizard paused, giving the demon an inquisitive frown. "Oh...? How so?"

"Before I escaped, I managed to read some of Ragath's hand."

"You mean..." Zhorghan began. He didn't seem too impressed. "You managed to sneak a peek? Wasting precious time, which was probably why you––" He paused suddenly when the demon puffed himself into a cloud of black smoke, then formed the short passage from the scroll in mid air.... "My mind is the gate to all worlds..." he said, reciting from the line.

"That was the beginning of the passage," Ohlar said, still floating up there. "Mostly overlooked by Shurlan."

"Aye...I see it now. But not even one as ancient as he would know what the Eternal referred to when speaking of his 'mind'. And only one scroll contains that answer, where Ragath must've slipped his hand. At first, we didn't know what it meant, either. But in time, we came to find out the truth. And it's just like what we're seeing now. Except that one word: mind. That is the key——the key to his home. Then...his home must be the gate to all worlds. But perhaps——" He paused when a sudden thought occurred to him. "Perhaps Shurlan hadn't overlooked this at all, Ohlar."

"But we have the only scroll where the Eternal makes this reference."

"Aye.... But what if Shurlan knew this all along...and was simply keeping it a secret? For isn't the coming of the Eternal inevitable? May hasten it...? If I was Shurlan, my thoughts would be the same."

"Breeding up wizards and witches for all eternity?"

"Aye...Aye..." said Zhorghan. However, he was too pre-occupied with his own thoughts to have heard the demon's comment. "Come, Ohlar," he said, rising up from his chair. He walked over to the cavern's wall on the far right, where an assortment of tuning forks hung. He grabbed one that was as big as his hand. "Let's not waste any more time. Shurlan might not have known what you were up to. But I don't trust the witch. She probably saw what you read."

From the base of Zhorghan's feet, a spark of electrical energy began to crackle and form. It soon snaked up around his body, then down an outstretched arm, where it collected into one concentrated mass. As the wizard's hand absorbed the energy, the tuning fork vibrated and made a low moaning sound while the electrical energy sparked and crackled all around it.

Soon, the wizard's hand ceased harnessing the powerful energy and reverted to its normal appearance. The tuning fork however, continued to glow brighter and brighter, and the low humming sound grew more intense till a great surge pulsed within the fork, causing a small explosion to erupt just a few yards from where they stood.

Then all became calm and silent once more.

Zhorghan lowered his arm, though the fork was still in his hard. His breaths came in heavy pants, and beads of sweat rolled down his cheeks....

In the moments that followed, a spark appeared where the explosion had once been. A few more followed, like flint when struck by an invisible hard. And out from these sparks, a big blue swirling mass––about ten feet in diameter–– suddenly appeared. Long, squiggly lines of electrical energy crackled all around it.

One of Ragath's portals!

The wizard hid the fork within the folds of his robe then walked right through it, vanishing from sight completely!

The demon followed closely behind him, stepping into the blue churning mass....

For a few seconds more, this portal remained, then it too closed within itself––leaving Zhorghan's carvern for the glowing balls of light to commence their aimless drift amongst the emptiness.

CHAPTER
TWELVE

"THE ETERNALS MOX and Baas..." the good-natured Mr. Lash began, while his class of twenty-three students listened. "...were considered more powerful than the other Eternals in those times. And they were certainly more revered because they controlled the two most important elements that ensure our survival, even to this very day. And these two elements, of course, are water and air. The Eternal Mox formed clouds from the very sea-water which Baas had provided for his use. And from there, Mox used the force of his winds to push the enormous clouds over the mountains where the rains fed the land and the rivers, and Pagaroth would make the water sweet, so the Eternal Baas could drink from the rivers' mouths to replenish his seas––" He paused when a skinny arm shot up in the air from the back of the classroom. "Aye...Syme?" He asked. His thin lips curled up into a patient smile.

"Mr. Lash," the tall, lanky Syme began. As a lykine from the Great Woods, he was indeed the tallest student in the room, being nearly six feet tall––at the age of just thirteen. When he leaned forward, both elbows hung over the small desk. "Is that why sea water tastes like salt?"

A round of laughter swept across the room, and a mop-haired boy gave the mischievous lykine a playful punch on his shoulder for giving him such a split.

The lykines (remnants of the Eternal Llok) were prankish creatures, especially in their early youth and adolescent stages. A trait which they'd inherited from Llok himself, who once played so many tricks on his sibling Eternals.

Because they were so gifted at magic, not a single year had gone by––since the school first opened its doors–– where Mr. Lash didn't have at least one lykine in his class. He learned that the best way of dealing with the Eternal's mischievous remnants, was to allow himself to become subjected to the childish pranks (no matter how obviously trivial). Suppressing a lykine's natural urges will only bring it out more, where he would seek more clever and nasty ways to create his mischief.

So instead of fuming and fussing at the boy's rude quips, Mr. Lash would occasionally play along. "Not quite so, Syme," he said. "But you're not too far off the mark, either. I'm not exactly sure why the sea is so salty. I think if you ask Mr. Cobber, he might have an answer for you."

Syme––still grinning––leaned back in his chair with some satisfactory, for he was allowed to secure his throne as the "class jester" for another day. And Mr. Lash was allowed to continue on with his lessons.

"We all play a part in history," Mr. Lash said. "It is the foundation upon which our own future stands. So it is very important for us to know our history. To learn about the Eternals, is to learn about ourselves. As they all depended on each other at times, so too must we support our fellow remnants. A perfect example of the Eternals' collaborations can be found in the deeds of the Eternals themselves.... For instance...without Baas's generous offering to Mox, then the Eternal Vlak would see his forest grow dry and die of thirst. And without Vlak's trees to replenish the earth with fresh air, then Mox would definitely be in bad shape. And this, in turn, would ruin all of Llok's creatures, and so on and so on...." When he stopped here, a big pillow-sized hand rose in the air. It had a thick long scar running across the heel of the palm. "Aye...Jhavon?"

"I have a question, sir," the young trunket said.

Since first joining their class several weeks ago, Mr. Lash found the trunket to be the most inquisitive among his peers. He was always asking questions. And in history, he found the trunket to be more learned than the others.

Though it was obvious that Jhavon had grown up on mostly myths and legends (as far as education was concerned), they'd been told with incredible accuracy! And yet, the trunkets were notorious disbelievers of the ancient times when the Eternals walked the land.

"You may ask your question, Mr. Trunsly." Mr. Lash was all too pleased to have him in the class.

"If the Eternals controlled everything and depended on each other, then how did they survive when Ragath destroyed Mox and Baas?"

It was a good question...one that wasn't asked too often.... The students were all eager to hear the professor's explanation.

"Well, Mr. Trunsly," he began. He walked over to the black-board behind his desk and drew what appeared to be a small rock. "Let's say that this——" he pointed at his drawing with a chalky hand. "––is Pagaroth's sapphire. Or Ragath's sapphire, depending on which side of history you see it from. And with it, Ragath caused the two Eternals to die. Now... in the absence of Mox and Baas, the world did go into chaos for quite some time. Catastrophic storms and floods plagued the world as they once did before the Eternals came to be. It was only through their power that the winds and seas were calm. So when these two Eternals vanished, their power disappeared; the winds and seas reverted back to their wild nature after that.

"Ragath had discovered that through Pagaroth's sapphire, he could harness any power in the universe, and this included the mysterious power of the Eternals themselves. So he used it bring the world's weather back under control.

"And as he went on to destroy the others, he used the sapphire's power to set things the way he thought they should be."

Jhavon thought about the professor's version of events, which totally contradicted the myths and legends that were told in the Land of Trunkets. Not that he ever cared for stories anyway. And though the professor's version sounded a bit watered down, it still made an interesting discussion.

The sound of an outside bell broke the silence, and the rustling of papers and loud speech began to take over as the students prepared to leave.

"One more thing before you go," the professor said. "I need a complete oration––from each of you––on your thoughts of Llok, by next week!"

There came a chorus of groans and muffled complaints all around.

"No no, none of that now," the professor went on. "We might not be using any scrolls in this class, but the library's filled with them. You'll find many copies of Llok's History in there...."

Being the only trunket in Pagaroth's school, Jhavon was seen as unique by all of his peers. And being the only one known to walk through the Red Forest and complete Shurlan's obstacle without any magic––he was seen in a kind of mysterious light as well.

Most of the students who attended Pagaroth's school were already born with their gifts, and therefore, were never required to complete Shurlan's obstacle. But the few who did however, knew the impossibility of the trunket's feat. In fact, many doubted that Jhavon had ever passed the obstacle. And like his admittance into Pagaroth, his admittance into school was seen as nothing more than another example of Shurlan's treatment for the boy. Perhaps he'd grown tired of the young wizards and witches over the centuries, and the trunket served as a novel sight to be seen on the grounds. Who knows...?

But despite the obvious feelings of envy and resentment that such childish imaginations are bound to spawn, there're still many others who were genuinely intrigued with the trunket and his mysterious origin. They were all curious about Jhavon's past. And long before his admittance into Pagaroth's school, tall tales of slain mox hounds were already in heavy circulation throughout the castle. Almost everyone knew of the outlaw trunket from the land of Ragath, who'd slain one of his own in cold blood, or self defense, according to which teller's telling the tale at the time. However, they all treated him differently. There were many (like Mr. Lash, and Julie) who were friendly towards him—but spoke with an air of wonderment and fascination in his presence. While some shunned and avoided him altogether.

Despite his itty-bitty size—which made him the smallest boy in all of Pagaroth—his reputation had grown far larger than any man's. However, he wasn't immune to the magical tricks and pranks that some saw fit to subject him to....

As he made his way to the next class, there came the sudden thumping, crasing sound behind him. And long before he could turn and see the two boys (dressed in brown robes) sprawled out on the floor, loud laughter erupted from all those in the hallway. The boys just laid there with confused and embarrassed looks on their faces. Beneath them, was a small puddle of frozen ice. A lykine's petty trick, that Jhavon himself had fallen victim to the day before. But since then, he'd encrusted the soles of his boots with tiny bits of rock. It made walking uncomfortable, and the sound of grinding stone always followed his footsteps. However, when walking on ice, they offered the perfect traction....

He looked on as the two boys tried to get up, only to slip and lose their footing again. A new roarous eruption of laughter came; all the students pointing and shaking their heads in pity.

Just then, a wave of warm air filled the halls and the ice quickly melted away. The crowd of students seemed to disperse in the same speed, leaving the two boys to get up and head to their class in peeved silence.

As to who had caused the heat could've been anyone's guess, for Jhavon had been rescued in the same manner the day before. But as to the perpetrator behind the childish prank, there wasn't the slightest doubt in the trunket's mind.

He scanned the crowd till he spotted the tall lykine leaning against the wall. A sly grin ran up the left side of his face as he raised a skinny arm in greeting....

Mr. Cobber taught math and science. He was a robust, middle-aged man, from a land called Danwhar. A brilliant teacher with a shock of salt and pepper hair, and a thick mustache that quivered above his lip whenever he spoke.

The acrid odor of chemicals filled his classroom. The walls were decorated with every mathematical equation known to the world.... For those who only focused on magic, this was their worst subject. But for Jhavon, Mr. Cobber's class was his favorite.

"Now class," Mr. Cobber began, after scribbling down some notes on a black board that was so wide it stretched from one side of his classroom to the other. "As we've already learned yesterday, beneath the surface of our world are things called 'plates' that move and cause the land to shake. And when the land shake, what is it commonly called?" he asked, then pointed to a little girl that rose her hand. "Ah.. aye, Morlah."

Morlah, was a young sorceress from the Land of Laap. Blind since the day she was born, she wore a thin black cloth tied around her head to cover her eyes. However, though impaired, she was just as normal as the rest of her peers. She appeared small and frail inside the large brown robe that swallowed her up.... Her twin sister Marlah (sitting right next to her) was identical to her in every way, save for the long black hair that flowed down past her shoulders, where Morlah's hair was perfectly blonde. She also had her sight, so she didn't wear any blindfolds the way her sister did. But where Marlah was blessed with the gift of sight, she was also cursed with the lack of hearing. And just like her blind sister, Marlah was born deaf.

Only by staying close to each other (at all times) had these twins adapted to their different worlds. Morlah, who possessed the keenest sense of hearing, used her ears to listen in on a world that would go unnoticed by Marlah in her absence. And in turn, Marlah used her sharp sight to see the things her sister could not....

"They're called 'shivers', Mr. October," said Morlah, in a very confident tone. Though she was only thirteen years old, she was already beginning to sound like a young woman. "But according to history, was it not Pagaroth who shivered the land?"

The professor's quivering lip went taut for a brief second as he smiled at the young girl. "At times, history tend to carry on carelessly with no regards to the facts, Morlah. But aye...you are correct. According to history (and not science) the Eternal Pagaroth shivered the land whenever he felt the need to move his mountains from here to there. But Pagaroth's been gone for thousands of years, and yet the land still shiver at times." He stopped here, looking at the blindfolded little girl, whose head followed his voice and footsteps. It was nearly impossible to read her blank expression. "Does history explain why?"

Morlah shook her head. "No.... But that's what Mr. Lash––"

"There's something that you all must learn about history," the professor suddenly began, cutting off Morlah's words. "History only serve as a memory to those with no recollection. And like memories, it tends to become distorted as time goes by. And yet, just as our memories are still so important to us, so is history."

"But if not Pagaroth, Mr. Cobber," Morlah said. "What other force in Hagaraak can cause the land to shiver?"

"I was just getting to that," Mr. Cobber replied. "As I mentioned earlier, there are plates below the land. Not the kind of plates that we eat from...but very large ones, made out of rock. And when these plates move, they cause the land to shiver."

"What makes the plates move, Mr. Cobber?" another girl in the second row asked. Though she tried her very best to speak softly, her voice was so high-pitched that it was heard outside the classroom. As a siren, it was the most she could do to prevent her lethal vocals from killing everyone in the room.

"Well, Emma..." the professor said. "The Eternal Pagaroth himself couldn't push these enormous slabs of rock on his own. So he used the flow of the earth's magma, which tend to became as slippery as ice when they run beneath the plates.... Some say that it was the movement of these plates that broke the world in three halves."

The school's curriculum was designed by Shurlan, to set such conflicting thoughts into the minds of the remnants. Each class––at times––tend to contradict the other; but not for the sole purpose of that. The curriculum was designed to suit the world's two main schools of thought: those who practiced magic, and those who probed into the mysteries of science.

Most of the remnants lived outside of Pagaroth, so their knowledge of the Eternals and the physical world were so infused together, very few were able to distinct real facts from myth.

In many lands, all things were attributed to the Eternals, for the sole purpose of bringing all living things into existence.

It was important for the students to know their world. To know of the power that exists apart from the Eternals. A power, that not even Ragath (for all of his scientific wisdom) could contain on his own.... And without this knowledge, a remnant can never reach his or her potential....

"But how could this be, Mr. Cobber?" asked the confounded young wizard, named Shurwath. "Everyone knows that Baas and Pagaroth split the world to prevent Ragath from leaving Hagar."

"That's partially true," the professor replied. "But the world wasn't just split to prevent Ragath from leaving Hagar. He made portals, remember? He could go anywhere; to a whole different world if he really wanted to. No Shurwath, quite the opposite happens to be the case here. Rather, it was to prevent the outside creatures from entering Hagar when Ragath sent the world on its unnatural course. For the togs used to wander into the Land of Laap at times. And the rykes often roamed near the Sea of Baas, where the rivers' waters are the most sweet." He stopped here to stare at all the rapt faces in the classroom before continuing. "And history is correct in all this.... But how do you suppose that Baas and Pagaroth broke up the world and split them apart? Surely, and I hope, you don't think they simply pushed them over the waters as if they were sail-boats."

The blank stares he got in return, confirmed that they all thought that much. In fact, all of his past students had once thought it that way. It was the general concept of the world. People often confused the forces of nature with the forces of magic.

"Surely..." he continued. "You don't think that something as big as a mountain can float on water?" he asked, feigning his astonishment. His narrow eyes opened wide. "Surely, you don't think Hagaraak floats on water.... No... it is on these very plates that the lands sit upon. And they move. It was Pagaroth who pushed these plates––so far away from Hagar, they eventually broke off from the land. And it was Baas who sent his mighty oceans to fill the gap. And long before Pagaroth came into existance, the land shivered on its own. So he never caused the land to shiver until the day came when he was forced to split the world.

"And this is why the land still shivers from time to time, even in the absence of Pagaroth."

CHAPTER
THIRTEEN

SHURLAN'S SCHOOL OF Merit operated in a four-year cycle, where the students explored their gifts in different stages of development. Different colored robes were assigned to each, according to how advanced they were. A student will usually wear a brown robe throughout most of his first year, then black during his second then green, and finally purple by the time he graduates. However, few exceptions were made for those considered to be highly gifted. In such special cases, a student's age becomes irrelevant when placed next to how powerful he or she can actually be. A direct remnant (as they're called) can don as high as a green robe in their first year.

Because of the school's focus on individual talent, each group of students were kept isolated from the other. The first year students (for example), wasn't permitted to mingle amongst those in their second year. And the second from the third, and so on.... The beginners were housed in their own dorms––boys apart from the girls, and so on.... There were four study libraries, each designated to an assigned group, where the content of the material were neither above nor below the students' ability to understand.

This method of isolation ensured that the students' development grew naturally, without skipping any steps along the way. One of the main problems Shurlan discovered during the school's earliest days, was the younger students who tended to pick up things prematurely from the older ones. And this posed a serious impedance with their learning, especially when it came to magic.

A first year pyromancer (fire wizard) not fully understanding the properties of heat, can not only injure himself, but others as well. And this posed psychological issues to the arrogant student, believing that he's already become a master in the field, and there's nothing more to be learned. The Copper City was filled with such half-wizards, clumsy witches, and wannabe sorcerers, who were born with their gifts but had developed them without the proper training.... They were like ship-builders, not knowing the ways of the sea.

Strict penalties were handed out to any student caught passing his or her knowledge down to the younger ones. The most cannon being expulsion from school altogether, though lesser penalties may stand in the right circumstances.

However, there were still a few places where all the students were permitted to meet, such as the main dining areas, or when in the gardens which is accessible to all those who lived within Pagaroth's castle.

On account of Shurlan's method, the school has been able to send at least thirty of the most skilled magicians throughout the lands each year for the past 3,000 years. 'Tis where the most powerful wizards, witches, and sorcerers developed their skills....

"The trunket claims that he can do anything!" Syme said to a group of boys. They were all gathered in the west wing of the gardens, near a small pond where countless lilies floated. Speckled ducks dipped their beaks below the pond's placid surface, while some paddled their way across to peck at the bread crumbs that drifted by. "And yet, he possess no magic...."

The lykine stood tall in his brown robe. He folded his arms and creased his brows, pretending to be in deep thought. He paced the soft grass in a comical way, causing his small audience to laugh at his antics. "Hmmm..." he began, staring up at the gloomy sky while tapping his chin with a long bony finger. "Tell us again, trunket. I don't think the whole class heard you correctly. Or maybe it was simply a jest. Tell us again, trunket. What can you do?"

"I can do any, and everything, Syme," Jhavon replied as he stood close by, staring up at the much taller lykine. Behind him, was Shurwath, the young wizard. Julie stood nearby, gripping tightly to her spirit-stick where the embedded gem glowed to a pulsating red to depict her growing irritation.

"Hmph!" the lykine said, before turning to his companions. "A blasphemer then?" he asked them. The boys all nodded in reply. A few "ayes" were heard being muttered within the small crowd. Syme then pointed to the sky, his long arm following a flock of geese through the air. "Can you fly without wings? Tell us, trunket. Can you fly?"

"Aye, Syme," Jhavon said. "That I can."

"Well, trunket.... Let's see this then. Let us see you fly."

"In good time, Syme. If you still wish to see me do such a thing. I won't use any magic of course––for trunkets don't possess any magic. But I'm sure there's a method to it. And if there's a method to it, then I'm sure I can find it––then I'll show you all that I can fly. Without magic!"

"Ha!" Syme laughed. "It's a jest I tell you. The trunket is a jester. He claims to fly, but he has no magic. He jests! How can anyone fly without magic? Unless he be some unknown remnant of Mox––which the trunket is definitely not. Nonsense! The trunket is a jester."

"It's no jest, Syme," Jhavon said.

"Aye...?" Syme's expression became more malevolent as he stepped over toward Jhavon and leaned in so close to his face that their foreheads nearly touched. "Is that so, trunket?"

"That's so, Syme."

"Well now...we still don't believe you. But if you must insist that this...this...method, you say can make you fly is no jest––well...I guess you have to prove it to us then."

"It's no jest, Syme."

"So you say, trunket. So you say.... But words are provided to both the powerful and the powerless. Are they not?"

Jhavon glared into the young lykine's green eyes. He was neither fearful nor intimidated by Syme, though his mounting anger was evident to all. "That they are, Syme," he said. "And it's such an unfortunate thing that words are unable to tell one from the other."

"Aye. Such an unfortunate thing. But deeds, trunket. And actions, can make such a distinction. You say you can fly. Is that not so?"

"Aye...it is."

"Well, prove it then. Prove it to us. Can you prove it us, trunket?"

"I can prove it," Jhavon was aware that he was biting into Syme's bate. But he didn't care.

"Very well, then." Syme walked back to where his companions stood. "Let's see this...this...flying of yours."

"I can't. Not at this precise moment."

The mischievous Syme feigned a great frown and rubbed thoughtfully at his brow. "Okay, trunket," he said, after a moment. "We know you can't just grow wings like Shurlan––my dearest kin––but in time, might you be able to do such a thing?"

"Aye. Given enough time, I can do anything."

"Aye...?"

"Aye!"

"Well..." said Syme. "How much time then?"

"Two weeks, Syme. Two weeks is all. Just atop the eastern wall. Meet me there around this time, two weeks from now. Then I'll show you that my words are just as powerful as my deeds."

"The eastern wall?"

"Aye."

They all turned to the far wall just then, and it seemed to go on forever as it surrounded the castle. It was a very long way to the top of the wall––even for Syme. "Very well then, trunket," he said, looking up at the great stretch of wall. It was like staring up at two morgah trees, with one standing on top the other. "Two weeks from now. Top of the east wall, it is. And I assume that you're going to show us that you can climb like a lizard as well?"

"If that is what you want. Then that is what you'll see, in time."

Syme gave a heavy sigh and shook his head in amusement. "I guess we'll have to take your word for it–– for now, at least. Till then, I have nothing more to say." And with that, he gave the trunket a sly wink, then he and his friends departed. But not before one of them found a flat stone and sent it skipping across the surface of the pond, barely missing a startled duck....

"Jhavon!" Shurwath was the first to chide the young trunket, beating Julie by a mere second.

"You allowed that jesting lykine to make you lose your wits. You should know his nature by now. No one takes him seriously."

"To have him make you pledge such silly promises, Jhavon," Julie added. "Is far beneath you. Now you must face more shame before the entire class, two weeks from now."

"I will not," said Jhavon.

"Are you serious about that, Jhavon?" Julie asked. "I know you can do things. Aaron said so himself. So maybe you can climb the wall. But you could never fly, Jhavon. Only if the Eternal Mox could give you some wings."

"And Mox isn't here," Shurwath said. "You'll never fly without magic."

"Climbing the wall should be easy enough," Jhavon said. "I just haven't thought of a way yet. And I'm pretty sure I'll be flying before two weeks time as well."

Both Shurwath and Julie exchanged worried frowns. Surely, the young trunket was bound to get himself hurt–– jumping from the eastern wall, where no amount of magic could save him from the ground's mortal lash.... They begged him to reconsider.

The trunket however, just smiled in return. "See....?" he said, giving them both a jovial tap on their shoulders with his pillow-sized hands. "I've figured it out already."

"Figured what out?" Julie asked.

"My own method, of course."

———●———

"My mind is the gate to all worlds, and all worlds lead to this gate," Zhorghan said, reciting the ancient characters that were carved into a mirror's golden frame. The eons of neglect had allowed layers of dust to crust over its once shiny surface. He stared at his own reflection, looking past the dent in the middle that made his face appear long and thin. "A most dubious and critical oversight, Ohlar," he said to the shadowy demon. "To rummage through the abode of an Eternal, seeking such frivolity as scrolls, when the real treasure sat right in front of them."

He swept a hand across the mirror's surface, causing the dust to fall of with a simple spell. The dent popped itself out, and his reflection was now perfectly clear. He stood there for a long time after that, mesmerized by the Eternal's mirror, uncertain of whether he should be seeing something other than his self....

———————•———————

The tall snow-capped mountains shot up in the sky as if to oppose the fridged winds that wailed and. howled with all nature's fury. Crags of ice and rock stuck out from impossible angles, like cliffs jutting out from other cliffs. Their icicles hung dozens of feet, like glass, carved in the shape of men's beards.

For leagues all around, the ground was white with fresh snow that shifted like sand in the strong wind. No animals on this world! Not yet. Frozen microbes maybe, deep in the ice, still awaiting their billionth year when a warmer sun might free them of their prisons.

It was an infant world....

It was here where a black dot suddenly appeared in mid air, like a blot of ink splashed on clear glass. It grew within seconds. Silver streaks of lightning snaked and crackled within the black void. The wind-driven snow blew in its way, only to be swallowed up inside——clinging to the dark robe of an Eternal who came walking out!

He stood still while his silver hair and beard whipped violently in the strong gale. His feet were bare, but they weren't affected by the cold ice. His sharp blue eyes shifted over the landscape, his face showing neither contempt nor approval of the cruel environment, before settling on the distant sun above the horizon. And judging from the angle it hung between a pair snow-capped peaks, he knew that he'd visited this world before.

But it wasn't exactly the same. That other world was hot, a complete desert. And it existed in another universe.

The dark portal closed in on itself behind him. Some five yards away, another one appeared where he took no hesitation upon entering. And just as suddenly, this portal closed in on itself as well.

The drifting snow hid his footprints, diligently correcting the desecration on the virgin ground....

CHAPTER
FOURTEEN

"BAHHH!" OLD HOLLAN exclaimed, shaking his head. His lips pouted, then pursed as if he just bit into something sour. "What do shadows know of such things, Shurlan?"

The two was sitting in the cluttered confines of Hollan's place, discussing the attempted theft in Shurlan's study. The lykine sat across from the old wizard in a big chair that might've been an old throne of some forgotten king. The metal on the armrests gleamed like dull copper under the light, however, if Hollan were to wipe at it with a damp cloth, there was hardly any doubt (in Shurlan's mind) that it would take on a more golden sheen.

"You're underestimating Ohlar's role, Hollan," Shurlan said. "This wasn't just some thief looking for treasure. He knew exactly what he was looking for. I was watching him. High in the ceiling, with the eyes of a serpant. He searched and searched until he found Ragath's scrolls."

"To do what then?" Hollan asked. "What do shadows knew of portals? Or anyone else for that matter? To conjure one, is a task for an Eternal. And not just any Eternal, either."

"The shadow is of no real concern here, Hollan. He's obviously in someone's employ."

"Obviously."

"Someone who showed him where to find the ancient text."

A deep frown creased the old wizard's brow just then. "Ragath's scroll you mean?"

"Aye," Shurlan replied. "I watched him as he read right from the text: 'My mind is the gate to all worlds.' He was so shocked at what he'd just read, he nearly ripped the scroll in half. And that's when I stepped him. I regret now that I hadn't done it sooner."

"You think he know what it means?"

"Aye."

Hollan began to look worried. "But that could only mean that he must have the other scrolls. Studying——"

"No," Shurlan said, shaking his head. "Not him, but someone else. It is true that he could've learned to read the script some time ago. But the one who studies them——take them apart and piece them back together, is the one who can bring us the most harm."

"Hmm..." Hollan said. His mind raced, searching his memories for hidden clues. "So we've gotten there too late after all. And after all these years, we're now starting to see the beginnings of it."

"Or the end," Shurlan said in a grim tone. "The missing scrolls...who knows what secrets they might be holding? And I assure you Hollan, the ones that I have contain nothing. No wander they were left behind."

"It was once said that Ragath had an apprentice," Hollan said. "Long before he attained the wretched sapphire. Legend has it that he had adopted a human boy from the Land of Laap. Some say Ragath kidnaped the boy, but I guess it doesn't matter much how the boy came to be. The thing is, no one has ever laid eyes on him, so the tale was considered to be just that: a tale. But who knows?" He shrugged. "We both know how true some tales can be."

"It's quite possible, Hollan.... I've heard of much stranger things. And I must admit, a secret apprentice would make a lot of sense. But we must also keep in mind that even this could be false, and pursuing some imaginary figure to no end, can take us more off course than we already are."

"That would certainly add more thorns to our branch."

"It certainly would."

Hollan sighed. "And what do Mor––"

"Stop!" The lykine's voice became shrill, but he was careful not to shout. "Don't say it," he said more calmly...his voice barely above a whisper. "Do not mention her name, lest she come floating in here like smoke from a torch. You know her ears are keener than a Biilath wolf's.... And to answer your question––no, she doesn't know. Nor do she need to. We're almost out of time, and I must have her focused on her task; not flying about looking for ghosts and shadows. Which she certainly will, if she ever hears about this."

Old Hollan gazed upon Shurlan's face and nodded. "I see that you still believe in those prophecies."

"More so," Shurlan replied. "Considering everything that's taking place. Ragath's return is inevitable. It's only a matter of time before he discovers the right portal that will bring him back to his world...our world. But there're others who wish to hasten things. As to whether or not they succeed, appears to be part of the prophecy as well.... After all these years, Hollan," he said, changing the gloomy subject to stare around the old wizard's messy room. "You still haven't cleaned this place up. I can recognize things that was knocked over centuries ago, and not a thought entered your mind to pick them up. You haven't changed at all."

"Ha!" Hollan let out a short laugh. "And I see that you're still in the habit of fretting over trivial things."

Shurlan allowed the wave of nostalgia to sweep through his mind and indulge in memories of times long gone....

"You know that boy of yours...? The trunket boy; Jhavon––if I remember his name correctly. He was here, just a few months back."

"Here...?" A curious frown fell over Shurlan's brow. "But how did he––"

"That son of mine brought him."

"For what?" Shurlan asked. He uncrossed his legs and leaned forward with interest.

"The trunket boy wanted three watches. Something to do with that Pag-be-damned obstacle you make those young lads go through."

"Hmm..." a more enlightened Shurlan mused. Those fierce eyes lit up for a moment. "So that's how he made it."

"Made what?"

"Words can't describe what he made out of those watches, Hollan. You would have to see them for yourself. But I'll tell you this, he could not have passed that obstacle without them."

"So he succeeded then?"

"Aye."

"So Rahjule brought us a magical trunket after all?"

"No, Hollan. The trunket has no magic. But he finished the obstacle as any wizard could."

"So, what is he?"

"A builder."

"A builder?"

"Aye," Shurlan replied. "And a thinker, an inventor, and a creator as well."

"An inventor?"

"Aye! Of all things.... He's young now, but there isn't anything that the trunket wouldn't be able to do as he matures and grew older."

"Well...if the greatest gods, magicians, and wizards couldn't stop Ragath from blackening the sky over Pagaroth for all eternity, then I guess we might as well try a trunket boy who knows how to build things from watches."

"The power works mysteriously, Hollan. The trunket was created to face his own Eternal in the end. Rahjule believed it. And who knows how long he must've been living in the Red Forest, but he did, and the boy showed up as predicted."

Hollan shrugged. "I guess the boy has some merit to him. The Red Forest says that much.... So what now?"

"We do nothing.... The time will take care of itself. Ours is almost up; we aren't mentioned anywhere in the times when things become new. The trunket's generation will be the last. They'll be the ones to see things to the very end. I don't know when, or how this will happen...but it will."

Hollan leaned back in his chair with a regretful sigh. "You know what, Shurlan?" he asked.

"What...?"

"Sometimes, I wish Rahjule had never written those Pag-be-damned scrolls."

None other than Jhekaath could've been the school's exercise instructor. He held many games––all non-magical activities––that encouraged the students to utilize their brawn as well as their wits. Competitive games, all combative in nature, very rough, very hands on. Whether one happened to be a wizard or a witch didn't make the slightest difference at all.

It was here, on the large open field at the school's southern wing, where the students suffered some of the most brutal injuries. Broken limbs (a severed spine, on one occasion) often happened to be the cause of some unfortunate soul, howling off the field in sheer agony. And on such occasions a senior student––specialized in the gift of healing––was always present during their training.

With the "healer's" magic, broken bones and torn muscles were mended in a matter of minutes. The wound, whether it be a five inch gash or a fingernail's scratch, will close up as if no injury had ever occurred there at all....

One such game was called: Rescuers. On one side of the field were the rescuers, while the catchers stood at the other end of the field. Then there were the captives, held in their bonds in the center of the field. Both the rescuers and catchers had six players each, but there were only three captives whose numbers were always half that of the other teams.

The players faced off in a 100 yard field. At the sound of a whistle, the rescuers must rush down toward the captives. It was the catchers' task to prevent the rescuers from ever reaching their hostages––by any means necessary. The catcher can grab, hold, scratch, punch, and kick...however, the use of magic was strictly forbidden on the field. Only one rescuer can free a hostage at a time, till all were rescued, or...if all the rescuers happens to get caught in the process. The team to accomplish their goal in less time, wins....

But the game of Rescue, along with all the others that require team effort, came 2nd to the most important activity. The main and most combative game: fighting with sword and shield. The only event where two participants combated each other. And most of the students' physical training were focused here. At times, the entire class period would be consumed by it, and nothing else.

No wooden swords, but real steel with blunt edges were used. Blows to the neck and head were forbidden, and the students did wear protective padding along their arms and legs, but that was as far as this particular rule went when it came to protection....

"You must always remember to keep your swords low and your shields high," said Jhekaath, while pacing back and forth with a shield in his hand. One of the senior students stood before him, armed, with the tip of his long-sword aimed at the ground––his purple robe flapping lazily in the calm wind.

Jhavon and the rest of the class all watched quietly while the instructor spoke. They stood in perfect formation, bodies erect, four rows––from the shortest in the front, to the tallest in the back. Each held their own swords, with the blunt tips piercing the trimmed grass on the field.

Jhekaath went into a low crouch and raised his shield. The senior student didn't waste any time, he moved in quickly. "Pay special attention to the movement of the sword," Jhekaath said, raising the shield just in time as the sword crashed into the side of it with a loud bang!

The violent blow didn't phase the instructor. He took two steps back, but the student matched the movement with two forward steps of his own. The student spun, swinging a side-swiping blow that might've cut a man in half with a sharper edge. The blade bounced off the shield, but the student never lost a step in his momentum. His sword came down like a hammer, banging off the surface of the shield again. This time, the instructor parried the blow, throwing his pursuer off balance, who answered immediately with a back-handed chop. But Jhekaath was much faster, he stepped into the chop and grabbed the student by his waist and elbow to send him sprawling onto his back.

"The most important weapon of defense when engaging the enemy," he said, while helping the student back to his feet. "Is not the sword or the shield, but your footing." He tapped his thighs with the shield. "Your stance. The way you position yourself in combat can determine whether you live or die. Always be mindful of how you stand. Knees slightly bent, one foot before the other. Always maintain your balance, and try to keep the enemy off theirs."

He broke them off into pairs, each focused on standing and maneuvering with the shields in defensive positions. "If you must step back," he said. "Don't do it as a retreat, but as an attempt to lure. And when advancing forward, don't look for openings, look for traps instead, because a skilled enemy could be attempting to lure you in as well."

The end of each day was spent conducting the same combative exercise, which left the students too sore and exhausted to do anything else. And not even the healer's magical touch could serve as remedy for physical fatigue...

———•———

It had long been to Jhavon's wonderment as to what actually made birds fly. He'd first thought that all flying creatures needed wings and feathers. But he would learn later on in life that bats and insects didn't have any feathers at all, and yet, they took to the air as well as any normal bird would. So that narrowed it down to the one thing that all flying creatures had in common: their wings. They all needed wings to fly.

The young trunket had once thought this to be one of life's undeniable facts (like snow being white, or rain being wet) till he learned––while delivering a fixed watch to one of Mr. Laan's customers in the country side––that not all winged creatures could fly! Like chickens––the same ones that went scurrying out of the way as he entered the customer's yard on horseback––was incapable of flying longer than a few seconds. He learned that this was due to the creatures' weight. Their wings were too small, and too weak to lift their bulky mass in the air for any significant period of time. Their breasts and thighs were too meaty–– too much marrow filled their bones. And this...he learned from eating many mid-moon suppers in the school's eatery.

But then there were certain creatures: vultures, hawks, mox hounds...that were much larger than any country side chicken, yet still managed to soar through the sky for many leagues. However, their wings were much larger in size and wider in span, like the mox hound...whose mighty wings were like great leafy branches....

So he reasoned, that the larger the creature, the bigger and more powerful their wings must be in order to fly.

Learning such things were inevitable to all intelligent trunkets. In fact, Jhavon already knew what it took to lift someone in the air; and more so than those who believed that only the creatures of Mox could fly. The challenge came in building his own personal wing that was big enough to lift all of his sixty-five pounds——if only for just a few seconds....

"And what would you ever need bamboo sticks for, Jhavon?" Aaron asked with a puzzled look on his face. The two laid sprawled in separate hammocks near Aaron's house in Shurlan's cottage. Both swung themselves slowly, nursing their fat stomachs that was stuffed with lamb's stew.

The trunket sighed as he laid there with his eyes closed. The effects of a full stomach always made him sleepy. "I'm thinking of building a frame," he said.

"Oh..." Aaron said, then kicked at the ground to send the hammock in a gentle swing. "A frame to hold up one of Julie's paintings?"

"No."

"Then what would a trunket like you need bamboo for?"

"A wing."

"A wing...?" Aaron rolled over on his side to stare at him. "A wing that could flap, like a bird?"

"Aye. That very wing."

"And what for?"

"To fly."

"Ha!" Aaron burst out laughing. He gave his thigh a good slap. "The trunket wants to fly...aye! Why didn't that come to me at once? Should've known that Jhavon, the great builder, would soon set his eyes on flying. Aye...! You're jesting, I hope."

"It's not a jest, Aaron." Jhavon said. "I'll make the wing. Then fly. I'll jump right off the east wall and wait for the wind to catch me."

"Or the ground to spank you!"

"Won't even get close to the ground."

"Because Morella will put a stop to it before you get the chance," Aaron's tone sobered up a bit. "She'll stop you in the air. You won't even know it."

Jhavon didn't say anything else at the sound of the elemental's name. It was no secret that her ears were everywhere.

"But even if this isn't so, Jhavon," Aaron went on. "I don't think there's any bamboo growing in Pagaroth. Maybe in Vlak's Forest."

"Guess I'll have to use plain wood then."

"But why favor bamboo so much?"

"Its lighter, its strong, and its more flexible. In Ragath, they grow everywhere."

"Hmm...and without this bamboo, your wing would be less flyable?"

"Not exactly. I'll just have to make a bigger wing to support the extra weight."

"So you still plan to carry on with this mad adventure?"

"Aye...I'll show them all that I too can fly?"

"Aha!" Aaron sat up on his elbow so fast, he nearly fell out of the hammock. "I suspected as much. For what would move you to do such things, if not for the urgings of some dare or bet? Maybe you have something to prove. In a world of magicians, the boy-inventor is seen as the weakest. And perhaps the dumbest as well, if he thinks he can fly."

"I'm not!" Jhavon snapped back. "Syme's only jealous that my papers always come back with better reports than his. I can never be dumber than Syme. In fact, I don't think that I've ever met anyone who could be just slightly dumber than Syme. I might be the weakest, but he's certainly the dumbest."

"Ah..." Aaron said, as though enlightened. "And so, our culprit has been named." He laid back down in the hammock. "The young lykine. King of all jesters! We all fell victim to at least one of them. Why should a trunket be any different? It's best to ignore him, Jhavon. He's a remnant of Llok. He cannot help but be a jest."

"He calls me a jest!"

"Oh, but you know better than that, Jhavon. How can you be a jest, after building that thing over there?" He pointed to the 100 foot platform in the distance.

Looking over at the platform now, it was hard (even for him) to believe that he'd actually built something like that. But the long scar across his palm reassured him that he did, along with the reminder that he'd almost lost his life going through the obstacle. "But they never saw that," he said. "Even if they did, they'll never believe that I made it. They all think that I'm Shurlan's pet."

"But I don't think so," Aaron said. "My mother don't think so, either. That's why she feeds you so much."

Jhavon laughed.

"It's true. Morella wouldn't allow you in the school if she thought you didn't belong there."

"But they don't know," Jhavon said, referring to his classmates. "They still think I'm a jest. And unless I show them different, they'll always think so."

Aaron sighed, then threw his hands up in resignation. "I listened. I spoke. I warned. But alas! I've failed.... If you think you have to prove things, then it's your pags-be-given right to do so. But I'm telling you, Jhavon. You'll be proving all sorts of nonsense to that jester until you leave this school and return to Ragath."

A surge of apprehension ran through the young trunket at the mention of his eventual return home. Back to the mox hounds and warders.

"And how did this schemer manage to convince you that you can fly?"

"He didn't convince me of anything," Jhavon said. "I told him that I can do anything; that I could fly if I really wanted to."

"Oh? And what caused you to attempt such a thing?"

"Because they doubted me. And he said that I couldn't."

Aaron frowned. "Is that all?"

"Aye...that's all."

CHAPTER
FIFTEEN

FROM THE LAND of Lagophar, was a very gifted boy named Ahnon, whom Jhavon had taked a good liking to—— or rather, it could've been he...who'd taken a liking to the young trunket. But either way, the two had grown very close over the long months. Ahnon was surprisingly small for a human boy. At the age of 13, he looked frail, and was barely taller than Jhavon.

With all of his clothing——robes included——custom made to accommodate his oversized hands, Jhavon never had to worry about looking silly because of his ill-fitting garb. But little Ahnon, however, wasn't as fortunate as his trunket friend——for all of his robes hung on his gaunt body like soaked bed sheets. And whenever the wind blew, his robe would flare like sails and threaten to take him high in the air.

Because of his size and apparent weakness, little Ahnon had been a constant target of Syme, before Jhavon's arrival to Pagaroth. And where the lykine's pranks might work just one time on Jhavon, little Ahnon always fell for the same old tricks. But this wasn't due to Ahnon's lack of wit, for it was nearly impossible to predict when the troublesome lykine might get an itch for a laugh.

Seeing that Jhavon was much smaller, and he didn't possess any magic, the mischievous Syme knew there was very little the trunket could've done to get back at him. So it was easy for him to forget all about the little "stickling" from Lagophar, and try his hand at new prey.

And it was this similarity, having one common enemy, that had brought the two together.

Despite his size, however, little Ahnon was by no means helpless. His gift was truly special and unique, though at this stage in his development it counted for very little. And being a mute from birth, he appeared as docile as a baby sloth.

Ahnon couldn't talk, so he spoke through the mouths of others––for this was his gift. Anything that lived (and possessed a vocal cord) he'd use as a vessel for sound. In the classroom, he usually spoke through the mouth of a willing student sitting right next to him. And outside of school, when no one else was around, he'd use the voice of nature; from the braying mule, to the squealing pig; from the chirping cricket, to the singing bird. All could possess the human gift of speech if Ahnon willed it to be....

"This History of Llok says..." Jhavon said quietly in the presence of Julie, Shurwath, and Ahnon, all seated at the same table in the school's study library. "That at the beginning, the Eternal Llok created all the animals first. Then he made the giants, then the humans, and the hairy togs. What do yours say?" he asked Julie.

Julie read from her own copy of the History of Llok. "It says, that in the beginning, the Eternal Llok made all the animals, the humans, the giants, and togs."

"How about yours, Shurwath?"

"Mine says: 'And Llok made all the beasts of the land, and all that live in it."

"Is that all?" Jhavon asked.

"Aye," Shurwath replied. "As far as all Llok's creations go."

"And yours, Ahnon?"

The little curly haired boy's lips began to move as he read from the passage. But no words came from his mouth. They came through Shurwath's instead: "'In the beginning, the Eternal Llok made all the animals, the humans, the giants, and the togs.'"

"Isn't that what yours say as well, Julie?" Jhavon asked.

"The very same, Jhavon."

"We have different authors, then?" asked Ahnon, through Shurwath's mouth.

Jhavon nodded. "They all amount to the same thing, though."

"So who's to believe that all the beasts were created first?" asked Shurwath this time. "Or whether the giants came before the humans? And since Llok loved the togs so much, how do we know that he didn't make them first?"

"And what of the lykines?" asked Julie. "The remnants of Llok. You'd think that they should be the first."

"It doesn't say," Jhavon said.

"The lykines," Ahnon began. "Would have to come after the creation of the togs, because in the History of Hagar, it says that the Eternals had intercourse with the things that lived in the world whenever they became drunk on togsmead. So the lykines, the treelings, you trunkets, the rykes, and everything else came after the togs."

"I think you're right, Ahnon," said Shurwath.

A broad smile crept across the mute's face as he gave a subtle nod in response.

"So it's as simply as this then," Jhavon said. "There're different wordings in each of our books. But they all lead to the same ends, I think. So there isn't much harm in that there. I don't think there's any importance in which order Llok created all the beasts, either. But——" he paused, holding up a fat finger. "It's very likely that the History of Llok was written by prejudiced hands. One author could've been a lykine, while a human might've written his own version. Nonetheless, they all seemed to agree on the way how things came to an end. So we can all sum up the History of Llok, without contradicting each other too much. I think we should stick to our own books——for now——and mention only what's truly relevant about Llok's history. Passages that contradict each other should only be summed up briefly."

There wasn't a class in Pagaroth's school that allowed both Jhavon and Ahnon to exploit their talents more, than during the afternoon's music session class. For Ahnon, it was choosing the worst voice in the room to produce the sweetest of sounds. Through him, any frog's throat will do, delivering the smoothest, gentlest tunes.

For Jhavon, it was the simple recreation of his musical instruments to suit his oversized hands and fingers. He made his flute longer, with holes spaced further apart. His harp and lyre were equally augmented to perfect scale——each note resonated around the room with the same excellence as their normal-sized counterparts.

It was a marvel to all (both student and teacher alike) that a trunket, with no prior experience in music, can make his own instruments. They marveled at his method of invention, much in the same way he marveled at some of their talent with magic.

Where Ahnon was gifted in controlling the voice of others, it was Ermma, a siren from Danwhar, who was the true master of sound. Even at her current age of 12, she held the power of seduction, hypnotism, and even death! with her enchanting voice. It was the only voice that Ahnon was strictly forbidden to use, lest he kill himself and everyone else in the whole class.

Because the students were left to develop their own gifts, there was never a central curriculum for magic in the school. Unlike the other subjects, magic was something that couldn't be taught. However, they did have special instructors who oversaw the development of each student's gift.

They were strongly encouraged to practice as much as they could. In fact, a student of Pagaroth's school spent most of his or her time preoccupied with magic, even Jhavon... whether he was aware of it or not. But for Ermma, this mode of preoccupation was constant.

Every moment of her life was spent on controlling the power that vibrated within her. Just speaking regularly, took considerable effort to bring her voice down to a level that wouldn't deafen or kill her audience. And this couldn't be any more true than when she was fast asleep––for just one utter, snore, or the slightest sound while dreaming, was loud enough to awake her entire dorm. Even her breathing had to be controlled while she slept....

Sirens were known to dwell all throughout the land of Hagaraak, however, their numbers were depressingly few. Because of their unstable powers, they're often shunned and feared in their infant years. Most are banished from their native lands, or dwell in distant caves. Others are simply killed at birth; the ear-splitting cries of the new-born infant betraying it to a deadly fate.... The life of a siren, is never good.

Through fear, they're often the target for a hidden archer, or a wizard's evil spell. In turn, a siren is a very cautious, unforgiving, and lonesome creature. The unfortunate robber, or would-be molestor, seeking to bring her harm, are doomed to the most horrible fate. For just five seconds, a single scream can burst the eardrums and hemorrhage the brain till blood pour from the ears, nose, and eyes.

Despite the ill treatment that was suffered by the rest of her kind, Ermma on the other hand, enjoyed a normal existance as any one of her peers at Pagaroth's school. This was due largely in part, because at twelve, she'd already attained a level of control wielded by most adult sirens. To add, her peers had never felt, or seen, the true devastation that a siren can actually bring.

Unknowingly, however––except for a privileged few–– Pagaroth's school could be harboring the most powerful siren in all of Hagaraak. Ermma had already reached such a high level in her gift, and at such a young age, it was nearly impossible to imagine how powerful she might become in the future....

"Just a few chips here and there," Shurwath said, inspecting a huge boulder one day. "And oh! Here––" he pointed to the base of the rock. "Here...the slightest of cracks!"

Jhavon, Julie, and Ahnon, all rushed to the spot where Shurwath stood.... Tiny flecks and small chips of rock laid scattered on the grass around the boulder. Though from a distance, it appeared untouched.

They each passed a hand over the small nicks and dents, feeling the sharp edges that remained on the rock's surface. At the very base, a thin crack had begun to form.

To affirm Shurwath's claim, they all turned and looked back at Ermma, who stood some fifty yards away. And even from that distance, they could sense her disappointment. Aye...she'd managed to shave some small pieces off the rock, but she had barely scratched the surface.

Ermma waved, signaling for them to come back. "Cover your ears," she said, once they all got close enough. "And stand clear."

They obeyed the siren's commands like humble servants, standing safely out of the range of her scream––which was quite some ways behind her. They plugged their ears as tightly as they could and waited for the faint (but unbearable) sound to come.

A single scream, in a concentrated wave––by any siren––was unheard of in the Land of Hagaraak. The nature of sound (for that matter) is never concentrated, but surrounds and spreads to the point where it grows weak and begins to fade. But Ermma was developing a different kind of power altogether; to encase her own sound within unseen barriers, or to throw her scream in one direction at a target of her choosing.

She took a deep breath, then opened her mouth wide as if she was about to shout. But instead of a word, a low high-pitched tone––like a soft whistle––poured from out of her mouth. It grew in volume, but just a few clicks before leveling off to an even tone, no louder than a bird's chirp....

The sound itself didn't present any immediate danger to those standing behind her. It was, in fact, quite harmless. However, it was the pitch of the sound that made it so irritating to the listeners. Even with their ears plugged, they cringed under the long, drawn out sound, feeling the blood beginning to crawl through their veins.

The danger laid in the direct path of the siren's scream. For though it might sound like a dull whistle on the outside, within the scream's invisible tunnel, was a sound beyond measure. One break in her concentration will cause the contained sound to break free and kill her friends behind her. Even if she were to close her mouth shut immediately, whatever remained of the scream (no matter how brief) could still have devastating effects.

From where he stood, Jhavon could see the air shimmer and wave as it shot from Ermma's mouth like rapid waves of vapor. The wave was two feet in diameter (though he'd seen Ermma form bigger ones). It settled directly in the center of the boulder, where the rough surface began to wobble. The boulder shook and vibrated, shedding small chips of itself on the grass.

Carefully...the siren closed her mouth shut again. The low whistling sound stopped, and so did the violent wobbling of the boulder as the tail end of the scream's wave absorbed itself around it.

Ermma's chest heaved visibly as she fought to regain her breath.

"Just 23 seconds," Jhavon yelled from where he stood behind her.

Ermma sighed, shaking her head with disdain. Her last wave had lasted nearly a whole minute. But this one wasn't even half as long. Considering the fact that her longest breath was over ninety seconds, and an average of sixty seconds for the ones that followed––she had every right to be upset with herself. She was clearly having a bad day.

Shurwath ran down the field to inspect the boulder. He ignored the fresh chips laying in the grass and stooped down at the base where the crack had formed. He used his finger to measure its length. "Nothing," he said, noting the crack didn't expand under the siren's recent assault. In a deary sort of way, he sympathized with Ermma, who'd engaged herself in a personal fight with the boulder that was twice her size. Each day, she attempted to blast the boulder to a million bits of tiny pebbles, but was only rewarded with fine chips and shavings.

"At least you cracked it this time," Julie said.

"It's no more than those small trimmings on the ground," came Ermma's curt reply. "After so many scream-waves, I probably weakened it. But I want to destroy the rock in one strike; not waste my strength beating at it."

———•———

When it came to struggles, Jhavon was all too familiar. The young trunket had been facing them ever since he was an infant. But where his old struggles came in the form of harsh weather and harder times, his new adversity came in the form of a lykine....

After one week, he had already managed to design and build a frame for his wings. It was triangular in shape, with a long stick running down the middle, and two more attached to each side for support. All he needed now was a thin cloth––strong enough to hold the wind....

"Make sure you triple stitch."

The words came from his mouth so suddenly, he turned toward Ahnon (who was standing behind him) with a dead-pan expression. "Just so you know," he said to the mute. "I've triple, and even quadruple stitched." To prove his point, he held up the brown cloth by the seam as a needle dangled from a thread in the stitch.

Ahnon stared at the seam, then shrugged.... "I just wouldn't like to see your wing stripping itself apart while you're still in the air."

"That is not going to happen," Jhavon said.

"You can never be too certain of anything, Jhavon."

"Well...I'm certain of this. I'm confident the seams won't come apart."

"How so?"

"Ships," Jhavon said. "I saw them all the time in Rag's Port. Some of the fastest ships are driven by sails that are all patched up. Many of them survive storms without suffering a single tear. I think my stitching will do just fine."

Since their project was kept secret from, all the teachers––especially Morella––the wings had to be built in Jhavon's room. The wings' frame, which now laid in a bundled heap against the wall, was easily constructed and bound together with rope. The brown cloth was stolen, or rather, "borrowed" from the tailor's workshop while he was distracted––and was now being stitched together to cover the frame.

For hours...the trunket sewed the cloth together, and though he was only a quarter of the way through by the time he went to bed, in his mind, the wings were already completed.

CHAPTER
SIXTEEN

"IS IT NOT the goddess, with whom Mox was in love?" mused a poetic Morlah, with her blind-folded face raised to the churning sky. The students were all gathered around her on the soft grass. An assortment of colorful flowers stood proudly in their beds near the trimmed hedges along the graveled walkways.

Ms. Wicket, the class overseer, sat quietly on a wooden chair nearby. She wore a blue pointed hat, and a long blue gown that reached down to the heel of her black deer-skin boots. She wore the stern face of a witch (which she really was) and showed no hints of warmth as Morlah practiced her magic.

And magic it was indeed, for the young sorceress was aided by her unique senses. None that offered any physical aid however, but a sense that allowed her mind to slip through time and see things as they once were, or what they might become.

"Is it not the goddess who saved men's souls?" the young sorceress continued. "Who formed the spirits from the winds of Mox, then placed them in all things that live? I'm told that Pagaroth's skies remain in gloom. I hear the thunder that follows the great flash. They tell me the clouds are gray, and sometimes black. So now, I know what these colors sound like...."

Morlah lowered her head and turned toward the flower-bed on her right. Though blind, it seemed like she was looking right at them. She stood for a moment longer before stooping down to place an open palm above the grass. "I know what yellow smells like," she said. Through the surface of the soil, a budding stalk came and bloomed into a yellow flower. "I know what red smells like," she said. And just as before, a stem rose from out of the ground to become a red flower. "And blue...and purple...and pink...and orange...and green...." Her nostrils flared as she savored the mixed fragrance of all the flowers she had just grown, while the rest of the class applauded her performance.

"That was very good, Morlah," Ms. Wicket said. It was the most encouragement she gave to any student. In magic, she was forbidden to teach. As class overseer, her only task was to ensure that the students work on their individual talents. Any attempts to assist or intervene would only hamper a student's development—no matter how bad he or she may be coming along. In the end, they always discover their own methods....

Marlah stood up next and took her twin sister's place in front of the class. "Where my sister cannot see, I cannot hear," she began. "But through the gift of sight I still know sound."

Though it was just mere words from Marlah's poem, the rest of the class knew otherwise, for nothing escaped the young sorceress's sharp eyes. She was the most skilled at interpreting the language of the body. At a mere glance, she can almost tell what's on a person's mind. And she was even more skilled at reading lips and facial expressions. It was a gift that had unfortunately made her the least liked of the twins. Her peers avoided her. And during class, when they couldn't, they covered their mouths whenever they spoke. And this, they did in the softest whispers, lest her twin sister catch their words with her sharp hearing.

"When the lightning flash," Marlah went on, pointing up at the gray sky. "I'm told that thunder rolls, angry and grievous through the clouds. The brighter the flash, the more you scare——and this tell my ears that the Eternal Mox had surely groaned." She took a deep breath and closed her eyes. "I know what the rain sound like."

Just then came the sound of rain. The students (even Ms. Wicket) were all forced to look up at the sky and search the clouds for what they knew to be impossible. Even though their clothes remained dry, the sound of rain all around played a potent trick on their minds.

"I know what the rivers sound like," Marlah said. The sound rain suddenly stopped, and the noise of rushing water took its place. "And the birds...the horses...the pigs...and the vicious cats." The last brought throat rambling snarls of leopards, and the loud roars of lions.

"Very good, Marlah," Ms. Wicket said. "Shurwath, is there anything you would like to share with us today?"

The young wizard came up to the front of the class and raised his left palm toward the sky. "Thanks to the goddess Laap, from whom I have descended, I've been blessed with the gift of spells. I may call the wind, the rain, and bright lightning from the clouds of Pagaroth." Much faster than the bat of an eye, a thin bolt of lightning shot up from Shurwath's palm into the thick churning clouds above. A bright flash erupted within, followed by hundreds of streaks of lightning that snaked their way all through the sky in a dazzling display for leagues all around.

The students all held their gazes up at the sky where the lively bolts danced and forked across the horizon.

Then...just as suddenly as it began, one of the greatest shows in nature came to an abrupt end, and the dark billowing clouds resumed to cast their dreary gloom.

"That was lovely, Shurwath," Ms. Wicket said, though she didn't look too impressed. "Had your bolt been any slower to leave your hand, you might've roasted us all."

A stunned Shurwath gave the class overseer an inquisitive glare.

Ms. Wicket returned the wizard's gaze with a cocked brow of her own.

"But..." Shurwath began, uncertain of what he should say at that point. "Surely, it was quick enough."

"Just barely," the witch replied. "Practice this spell more, Shurwath. Nature can be a playful thing at times. But its unable to distinguish a babe from an adult. Such games can prove deadly to a witless wizard."

"Aye, Ms. Wicket," Shurwath said lamely. Though Mr. Cobber had instructed them well on the dangers of lightning, he thought his bolt was small, and harmless to all those around him––and indeed, it was. But the harsh criticism that came from Ms. Wicket did much to bring the feeling of failure to the surface.... He took his seat among the rest of the class in stiff silence.

A sharp snicker broke the dull mood that lingered in the air.

Ms. Wicket swept her fierce eyes quickly across the heads of the students until they settled on the lykine like a ton of steel.

Realizing that he'd been caught poking fun at a fellow student, Syme tried to compose himself while stifling the last fit of laughter that threatened to slip through the tightness of his pursed lips.

"Did I just tell a joke, Syme?" asked the witch. "If I did, I was not aware of it. Nor do I think that the rest of the class picked up on anything funny about my words." Unlike the other teachers, Ms. Wicket had no tolerance for the lykine's tricks. She found those who toyed with magic were neither appealing nor amusing.

"No, Ms. Wicket," a nervous Syme replied.

"Good," she said. "Maybe you're fit to give us an equally wonderous, and safer, demonstration of your magic."

"As a matter of fact, Ms. Wicket—" Syme jumped up at once and made his way to the front of the class. "I do." With one hand on his hip, he searched the sea of faces before him until he found Jhavon's (who returned his conniving leer with a wary look). "I come from the Great Woods," he began. "The Land of Llok, the god of beasts, so blessed I am, with gifts like these."

Slowly, Syme's body began to swell and grow fat. Thick brown fur bristled from the surface of his pale skin. Huge claws replaced his hands and feet, and his grinning face morphed into that of a bear.

Fully changed, the grizzly bear stood up on his hind legs at an impressive 10½ feet tall, dwarfing the little old witch that sat virtually unphased by its formidable presence. It then thumped on its chest with those big claws and let out a great roar.

The intrigued students all gasped in wonder and delight, for this was the first time the young lykine had morphed into anything that huge. However, as the wave of excitement began to recede, their applause soon followed and their fascination grew as they waited to see what Syme might turn himself into next.

The bear then shrunk down to the size of a horse. Huge black wings sprung out from the sides of its back, sending loose feathers through the air in wild loops. Two gnarled horns curled out from the back of its head that was already beginning to resemble that of a large predatory cat.

With a single flap of its mighty wings, it leaped up and hung effortlessly in the air. The strong breeze caused the students to shield their eyes from the dust as the hideous beast rose higher. It jerked and reared its head, then gave a loud ear-splitting shriek.

"A mox hound!!" One of the students shouted.

They all watched (though Jhavon was too terrified to think) as the hound made tight circles above their heads. It kept those big yellow eyes fixed on the young trunket—then suddenly, its huge black wings appeared as if they were shrinking, fast! The hound flapped frantically as it struggled to stay in the air. A long grievous shriek escaped through the fanged mouth while it shook its head back and forth in extreme pain. The sharp claws soon shrunk and became the lanky arms of the lykine once more. The hound's face shrunk down to the size of mellon, reluctantly giving way to Syme's features, which were contorted and disfigured with agony.

The students, realizing that something had definitely gone wrong, were now beginning to look worried.

Syme's shrinking wings were the last to go, leaving his body to fall the rest of the way to the ground. He struggled up to his trembling hands and knees. Sweat matted his hair to his face. The heavy panting of his chest betrayed the fact of how weak he'd become....

"It is true that the Eternal Llok, created all the beasts," Ms. Wicket said, to the panting Syme as much as she was addressing the class. She remained seated, indifferent to the lykine's distress. "But he didn't create any abominations. And that is one thing a lykine cannot attempt. The unnatural anatomy of abominations do not work well with that of any remnant. And I see, Syme...that you haven't learned this until now."

The lykine vomited on the grass as she said this. The ground instantly soaked up the foul liquid.

"It comes a surprise to me, Syme," Ms. Wicket said, "I thought you knew the laws that govern your own kin. Not even Shurlan can accomplish the feat you just attempted."

The exhausted Syme fell back down on his elbows; his arms now too weak to support his own weight. He could only manage to shake his head before vomiting on the grass again.

"Well now you know, Syme," Ms. Wicket said. "No matter how powerful a morpher can become, he'll never be able to morph into an abomination. Their flesh and bones don't match. You must remember this. The instant you turned yourself into that creature you began to die. And had you not been able to return to your natural form, you would've died as a mox hound. Their hearts beat too fast, and their muscles require more blood than your little body could supply."

Syme looked up at the old witch just then, surprised that she knew what was going on inside of him. "But...how..." he faltered. "How do the——"

"Because they're abominations, boy!" she snapped, not caring what he meant to ask. "They're not made like you, or me, or anything else. They defy life, they defy death, they defy the laws of nature itself!"

———•———

The demon was mindful enough to stand a good ways from Zhorghan as he faced Ragath's floating mirror. "Maybe it means something else," he said to the old wizard. He looked concerned, because he knew Zhorghan had become so desperate, he would try anything in order to find the answer to the Eternal's riddle——even if that meant putting both of their lives at risk. He wanted so badly to inform the wizard that maybe they'd misinterpreted the meaning of the passage. But he feared he might insult him and cause him to become more stubborn in proving his point.

"That is quite possible, Ohlar," Zhorghan replied, while keeping his gaze fixed on the hovering mirror. "But you're wrong. What else would Ragath need this mirror for? A mirror that leads to all worlds. An Eternal, who already possess the power to erect any portal?"

"And that's the very thing, Zhorghan," the demon said, glad for the opening to insert his own opinion, and possibly prevent the old wizard from making the one mistake that might end their lives. "Ragath is an Eternal. He used his own methods that none of the others could've figured out. No one ever knew the secrets to his design. Only he had such power. You may be right in your assumptions, but wrong in your calculation and estimations."

Zhorghan abandoned his reflection in the mirror and turned to Ohlar's black figure. A deep frown in his brow betrayed his irritation with the demon. "Wrong in my calculations?"

Ohlar returned the old wizard's gaze, but made no reply.

"After all these eons?" Zhorghan went on. "You're starting to think like a tog, Ohlar. How could you say that only Ragath has the power to erect portals? Then what have I been doing all this time?" He raised the tiny tuning fork in the air. "Eh?!"

"That's not what I meant," the demon said. "There's no doubt you've been able to duplicate the Eternal's feat with your magic. But that's such a low level, Zhorghan. Even you must admit to that. As powerful as you are, you're still restricted from leaving this world——and at such a limited range at that. But if this gate is the one that leads to all worlds, do you think your power is as strong as Ragath's? You're barely strong enough to open a gate to Pagaroth."

A violent twitch jerked the side of Zhorghan's cheek to disturb his stern expression. However, he didn't bother to hide the nerve that had obviously been pinched by the demon's criticizing remarks. But the truth——he knew——never held any regards when it came to being offensive. "You may not think like a tog after all," he said, curbing his mounting anger. "But you're no braver than your predecessors, either. Had I lacked such daring as you, I would've never been as strong as I am now. And I think you take that for weakness."

Before Ohlar could utter a single word in response, the old wizard spun back around to face Ragath's mirror. And at that instant, a surge of raw energy erupted at his feet.

"Zhorgan! No!" the demon pleaded as the crackling veins of electric energy was now flowing through the old wizard. "You fool! That was not what I meant!" But he knew his words were falling on deaf ears as he watched Zhorghan extend his arm and aimed the tiny fork at the mirror's surface.

For a brief moment, dead silence fell upon the entire cave——so much so, the demon thought he was deaf. But only a few seconds followed before a loud high-pitched sound came from the fork that was now vibrating in Zhorghan's hand. He stumbled back, while keeping his eyes glued to the mirror. And if this moment happened to be his last one alive, he wanted to at least enjoy the show....

The fork's sound and vibrations grew more intense (causing the demon to cover his ears) as Zhorghan continued to put all his power into the tiny instrument. A bright blue spark exploded ahead of it——prematurely, it seemed. But then another one followed, much stronger than the one before, sending a shower of blue sparks flying through the air. A blue beam of energy shot out from the fork just then, illuminating the entire cave as it slammed into the surface of Ragath's mirror!

Ohlar looked on in frozen fear, expecting the beam to bounce off the mirror's surface and explode into the walls, crushing them both beneath tons of rock. However, as to what was actually taking place, the demon had never thought it possible. For the beam was going through the mirror. Not through, as to come out on the other side––but into another world!

The beam's size shrunk after a while. The wizard let out an agonizing groan as the tuning fork's vibration stiffened and the blue beam sputtered out of existence. Zhorghan collapsed to the ground.

The demon flew across the cavern to his aid. He turned the exhausted wizard on his back to find him unconscious, but alive. With a few days rest, and some magleaf tea, he should be strong enough to walk again.

He turned to look at the mirror, but it wasn't there. It had fallen on the ground when the wizard used up most of his power. He walked over to where it was laying face up, and to his utter astonishment, the mirror had changed. No longer did it reflect things––the way all mirrors should. Instead, its surface was pitch black, dotted by countless stars and galaxies. "By the hand of Mox!!!" he exclaimed to himself, transfixed by the tiny universe contained within Ragath's mirror. "'My home is the gate to all worlds.'" He recited the passage once more, slightly hoping that it might invoke some kind of response from the mirror. "Until now, no one had any idea what the Eternal meant." He then turned to the unconscious Zhorghan, still laying on the ground. "Not even his own apprentice."

———•———

A crowd of excited students were all gathered at the eastern wall that surrounded Pagaroth's castle. Before them, Jhavon stood with the wing he made from the tailor's cloth and sticks. From end to end, the wing spanned nearly ten feet, and was light enough for the trunket to carry——but so big that it dragged on the ground behind him.

"And the jester's here today, to perform the biggest jest of all..." Syme said to the crowd. He'd sobered (just a bit) since his botched attempt to transform into the mox hound. However, he still hadn't given up his old tricks and taunts upon those he considered to be weaker. In fact, the lykine's most recent mishap had only brought feelings of sympathy from the others. And not only did his painful ordeal award him with some extra attention, it also brought a certain degree of respect as well.

"Nothing but some old rags tied to sticks." The lykine jabbed at the wings's tight cloth with a long finger. "Where did all the feathers go, trunket? Or did you pluck your own wings?"

A wild burst of laughter erupted from the crowd.

"It don't need feathers, Syme," Jhavon replied, ignoring all the laughter around him.

"Oh...?" asked Syme. His face, a mask of pure skepticism. "Is that so, trunket? Then tell us; what flies without feathers?"

"Bats!" Jhavon spat, proudly shifting the wing's weight on his back. "And not only bats, but flies and grasshoppers. And the same goes for all the flying insects, you...dung-for-brains. Anything else you need answered?"

Syme's tight grin slowly softened at the insult. Had it not been for the school's strict rules against fighting, he might've struck the young trunket.

Those who stood in the crowd must've sensed this as well, for their laughter had suddenly died down and they all became quiet. They waited in suspence——anticipating some kind of tight—as the tension continued to build between the two....

"Alright then, trunket," Syme finally said. He forced a smile that was obviously hard to maintain. "I have to admit that I never thought of such things. Very rarely, do bats and insects cross my mind. And I think you're right; bats and insects do fly through the air, so fast, that their featherless wings are hardly ever seen.... But tell, trunket. Can this... thing...flap as fast as the slowest bat? Can it even flap at all?"

Jhavon sighed with mild frustration.

"What...?" Syme brought his head closer to the trunket so he could better hear his words. "What? I didn't hear you. What was that...? Did you say no?"

"That's right, Syme. I said no.... I did not build my wing to flap. I built it to fly."

The crowd of students all burst into laughter again, and the playful Syme (tension gone) assumed his natural mood.

"Hmph...!" the young trunket fumed. He turned his back on the mocking crowd to gaze up at the height of the daunting wall. It was so high, he had no plans on climbing it at all. "Shurwath!" he called over the din of laughter.

The young wizard had been standing beside the crowd, along with Julie, Ermma, and Ahnon. They were the only ones who didn't share in the crowd's amusement.

Shurwath walked over to where Jhavon stood. "Are you still sure about this?" He spoke just loud enough for the trunket to hear. "You see how ridiculous all of this looks. You cannot possibly expect to fly an inch with that thing. You'll only succeed in falling to your death."

"Just get the things ready," was all Jhavon had to say.

Shurwath frowned. "But this is foolish," he said. "He's obviously trying to get you expelled. And this stunt can very well do the trick, even if you do somehow manage to fly. Can't you see that?"

"I can't get expelled, Shurwath."

"Oh...?" the young wizard wore a doubtful expression. "You've obviously let your imagination get the better of you; more so than that jesting lykine. What makes you think such a thing?"

"I have my own reasons, Shurwath. You have to trust me. Just get the things ready before Ms. Wicket, or Ms. Mmm––" he paused, mindful not to mention the elemental's name. "Before someone come and start asking questions."

"Very well, Jhavon," Shurwath said, with a sigh of defeat. "But Julie says that she's not sure if she's strong enough to catch you if you start falling. Maybe I can turn the ground to water, but it's up to you to know how to swim after that."

"I don't need any of your magic," Jhavon said. He was becoming impatient. "I just need you to hurry up and get the things. Go on."

Shurwath walked back toward the crowd. "Alright, alright! Get back everyone. Get back! Watch out!"

The crowd simmered down once more and obeyed Shurwath's command. Even the mischievous Syme began stepping back.

"And I have a wager for you, Syme," Jhavon said.

"Aye...? And what wager is this, trunket?"

"That if I do fly, then you have to mount my spotted gray."

"Aye!" Syme replied. "I'll agree to that, trunket. I'll mount your spotted gray, the day I see you fly. But I don't think that day's today."

When the crowd moved back at a safe enough distance, Shurwath turned back around. "Ready, Jhavon?"

"Aye!"

Shurwath stretched his arms forth just then. His face went blank as he tilted his head up to the sky and began muttering a spell under his breath. It seemed like the wind had stopped blowing as everything around him became calm, and the seconds ticked by without anything happening at all.

But then a faint, booming sound, interrupted the silence. Though distant, the sound gradually grew louder and appeared to be approaching them from the west.

A student tapped the shoulder of another and pointed in wild astonishment at what she was seeing.... At 200 yards away, it looked incredibly tall. It quickly closed the gap with each giant leap, and each time it landed on the ground the deep echoing boom grew louder.... At 60 yards, the thick gnarled bark could clearly be seen on what was now evidently the trimmed trunk of a very large tree. It was at least 20 feet in diameter and dozens of feet tall. As it hopped over the heads of the marvelled students, huge dark rings spiralled on the surface of the severed stump––too many to count during its brief passage; however, it did reveal an age that stretched back into the ancient times.

"A trunk from a Morgah tree!" Syme said, trying his best to appear unimpressed by the young wizard's extraordinary feat. "Anyone who knows their geography will know that Mharadaath is the forest world where the goddess Morgah once ruled."

The students all stared with dubious looks on their faces. Some of them were shaking their heads. It was obvious they hadn't heard of the legends of Morgah since the teachings of Mharadaath––and the third continent–– won't be given until they were all in their fourth and final year in Pagaroth's school.... Syme must've been listening to the tales shared amongst the older students around the gardens. (And it was equally apparent that Shurwath had been doing the same as well––perhaps more so, since he knew the location of where this behemoth of a tree trunk was kept.)

The giant log made its last leap and caused a slight tremor when it landed, showering everyone with pieces of rotted bark, dirt, and dozens of tiny insects. The stench of decayed wood fill the air.

Jhavon guessed the log to be standing at least 100 feet from the eastern wall. However, it was hard for him to decide how much taller the log actually was. It was much taller than the eastern wall––he knew this for certain. And from where he stood, it appeared to be tall enough for the task.... "Alright, Shurwath," he said to the young wizard. "Let her down...easy now."

Moments passed and the monstrous log still remained poised where it stood, sturdy and unmoving. Angry shouts could be heard coming from the top of the wall as the guards began to arrive on the scene. There was a sense that the entire castle had been alarmed, which Jhavon had anticipated. It was even expected that the enraged teachers and elders should be arriving soon. Only the sheer distance of the eastern wall from the rest of the castle, had given them the advantage of a head start. This much he had anticipated well in advance––which was why the most isolated section of the grounds had been chosen.

There came a sudden guttural sound as the log began to lean forward, digging its base into the soft soil beneath. It gained momentum as it fell, but not much, because it slowed down as the upper half neared the top of the wall.

Overwhelmed by their own fright, and the sheer size of the rotten log that threatened to crush them, the guards scrambled to get out of the way. The last man barely cleared its looming shadow as it came crashing down upon the wall's ledge, pelting bits of rotten debris in every direction.

Without a moment's time to waste, Jhavon dashed toward the fallen log, slowed only by the pull of the wing mounted on his back. Up ahead, a broad plank was laying on the ground, a dozen yards from the log's base. It had once served as a marker for where the log must stand. Now it must serve as a ramp for him to run up the 45° incline. And as if on its accord, the plank made a sudden leap off the ground and landed onto the log's base with a single bounce.... In his mind's eye, he could clearly see Julie aiming her spirit stick at the thing, eager and too glad to be doing her part.... He slowed his pace while making his way up the ramp, careful not to be thrown off balance by the small wobbles as he ran across the middle before hopping on the much larger ramp, which was the actual log itself.

This amazing feat of power and cunning had caused great excitement to build inside the students who were witnessing it all. The enormity of what they'd just experienced had left them craving for more, eager to see what the young trunket was going to do next. Thus...all their taunting and ridicule soon turned to cheering and support––the total opposite of what Syme had expected (but deep down, even he wanted the show to go on).

192

"It's Ms. Hugh!" a little girl suddenly shouted.

When some in the crowd spun around, they saw that it was indeed the music teacher, along with what appeared to be the entire school's faculty, storming across the grounds toward them. And not the teachers, but most of the older students as well—creating a huge array of black, green, and purple gowns, with a few specks of white (worn by some of the elder wizards who lived in the castle) dotted here and there.

Perhaps it was the sight of this incoming intrusion that fed the students' fiery emotions even more, and caused them to cheer on the trunket in rebellion, urging him on as his tiny body continued to sprint up the length of the giant log.

Jhavon was well aware of all the commotion that was happening below. He managed to steal a few backward glances to see the teachers—and quite possibly the whole school—gathered on the grounds. Some of the older students (ordered by the teachers) scrambled up the plank to chase after him on the log. But he was already too far away to be caught.... Some fifty yards up ahead, the guards had repositioned themselves along the wall, anxiously waiting for him to near the top. But he'd anticipated this as well; the general assumption being, that he was trying to escape. What else should they expect from a powerless trunket?

He was almost near the top now, and his legs were beginning to burn, which slowed his pace. The brittle bark that crumbled under his weight became more of an obstacle for his tiring body. He turned around more often than necessary, checking to see how much his pursuers had shortened the gap. They were gaining, though not by much.

Their long dash across the grounds had already drained most of their energy before they made it to the log.

A murky mist swirled from the west and whisked quickly along the top of the wall. Like smoke blown from a giant's mouth, it shot past the awaiting guards––fogging their vision––as it made its way down the log.

"And just where do you think you're going?" Morella's enchanting voice came through the mist. Her smoky face looked as angry as it could ever be.

Startled, the young trunket froze in his tracks; his labored lungs grateful for the much needed rest.

"What is the meaning of all this, Jhavon?"

"Noth--nothing..." Jhavon replied between breaths. "Just trying an expe--experiment is all."

The smoke swirled inside Morella's disbelieving face. "An experiment...? You call almost destroying the eastern wall, and nearly killing the castle's guards, an experiment?!"

"Aye," Jhavon replied. "Just different, is all. A different method. None would've caused any real harm to the wall, or to the guards, as long they were careful to stand clear––and they did." He looked back and saw that the older students were almost upon him now. He couldn't allow them to catch him and haul him back to the ground.... From where he stood, he judged the drop to be at least 150 feet; enough room for him to make his flight. He began moving closer to the log's edge––

"Jhavon!!" Morella yelled. Her windy voice shrieked in terror for the boy. "You mad little trunket! Don't you––"

But Jhavon, hands gripping the rope tied to his wings, had already ran and jumped off the side of the log! His body dipped out of sight.

With a frightful gasp, Morella swirled up into the air, stopping all sound, movement, and time....

The startled guards stood frozen on the wall, their faces filled with wild-eyed shock as they leaned over the wall's ledge to catch one last glimpse of the falling trunket. The great crowd below stood fixed in time; their suspended expressions' a mixture of shock and excitement. A streak of lightning was held in mid stride, and the frozen clouds now appeared like one solid rock in the sky.

Morella flew down to where Jhavon had jumped. He had barely cleared the log, and his wing was already pointed toward the ground. His face was in a state of frozen determination. His body held well poised and balanced, even at such an odd angle of descent. "What is this madness, boy?" she asked the young trunket, while studying the way his body was positioned.

"Morella!"

The sudden sound of her name being called (in such a harsh manner) had taken her unawares. Very few were powerful enough to remain unaffected by the elemental's time-freezing spell (the shadowy demon, Ohlar, being one of them). However only one of them lived in Pagaroth's castle.

She flew up over the log, leaving Jhavon's body suspended in mid air. Her misty form stopped just a few feet before Shurlan. "Look at what the trunket has done!" she said. "Out of all the ways to put an end to his own life, he decides to do it for all to see."

The ancient lykine stood (unmoved by Morella's dramatics) on the lumpy surface of the log. "I would hardly think that is the boy's intentions, Morella," he said.

"Oh...?" Morella asked, not pretending to be surprised at all. "And this isn't some...clever trunket's ploy to escape Pagaroth by his own means, either? Or maybe you think it's some kind of experiment as well?"

"Escape...?" Shurwath looked amused at Morella's outrage. "Is that what you think all this is, Morella?" He pointed to the giant log, and then at the big assembly down below. "Surely, Jhavon would've chosen a subtler method than this. And I'm hardly one to believe the trunket is bold enough to disobey Rahjule's instructions, much less leave his horses behind. So perhaps it's just an experiment, as the boy say it is."

Morella scoffed at this, causing a puff of mist to shoot through her nostrils. "I feared you might've seen that much." She shook her head with a dreary sigh. "Looks like the trunket wants to fly now. As if those things he created in your old cottage wasn't enough.... What in all of Hagaraak could ever push the boy to jump off the castle's walls?"

"It's in his nature, Morella. The trunket is a creature who follows his mind. The rest of us, who rely only on our senses, will find this too difficult to understand."

"You sound as if you approve of all this."

"Not in the least, Morella," Shurlan said. "You should know better than anyone else that I never tolerate a student's disobedience. But he didn't hurt anyone in doing so––nor was it his intentions. I'm pretty sure we can find some suitable chores to occupy him over the next few moons, for the little damages and disturbance he and his friends have caused here today. But that's as far as it goes. No matter in what form it may come, we must not interfere with a student's development."

Morella didn't reply at once, she studied the giant log and the part it played in the strange construction instead. The assemblage, in its own simplicity, was the purest of all trunkets' design. No special magic. No hidden power. Just simple things put together, that worked as if they moved by the hands of the Eternals. His ancestors had waged great wars with similar things; defied the Eternals with clever inventions. "I'm disappointed in Shurwath, for aiding the trunket in all this. He's such an honorable boy. But I suppose the trunket's a master in the art of pursuasion as well."

"Or maybe Shurwath felt right to aid a friend by all means," Shurlan replied. "Shurwath is a good boy...you said so yourself. I'm only surprised that he actually managed to find and then dig up this old wood." He tapped on the log with his foot. Though rotten, it was still hard as a rock.

The morgah tree was once a gift from the goddess Morgah, to Pagaroth, during the castle's construction many eons ago. The goddess had commanded a single herd (32 in all) to march from the great forest world of Mharadaath, all the way to the Hagar (when the world was still one).

This was how the great main gates of the castle were made. The same went for all the fine woodwork found on the windowsills, doors, door-frames, and most of the furniture. Virtually indestructible, they lasted all throughout the millennia, and still remained as fresh as the day they were built and polished.

"How do you suppose he found this?" Shurlan asked, motioning to the log under his feet.

"Just one or two were left after the castle was built. Pagaroth buried them in the land so they may feed off the rich minerals there." She spun around, pointing in the direction the log had hopped from. A line of huge circles were left printed on the grass in its wake. "Just beyond the southern walls.... How the boy became strong enough to lift such a huge thing from out the earth, is quite interesting. But as to how he could've known they were there, is a great mystery to me, Shurlan. A mystery, that I would engage myself in solving, when this is all over."

"Hmm...." Shurlan said thoughtfully. Though he had a faint idea where Shurwath might've received the location of the buried logs, the hidden strength of the young wizard occupied his mind even more. A cold shiver ran down his spine as a particular revelation of the prophecy came to mind. A warning, that the inevitable days were soon to come. "Keep a close eye on Jhavon," he said. "Unless he falls, don't interfere with the experiment in any way. The boy's success may benefit us in more ways than we can possibly know." As he said this, his body shrank down to the size of brown hawk and to flapped away....

———•———

The wind rushed into his face, and the ground was coming up fast! The wing created a strong drag as it fought to catch the wind. Then suddenly, he could feel his body leveling off. The rope dug into his hands and chest as the wing caught full sail.

He knew Morella had to be right behind him somewhere. He was certain she was going to try and stop him at any moment and bring him safely back to the ground. But after the moments went by without him feeling her presence, he brought his mind to focus on controlling his path of flight.

Mimicking the actions of birds, he tried to lean his body to the side in order to turn. But nothing happened. He kept on going straight. He swooshed over the crowd below as his altitude continued to decline, and soon, he encountered his first problem. He didn't know how to slow himself down!

It was his one and only miscalculation. He didn't have any means of controlling his flight. He'd once thought it was just a simple movement of the body––the same way he saw the birds do it. But now, he realized that he'd been terribly mistaken. Rather, it was the movement of the wings, that caused the birds to make their turns!

———•———

On the ground, both student and teacher alike all marveled at what they were seeing. They found it strange that Morella had just allowed the boy to jump off the log, then simply vanish the way she did. They were all certain she would put a stop to everything as well.

They all cheered (the students) as the trunket swooped down directly over their heads. As he did, his eyes seemed to connect with each one of theirs. And then he was gone... across the grounds––and smack-dead into the southern wall! The delayed sound of his collision came seconds later....

CHAPTER
SEVENTEEN

IN THE LAND of Lagophar, one thousand leagues west of Pagaroth, stood the Wolf Mountains: a cluster of snow-capped peaks, where the daunting crags jotted up into the sky as far as the eye could see. There, the ice glimmered under the sun's light like studded gems sprinkled all over the rock. An assortment of pine, spruce, larch, and hemlock covered the base of the mountains like the hems on a rough green dress.

Here, the sky was spared of Ragath's curse. A grateful sun sent its rays through the leaves of the evergreen trees in the forest. Here, the sounds of nature rejoiced to the wonders and blessings of daily life....

"Fhar!" a boy shouted after his pet wolf that went sprinting down a narrow stream. The wolf hopped and lunged from one icy rock to another. It moved so swift and exact, it appeared like a white blur, leaping from one side of the stream to the other. Then, with a sudden springy vault, it cleared the high bank and vanished into the snow-covered ground that matched its white fur perfectly. Not once did its paws touch the surface of the icy water.

"Fhar!!" the boy yelled in vain, then swore an expletive oath under his breath before chasing after his wolf. Luckily, he was already on the same side of the bank.

The white wolf's paw prints were as big as a bear's. So he followed them (easily enough) as they twisted and turned around so many trees, one might've thought it was chasing a rabbit. Some ways further ahead, drips of blood began to appear in the snow as if the wolf had cut its paw.... He followed the blood until he could barely make out the lump of white fur up ahead. And had it not been for its pink ears that twitched as it raised its awesome head, he might not have seen it at all.

"What is it, boy?" he asked softly, as he eased up to the side of the wolf. It seemed distressed as it glared into the dark tree-line directly in front of them. It made a vicious snarl, revealing sharp long fangs that dripped slimy saliva. The thick white fur bristled on its back like fine needles. The pink ears twitched again, awaiting the slightest movement to pounce at.

"What is it, Fhar?" The boy was growing more suspicious by the moment. "Fhar?" He stroked the thick fur while staring into the thicket. "Come boy." He grabbed a handful of fur and gave it a light tug, but the wolf wouldn't budge. "Let's go."

As if sensing––and becoming irritated––by the boy's own fear, the wolf's snarl became more fierce. It moved forward, slowly dragging the boy along with it.

A vague outline moved near the brush. The boy's eyes weren't as keen as the wolf's, so he disbelieved them at once. The wolf however, spotted the anomaly upon first sight; its muscles tensed along its back and powerful hind legs before it darted toward their invader at the blink of an eye!

The boy watched in shock as the wolf hurled itself through the air, its huge jaws gapping wide open to clamp down upon the creature's neck....

———●———

The main gates at Pagaroth's castle swung slowly outward, just wide enough to allow a lone figure to come cantering through on a black horse.

He dismounted when he reached the courtyard, then grabbed a brown sack that was tied to the saddle and hoisted it over his shoulder.

Before he could turn around, one of the handlers had already appeared by his side to take hold of the reins and walk the horse over to the stables. The handler burned his hand when he gave the steed a gentle pat along the side of its neck. It felt as if hot water boiled under the black skin. "Kicking her a bit too hard, have we?" the handler asked. He felt sorry for the poor creature, though it didn't appear to be exhausted.

The rider didn't respond. But when he turned to look at the handler, the wind blew at his dark hood and revealed a small portion of his face; enough to change the handler's aggressive tone.

"I...it...it was just a jest, sir..." the faltering handler said, with a nervous laugh. He cast his fearful gaze to the ground, lest he should appear rude by staring.... He gave the horse a gentle rub once more. "Strongest beast in all of Hagaraak."

But the rider was already halfway across the courtyard, heading toward the great staircase that lead into the castle....

It was a rare sight to see a treeling outside of Vlak's Forest. And for one to cross the impenetrable Hills of Pagaroth and venture into the accursed land, was perhaps unprecedented in the history of its kin.

These remnants of Vlak, had inherited most of the Eternal's gifts: power, immortality, and the uncanny ability to get their nourishments directly from the soil. Unlike their distant kin: the rykes and the lykes, whose forms appeared more tree-like...a treeling was mostly made up of flesh, blood, and bone. It was only their smooth skin, which was pale, hard, and shiny, that gave them the appearance of being made of polished wood. Like a life-sized wooden puppet, perhaps....

Their limbs can stretch to incredible lengths––and if a treeling so wills, he could be as tall as the main gates. They can make their fingers become like fine needles, or flatten their arms as thin as swords.

They had big owlish eyes that were set deep in their eye-sockets, which never blinked because treelings didn't have any eyelids. Because of their solid skin, they didn't have any pores, so they never sweat––nor did they grow any kind of hair.... This, along with their slim, elongated faces, made the treeling a very disturbing creature to set eyes upon for the first time....

Lhonaan made his way through the castle's broad halls as though it was his own home. Below the glowing, wall-mounted lamps, his pale hands and face contrasted perfectly against his black hooded robe.

He rounded a corner then went up a narrow flight of winding stairs, where he was soon met by two armed guards who nearly gasped when they saw his white chiseled face. They did their best not to show any fear as they bid the creature to follow them down the corridor to a pair of polished wooden doors that suddenly swung open upon their approach....

———●———

"Okay then..." Shurlan said; Lhonaan entered the room filled with twelve wizards, witches, and sorcerers. "It seems that everyone's present now."

Not caring for the lykine's tradition of proper decorum, Lhonaan decided not to wait for the formal greetings and introductions to begin. He slung the sack off his shoulder and pulled out the severed head of a hideous beast, allowing the stench of decaying flesh to fill the room.

The suddeness of the offensive smell, coupled with the treeling's rash display, left many of Shurlan's guests appalled and disgusted at the same time.

"This..." the treeling began, holding up the severed head for all to see. He spoke in a deep sonorous voice, despite his thin appearance. "This is what have been slaying so many of my kin over the last few days." Aside from the upward jerks of his long nose whenever he spoke, his expression remained blank.

"But this is not the same creature that devastated my land," a white bearded wizard said.

"Nor mines," someone else added, quickly followed by a few others.

They all stared at the beast's severed head, trying to make sense of the rows of sharp long teeth and pigish snout. However, what caused the most fear around the room was the sheer size of the beast's head. From where they sat, it was nearly half the size of the treeling's body. Just one snap from those powerful jaws could easily rip the treeling in half. And in all likelihood, that was precisely what the beast must've been doing to all the creatures that lived in Vlak's Forest.

"And that is all to your luck, then," Lhonaan said to all those present in the room. "For if it had, many of you might not be sitting here today."

A few disapproving grunts could be heard around the room.

"Do you have any idea what this creature might be, Lhonaan?" asked Shurlan.

The treeling shook his head. "In all the days that Vlak have given me; and in all my roaming across these lands, I've never seen this creature. I'm certain they don't belong in our world. Nor are they of Gargaath, or Mharadaath."

"They...?" a witch with a shrill voice asked. "You mean, there're more than one of those things?"

"Aye." Lhonaan replied. "A whole herd of them came through our forest, killing and eating everything in sight!"

The room broke into an apprehensive clamor. It was true, all their lands have been invaded by strange creatures, seemingly from different worlds. But none were as fierce in appearance, nor as vicious in killing, than what Lhonaan was describing to them now. And what if this creature invaded their lands next? The thought was disturbing to everyone, especially the sorcerers who lived in Danwhar, where the vast swamps made their numbers few and far between.

As though satisfied his demonstration had drawn the desired effect, Lhonaan stooped down and shoved the severed head back into the sack. Wien he tied it shut, the foul odor left the room at once.

"As tragic as all of these happenings are," Shurlan began, addressing his terrified guests. "We all knew they were bound to happen––and for thousands of years we've been preparing for when these days finally come upon us. And such days, as you must surely know, are upon us now. Has been for the past two years, and will continue to be until Ragath's return."

A cold silence snuck into the room, as all eyes were fixed upon the lykine...eyes doused in fear. And this angered Shurlan as he returned their frightful stares, realizing that the battle was already lost before it had even begun.

As powerful as most of them were, they'd grown soft over the eons. None of them (besides a priviledged few) had taken the prophecies seriously. They'd long became accustomed to the notion that they would live on their lands forever, though it was written that they would not!

It wasn't the strange sightings and attacks that caused their apprehensions, for any skilled sorcerer could've beheaded the beast inside Lhonaan's sack. Rather, it was the return of Ragath that summoned their most dreadful fears. For no mortal, or remnant––no matter how powerful–– would ever come close to killing an Eternal. In was a fact that spelled doom for all those present.

"Well..." an old prune-faced wizard began. "This could only mean that someone has succeeded in opening the gate that lead to all worlds."

"Aye," Shurlan replied. "Some time ago, a shadow named Ohlar, snuck past our guards and entered my study with his eyes set on one of Ragath's scrolls."

"A shadow?!" the wizard asked, prompting the other guests to raise the clamor in the room once more.

"Why would a shadow be concerned with anything belonging to Ragath?" Lhonaan (who was now seated) asked. "From what I remember, the remnants of Mox despise Ragath, for what he did to their Eternal."

"That's true," Shurlan said. "But Ohlar's a rogue. Nor is he a remnant of Mox, but an abomination. It's possible that he's conspiring with someone else. Someone, with great power, and vast amounts of knowledge when comes to Ragath and his writings."

"So I'm guessing this shadow wasn't captured?"

"No," Shurlan said, shaking his head. "Whoever sent the shadow, knew where the scrolls were. I was here when he entered the study. I watched him read the ancient words. They must've known about the gate before coming here."

"So someone's been helping Ragath all this time?" a sorcerer asked.

"That much is certain," Shurlan replied. "It's rumored that Ragath once had an apprentice, and it's quite likely (if he exists) that he's the one who's secretly against us now. It's impossible for Ragath to have opened these gates from outside of this world. So our general assumption must be that Ragath's apprentice is the one responsible."

"And in doing so, he's allowing all sorts of creatures to wander into our world. At least until Ragath finds his way back."

"Aye..." said Shurlan. "With all the gates open, it's only a matter of time before he finds the right one. And as much as I regret saying this, it would be much sooner than later. The Eternal can come stumbling through one of these gates at any moment." He stopped here, expecting more questions, but surprisingly, none came. He need not guess what were running through the remnants' minds at that particular moment, for he knew his own thoughts were the same as theirs. The only thing one could think of when knowing the end is near....

———●———

While the most powerful remnants in Hagaraak held their meeting, another meeting——of less importance——was taking place near the castle's stables....

A small crowd of first-year students followed closely behind Jhavon as he walked his spotted gray out of the stables. The crash from his short flight had left most of his bones broken, and he was unconscious when the healers came to his aide and mended him back together as good as new.

In the trunket's mind however, his flight was a failure. His wing lacked the ability to steer; not to mention the frightful experience during the entire ordeal.

But that was not what his peers had seen on that day. He was too high up in the air for them to see how he struggled to control the craft. In their eyes, he looked as relaxed as any bird in the sky. His path of flight appeared as perfect as any other, save for his sudden crash, which they attributed to the trunket's inexperience with his new invention.

And to add to his new-found fame (and notoriety), the young trunket had blatantly defied Morella to her face. A feat that was yet to be accomplished——by any other——in the history of Pagaroth's School of Merit. So not only did he earn the respect of his peers, but that of the old students as well.

"As promised, Syme," Jhavon said, holding the spotted gray by the reins. "I told you that I can fly without magic... and I did. Now it's time for you to own your claims. You said you can mount my spotted gray, if I show you flight––and I have."

"And that I can, trunket," Syme said. "There isn't a horse in all of Hagaraak, that a lykine cannot mount. But first..." he held up a long finger. "How do I know that your horse is not yet tammed, and is still wild and unruly? Prove to me that this horse isn't pinched, and has been broken in. If you can do this, I'll gladly mount this horse that everyone says is from the Red Forest."

Syme knew all about the legends of the enchanted forest. He also knew that Jhavon had never ridden the spotted gray. Which told him that the trunket was incapable of mounting his own horse.

However, it was only through his respect for the old man––the true owner of the spotted gray––that Jhavon never bothered mounting the horse. But he often wondered if he could. "Very well then, Syme," he said, after a deep sigh. He motioned for Shurwath to help him up, seeing that he was much too small to mount the horse on his own.

With a calm wave of his hand, and a spell's soft whisper, Shurwath caused the little trunket's body to lift effortlessly in the air until he came directly above the horse's saddle. He waited patiently for Jhavon's approval to lower him down, before bringing the trunket gently upon its back.

The sudden, unexpected weight on its back, sent the spotted gray shying off to the right with a disgruntled snort.

Jhavon rubbed a soothing palm along its neck. The spotted gray pawed into the ground with a stomping hoof while jerking its head up and down.... The students all looked on in quiet suspence, half-expecting the horse to buck and rear up on its hind legs to throw the trunket. But quite the opposite happened (to everyone's surprise) when the horse gave one last shake of its head before calming down. Soon, it became humble and obediant under the trunket's command——so much so, that it even allowed him a friendly trot in a circle.

"There, Syme," Jhavon said, bringing the horse to a stop with a grateful pat along the side of its neck. "The spotted gray is as tame and broken as any other horse in these stables. I've proven that much. But that don't mean you'll be able to ride her the way I just did. I warn you now, and I'll hold nothing against you if you refuse this. Maybe I can think of something else for you to do, other than riding this horse." Without Shurwath's help, he dismounted.

"Nonsense!" Syme stepped to the front of the crowd. So subtle was Jhavon's dare, he failed to notice the amount of resentment it stirred inside of him. And this caused him to be careless. "I've ridden much wilder beasts than this one. It looks peaceful enough.... My thanks to you, I must say."

Even as Syme took the reins from Jhavon, the horse was already beginning to shy away. Its big brown eyes glowered at him with grave warning. And when Syme returned the mount's gaze, he felt as though he'd fallen into a deep dark well. He couldn't describe what he saw or felt, but he knew, deep within his soul, that the spotted gray would never allow him to mount....

"Well, Syme?"

The sound of Jhavon's voice seemed to pull him from his trance. "Just a minute, trunket!" he shouted, unsure of what else to say. "Just admiring the form is all. I must admit, this horse of yours is one of the beauties." He turned his attention back to the spotted gray, hoping the beast sense his admiration.

At the slightest touch, the spotted gray reared up on her hind legs with a grievous neigh. The suddenness of the violent tantrum startled Syme, but he quickly recovered, holding tightly to the reins.

The horse came back down and swung its powerful neck so that its head crashed into Syme's face, knocking him senseless onto the ground.

It reared up again, and before the dazed lykine could roll out of the way, it brought its front hooves smashing down onto his body.

CHAPTER
EIGHTEEN

WHETHER A STUDENT be a witch, wizard, lykine, or trunket, each possessed their own gift that developed in stages. Growth and development varied within each. Some students are physically stronger than others, but may develop their gifts at a much slower pace. And vice versa....

And the teachers, such as Ms. Wicket, whose roll in a student's development is strictly passive, treat such problems in the gentlest of ways possible. Since each student's temperament and progress in class are made to be reported from one teacher to the next, none of their overall dispositions toward potential and aptitude are ever missed.

The teachers must not only know each student's talent and ability, but must also be aware of their progress in other classes as well. Only then, can the teacher's involvement in the student's life have the most potent effect.

Students lacking in physical prowess are pressed harder than their peers by Jhekaath. Those who are slower in their mental faculties receive more attention from teachers like Mr. Cobber and Ms. Haph. And those who're seen struggling to develop their magical gifts, are subjected under the keen eye of Ms. Wicket.

The latter, in particular, is a tender (and sometimes) special case. It's been known that physical stress, in some extreme cases, can serve as an excellent platform for boosting one's magical abilities. Such a fact might seem feasible to any individual, and yet, will choose to follow its own specific guidelines in other cases. Some students are perfectly susceptible to such methods, as their talents bloom freely under the physical strain. While in others, there seem to be a limit as to how far such methods can actually be helpful before it becomes ineffective and the student must continue their development through their own methods. And in others still, it might take the most stressful of all physical endeavors––like a near death experience––to bring out even the most minute change in a student's magical ability....

"Shields up, swords low," Jhekaath said to both Ahnon and Syme, as they face each other. They both held on to their swords while taking their stance; one ready to engage, while the other prepared to defend. "I said shields up, Ahnon!"

The mute raised his shield just below his eyes. The tip of his sword kissed the dirt as he kept his gaze fixed on Syme.

The taller lykine was bent in a low crouch to accommodate for Ahnon's smaller size. He kept his shield recklessly low at the waist, defying Jhekhaath's command. A nasty scar ran along the left side of his cheek, from the corner of his mouth, all the way back to tip of his left earlobe. And despite some broken ribs, a broken jaw, and a cracked skull that he'd suffered while being trampled by Jhavon's spotted gray, that long scar on his face was the only reminder of his terrible mishap...thanks to the school's gifted healers.

Since his failure and embarrassment at the hands of the young trunket, it appeared that Syme had abandoned his childish pranks. Due either to his new disfigurement, or the horror of his latest experience, the mischievous smirk that once played on his face was now gone. His expression had taken on a more serious, or even malicious look since then. Very seldom did he smile; he don't laugh as much either. He kept a raw disposition, and his attitude rubbed off coldly on others. And at least to his peers, it seemed, he would remain in this bitter frame of mind for a very long time, whether or not he got over his defeat––

"Engage!" Jhekhaath shouted, prompting both students into action.

With his long legs covering the short gap, Syme came quickly within striking distance of Ahnon. He swung his sword in an upward slash, but the blow was deflected as Ahnon brought his shield forward––then up, in an attempt to throw his off balance.

Syme felt the sudden shift in his weight, so to correct his awkward position, he went into a spin while countering with a back-handed slash.

It was a clever strike...but the mute's eyes and intuition was quicker. He raised his sword and blocked Syme's attack, quickly countering with a thrust to the neck, but was parried away. An unexpected blow slammed into his shield as Syme dealt a powerful kick with his foot. The force of the blow sent Ahnon back a few steps. In an instant, Syme fell upon him again; this time coming in with a low chop that might've broken Ahnon's ankle if he hadn't jumped in the nick of time. However, this lost of ground would cost Ahnon even more, because he was forced to bring his shield up again.

From the sideline, the students watched the ensuing battle. They all seemed to cringe each time Ahnon barely escaped a shattered rib, or a smashed skull. It was obvious as to who was dominating the competition.

Jhavon didn't like it... His friend was clearly out-matched by a much larger opponent. The lykine stood at least two feet taller than Ahnon. And he was much stronger. He wondered when Jhekhaath would decide to put a stop to it....

A downward chop came crashing down upon Ahnon's shield, causing the mute to drop to one knee under the heavy assault. The blow felt as if a huge stone had fallen from a high place and smashed into his shield. He pushed off and regained his footing. He was starting to breathe heavy as the eve of exhaustion began setting in. The muscles in his little arms were beginning to ache from lifting the heavy shield. And when he looked at Syme, all he could see was pure rage and madness. He could feel the lykine's hatred with each blow he blocked with his shield.

Sweat poured down Syme's face as he pressed on, raining down relentless blows upon his opponent.

Ahnon was forced to thrust his shield upward, again and again, as Syme now loomed directly overhead. He braced when he saw the lykine pause for one last swing (it seemed), but when the expected rattle of his shield never came, he knew––in that moment––that he was in trouble. And before he could bring his shield back down in time, the vicious blow cracked into his hip bone!

The mute's face grimaced with unspeakable pain, but no sound came from his yawning mouth. He dropped his sword and retreated on one leg, while barely managing to deflect a blow to his head with the shield. But another blow quickly followed, breaking his upper right arm this time.

He dropped his shield, stumbling backward, then fell to the ground in agony. With tears streaming down his face, he looked up at the lykine who would've killed him by now if the edge of their swords weren't dull.

Syme approached the wounded mute as he lay helpless on the ground. He felt no pity for Ahnon. All he felt was the need to seek revenge and a great urge to get back at the trunket and his friends who had caused him so much harm. "Syme!!!" He paused, surprised that he called his own name. But then he noticed Ahnon, staring deep into his eyes. "Don't you dare use my voice," he growled at the pleading mute. He kicked him on his injured hip––and immediately, he too began to howl in pain!

Syme dropped his sword and shield as a severing pain entered his upper right arm...so unbearable, that he too collapsed to the ground....

Jhekhaath walked over to where the two boys laid on the ground. He looked down at Syme as he writhed and squirmed in pain. Then over at Ahnon, who had now curled himself into a ball, crying, as great sobs shook his body. "Alright now," he said, kneeling down next to the injured mute. He placed a comforting hand on his shoulder. "You can stop it now. Magic is against the rules in my class."

———•———

His bare feet walked upon the surface of a distant sun, in some unknown part of the galaxy. Great walls of fire swirled and blazed all around him. And yet, not so much as a single thread on his garment was singed. Not a single strand of his hair was set aflame.

Before him, was a portal in the shape of a black cube....
A portal, that he himself didn't erect.

Someone had opened all the gates!

When he stepped through, he had instantly entered a
new world. A rocky, deserted one. And just like before, a
portal stood just a few feet beyond.

For the first time in eons, a smile stretched across the
Eternal's face....

CHAPTER
NINETEEN

.... Four Years Later

THE STRONG WIND blew in his face as he flew over a sea of lush green fields. The trees of a wooded area blew by in a vague blur beneath him. He brought his arms inward to make the wings flap, causing his body to lift higher in the air. With perfect timing, he stretched his arms out again and the wings caught the rushing wind to hold him up in the sky like a looming hawk.

Since his first flight four years ago, he'd made some significant changes in his invention. Most of these improvements however, didn't go into the wings itself, but into creating the accessories needed to keep his back and legs straight. Some time ago, he'd come to learn that his body grew tired very quickly during flight. Just keeping his legs aligned while working the wings with his arms, required a lot of strength——and this had only awarded him a very short time in the air.

After many attempts at trial and error, what the trunket (now a senior student) would finally end up with, was his own special garment, designed for flying. Interlocking rods were stitched into the rough leather, and ran along the length of his spine and down the back of his legs. They were made to lock themselves in place whenever Jhavon stretched himself out. They helped keep his spine and legs in place while his arms remained free. And only by twisting both ankles, can the rods become unlocked to free his legs (something the trunket would eventually call his "landing maneuver") whenever he needed to make a landing.

With this built-in mechanism, the trunket saved most of his strength and stayed in the air for a much longer period of time. He chose to remake his wing with leather, because he found it was stronger and provided less friction. A single rod ran through the center of each wing. And instead of having one big contraption attached to his back, he now had two smaller wings that were specially made for each arm.

The garment itself was a one-piece suit that he could put on like a regular pair of trousers, then laced up the sides and along the arms to avoid the trunket's huge hands. Then the arms went through five loops that were fastened along the wings with leather straps.

His most significant challenge came with the guidance of the wing itself. A steady flight depended on his arms being leveled at all times. One falter, or the lowering of either arm would send him veering off in one direction, or spiraling out of control. And since no imaginable feat of engineering could solve this problem, the trunket still had to rely on his physical strength to keep himself in the air.

He soon learned that natural flying was a mixture of both strength and skill. With time, experience soon followed, and he learned how to balance himself in the air while conserving his energy. He learned not to fight against the wind. And when a falter in his posture caused him to drift off course, he no longer struggled to keep his weakening arms up, but simply lowered the other to veer himself back on the correct path. And in time, he grew stronger still, developing the muscles in his arms that kept him in the air for as long as he liked....

———•———

Jhavon soared high over the rolling hills. The great walls ran around the castle in a neat circle, save for when it met the main gates; their straightness gave the wall's round shaped a "dented" appearance from above. The gray slants and steeples that made up the castle's many roofs, formed their mountains and hills in their own sort of way.

The pleasant smells of baked and cooked foods flooded his nostrils, causing his mouth to water. He made great circles around the castle, gradually lowering his altitude. He swooped past the four watch-towers where the guards (who were nestled inside) paid less attention to him each time he flew by. And the people below hardly paid any attention at all! They'd all grown accustomed to seeing the flying trunket, flapping his wings high above them.

As he approached the incoming roof, he twitched his ankles and his legs came free. The sudden change in posture drug his body down. To compensate, he flapped and slowed his descent until he landed gently on his feet.

He squatted there a while——on the roof top——gazing down on the tiny people below. The flight had left him a little exhausted. His breathing was heavy, and his heart thumped rapidly. There was a comforting burn in the muscles that bulged in his arms.

Though he'd grown, the trunket wasn't one to keep himself groomed. He allowed his hair to grow long and wild with no restrains, save for the single string that kept it tied back in a bushy ponytail. For the first time, a bead of sweat began to trickle down the side of his face, disappearing into the thickness of his black beard. His long black curly hair fell over his shoulders, swaying to the rhythms of the wind.

There came a sudden flutter from above as a light-brown hawk landed nearby. It skittered across the roof and came to his side, its head cocked to one side while a fierce eye studied him intently.

"I wonder how you found this one?" he said, staring down at the hawk. He noticed the black and white blotches decked on the brown feathers. In some places, the three seemed to blend. "A pretty one at that!"

The curious hawk continued to stare; its black beady eye appearing to show contempt for the trunket's artificial wing. It let out a shrill cry.

Jhavon winced. "Not so loud, for Pag's sake!! A trunket's ears can only take so much."

The hawk skittered over the toward the roof's edge.

"Hold on...let me catch my breath."

The hawk seemed eager to leave. It let out another scream, before it went flapping off the roof.

"Oh, alright," Jhavon said, standing up in a lazy way to stretch his arms and legs. "This better be important." He broke into a short run and dove off the roof. He threw his arms and legs back––all in one swift motion––and was airborne once again as the suit's mechanism locked his legs in place.

He focused on the hawk's tiny body as it continued to glide downward, before rounding the side of the castle.... It would eventually lead him to the gardens, where Ahnon and Shurwath stood. Ahnon stretched out a gloved hand, and the hawk landed there as light as a leaf.

Jhavon circled the area twice before landing on the soft grass.

"You don't look too tired to me," Ahnon said (through Shurwath's mouth) as he stroked the hawk affectionately along the back of its head.

"And you two don't look like you're in distress," Jhavon said, freeing his arms out of the wings' extra weight. "Or maybe it's someone else this mighty trunket must save."

Shurwath laughed.... At seventeen, his features had developed quite handsomely. A light-brown beard was just beginning to form on the lower half of his boyish face. "Not us, Jhavon," he said. "But old Hollan appears to be in some dire need."

"Hollan?" Jhavon frowned, as he wrapped, then tied the two wings together with leather straps. He gave Ahnon a puzzled look.

The mute's 5½ foot frame had remained as thin and fragile as when they were first-year students. And other than a pair of thick eyebrows, a thin mustache was the only sight of facial hair on his face. "Aye," came the curt reply through Shurwath's mouth. "And it sounds urgent at that." He then raised his gloved hand and sent the hawk flapping away....

———●———

Old Hollan had taken a keen liking to Jhavon, and out of sheer curiosity about the trunket's progress, he often invited him down into his cluttered room for long talks over strong pagsroot tea.... "My apologies if I interrupted your flying," he said. A small cup floated off his table across the room and into Jhavon's awaiting hands.

"No need for apologies, Hollan," the trunket replied. He took a sip of the hot, sweet beverage, and smacked his lips. "I was just about finished with my exercise when I received your message."

The old sorcerer just stared at the trunket, who appeared so tiny in the large chair. He entertained the thought of the trunket being a future king in some distant land. But just sitting there in his purple robe, lost in the strong effects of the pagsroot tea, Jhavon was just a child in a man's seat. He followed his gaze till it settled on the finger of an old armored glove, sticking out amongst the cluttered mess on the floor.

Hollan chuckled when he saw it. The finger was unusually fat, and formed a long iron spike at the tip.

Just by the looks of the glove's over-sized finger, Jhavon knew it was made for the hands of only one race of creatures.

"There was once a warrior...." Hollan said.

The sudden sound of the sorcerer's voice interrupted whatever deep thoughts the trunket had at the moment. He turned to Hollan. "My apologies, sir," he said. "I didn't quite pick up on what you said."

Hollan nodded down at the glove. "It once belonged to a trunket, named Rhonaak."

Jhavon's eyes lit up at the sound of the warrior's name. He'd learned much about his role during the wars of the Eternals. "Rhonaak, you say?"

"Aye."

"Impossible, Hollan. That glove would have to be thousands and thousands of years old."

"That throne you're sitting on is older than that, boy," Hollan barked. "Are you implying that old Hollan's a jest?"

"Oh no," Jhavon straightened up in his seat. "Not that at all. It's just...the war of the Eternals was just so long ago."

"Means nothing, boy."

Jhavon sighed. "I've heard of Rhonaak. The trunket who led his army across the Ghi River into Warriors' Mountain."

"And that he did, boy."

"Did...did you––" the trunket began, not sure if he should ask the old sorcerer. "Did you ever see Rhonaan, sir?"

"See him...?" Hollan seemed taken aback by the question. "See him? I fought against the pag-be-damned beserker myself––" he paused, staring into the trunket's wondrous eyes. "Killed him with my own sword."

The sorcerer's gaze was too hard to hold. Jhavon broke off to stare at the glove again, thinking how much the bent finger resembled a broken claw. He half-expected the famous warrior to be laying under all the clutter. "It's said that he only had one arm."

"Aye," Hollan replied. "Didn't stop him from cutting men in half like logs."

"What was he like, Hollan?"

Hollan grunted as he leaned back in his chair. "Hmm... let me see if I can remember Rhonaak correctly.... What did they tell you in school?"

Jhavon shrugged. "Just another warrior who fought during those times. No different from all the others."

"Is that all?"

"Just about."

"I often wonder what good is all this schooling for," said Hollan, giving a sardonic snort. He sighed, pointing two fingers at the glove, causing it to rise slowly out the rubble. The whole glove was huge, bigger than the trunket's own hands. The armored fingers were nothing but long claws, and sharp spikes stood on its knuckles.

Hollan pointed somewhere else, and a racketing sound soon followed as a short armored leg came floating out of the clutter. Another leg came from somewhere else. Then came the upper and lower torso, with ancient engravings etched into the rusty armored plates——too ancient for the trunket to understand what they meant. And upon each shoulder-plate, two iron spikes stood, now rusty and worn from age and decay.

From somewhere in the back of the room, the stiff armored arm came drifting right past Hollan's head to fit itself into the armor's left shoulder socket with a grinding sound. The lone glove then joined itself into the arm's gaping wrist. The armor's right shoulder-socket however, remained empty. "Now, if I can only remember where I put that thing." Hollan said to himself, looking all about the room. "Ah-ha!" He pointed to the left, somewhere beyond where Jhavon was sitting.

There came a dull clank, like the sound of a piece of metal being dropped. A large helmet, with a razor-thin crest curving across the length of the skull, came floating past the awe-strucked trinket. It came over the headless armor, then rotated until the empty eye-sockets appeared to bore into the trunket's soul.

The completed armor was no taller than Jhavon. But the sheer mass of the body was much larger than any trunket he'd ever known. The squat thighs and legs were as thick as Jhavon's whole body. The shoulders were as big and round as cannon balls, and a bulging barrel could've been its chest. The single arm was equally great and astonishing in size and length. The empty helmet showed only a vague definition in its carving, to depict what the legendary warrior had actually looked like.

Jhavon became startled by the armor's sudden movement. The shoulder's rotating disk made a series of squeaks and crunching sounds. It bent down like a teetering puppet to work out the joints in its knees and hips.

"Even way back in those primitive times, the trunkets had mastered these kinds of inventions," Hollan said. "Even their horses were fitted with armor. Hard buggers to kill...."

Jhavon was at a loss for words as he stared at the empty armor, bending and stretching out its rusty knees. He tried to picture the ancient warrior in battle.

"Oh..." Hollan said suddenly. "I almost forgot." A big rusty axe shook its way out from beneath all the rubbish. The rusty head was still attached to the rotted handle. It drifted over toward the empty armor and was snatched out of the air by the lonely arm. It swung the axe in a skillful combinations of chops and twirls, before standing motionless in the room once more. "Now, that's the closest that you, or anyone else, would come to seeing what Rhonaak was like in his time. And as for his many victories in the battles during the great war, well...that's quite another story––way too many for me to tell. We could be here all night."

———●———

A smooth flat stone skipped across the surface of the pond before vanishing into a black swirling hole that churned above the water.

"Ha!" a mail-cladded guard pointed. "You see that? Right on the first throw!"

His comrade stood close by, aiming his drawn bow at the portal. Both waited in silence, and none dared drop their guard or take their eyes from the spot where the stone had just vanished.

There was just a faint twang at first, zinging up through the portal's black threshold. The guards became startled upon hearing the sound as potent adrenaline shot through their bodies. One of them hurled a long spear across the pond, then gasped in shock when it stopped just halfway inside the black hole. For a moment, the weapon stood motionless, as if held in place by the portal itself. But then it began to twitch and bob in the air as an agonizing wail pitched from the mouth of some unknown beast that came staggering out with the spear lodged deep into its side. The clawed feet scratched at the empty air and the beast fell into the pond with a lame splash.

The other guard let his arrow fly right into the creature's neck, while it struggled to keep its head above the water. The long grotesque arms fought to keep its heavy body afloat. A second bolt pierced its head, right below where a curved horn protruded. A third shot into its eye, and that seemed to make the creature swallow a mouthful of water, for its grievous screams did cease for a moment before starting up again.

Content that they'd wounded the beast to the point where it couldn't save itself, the two guards just stood by and watched with pleasure until it drowned....

"A dangerous game you two enjoy."

The guards spun quickly around at the sudden sound of the strange voice. One of them had already drawn his bow, and sheer panic caused him to release the bolt.

Rahjule stood behind them with his black cloak draped over his shoulder. The arrow's shiny head turned to dust the instant it touched the cloak, leaving the naked shaft to fall harmlessly to the ground where it sank into the earth.

The two guards became surprised––fearful even. "Holy Pagaroth!" one finally managed to utter, once he realized that he'd nearly shot the remnant of Pagaroth. They both dropped down to their knees.

"Never take your eyes off the gate!" Rahjule said, pointing toward the portal's gaping hole. "What if some flying abomination came out?"

They both scrambled back up to their feet again––bow and spear drawn, as if anticipating the oncoming attack at any second. However, their faces became filled with confusion when they realized the gate that they'd been guarding over the past four years (slaying any creature that came crawling out of it) was suddenly gone! Only the empty air remained above the calm waters; and what was supposed to have been natural, felt otherwise.

The guards had to force themselves to remove their eyes from the spot where the portal had once been, to the spot where Rahjule had once stood. But they found nothing there as well! Just the shimmering ground that solidified right before their eyes....

CHAPTER
TWENTY

VERY FEW KNEW of the scrolls that prophesied Ragath's return. But only one knew about the "gate keepers" (because he employed them) who stood guard at every portal that'd been erected all across the Land of Hagaraak....

A hazy mist oozed over the window-sill and poured into Shurlan's study. The compused lykine just leaned back in his chair with steepled fingers.

"Reports have been coming in from all over the lands," Morella said, floating up gracefully to his side. "That gates have closed.... All of them."

"If one closes, then all will close," Shurlan said, staring up at the dark churning clouds through the window.

"So, the day has finally come...?"

Shurlan didn't react to Morella's apprehensive words. So too, were his eyes blind to the worried expression on her face, for his mind had already become too enthralled with his own day of reckoning.

———•———

As the glowing balls of light came together to form one bright cluster, they slowly dispersed at the slightest touch, scattering themselves all throughout the cavern again.

Long slanting shadows bent around the solid objects on the ground. The stalactites' crooked fangs stood proudly in the high ceiling as the lights crept by, before retreating back into the shadows once more. Then, as if coming to the limit of their airborne migration, they would retract themselves to form another cluster, then slowly disperse at the slightest touch in a repeated pattern.

Ignoring the fact that his magnetic presence was the cause of this... this...strange work of polarity, the Eternal, Ragath, sat upon his ancient throne that was made from solid gold. His blank face was an unreadable mask that had been staring into the cavern's far wall for an entire week, and not once did he move, flinch, or bat an eyelid....

"This is hardly what I expected of the dreaded return of Ragath," Ohlar said, whispering softly into Zhorghan's ear as he drifted by. His black smoky form billowed up into a chair nearby. "Surely, this is not what the world's been––" But his words were cut short when Zhroghan threw up a silencing hand.

For days, the old wizard had submerged himself into the text of the ancient scrolls. "The world know nothing of the Eternals," he said, without looking up from his reading. "There's no mentioning in the prophecy, anywhere, that Ragath will destroy the world upon his return. But that is the general assumption––is it not?"

The demon didn't bother to reply. Very few were as gifted, and priviledged to be favored by any Eternal, as Zhorghan.... This much, he had to admit to himself. But there was something very odd in the Eternal's silence. He hadn't uttered a single word––to anyone––when he stepped out of the mirror's portal that Zhorghan had prepared for him four years ago. And not one time did he acknowledge the presence of his apprentice when they'd both stood, stunned by his sudden appearance in their midst.

"So tell me, Ohlar," Zhorghan went on. "What were you expecting of this day, after all these centuries?"

The demon shrugged.

"Another breaking up of the world, perhaps?"

"Perhaps," he said, in all honesty. "Considering the fact that he'd left the world in so much chaos and destruction. It's only natural for one to assume that Ragath might want to seek revenge on all the remnants of the Eternals."

"Revenge...?" Zhorgan seemed taken aback by the comment. And this time, he did turn away from his work to give the demon a questioning frown. "Who is there left remaining for my Master to seek revenge upon? Or haven't you noticed that Hagaraak has been a godless land for many eons?"

"Or maybe we're all simply mistaken, Zhorghan," Ohlar replied. "But you do understand how easy it is for one to fall into such errors?"

"Aye," said Zhorghan. "Men would always be subjected to wild thoughts. But we're not mortals, Ohlar. We've seen what changes can occur between the passage of so many years."

"You speak true, Zhorghan."

"And yet––" The wizard cocked a thoughtful brow. "You were expecting certain things to happen at the hands of an Eternal."

"I admit that much."

"And do you now see how your expectations have led you to error?"

"Aye. I see that now."

"So tell me, Ohlar. What do you know of Ragath's sapphire, other than what you've already read in the scrolls?"

"Can't say that I know too much about it, beyond the power it contains. Ragath wanted to change the world——"

"Change the world?" Zhorghan stopped him at once.

"Aye...."

"Hmm...maybe you knew less than I thought, Ohlar. How long have you been amongst the Eternals before the splitting of the world?"

The demon shook his head. "Not very long. I was barely coming of age when Mox was destroyed."

"Destroyed...? Well...I wouldn't say destroyed. And there're very few alive today who understand why certain things ceased to be. But allow me to be the first to tell you that none of the Eternals were ever destroyed. Even Pagaroth and the meddling Laap still live, though not in this world.... There was a time when the Eternals weren't needed at all. Did you know that, Ohlar?"

"It's hard for me to even picture such things in my head."

"As hard as is it to believe, such a time did exist. Long before we came to be. The Eternals were created by an awesome power. A power too great to imagine. It's this power that my master had captured within Ragath's sapphire. And I had witnessed him do this with my own eyes. The power that created the Eternals, wielded in the palm of his hands.... And do you know why he was the last to be created?"

"It's written that Ragath's purpose was to find a netherworld for all the lost souls."

232

"But that's all that was ever written, Ohlar," Zhorghan said. "The true purpose of my master's existence is even harder to accept."

"The purpose of my being is not important." Ragath's deep voice resonated all throughout the cavern.

Startled out of their wits, both Zhorghan and Ohlar spun around to face the Eternal, still seated on his throne. But nothing had changed in Ragath's posture. The sound of his voice still thrummed along the surface of the walls and ceiling. "You could never be more correct in such a matter," said Zhorghan, with all the reverence his tremulous voice could muster.

"You speak of Pagaroth's stone," Ragath said. "Did you know that its been partially pieced back together?"

Zhorghan raised his bushy brows in surprise.... So that's what Ragath's been doing all this time, he thought. The Eternal had been learning of all the events that had occurred over the eons while he was gone. "I didn't know it was possible to recover the lost shards," he said. "They'd been scattered all across the earth; some is said to have landed on the highest of peaks, and have sunken down to the deepest parts of the sea.... But then again, it would make sense that Rahjule could've dedicated many millennia to finding them. That sight explain why he hasn't been seen in such a long time."

"The remnant of Pagaroth still live?"

"Aye."

"Then it's obvious that he has plans on keeping them from me."

"Obviously," said Zhorghan. "Many preparations have been made for the day of your return.... But how do you know the stone is just partially whole? The task should've been easy enough for Rahjule to have recovered all the shards."

For a brief moment, it appeared as if Ragath wouldn't bother to explain anything else to the wizard until he noticed the tiny blue specks beginning to sprout up from the ground around them. Even in the dark shadows, they clung to the walls in a glittering mass before swirling up into the air like a swarm of blue embers. The spray of glimmering blue dazzled the entire cavern as they drifted over toward Ragath, settling just inches above his awaiting palm before fusing themselves into a small gem.

Ragath held it up for his astonished apprentices to witness. "Because..." he said. "This is all that he left for me to find."

———•———

The festival of Ghaan (or the festival of creation) is held each year on the last day of the winter season. And on this day, the harvest were incredibly bountiful, regardless of whether the land had been tilled or not. The citizens all don the costumes of their favorite Eternal, to re-enact the doings of their time. They held great feasts, then sang and drank until the festivities is ended by sheer exhaustion.

By midnight, almost everyone is Pagaroth's castle had fell into a drunken stupor, induced by countless jugs of ale and mead. The guards were all slumped at their places of post. Rubbery legs were sprawled all over the ground, with hanging chins propped gently on heaving chests. Only the lively flames of torches flickered on with indifference, keeping the harmless shadows at bay....

None was aware when a dark portal had opened, blowing out a black cloud of smoke....

A soft giggle sounded in the shadows that hid the gardens. From out the darkness, a hooded figure came, running gleefully from where a trimmed hedge faced the torch's light. She spun around under the hovering flame to make sure she was still being pursued. But the darkness beyond the hedge remained as still as the silence that accompanied it.

Her face flashed with excitement when she caught a shiny reflection in the corner of her eyes. She yelped! realizing that capture was so close, then went skittering across the loose gravel (toward a portico along the castle's wall) as she held up her dress to keep it from dragging on the ground.

Her breathing was fast and heavy when she reached the wall. She fixed her eyes on the white gravel under the dim light of the torch, hoping to spot her pursuer––secretly hoping that he would find her...here.... She made a sound, as if by mistake, to give him a hint that she was near by. But soon, her breathing slowed, and her racing pulse eventually dropped back down to its normal pace.

She was beginning to grow impatient...just standing there...in the shadow of a lonely portico––

"You're not much of a good hider, you know."

The suddenness of the lykine's voice (whispering softly in her ear) nearly startled her half to death. However, the familiar touch of the gentle hands on her waist brought back her senses, her zest for life––and love....

She turned slowly around and allowed herself to fall into the warm embrace that no amount of cold may hinder––

Except for the damp nose that brushed up against her forehead.

"Oh, for pag's sake!" she snapped, leaning back to wipe her forehead with the back of her hand. She waved a finger, causing a small flame to spark into existance in the palm of her hand. The weak light cast their faces in a soft amber glow.

The long face of a fox stared at her. Two pointy horns stood on its head, between a pair of tall ears.... It was the closest resemblance to his Eternal that any lykine could achieve.

"I had enough of Llok for one night," she said.

The fox frowned, knitting its bushy brows. Its jaws opened (just slightly) to reveal some pointy teeth inside. A long nasty scar ran from the corner of its mouth, all the way back to its pointy ears as it made a low whimpering sound.

"Come on then," she urged him, landing a playful punch on his chest. "I told you that I'll never kiss a dog. And I mean it."

One last grunt came from the fox as the horns sunk back into its head. The long snout began to recede, and so did the light-brown fur, leaving the hideous scar to stretch on Syme's face. "Even if you know what lies inside the dog?" he asked, staring into her dark eyes. The years had caused his face to appear grim, a bit menacing even. Especially with the scar's rough tissue growing into the left side of his bottom lip——dragging it down a bit——adding further disfigurement to his features.

"You know what I mean, Syme," the girl said. The outline of her pretty face was partially hidden by the large hood she wore. "Stop being so sensitive."

She was used to it, though. She knew what lay behind Syme's unhappy face, was a warm and joyful spirit. She closed her palm to extinguish the flame. They kissed with passion under the portico's shadow.

"What is it, Shaan?" Syme asked when she stopped kissing him all of a sudden. He could feel her grip tightening on his robe.

"Something's lurking, Syme," she replied.

"Wh––" He felt it too! A warm sensation brushed his skin.

"It's behind me, Syme!"

He drew her closer in the darkness, and they both took a silent step away from the intruder. "Give whoever it is, a little singe," he whispered in her ear. "That'll teach them not to sneak up on lovers."

They timed their movements before Shaan spun quickly around!

A bright ball of light flashed before Syme's eyes when his woman caused a blanket of fire to spread over their heads. He had to duck down low to prevent his hair from going up in flames. However, what they saw before them was hardly what they expected.

"Shadows!!"

All around them! Black inky clouds, with blazing red eyes.

Not knowing what else to do, the frightened Shaan blew a gust into the encroaching mass. But the demons simply changed their misty forms into solid black creatures. A long black shaft (like a spear) shot out from one of their hands and pierced into Shaan's unguarded chest!

The witch gave a painful gasp before her body became limp in Syme's arms.

"Shaan!!!" The shock of what had just happened left the lykine stunned and speechless. So much so, he didn't notice that the fire had died along with her, leaving him in darkness with her killers.

His reaction was pure rage after that. And without him being aware of it, his body began to grow. He swung a gnarled, mutating arm toward the glowing red eyes that simply wavered as though his vision became blurred.... A sharp point hit his side, but it barely scratched his thick armored skin.

He brought his arm down and broke the spear. But another mad swing at the glowing red eyes went wildly through empty air. The force of multiple stabs sent him stumbling backward. And trough unharmed, he felt the ground suddenly become soft as some of Shaan's ribs snapped under the weight of his own foot.

More rage surged through him and a long agonizing howl poured from his giant mouth. He ignored the soft pinches of the demons' spears that bounced harmlessly off his body, then charged right through them as they puffed themselves back into untouchable smoke....

———•———

The tremulous sound of a great horn stirred the trunket out of his drunken sleep. The ill-timed ringing of bells dragged his mind from its hazy grogginess. However, it was the sound of the terrifying screams and pandemonium that caused him to jump out of bed!

"Pagaroth is under attack!!!" came the shouts from outside.

"They're inside the walls!!!"

"Monsters!!!"

"Jhavon!"

He spun around at the sound of his own name. There was chaos all around the dorm. Students hustled out of bed, throwing on whatever clothes they could find, while others scrambled out through the door.

"Jhavon!"

A hand grabbed his shoulder. It was Ahnon. He looked as frightened as he'd ever been. He stared deep into Jhavon's eyes. "Something's attacking us."

The words popped into his mouth. He now understood why he couldn't see who was calling him.

"Get up, Jhavon! We must leave now!"

Confusion still boggled the trunket's mind. "Who... who's––"

"No time to explain! We must leave here at once!"

A horrible scream came from the other side of the dorm.

"Let's go, Jhavon!"

The trunket rolled out of bed on shaky feet and threw on his purple robe. Their dorm was in complete disarray as they were the last few to leave. Sheets and clothes were strewn all over the floor.

As they rushed through the door, he noticed Ahnon holding a flashy dagger in his hand....

———●———

Armed guards (bearing torches) spilled through the castle's gates to join the wizards, sorcerers, and witches, in their fight against the otherworldly creatures that had suddenly invaded their land. Black portals would swirl in and out of existence, allowing herds of demonic beasts to come lumbering through.

With each creature that was slain, another––more hideous it seemed––would come crawling through a portal, only to be struck down by a wizard's lightning bolt. Some bore no resemblance to any creature on earth...just transparent blobs of raw energy, impervious to any sorcerer's magic.... These, were the hardest to kill, and in turn, killed the most easiest of all.

A small bird flittered by overhead, then morphed into a hulking rock bear just before it landed in the midst of the battlefield. It was a formidable creature, standing well over ten feet tall––found only in the realm of Vlak's Forest. Its hard gray skin was as smooth as a whale's, and it showed off the large rippling muscles that gave it its rock-like appearance. It charged into the creature's side, sending it whirling to the ground where its innards poured out through a gaping wound.

While the guards closed in to finish off the beast, the rockbear turned on three demons, slaying all with teeth and claws.

A portal opened up nearby and pulled a wizard right through. When the bear saw this, it reared up on its hind legs. Its long bloody snout shrunk, and soon, Shurlan's face appeared. "Beware of the gates!!! Beware of the gates!!!"

Pag' help us! Shurlan thought to himself. It was all happening too soon. He studied the battlefield, noticing the human guards and younger students were dying the most. Even some of the elder wizards were beginning to fall. And yet, more portals opened from where more creatures came.

They were losing.

The sky churned above them all, and several bolts of lightning came striking down upon the heads of many creatures, causing a gory rain of blood and meat to shower the battlefield for a brief moment. Another bright bolt flashed from Shurwath's hand and went crackling across the yard to electrocute two incoming demons.

He saw a witch shudder, then fall. The air shimmered where she once stood, before moving on to kill another guard in a similar fashion.... Shurwath shot his bolt at the apparation, but all it did was absorb the electric shock.

———•———

Morlah grabbed her twin sister by the shoulder to get her attention in the midst of the chaos. They stood on the southern end of the castle at the 7th guard tower. A vicious fire-wielding reptile had just set fire to a shed nearby. Tall flames were beginning to consume the roof as it fed ravenously on wood and straw. The dead littered the ground all around them.

Marlah was too busy fighting off the hideous creatures to notice her sister. But when she finally did, she feared Morlah had been hurt. "What is it?" she asked over the deathly screams. But she became distracted (once again) when a sudden sensation caused her to look where a scaly creature was chewing on a dead woman's neck. The flesh was torn from her face.

With the sudden wave of Marlah's hand, the creature yelped——then froze. Its body rose an inch above the ground, then tore itself in half!

"Are you hurt, Morlah?" she asked again, searching her sister's body for any signs of blood.

Morlah's lips began to move.

She read them carefully. A puzzled frown fell on her face. "You can see them?"

Morlah nodded.

"See who, Morlah?" she spun around to see what came behind them.

Morlah shook her head in frustration and grabbed her sister's hand again. She pointed westward, toward the main gates.

Marlah was still confused. Though she studied the area where her sister had pointed to, she couldn't make out anything too different from what was happening all around them. At least they had a big fire that gave them light. It was much darker by the main gates, save for a few dying torches that lay on the ground next to the slain guards. "Are you for certain, Morlah?"

Her sister replied with a grave nod.

"Okay then," Marlah said, taking her sister's hand. She led the way west, along the great walls, till they came to a dark area. "You'll have to lead us now," she said to the blind sorceress. "My eyes are no good to us here."

Morlah used her powers to lead them through the dark, with more ease than Marlah had done under the fire's light. As they went past the 8th tower, the castle's courtyard and main gates came into view. There, the fighting was more intense, and it appeared as if the dead had carpeted over the entire grounds.

Morlah paused between the tower and the main gates—— as if scanning the battlefield for someone——before she found them in the midst of the fighting guards.

A large beast came charging toward them just then. But without so much as flinching in the monster's direction, the blind sorceress held out a hand as she whispered a spell that sent the creature flying over the great wall with a whining howl.

Some ways ahead, they helped a soldier cripple a nine-foot demon, before she stopped and turned to her sister. She pointed off to the side at a clear wobbly thing that looked like a bubble of floating water as it slammed into the body of an unsuspecting wizard. The wizard shuddered, then dropped dead to the ground.... "We have to kill them," she mouthed the words to her sister.

Marlah gave her a sly wink, which she knew would go unseen by the blind sorceress. They turned to the floating blob of energy while summoning a wicked life-sucking spell. The apparition appeared to freeze in mid air, then for no apparent reason, it began to shrink down till it was no more.

They moved through the throng of battle, ignoring the death that was happening all around them, while slaying everything that stood in their path. They sucked up the second apparition much easier than the first, growing stronger each time. It was then that Marlah realized her sister was attracted to the energy emitted by the strange creatures. So she followed her trail with the same thirst and hunger as the demons who craved their blood.

She followed Morlah all the way into the courtyard, where a huge rock bear tore into the throat of a hideous creature. The mighty bear reared up on its hind legs, and Shurlan's face suddenly appeared where its mouth had been.

"Beware the gates!!! Beware the gates!!!" she heard the ancient lykine say, before his face morphed back into the rock bear and went charging back into the thick of the battle.

Morlah stopped and pointed toward another apparition. It had just killed a witch, then absorbed a lightning bolt from Shurwath. It began to move——fast. But she locked on to it just in time, feeding off its energy until it was no more. They then moved on the next one, not caring to receive the young wizard's gratitude.

———•———

Sheer terror had caused the trunket to freeze in his tracks as he and Ahnon ran out of the castle into the courtyard.

Shurwath stood before them, calling lightning from the sky to rain down on the enemy. He shot his bolts into some demons and burned them dry. He then turned his magic onto some unseen thing that came flying at him, but then it began to shrink and it suddenly vanished.... It had given the young wizard quite a scare.

On the grounds before the main gates, beasts as large as trees brought their feet and claws crashing down on the guards below. Only the magic from the wizards and sorcerers kept them at bay. He looked over at Ahnon, still holding on to his little dagger, but was now unsure it would be of any use on the giant creatures. But then the mute reached out with a hand, causing a nine-foot demon to pause in mid swing (aimed at a sorcerer's head), to look directly over at them from all the way across the grounds!

Ahnon made a brief scan of the battlefield before pointing out another demon that fought two human guards. The first demon charged into its kin, catching it unawares with a sharp-clawed strike to the throat. The creature was dead before the demon marched off in search of something else its own size.... The effort was keeping Ahnon's attention so engaged, that one slip in his concentration would cause him to lose control of the creature.

Unarmed, and without magic, the trunket felt more vulnerable than the human guards. And more useless at that!

He spun around and ran back into the castle....

———●———

The enchanted gem stone on Julie's spirit stick glowed a furious red as she invoked her most powerful spells at the shadows that drifted in and out of the castle's rooms and libraries.

Very few shadows were seen on the battlefield, since they were all given the task of invading tie castle's interior. The sounds of things breaking and crashing to the ground filled the halls. Smoke, from lit fires, puffed lazily through the creases of closed doors. An occasional scream would sound (from anywhere) as some poor soul died defending their own life.

"They're destroying the castle, Ermma," she said. Fiery tears streamed down here face. Her spirit stick flashed and sent a great burst of magic surging through her body, then out through her outstretched arm. A black cloud of four incoming shadows succumbed to the witch's power and fell to the floor in a harmless pile of dust.

The sight of fire and smoke were all around them now. Black filmy ash floated down from the higher floors. The once glossy tiles were now littered with ash, debris, and dead bodies.... The castle's interior was now in ruins. Even the little floating flames that once served as useful lamps, now appeared to contribute to all the destruction. They simply hovered and flickered, oblivious to all the atrocities taking place.

A loud explosion came from around the corner in the hallway. Two shadows shot by in the wake of flying glass and smoke. The sound of the crackling flames intensified. Something big crashed down on the floor.

The smoke in the halls were beginning to thicken!

Ermma grabbed Julie's arm with an urgent tug. "We have to go!" she yelled. "There's nothing left to fight. Not even the shadows could stay in here much longer."

Julie followed the siren through the burning halls. Flames were already eating away at the walls. In some places, she was forced to conjure wind-spells in order that they could make a dash through the tunnels of fire; through the smell of roasting flesh and wood....

They came out through a door on the northeastern side of the castle in a mist of black smoke. The cold fresh air brought a welcoming sensation in their lungs when they heard the monstrous cries of beasts in battle near the gardens.

"A ryke!" Julie said, with a growl of pure hatred. "Probably came here with the shadows. Let it die." She began to walk away in the opposite direction, but then stopped when she realized Ermma wasn't following her. "Are you going to help me with the others, or are you to stay here and listen to a dying ryke?"

Ermma just stood there, staring into the darkness. With her keen hearing, she followed the violent sounds as the ryke continued to thrash through the rows of hedges.

"Well...?" Julie was becoming impatient.

"It don't sound like its dying," Ermma said. "Having a rough time, maybe. But not dying."

Julie paused to get a better ear of the violence. Only the unmistakeable grunts and snarls could be heard coming from the ryke. But nothing more, save for the rumbling and thrashing in the grass, and the occasional snap of a bone or two. But no dying wails and cries, human or otherwise. "Something's...attacking it?"

"Or something's being attacked," Ermma said. "I'm sure I can put any ryke on its knees. And whatever its fighting can't be that strong, or the battle would've been over a long time ago. How dangerous can it really be for us to just go down there and have a look?"

Julie weighed the odds in her mind. It would be silly for them to die in the dark––she'd rather perish in the burning castle first. However, Ermma did have a point. Whatever was out there couldn't possibly be much stronger than they were, since it was having so much problems with the ryke. And either way, she'd have the pleasure of killing them both. "It shouldn't take us that long."

A mischievous grin stretched across Ermma's face. "Not too long at all."

With the sight of her dead friends and teachers still fresh in her mind, Julie led the way. She'd suddenly grown an insatiable thirst for her enemy's blood.

A bright light shone from the stone on her spirit stick, illuminating the path before them. Torn shrubs and uprooted flowers were strewn all over the grass. And just a few yards beyond, they could see the hulking ryke, surrounded by over a dozen black creatures.

"Shadows!" Ermma dashed forth with more speed and vigor than Julie thought she had. When she came to a sliding stop she opened her mouth as if to shout, but no words came. Not a sound. Instead, long waves caused the air before her to warp and shimmer.

The shadows all seemed to freeze in place, as if hypnotized by the young siren's voice. A few shadows puffed themselves into smoke then scattered, while their comrades fell dead to the ground. But their flights were all short as they flew up in the air, only to fall back down as sprinkling dust.

Now alone, the confused and disgruntled ryke began thrashing all about, searching for the enemy that'd long drifted away as harmless smoke. He seemed oblivious to the bright light that shone all around. His face and body covered in thick bark. His black beady eyes, barely visible under the wooden, droopy brow.

The sudden clangs from the bell towers seemed to bring him out of his madness. And for the first time, he appeared to notice the bright light from Julie's spirit stick. He watched the gem as it grew dim, and the witch stretched out her arm to cast a deadly spell.

But then the ryke did something that surprised them both. It spoke....: "Rykes are sacred to the goddess Laap, Julie," it said, in an all too familiar voice. "You learned that in your second year. But then again, I'm not surprised. You always slacked in your studies."

Julie gasped in shock, then quickly dropped her arm as the ryke's grotesque form dissolved away into a tall and graceful lykine. "Syme!"

He was limping. Badly. He had to hold his ribs when he moved, walking past Julie and Ermma without uttering a single word. He went under the wall-mounted torch that showered the gravel in a circle of light, disappearing under the darkness by the castle's wall.

They followed slowly behind him, fearful that he might suddenly fall into another fit of rage. The light from Julie's stick showed him kneeling next to a person's body along the wall. They could hear him sobbing.

Ermma covered her mouth to block the deadly gasp when she saw who Syme was holding in his arms.

Julie dropped her spirit stick when she saw her dead sister's face.

CHAPTER
TWENTY-ONE

"HOLLAN!" JHAVON CALLED, as he ran through the winding passageway under the castle. Down there, the ringing bells and dying screams were completely blocked off by the thick walls. Surely, all the chaos happening above had gone unnoticed by the old man. He was probably enjoying the effects of some freshly brewed pagsroot tea.

"Hollan!"

As the light that shone through the doorway finally came into view, he didn't waste any time in entering Hollan's place. He shouted inside the empty room, half-expecting old Hollan to come shuffling around the corner at any moment. "Hollan!" His impatience caused him to dash across the cluttered room.

Rhonaak's armor still stood in its place from his last visit. He brushed up against the cold metal as he rushed by, though he was too much in a hurry to notice it at the time.

He tripped over something that held up a pile of junk and it came crashing down behind him. The loud clattering was enough to make him freeze in position as if he was disturbing the only place left in the castle where some kind of peace remained.

He continued with less caution this time, kicking over whatever laid in his path. He went behind the little room where he saw Hollan disappeared into so many times before. But there was nothing but junk and clutter there now. No mattress, no chair in sight. No Hollan.... The place was empty!

It was then the thought occurred to him that Hollan had more than likely been alerted of the invaders, and was already in the midst of battle. And the more he thought of this, the more plausible the idea seemed, and the more he cursed his own stupidity for not thinking about it sooner. He cursed himself for running out on his friends when he should've been helping in any way he could...magic or no magic. Shurwath and Ahnon were probably—

He cursed again for thinking such dreadful thoughts, then ran out of the small room, kicking at the junk that litter at the floor. He swatted at Rhonaak's armor as it stood in his way. However, bone connected with metal that didn't so much as budge under the careless blow. "Ahwooo!!!" he wailed out, grabbing his throbbing hand. He gave the rusty armor a cold stare. He gazed into the helmet's hollow sockets, pretending to stare into the warrior's eyes. "Our Eternal has returned to kill us all," he heard himself saying. It was the first time the thought had ever occurred to him since the beginning of the assault. But who else could be responsible for opening the portals, other than the god of portals himself?

New reckoning seeped into his mind just then.... The times in which Rhonaak...this...armored trunket once lived in, has now returned. Times of relentless war, but much worst, because there aren't any Eternals left to oppose Ragath. His Eternal...! The Eternal of all trunkets!

He wondered what held the armor in place, if Hollan wasn't there to hold it up with his magic. The huge clawed goves still gripped the axe's handle, which was as thick as a small log——and the double-bladed head looked heavy enough to send the whole thing tipping over on its side. And yet, it stood as firm as if the trunket warrior was actually standing inside of it.

Both blades on the axe gleamed with a (newly) sharpened edge, though Jhavon couldn't recall seeing the blades as clean and shiny as they are now. It looked as if someone had taken great care——and time——in dusting the whole thing off. They even polished it up a little. He didn't have any doubts as to who that person was. The oil could still be seen where small drops had been used to lubricate the limbs and joints.... There wasn't any doubt in the trunket's mind what Hollan had expected him to do if he ever came back down to his room and found the armor (which Hollan somehow knew he would).

With a self-calming sigh (and a determined mind), Jhavon took Rhonaak's helmet from the armor's shoulders and lowered it down on his own head....

———————●———————

The heavy metal, along with the armor's ill-fitting joints, made walking a strange and tedious task for the young trunket. The axe's handle, which was actually carved from the branch of a morgah tree, was surprisingly light in weight——despite its huge size. However, it fitted comfortably in the trunket's hands. It was the broad head of the axe (weighing fifty pounds) that carried all the weapon's weight.

The castle was already on fire when he made it back to the surface. Tall flames hugged the walls, emitting heat and stifling smoke into the halls. The armor protected his skin from the flames' fiery touch, but did nothing to keep the air around him clean.

The wave of fresh air swarmed around him like an artic breeze as he stumbled outside through the northeastern door.

He was yet to decide on his next course of action when a white light illuminated the walls and grass to his left. The trimmed hedges of the garden was awashed in it, which he thought strange because he was sure he'd taken the southern exit, much closer to the battle. He wanted to join the human guards, whose weapons were similar to his. He had no plans on coming this far.

The howl of a ryke reached his ears, followed by someone shouting: "Shadows!" The siren's pitchy voice was unmistakable.

He hoisted the heavy axe over his shoulder and hobbled over to the sound of his friends in battle. By the time he rounded the bend, he was nearly out of breath, and Julie and Ermma were already following Syme toward the castle's western wall.

The light from Julie's spirit stick showed Syme holding someone in his arms. Their heads were all bowed, as if in mourning.

Syme's keen sense came alive upon his approach. He spun around in the trunket's direction, alerting the others. Julie shone a blinding light in Jhavon's eyes, while the air around him was already beginning to cook. His skin tingling.

"It's just me, Ermma!" he shouted to the siren. "It's me! Jhavon! Stop!" He took off the helmet. His face shone in the bright light.

"Jhavon...?" Ermma sounded a bit relieved.

"Lower your light, Julie," Jhavon said.

Julie's spirit stick dimmed down to a soft glow.

"Jhavon...! I almost——"

"I know, Ermma," he said to the young siren, who gave his bulky frame and awkward hug. "I was feeling the beginnings of it."

"I thought you was one of those monsters.... What is this?" she asked, noticing the armor for the first time. "Where'd you find this old thing?" Her hands fell on his bare right arm. "And what happened to the other sleeve?"

"I found it in old Hollan's place. It once belonged to a one-armed trunket warrior. There's only one sleeve for this particular armor."

The lykine was looking up at him. He still held Shaan's dead body in his arms. Two long streams of tears lined his face.

Jhavon let the axe fall, and moved in closer. "What happened?" he asked in a nervous voice, fearing it might be someone dear to him. His heart sank when he saw Shaan's face, and the gaping wound in her chest. He looked over at Julie. "I'm sorry," he said, his words barely audible.

"It was the shadows," said Ermma.

They all fell silent again, ignoring the bells, the burning castle, and all the death that were taking place at the castle's gates....

"It's Ragath," Jhavon finally managed to say. He felt their heads turning towards him.

"What?" asked Ermma. "Why do you say Ragath? It's just a few shadows, coming here to raid us."

"Ragath brought the shadows," Jhavon said. "They came through the portals."

"Portal?" asked Syme, looking up from his dead love.

"Aye," the young trunket replied. "Ragath's portals. Hundreds of them."

"So Ragath's here?" came the fearful question.

"Aye."

"And what of the others?" asked Syme.

"Fighting," Javon said. "I went to warn old Hollan, thinking he was all by himself down there, but he was already gone. He must've knew that I might come to fetch, because he left me this armor."

They all stood and waited for a brief moment as Syme did the most unexpected thing and kissed the dead witch on her lips. He then mouthed a few words that no one else could've heard, before gently lowering her body to the ground. He crossed her two limp arms together across her chest to cover the mortal wound, then stood up. "I guess we can't just sit here all night," he said. "There's more things going on, and I should think we're needed elsewhere."

Jhavon went to retrieve his helmet and axe. When he returned, he noticed Syme staring at the bulky contraption on his body.

"A one-armed trunket warrior, you say?" the lykine asked, a bit too skeptical for Jhavon's taste. "Then I suppose he wanted you to have one arm as well."

"More suitable for this sort of armor...don't you think?" the trunket replied....

They headed west, toward the main gates.

As they approached the second guard tower, past the stables, it confounded all—except Jhavon—to see that it was totally enclosed with large boulders. They boxed the entire structure, appearing like a hastily constructed tomb, built to protect the defenseless horses inside.

The trunket only knew one person who could erect such thing in so short of a time-span. Years ago, during the many cold nights spent in the open fields under Pagaroth's dark sky.

"What do you think it is?" asked Julie, as they ran past the entombed stables.

"Some abomination's trick perhaps," Syme said.

The sounds of battle were growing much louder. The desperate cries of men, women, and beasts, becoming more distinct, heightening their apprehensions for what awaited them.

Each quickened their own pace in silence, secretly contemplating their own means of survival.

They were nearing the castle's northwestern wall now, and still, things remained fairly dark, save for the occasional flash of some wizard's magic that revealed the large monstrous figures up ahead.

Syme's body began to grow with bone-crunching sounds as he morphed back into the hulking ryke.

The dim glow of Julie's spirit-stick began to throb and pulse, betraying her mounting emotions before battle.

"Spread out!" Syme said to Julie and Ermma.

The two obeyed the lykine's command without complaint, taking the lead as they broke off to his right.

Syme looked over at Jhavon. "Stay close to me, trunket," he said. "I would hate to see you lose an arm like the owner of that armor you're wearing."

No reply came from Jhavon, who still struggled to keep his balance under the armor's weight. The muscles in his legs were already beginning to burn after the short run to the main gates.... The warrior, Rhonaak, must've been as strong as a giant, he thought. He hoisted the mighty axe on his shoulder, gripping the handle with both hands....

As they cleared the northwestern wall, Julie caused the gem on her spirit stick to become so bright that it illuminated the entire battlefield as clear as day.

Syme broke off into a quick sprint, though the sheer size of his bulky frame appeared to move slower than everything else. He was fast enough to come up beside an unsuspecting beast nonetheless, bashing the creature's head with a spiky fist before it had a chance to react. Pure adrenaline rushed through his body at that point, and a mighty rear erupted from his mouth as he caused countless thorns to stick out on the surface of his body––from head to toe––like a living cactus!

Upon seeing this new foe enter the stage of battle (and fearing it perhaps), the larger monsters all rushed upon the ryke at once, with the same insatiable thirst for blood as they did with the weaker human guards. They pounded on the prickly ryke, only to be fended off by Syme's merciless blows.

The trunket, probably too small to be seen (or bothered with) in the midst of these clashing giants, took the first swing of his mighty axe at the back of one of the creature's heel. To his complete surprise––and perhaps, the beast's as well––the weapon's incredibly sharp blade sliced right through the creature's foot, severing it completely. The grieving beast fell backward while blood spouted from its pruned stump. And before it had the chance to turn on its side, the trunket was upon it again, letting the blade of the heavy axe chop into its throat!

Through a sweet combination of adrenaline and a dire need to stay alive, Jhavon was now working the armor with a lot more ease. Gone, was the fatigue in his arms and legs, and he wielded the mighty axe as if he was the dreaded Rhonaak himself.

It came as no surprise to see how readily their four years of combative training came back to them at such a time of need. They weren't weak, or cowardly, by any means. During their schooling, they'd all suffered their fair share of broken bones. They were all familiar with physical pain and violence. And they all knew how to inflict it as well....

Sometime during the bright flash that came from Julie's spirit stick, the great wall along the 8th tower began to collapse. And without the wall's support, the main gates came crashing down—killing both friend and foe alike.

As if possessing a mysterious power of their own, the huge boulders that once made up the wall began reconstructing themselves into fifty rock-giants, each standing at least 100 feet tall. From one massive rock to the other, they formed, turning this way and that way (as if confused on where to actually go) before heading toward the battlefield. With each step, came a thunderous boon! and tremor. Their heads were nothing more than a solid block, with no features or distinction of a face at all. But their hands were like huge mallets, attached to a chain of rocks on their shoulders.

Upon seeing this new army of incoming giants, all took steps at some form of retreat, save for the invading creatures who had no understanding of the world they saw as alien. And neither did they attempt to evade the rock giants' feet that came crashing down upon them....

A loud crack suddenly boomed in the sky above. Jhavon looked up to see the clouds beginning to part, and for the first time in four years, he saw the bright stars twinkling in the heavens. However, they quickly began to change as they appeared blurry, and smudged, to the point where they were nothing more than white swirling streaks in the night's sky.

An awesome wind kicked up and grew stronger by the second. Breathing became harder as the vacuuming wind pulled the air from his lungs. Soon, bodies (both live and dead) were lifted off the ground and hurled up into the sky toward a swirling mass with the sounds of fading howls, screams, and roars in their wake.

He found his own body beginning to rise in the air, and by then, it was already too late as he realized that the Eternal, Ragath, had opened his portal in the sky to rid the world (his world) of Pagaroth's castle, once and for all!

Jhavon screamed as his little body flew up towards oblivion, fearing the unknown that awaited on the other side.

A rock-giant appeared just in time, it seemed, with its huge body looming directly above the trunket. It stood unmoving under the portal's vacuum, collapsing its own body around him, forming a small rocky fortress on the ground.

CHAPTER
TWENTY-TWO

HE JUMPED FROM out of his sleep when a large clump of moist dirt fell on his face. A natural reflex caused him to slap at it with a gloved hand, but was instantly awarded with a bruised cheek that proved to be a lot more painful than the dirt itself. He swore an expletive oath, then shook his head free of the loose earth as he plopped himself up on one elbow. He could smell the rich soil, but he couldn't see, because it was still pitch black all around.

There came a crunching sound, as if something heavy was being lifted off the ground. Then the flood of gray light stung his vision as the rock giant began to rise and reassemble itself with a series of loud clicks and clacks. More loose dirt rained down on upon him as the giant became whole and ambled slowly away.

It had been laying on top of him the whole time!

He gazed at the giant moving down the field, where several other boulders were also reforming themselves. He noticed where every rock-giant rose, a confused figure in purple robes sat beneath, brushing at their hair and garments. A strong wave of relief surged through him when he saw Shurwath standing up in the midst of the milling boulders, slapping his beloved hat against his thigh.

That horrible dream was no dream then, he thought resentfully. The broad expanse of the open field stretched out before him. Nothing but grass and distant hills as far as the eyes can see. He remembered the collapse of the walls and the main gates, and what was left of the walls were still walking around in the field.

He turned around, expecting to see the charred remains of Pagaroth's castle, but was astonished when he found nothing there! Just the rolling hills that stretched beyond where the main gates once stood. But then he realized that he was looking in the wrong direction, so he spun back around.... Not that it would've mattered anyway, because it wasn't there either.

What had once sat on the land for thousands of years, was now gone. Nothing remained! save for the gaping hole in the ground where the gutted foundation lay in ruins.

Loose dirt and pebbles trickled down the inside of his armor as he rose to his feet. And as a result, a fiesty itch flared up on his inner thigh. Foul words spilled from the trunket's mouth, cursing the wretched gloves and armor, yearning (but not daring) to take it off.

"Stop wasting precious time, boy," said a rough (but very familiar) voice behind him.

Jhavon looked up and found Rahjule standing there. His face was just as old, and wrinkled, and mean, as he'd last remembered it. The long white hair and beard flowed from his head and chin, spilling over his shoulders and chest. The black cloak was draped over his shoulders, and flowed all the way down to the ground. "Sir!!" he shouted with glee. Without thinking, he rushed up to the old man and embraced him with an awkward hug, but the cloak became a solid wall at the slightest touch, coldly rejecting his affections.

"This is no time for joy," Rahjule said. "Haven't you lost most of your friends today?"

The trunket appeared taken aback by the old man's harsh words.

"Well, boy?" Rahjule pressed on. "Didn't Shurlan teach you anything here...? Or did you not learn...? Which is it?"

"The instructors taught me well, sir," Jhavon replied. "So I learned well."

"So why rejoice in these times? You say you've learned well; so I must assume that you already know that Ragath is out for your head."

"My...my head?" Jhavon looked confused. "But why would——"

"Why what, boy?" the old man growled, sounding frustrated. "What do yo mean? Haven't you been studying my scrolls?"

"I've studied all the scrolls, sir."

"And yet, you don't know this day?"

"Aye.... Ragath's returned to reclaim the stone of power."

"That much is already too obvious, boy. A no-brain tog in the Land of Gargaath, know of Ragath's return by now.... You've forgotten your lessons."

"No, sir. I remember all I was taught, from the first day of my beginning years until now."

Rahjule wasn't convinced. His blank face gazed across the horizon, as though expecting something to fall from the dark clouds in the distance. "Tell me, boy," he said. "How many of your friends are left alive?"

Jhavon turned around to look at the small group gathered behind them. They all wore uncertain looks on their faces, as if they weren't sure of whether or not they should join them. He counted: Julie, Ahnon, Syme, Shurwath and Morlah.... No one else was left alive, save for the horses in the stables that were protected by the rock-giants. "Just six, sir," he said softly, realizing how much had actually been lost. "And myself, makes seven."

"Which one of you can turn the heavens?" Rahjule asked.

The trunket frowned. "Sir...?"

"You heard me, boy."

"I...I don't know."

"And which one's the soul demon?"

Again...Jhavon was shaking his head. "Never heard of such things at Pagaroth's school, sir."

"Then where's the queen of the night? And the king of the woods? Or the oracle? And the one too whispers death?"

Jhavon shook his head at all the old man's inquiries.

Rahjule sighed. "No wonder you all stand there looking foolish. You, in that ridiculous armor, and they in those silly robes. You've all learned nothing! Shurlan raised you all up as weaklings. And he taught you nothing!"

"This armor once belonged to the famous trunket warrior, Rhonaak," Jhavon said proudly, ignoring the old man's criticism.

Rahjule glared down at the trunket just then. His silver eyes made a quick, but careful study of the rugged armor. "And where'd you learn of such things, boy? Surely not in that...school. Some trunket's folk-tale perhaps."

"Old Hollan, sir…. He told me many tales of the mighty Rhonaak. He even told me that he killed him. Then he left me his armor."

"Has been saving that old scrap for all these eons has he?"

"Aye…. He sharpened the axe and cleaned it up for me."

"Ha!" Rahjule exclaimed. A fine hint of a smile appeared on his face before it vanished. He shifted his gaze over to the others instead. He noticed one girl holding a staff that glowed bloody red. "All's not lost then," he said softly to himself. "Perhaps Shurlan had his own methods."

"His own methods, sir?" Jhavon was still confused.

The old man appeared as if lost in thought as he looked down to address the trunket once more. "I see you haven't grown an inch since I last saw you."

"Just a foot, sir," Jhavon said. "I'm a little over four feet tall now."

"Never mind that, boy," said Rahjule, in a sudden change of tone. "We've wasted enough time here. Go get our horses ready."

———•———

They were both bewildered and saddened at the loss of their home. The fact that some of their closest friends, along with everyone they knew had been killed and taken from the world so suddenly, seemed unbelievable. And yet, it had happened…. None knew this to be more so than the blind sorceress, Morlah.

"Are you certain of it, Morlah?" asked Ermma, her eyes already welling with tears.

Morlah replied with a grave nod. Her blindfolded face was tilted up at the gray gloomy sky (where Ragath's portal had once swirled) as if searching beyond the accursed clouds. "It is for certain, Ermma," she said. "I can't feel my sister's presence anywhere on this world. She's gone with the others, to whatever realm Ragath sent them to. I hope they aren't suffering."

"Oh, Morlah," Julie cried, with a tremulous voice. Long tears streamed down her face.

Shurwath, Syme, and Ahnon stood quietly nearby; each preoccupied in his own private mourning.

"She was with me the whole time," Morlah went on. "Our hands were joined in power, and hadn't been broken––not once. She should've survived with me. Covered up by those..." her voice trailed off as she turned toward the rock-giants that were now huddled together like a group of chiseled monoliths. "Those rocks...they should've protected us both."

"But they didn't," said Syme. He faced away from the others, so only his long black cape was seen. The light wind drew the smell of blood and stale mead from the cape's fabric. A testament to the brutal carnage that ruined the previous night's festivities.

"And what's that supposed to mean, Syme?" spat a hot tempered Ermma.

She moved to confront the insensitive lykine, but a swift hand haulted her pace.

"He meant no harm by it, Ermma," Morlah said, nearly dragging the fiery siren back to her side. "I can sense that his pain and loss is as deep as ours––perhaps deeper. And he has a point. My sister should've survived with me, but she didn't.... The man behind us...is the one who move the rocks. He allowed all the others to be destroyed, while deciding to save only us. There must be a reason for this."

The others turned around and saw the old man in deep conversation with the trunket. They knew he couldn't be a teacher, nor was he one of the cooky old wizards that used to saunter around the castle's grounds and conducted strange experiments inside the labs.

Besides the horses in the stables, there were no other beasts to be seen for many leagues around. And yet, the old man appeared as fit and well rested as one who didn't travel at all.... So where did he come from? Was what they all seemed to be asking themselves.

"Jhavon's in no danger," Morlah said, sensing their concerns.

"Is he one of Ragath's minions?" Julie asked; her spirit stick glowed to a fiery red.

"Not of Ragath," said Morlah. "But of Pagaroth, A remnant of Pagaroth. Much older than Shurlan."

It was at that moment the old man's eyes fell upon them. Suddenly, his expression changed and became as soft and placid as the deep lines and wrinkles in his face would allow. He appeared to say something funny to the trunket, because he broke out in a curt chuckle. Then they saw the trunket heading toward the stables, leaving his axe and helmet near the man's feet.

Ermma was the first to grow impatient, stalking over toward the old man, forcing the others to follow closely behind. Her voice was primed for destruction as she stopped just a few feet from where he stood. "What business do you

266

have here?" she asked, her voice sounding fine, clear, and as thin as twine.

It was the sweetest sound Rahjule had ever heard in his long life, but he also knew it was the deadliest. He could barely suppress the wry grin from ruining his composure. The fact that he stood before the most powerful siren in all of Hagaraak, didn't bother him in the least. Shurlan might've created a monster, but she was yet to know her real power. She posed no threat to him...for now.

"Answer me, old man!"

The pitch in Ermma's voice rose with enough force to split a man's eardrum. However, it only caused Rahjule's black cloak to shimmer. His face shifted, then reformed itself like stirred up sand as he relished in the sweetness of the siren's mild scream. He wanted more. He yearned for it! He secretly wished for her to scream at him with all her might.

The sound of the galloping horses broke his concentration, but he kept his gaze fixed on the siren's impetuous face.

Ermma became distracted as well, and she took her eyes off Rahjule to stare at the incoming trunket on his brown colt––with seven other horses in tow.

Rahjule was a bit disappointed with her carelessness. He thought a quick dirt-blast to her face should teach her a lesson in vigilance, but they were seriously running out of time....

Jhavon reined in close and made a clumsy dismount off his horse. The brown colt had grown up to be a large and powerful adult. Hard rippling muscles could be seen bulging in its hips, thighs, and shoulders. Over the years, he'd trained it to stoop down on its hind legs in order that he could more easily mount and dismount.... He grabbed his helmet and axe off the ground, while the spotted gray ambled over to its rightful owner.

"She look a little fat in the ribs, boy," Rahjule said, taking the horse by the reins as he scrutinized every inch of the beast. "What have you been doing...giving it too much food, or less freedom?"

Jhavon threw on his helmet. "I might've been a bit too generous in my feeding at times."

"Hmph!" Rahjule said, as he mounted the spotted gray. "She'll have to run it off then." He turned her southward and kicked her into a slow canter.

Jhavon rubbed gently along the colt's side and brought it down on its hind legs so he can properly mount it. As it rose back up, he sat the axe on his shoulder and stared at the others, who were all looking up strangely at him. They didn't know what else to expect, nor were they sure about what they should do next. "Come on," he said to them. The bulky helmet made his head look massive. "The old man isn't much for words, but he guides well. You can trust me on that."

"But this our home, Jhavon," Julie said. "We can't leave here."

"And where do you suppose that man's taking us?" asked Shurwath.

Jhavon shrugged, then studied the direction Rahjule was taking. "Through the Hills of Pagaroth."

"He's insane!" Ermma said. "No one travels through those hills. They're infested with demons and abominations."

"He has his methods," Jhavon said.

268

"Well, you can follow that mad man all you want, Jhavon," Ermma shot back. "To both of your deaths, perhaps. But I'm not leaving Pagaroth."

"Look...." Jhavon pointed toward the gaping hole in the ground where the castle once stood. The rock-giants were moving toward the empty space, and one by one, began to collapse themselves into the hole until the very last boulder filled the top. A sheet of dirt then came sliding over to cover the grave completely. Tall stalks of grass could already be seen growing on the leveled ground, erasing any signs to indicate that anything had ever stood over it.... "Don't you see?" He asked them. "The Eternal Ragath has returned. All that lives throughout the three realms are under his rule now. Pagaroth is no more."

———•———

Night fell as quick as the dawn on that day. And without the shining lamps and magical flames that once kept Pagaroth's castle well lit, it would be the darkest one they experienced in the last four years.

As he'd done with the trunket those few years ago, Rahjule found the perfect cave for them to camp the night in. Small fouls presented themselves from out the brush, which he commanded the trunket to decapitate (with Rhonaak's axe) very quickly, lest the docile creatures "change their minds." Fruits were plucked from unusual trees, and vegetables were uprooted from the hardest soil. And after the pleasant feast, they thanked Pagaroth for blessing the land, then settled in for the rest of the night.

But it was at times such as these, when the mind's at ease, that the most unpleasant events are recalled. When stuffed stomachs and lazy limbs cause the mind to wander....

"I only noticed Shurlan," Ahnon said (through Jhavon's mouth). The campfire that blazed inside the cave emitted a cozy warmth. "Don't know what happened to the elders before that; especially Morella."

They all expected to see the elemental come whirling into the cave at the sound of her name. But no such thing happened. Nor did she appear any of the other times when Jhavon and Shurwath tried calling out to her.... According to Morlah, she was gone from the world as well. And so was Hollan, Ms. Wicket, and all the other respected instructors.

"Only Shurlan still remained to fight," Syme said.

"Some mystery still reside in all this," Jhavon said. "We all know that Shurlan, Morella, and Hollan, had all fought in the war of the Eternals. History tells us that much. But what threat could they ever pose to Ragath, without the other Eternals? And why destroy Pagaroth's castle?"

"Revenge, maybe," Shurwath suggested. "Pagaroth did set him back a few thousand years."

"No..." the trunket said, shaking his head. "Revenge is too petty of a thing. And revenge on who? The Eternals are all gone."

"The demons were raiding all the rooms in the castle," came Ermma's fine voice, from where she sat on the ground. "There were looking for something."

"Scrolls and potions?" Jhavon asked. "Ragath wrote most of those scrolls himself. And what use would he have for any potion?"

"Why not ask your old friend sitting over there?" Ermma said. "He seems to have all the answers, even though he hasn't said a word to us all since leaving the ruins."

They all turned to look over at Rahjule as he laid comfortably on the ground with his veiny hands folded across his chest. They'd followed him a good ways, as he led them safely to this cave where he prepared a fine feast for them, but that was the extent to his hospitality.

"He seems to speak to you only," Ermma said to Jhavon. "Why can't you see if he can give us some answers?"

"You'll come to know all things in due time, siren," Rahjule said. The sound of his gruff voice was so unexpected, it took than all by surprise.

"You still haven't told us anything," Ermma spat. "What's going on?"

"Hmph!" Rahjule snorted. "After all that has happened, you still can't see things for what they are...."

There was a long pause that followed as they all waited for Rahjule to continue...but he didn't.... Ermma fell back with a sigh of frustration.

"The end of our world is approaching, siren," he suddenly said, reviving everyone's attention. "Or didn't they teach you that in school? You do know that Ragath's been resurrected, do you?"

"Aye," they all seemed to answer at once.

"Then you should already know what's happening. You must let your schooling be your guide from now on. Open your minds, and the answers will come. And don't concern yourselves with Shurlan and the rest of the elders. They've been sent to the realms where their Eternals reside. You do yourselves no good by worrying about them. So rest, and bother me no more tonight." And with that, Rahjule rolled over on his side and fell asleep at once....

Camp was broken just before dawn as the black sky faded to an ashy gray. The charred remains of the campfire had sunk into the soil without a trace. And all––except Rahjule and the trunket––gazed in astonishment when the empty cave collapsed in on itself and assumed its former arrangement on the landscape's natural setting. Even the laden fruit-trees were gone, probably withered away into the soil while they slept....

They rode mostly in silence as they followed Rahjule on his spotted gray. Occasionally, a variant bird would swoop down and land on Ahnon's shoulder. The two would then exchange looks, as if exchanging words, before the bird went flapping up into the sky again.

"The Hills of Pagaroth is fifty leagues across," the mute said (through Jhavon's mouth). "About two or three days travel."

"Oh...?" said Syme. "Is that what your little birdies tell you?"

"Aye," Ahnon replied. "And none too easy a crossing at that. We'd be lucky to find footing for our mounts."

"I'm sure no remnant of Pagaroth can be impeded by such things," said Ermma, loud enough to ensure her jesting words reach Rahjule's ears.

"It can't be all that bad if he's taking us through," Shurwath said.

"Where do you think we'll go after that?" Jhavon asked Ahnon.

"It's hard to know for sure," the mute replied. "My friend tells me there're many lands beyond those hills: the

272

Marshes of Baas, the Lake of Pearls, Vlak's Forest, and the end of the Ghi River."

"We're heading south," Jhavon said. "So we are definitely not going to the Marshes of Baas."

"Aye," said Ahnon. "So that only leaves the three most southern places."

"All the better," Julie said. "I'd rather be in a dry forest, than a wet marsh."

It wasn't until late afternoon when the first peaks of Pagaroth's hills revealed themselves in the distance (about 20 leagues away). There, the accursed clouds seemed to churn with more intensity, and the lightning flashed with greater fury. The hills stood like stubborn dunes, all clustered together to make their lands impassable. Their white jagged peaks appeared like a forest of thorns under the dark clouds. And even from such a distance, there wasn't anything––in all of Pagaroth––that looked as formidable, frightful, and forbidden as those hills....

The approaching night had almost blackened the sky when Rahjule finally decided to stop. He rose their cave from out the ground, and the horses were the most eager to retreat into the shelter.

CHAPTER
TWENTY-THREE

SHE FLED AT the mere sound of the wind's haunting wail that scraped over the edges of crags and cliffs.

She shouldn't be alone in this world.

Nothing seemed to exist there.

And yet, she could feel them. Sense their evil! Like dirt, when it clings to the skin.

The evil was there.

Deep, and ancient, residing all across these lands.

So she fled; trying to beat the wind. The darkness was all around. Not from the night's sky, but her own darkness from birth.

A strange sense reached out to her. Just one of many. And from the many, formed one. Their faces flashed in her mind. The one of many. One by one. Each the same. Gone, were the eyes and mouth. Only the nose remained. Long necks and oval heads. No eyes, just plain skin, yet they faced her accusingly. No––they were warning her. No mouths, just plain skin over bone––

Morlah jumped out of her sleep with a frightful gasp. She could feel the sweat on her face, running down her neck and back. She threw her awareness around the cave but only sensed the horses and her friends while they slept.

The evil was gone.... But what a terrifying dream!

"Hmmm," came Rahjule's voice nearby all of a sudden. "Who shall reveal themselves today?" he asked, in his most amusing tone. "Is it the Soul Demon, or the Oracle?"

"I'm no soul demon," said Morlah, turning towards him. "Nor am I an oracle. A sorceress from Lagophar, I am."

"That's not what the Mhogs seem to think, young sorceress."

"Mhog...? I know of no Mhogs. Nor do any Mhogs know of me.... And what is a Mhog?"

"The ones who just disturbed you so; in your dream. Did you see them?"

"The ones with no eyes?"

"Aye..." Rahjule replied slowly. His face took on a conspiratorial expression. "And what else...did they not have?"

"Where any creature's mouth should be, was not."

"Aye..." said Rahjule, nodding his head. "Creatures having no eyes and mouths. Aye...those are the Mhogs I speak of. Telepaths."

"But how do they––"

"All things that live, have their own methods of doing so. The trees have neither eyes, ears, nose, nor mouths––and yet, they outlive the most ancient of men.... Is it not so?"

"It is."

"So, tell me young sorceress. What did the Mhogs tell you?"

"Danger awaits.... An evil presence know that we're coming. We shouldn't go through the hills."

"But we must. The Hills of Pagaroth, stretch all the way from Lagophar to Laap. Then we must cross the Ghi River. Such a journey could take months. Ragath might have the power of the whole universe in his hands by then…. We'll pass through the hills safely enough. The Mhogs tend to take things a bit too extreme for my likes. And look…it seems they're pleased with scaring Ahnon as well."

Soft groans could be heard coming from the dark corner of the cave. Morlah sensed that it was indeed Ahnon, though his dream didn't appear to be as frightening as here.

"The Mhogs," Rahjule said. "They're such pesky creatures. So uncaring to one's privacy. But only to those who are gifted with the power of the mind—as they are. Only then can some form of connection be made. So I'll ask you again, sorceress. Which are you…the Soul Demon, or the Oracle?"

"I'm…I'm no demon, old man. I'm a sorceress, nothing more."

"Hmph!" Rahjule laid back down on the ground. "I suppose that should answer everything then." And he said no more.

Morlah shifted her senses from the old man, back to Ahnon. She tried to sense the mute's emotions, but found that his mind was protected by some… mental shield. She could only sense the Mhogs; those horrible things! They must be very powerful, she thought with weary sigh, as she eased her head on the ground.

———•———

The Hills of Pagaroth became more distinct with each passing hour. The rocky mountains and sparse trees were coming into view. Within just three leagues, their massive formations blocked out the gray horizon.

Despite the Mhogs' unpleasant visit in his dreams, Ahnon showed no signs of the terrible ordeal he experienced the night before. He rode on in silence, as usual, gathering bits of information from the little birds that flew by.

Morlah could sense that a trouble stirred deep within him, though. However, she decided it was better not to ask.

Rahjule didn't pay either one of them the slightest attention––or at least, he pretended not to. His main focus remained on what laid directly ahead. They've been riding on a slight decline for the past league and a half, and it was now becoming steep. The trees appeared to lean backwards. The horses' gaits became unsteady.

They'd hardly noticed they were amongst the dreaded hills till they found themselves surrounded on all sides. Sharp jagged crags loomed dangerously overhead, threatening to send a loose boulder crashing down in their midst at any moment. The strong crosswinds moaned and howled as they fought to squeeze through the tight spaces of the clustered mountains. A sound so chilling, it caused Rahjule's company to become wary at every turn.

Julie's spirit stick glowed to a cautious mauve. The cold wind made her shiver inside of her purple cape. She looked over at Morlah, noticing her expression was becoming more uneasy. "What's out there?"

"Things live in these hills," Morlah said. "Abominations. Things that dwell in the night. They feed off the flesh of others...and themselves...when they can't find nothing else to sustain them."

Shurwath let out a soft, but apprehensive sigh as he scanned the surrounding hills. Behind each crevasse and corner, there seemed to be a pair of hungry eyes. "How much further, before we cross these hills, Ahnon?"

"About fifty leagues," the mute replied.

"And how far have we made it through so far? About ten leagues is my guess."

"Not even close, Shurwath. We've only traveled about two, but no more than three leagues since entering the hills."

"All the more sights for our pleasant viewing then," Shurwath said, regarding the frightful environment with wary eyes.

"Aye...."

"We're treading upon the domain of the damned," said Morlah.

"I think we already know this," Shurwath said. "And look there——" He pointed at Rahjule, who was riding up front. "The old man don't look too worried. Asleep in his saddle, if I don't know anything else."

They all looked over at Rahjule. And indeed, his head did appear to be slumped forward, as it swung lazily from side to side.

Only the rocky landscape changed as the hour went by, as did the howling wings that grew more or less audible—— but never totally silenced. The small birds stopped flying by, due to the more predatory kinds that began circling above.... Occasionally, a black raven would land on Ahnon's shoulder, then go flapping up into the gray skies again.

At one point they came to an area that was less rocky, where the grassy hills came into view with an assortment of pine, larch, and hemlock scattered about in a few places. The howl of the wind itself was now above them, blowing into the hollow pockets of the rocky mountains....

Rahjule suddenly stopped.

However, it was Morlah who sensed it first. "Abomination..." she hissed between clenched teeth.

"Show me!" said Syme, already hopping down from his horse.

"High up in the hills," Morlah replied, pointing to the edge of a rocky formation.

A creature with two horns on its head could be seen stooping down atop the hill. It wore a long black cloak (similar to Rahjule's) that draped itself around his body as he watched them in silence.

"Get back to your horse, boy," Rahjule told Syme. He signaled to the creature with a wave of his hand. "There's nothing to harm you here."

Even at such a distance, the creature's huge body was still noticeable under his cloak as he stood up. He ran down the side of the hill where he hopped a protruding cliff just a few yards away. He landed with a bone-crunching thud as his gnarled hooves met the solid ground, before setting off in a slow trot towards them. And with strides as long as ten feet, he was standing before Rahjule in a matter of seconds.

"It's an honor that we meet again, Rahjule," the creature said in a deep, but cheerful voice as he made a reverent bow. He stood at least eight feet tall. Short black fur covered most of his neck and face. His horns were as thick as a man's thigh, and very pointy at the tip. He had brown eyes that were hooded over by thick brows. A hog's nose, with two fat tusks coming down from the roof of his mouth, and a long white beard flowing from his chin.

"It is likewise an honor Phallock," Rahjule replied, giving a curt bow of his own.

"The news have already reached us," Phallock said. "My sympathies go out to you and the surviving remnants."

"All the lands must've heard the news by now," said Rahjule. "The trees still mourn the dreaded day."

"Aye..." Phallock said. His dark eyes fell upon the spotted gray. "And I see that Llanx is still her old self."

As if to agree, the spotted gray pawed at the ground and gave an affirmative snort.

Phallock chuckled. "The trunkets haven't destroyed the Red Forest as yet, I see."

"They'd have to walk on solid ground first," Rahjule replied.

"And the chosen ones?" Phallock regarded Rahjule's company with a quick glance.

"Aye," Rahjule said. "That they are. All seven of them. Nearly lost the lykine, though. But then again––" he paused, considering the thought. "Maybe I shouldn't say that I nearly lost him. Perhaps it couldn't have been any other way. Everything is as predicted."

"I see," said Phallock, now staring at the students. Then he leaned closer to Rahjule and asked softly: "Which one of them is the soul demon?"

Rahjule whispered the answer back to Phallock.

The creature looked taken aback by Rahjule's response. A deep frown fell on his ugly face. His eyes shifted over to the soul demon, then back to Rahjule again. "A little frail... is he not?"

"That he is," Rahjule said. "But he is the soul demon. He don't know it as yet, though."

"Hmm..." Phallock said. A large back hand, with long devilish nails, eased out from inside of his cloak to stroke at the pointy white beard on his chin. "Either Ragath's too early, or that one is a bit slow in development.... Is he not?"

"Which one? Ragath, or the demon?"

Phallock shrugged. "Either one will do, I suppose."

Rahjule shifted his weight on the horse. "Ragath's return is precisely on time. All's well on his part...unfortunately. And it's not just the demon who needs development. I'm afraid they've all been plucked a few years before their time."

"Pagaroth help us all then."

"But I think it was intentionally done," Rahjule said. "Shurlan's own method, I think. He intended for me to complete their schooling. They were left to develop along with the passage of their destiny."

"A bold plan."

"But none too foolish. I'd rather have a timid novice for a companion, than a master who's none too smart."

"Hmm.... Which is why I thank the gods that these things were left up to you and Shurlan, instead of me. Too many mixed up things for one mind to consider."

They both shared a short laugh....

For the rest of the day, Phallock led them through the forest of clustered hills. They moved swiftly, in order to beat the night's approach, pushing their horses as hard as they could over the rocky terrain.

The swift-foooted Phallock made it hard for them to keep up, for he ran naturally among the rocks. With each leap and bound, his black cloak would fan out to reveal a long, stiff tail bobbin out from under his lower back.

They arrived at his den––a cave dug into the lower incline of the hill––just before nightfall.

Phallock's den looked more like the interior of a king's palace than anything else. The floor was incredibly smooth, and shiny. The walls were decorated with all kinds of intricate carvings. Sculpt faces, both beautiful and hideous, gazed down upon them with timeless expressions––their flawless details forever etched in stone.

Dozens of golden poles stood all around, where fiery torches sat atop to give the cave its buttery glow. The warm light gleamed off the golden legs of tables and chairs. Big cushions, made from fine silk, laid upon the thick fur of ancient beasts that served as soft rugs.

A tall statue of a majestic creature stood poised at the center of all this luxury. It was humanoid in appearance, with feminine features. Her beautiful face tilted up toward the stalactites that hung from the ceiling. A lonely horn, just six inches long, protruded from the middle of her forehead where curled locks began to flow and whip, as if disturbed by an unfelt wind. Great wings came out of her back and spanned an amazing thirty feet wide. Her slim delicate arms were captured at a graceful angle that seemed impossible for any other sculptor to duplicate. In her right hand, she held a godly scepter, studded with gems of all kinds. An elegant dress hung from her shoulders and fell all the way down to her bare feet. Two handfuls of firm breasts sat taut on her chest, where two pea-sized nipples had been captured as well. A thin stream of water arched out of her pouting mouth to land and make gurgling sounds in the shallow pool that surrounded her.

The students all marveled at the impossible setting of the whole place, for everything they set their eyes upon was a work of pure art.

The two elders, however, carried on as if they were in a plain old natural cave. They dined, and drank till their heads became too groggy to stand——or think, for that matter....

"So what's the trunket's name?" Phallock asked Rahjule. He tore a roasted wing off a fowl's impaled body and stuffed it into his mouth.

"His name's Jhavon," Rahjule replied, reeling off the effects of the strong mead.

"A spell weaver?" asked Phallock, staring across the room at the trunket. The warm bath from the pool was a pleasant welcome to them all. The healing water served to refresh their bodies as well as their spirits. And after a hearty feast, they couldn't be more settled in, and comfortable, even if they were still living at Pagaroth's castle.

"Trunkets don't have any magic," Rahjule said. "Or have you forgotten who's who over all these eons?"

"Just curious," Phallock replied. "One would easily think the trunket must have something...special, if he's to face an Eternal."

"He does."

"Aye?"

"Aye."

"And what is this special power, if he's not some kind of spell weaver?"

Rahjule gulped down a mouthful of mead. "Pagaroth's stone——" he paused to refill his mug. "It favors him. He can weave all the spells, if he so chooses."

"Hmm..." said Phallock, while stripping the meat from the wing's bone. "May Pagaroth be with him then."

"I wish the same."

"Aye...."

They ate and drank in silence for a while until a sudden burst of laughter disturbed the peace.

Phallock's train of thought was reverted back to the trunket. "I thought you would've buried that thing deep in the liquid fires by now."

Rahjule followed the creature's eyes. "The axe?" he asked, looking over at the armored trunket. "No.... That wasn't my doing. One of Hollan's relics. He favored the boy greatly, you know."

"Hmmm...vicious times, those were," said Phallock, as he allowed his mind to drift back into the past. The trunkets were different creatures back then. Warlike. With machines, and weapons, such as the armor he was looking at now. The one that belonged to the dreadful Rhonaak. "Does he know who's armor he flaunts?"

"Aye.... And very much so. Hollan told the boy everything, and quite possibly against Shurlan's wishes. But you should see the boy in battle, Phallock. He's fearless. Weilds an axe as any warring trunket should. I watched him chop down those giant creatures with my own eyes. Hacking off heads and limbs as if he was proning a tree. He's a fierce warrior, Phallock...." Rahjule then drained his mug, but quickly refilled it again. "If only he was missing an arm...."

————●————

"Who would've thought," Shurwath said, as he was reclined on a large fluffy pillow. "That we'd be riding along with the great Rahjule...one of the last few remnants of Pagaroth."

"I think Morlah knew who he was," Ermma said.

"No," said Shurwath, shaking his head. "It's not the same. Morlah only sensed Rahjule's presence after Ragath destroyed Pagaroth's castle. And even then, she still didn't know who he actually was. She couldn't have known all along."

They all turned to the blind sorceress, who was laying on a comfortable cushion. Her arms were kept folded across her chest while she remained as stiff as a log. It was hard to tell whether or not she was asleep.

"Morlah," Shurwath called. "Did you know the remnant of Pagaroth would be among us?"

"I have no time for these silly musings of yours, Shurwath," Morlah said. "But no. I didn't sense him until the day I lost Morlah."

The mentioning of her sister dampened the mood. A moment of unpleasant silence followed.

"And what about this...Phallock creature?" asked Julie, attempting to change the subject. She too, had lost her sister, and preferred not to dwell on it. "I never knew an abomination can have such..." she gestured toward the carvings on the walls, and the gold-trimmed furniture. "Things."

"It's all so beautiful," Ermma said. "I wonder who's hands could've molded such crafts?"

The trunket looked up to study the carvings, then shrugged. "He made them himself."

"I suppose it's possible," Julie said. "He surely had more than enough time for the task. But time, and skill, are two quite separate things. Phallock's hands aren't those of a sculptor's or painter's, for he has claws...like a cat. Do you still think that all these masterful works of art were wrought by his hands?"

"Aye," came the trunket's reply.

"That's only a guess, trunket," Syme said. "No one but Phallock, knows for certain how many hands made these things."

"Just one hand did all the work, Syme," Jhavon said.

"How so then?" asked Syme.

Jhavon sat up on his cushion and pointed to a wall where a cluster of ancient figures were carved. "The telling is simple," he said. "It's obvious that the artist carried out these works using his own distinct methods. And you could see it being used everywhere within this cave. Look at the carvings...though they're all quite different and unique from one another, the style of their design are all the same. And those similarities are most evident in the hands and fingers. You could see where the same methods were employed in creating their shape."

The carved figures that the trunket spoke about were all fused within the rock with their upper torsos protruding as though trying to escape their entrapments. Most of their fingers had long fallen off, exposing the stubbed joints along the knuckles. But it was the curve in the palms, and the bending of the wrists, where the trunket revealed the similarities in Phallock's signature touch.

"Then there're those symbols," Jhavon continued, pointing up to a different section on the wall. "Again, you see the curves and angles all being identical to one another. Like texts on a scroll, written by the same author.

"Then there're the many bulls and rams that Phallock seems to favor so much. Their horns are all attributed to the Eternal Mox. You can see exactly where he decided to make his bends, as though it was a sacred rule in his method when and where he should do so. All these are the signs of one hand's signature.

"Then we have the lovely fountain that appear to be the center of all things. The only difference about this sculpture, is the material out of which she was made. Phallock used pure marble to create her. He even fashioned her on the inside, so the water could spout from her mouth to feed the pools, canals, and baths, all throughout this cave. Phallock gave this one special authority, and placed her above all his other creations. This is evident by the sceptor she holds. It's almost as if she knows that all within this cave are her subjects."

"Do you think she was real, Jhavon?" asked Ermma.

"Aye," the trunket replied. "She had to be, for one to command such devotion in Phallock, that he placed her above all the others. She dons the wings, and a single horn, to show that she was ones a remnant of Mox. But she's no abomination, because the life-giving water that flows from her mouth, indicates that she once had a spirit. The jewels on her sceptor could've been gifts from Pagaroth. Aye...I should think that this...whoever she was, had been alive at one point."

"Then you think wrong, boy," came Phallock's slurred voice from behind.

"Wrong?" the bemused trunket asked.

"That's what he said, trunket," Syme said, "Your guessing was quite the enjoyment, though."

"I wouldn't say that his guesses were all wrong," Phallock said, coming around to stand beside the statue. His strides were as graceful and elegant as any cat's. "He was right about me being the creator of all these marvelous things you see before your eyes. When you live to see 10,000 years as I have, you'll come to know boredom as I do. But this…" he paused to gaze up at the marble statue that loomed before him. He rubbed his paw gently along the huge wing. "This is no creature that had ever lived," he said. "She's but a mere representation of the Eternals. The wings are symbolic to the Eternal, Mox…but not the horns. Those go to Llok. The expressions of the face and body are representations of Vlak. Notice how the arms are bent like branches; her hair, wild and free, like the leaves blown in the wind. Water flow from her mouth to feed the bath and pools, the same way Baas used the rain to feed the rivers and lakes. Her feminine gender can only be attributed to the goddess, Laap. And the jewels on the sceptor, once hidden so deep in the ground, pays much hommage to the Eternal, Pagaroth. In these things you are right about, Jhavon…as well as her position of being superior to all my other works. But in truth, she's just a representation of all the Eternals combined to form one being."

"And this is what you supposed this…one being…to look like?" asked Julie.

"Well…" Phallock began. "I never thought that such a being would look exactly like what you're seeing there. She's merely a visual representation of a power that rule over all: the beasts, the land, the sea, the sky, the trees, and everything else that make up our world. And I don't think such a power would be inclined to adopt any one specific form."

"Stop confusing them with all your mystical talks, Phallock," Rahjule said from across the room.

"Ah..." said Phallock. "At last! The mead speaks."

"It's not the mead that speak," Rahjule said. "Just one, still possessing good sense."

"Well," said Phallock, as he gave one of his tusks a quick lick with his tongue. "That just lets me know you're incapable of seeing the beauty behind such creations."

"Perhaps I am. Perhaps I never understood the meaning behind such things."

"Maybe you should have taken some schooling along with these students."

"Perhaps," Rahjule shot back.

Phallock laughed. "You're always so serious, Rahjule. Even about the most trivial things."

"Nothing's ever truly trivial, Phallock. Especially when we have an Eternal, bent on changing things for the worst."

———◆———

With Phallock as their guide, all fear and apprehension dissolved from the student's minds. The close cropped hills that formed so many dark passages, didn't appear as formidable. And though the howling winds still raged, they ceased to haunt.

There was an easiness about him that brought them comfort, as he moved across the landscape at a modest pace. Since sunrise, they had only traveled just a few leagues. As midday approached, they came upon the sounds of horns blaring in the distance. Long, sonorous drones. Some sounding more faint than others.

"The Mheekhas!" Phallock shouted from up front. However, he didn't appear to be alarmed. "Their tribes roam all over these hills. I believe that the Chronhox and Ghallem tribes share these lands, if I remember correctly. Then you have the Sophs, the Khaphs, and the Pynes, dwelling in the surrounding areas. Peaceful creatures really...unless they consider you a threat."

"We've been spotted then?" asked Shurwath.

"Aye," Phallock replied. "Just a warning to their kin that strangers are passing through their lands."

"Shouldn't you have sensed them, Morlah?" Ermma asked the blind sorceress.

Morlah shook her head. "I can't sense anything," she said. "Even though I hear the horns. I think the Mhogs must be..." her words trailed off suddenly as she became silent.

"Who?"

"It's nothing," she said. "Just a name that came to my dreams one night."

"Well," Ermma said. "If you couldn't sense these... Mheekhas, then they probably saw us from far away. I'd hate to know that these things surrounded us so easily, without either one of us being aware. This could've easily been an ambush."

Morlah didn't reply. Her mind was focused on the distant sounds. Plus something else had been plaguing her mind since they'd left Phallock's den. She was beginning to think that something had taken away her power; or was somehow suppressing it. She squeezed tightly on the reins of her mount, seeking comfort in the beast's strength that moved beneath her, while searching the blackness for any signs of light.... For the first time in her life, Morlah was truly blind!

They spotted the first Mheekha, standing on the cliff of a nearby crag. The beast was shorter than what they'd expected, but it had a wide body, and it still looked strong enough to rip a man apart. Though thick gray fur covered its entire body, a tuft of long white hair flowed from its head. Black beady eyes pierced through its furry face while it followed their every move.

The Mheekha suddenly raised its head to the sky and opened its mouth. The sound of what they all thought (except Rahjule and Phallock, of course) was a blaring horn came pouring out.

"Loud creatures," said Jhavon, with a slight cringe.

"I hope you didn't think they were music lovers!" Phallock shouted back.

The Mheekhas suddenly appeared by the hundreds, coming down from the hill tops. Some stood on the nearby cliffs, showing off their long spears and swords. Their gray, oblong bodies, dotted the rocky landscape as they watched the strangers ride by.

"These are the Ghallem tribe," Phallock said. "You can tell by their gray fur. I think the Chronhox is black, though...not quite sure. I know the Sophs are brown, and the Khaphs are...white...aye, I think they're white...."

As they rode by, Jhavon stared at the Ghallems, and couldn't help but feel that all their eyes were focused solely on him. Their furry, unreadable faces told nothing, and yet, he felt the vague sense that they expected something from him. They followed him with their eyes as he rode by. And for an entire quarter of a league, he encountered those wanting eyes on each Ghallem he rode past.

The trunket sped up to the old man's side. "Are they always like this?"

"Like what?" Rahjule asked.

"Always so quiet. Staring...."

From the corners of his eyes, Rahjule regarded the mass of Ghallems that were gathered along both sides of the hills. "Seems like they've been studying their own prophecies, boy."

"What prophecies?"

"Hmph!" Rahjule scoffed at the trunket's lack of knowledge. And yet, he thought, maybe it was better for them. At least that was Shurlan's intent. "Whatever prophecies their wise ones told them," he said instead. "How should I know what's written in their scrolls!?" And that was all he had to say on the matter....

They rode on for another league before they left the last Ghallem behind. This time, the solitude of the empty hills was a much welcomed sight. At nightfall, Rahjule prepared another cave, though it didn't come with the exquisite luxuries of Phallock's den....

"There once lived a priestess," Phallock began, after another pleasant feast. He held his mug of mead close to his chest as he sat, leaning up against the cave's wall. The light from the small campfire cast his horns' shadows like two crooked hooks on the ceiling. "A priestess of the Eternal, Baas. Her name was...her name was..." he frowned, then looked over at Rahjule. "What was that priestess's name?"

"Which one?" Rahjule asked, while laying on his back. "Baas had many."

"Oh––the one who rode the waves from Lagophar to Mharadaath," Phallock replied. "The one who––"

"Lysha."

"What...?"

"Lysha's her name," Rahjule repeated.

"Ah..." said a satisfied Phallock. "Lysha. Aye! That was her name.... Lysha, the priestess of Baas. I mustn't forget that name for another 1,000 years. And neither should you," he said, waving his cup (without spilling a single drop of mead) at Jhavon, and all the others who were gathered near the fire.

"We've heard of Lysha," Shurwath said. "Every 2nd year student is learned of the famous priestess who commanded the waves that took her to Mharadaath."

"Hmm..." said Phallock, taking a few gulps. "So you have."

"Aye," the young wizard replied.

"Why did she go all the way to Mharadaath for then?" Phallock asked.

"To save the goddess Morgah, from Ragath," Julie said.

"To do what?!" A deep frown fell over the creature's face.

"To save Morgah."

"To save Morgah?"

"Aye," said Jhavon.

"And how was Lysha supposed to save a goddess?" the confused Phallock asked.

"She hid the goddess in a lake," Jhavon replied. "That's now called Morgah's Lake."

Phallock suppressed a hiccup and looked over toward Rahjule. "All the mead must've muddled up my memories over the years then," he said. "For I recall certain events in my mind that are quite different."

"Your memory's not at fault here, Phallock," said Rahjule, without turning around. "It's their learning."

Pure confusion washed over the creature's face as he turned to regard the students, then back over at Rahjule.

"Their learning...? But Pagaroth's school is the best in all of Hagaraak. Designed to––"

"It was intentionally done," Rahjule said. "Shurlan designed it that way. He didn't teach them everything, lest they become too vain and arrogant in their knowledge. And not only that...one can become quite timid and cowardly if he comes to know certain things all at once. Especially if they know things as we do."

"So he taught them the wrong things, because the truth might discourage them?"

"Not exactly," Rahjule said. "Certain things are better off left not mentioning. They weren't taught the wrong things, for Lysha did ride the waves to Mharadaath. And they did end up going into Morgah's Lake. But that's the extent to their knowledge on that matter. As to what caused them to hide in Morgah's Lake, was intentionally left unsaid."

Phallock swallowed a mouthful of mead, then shook his head. "So they're blind to certain truths then?"

"Aye," Rahjule replied. "Ignorance can have its advantages too. For instance...the trunket boy over there."

All heads turned to Jhavon.

"Through all his schooling," Rahjule continued. "He had never heard of the warrior, Rhonaak. But outside of school, he did learn, and now he wears his armor.... Somehow, Shurlan had foreseen these things. Perhaps he had noticed the discouragement in the earlier generations when the method of his schooling was still young. So he made some necessary adjustments."

"I suppose four years is too short of a time to learn what took us centuries to understand," Phallock said.

"I think that's what Shurlan figured out as well," Rahjule said. "He wanted them to learn and develop along with their destinies. Their schooling was only meant to be basic. They're now engaging in their real schooling. The same way we learned: through experience."

"So they really don't know what happened at Mhraradaath?" asked Phallock, with a certain gleam in his eyes.

"I doubt it."

"Good then...." Phallock brought the mug up to his mouth. "It's time I fulfill my part in all this––as small as it is––and fill in the tiny gaps for them."

Rahjule didn't reply.

"Our story is a real long one," Phallock said to the students, who were all wearing confused looks on their faces. "And yet, to know as much as you do in such a short time is quite amazing."

"I always knew there was more to the whole story," said Syme. "More to the world. More to the Eternals, than what they were teaching us."

"Aye," Phallock said. "Much more."

"More to who we really are as well," Morlah added.

Phallock shot a nervous glance at Rahjule just then. "That would be another lesson," he said. "And from another teacher. In time, you'll be given all the answers you seek." He didn't want to be the one who ruined the fate of the entire universe by mouthing the wrong words. "But tonight..." he went on. "You will learn what really happened in Mharadaath. You see...it wasn't just trunkets and their war-machines that threatened the world––no offense to you,

Jhavon. But had it been that easy, Ragath would've fallen, and the Eternals might still be here today."

"So there were others?" asked Shurwath.

"Aye," Phallock replied. "The trunkets were one race against so many in the world."

"So who were their allies then?" Jhavon asked. "The giants, the treelings, the remnants of Mox?"

"None that inhabits this world," Phallock said. "Ragath brought strange creatures from other realms to assist him. The trunkets were only entrusted with defending their own land. And I must admit, it was a fight they won squarely.

"But anyway––" He paused to refill his mug. "The world was still one when the war began. But Vlak, Llok, and Mox, were already gone. Ragath was bringing huge armies of creatures from different realms to fight the remaining remnants. But these weren't the kind of creatures you saw at Pagaroth; those were hungry beasts with no brains. These creatures were different. They had magic! and the brains to go along with it. They were powerful, and they looked like men––but they weren't. They were bent on destroying all that lived in the world. Maybe Ragath had promised them eternal life, or unlimited power of some sort.

"The Gallgaliums, was the name of their race...aye, if my memory serves me correctly. The Gallgaliums. Eyes white as snow. Not a strand of hair on any part of their bodies. But strange power coursed through their veins. They caused things to become...undone."

"How so, Phallock?" asked Jhavon.

"Well..." Phallock said, as he cleared his throat. "The Gallgaliums were creatures that were made up of raw energy.

A careless wizard might've found himself floating through the air in millions of tiny pieces. And that's what I mean when I say they made things become undone."

"But how come we never learned about these Gallgaliums?" asked Shurwath. "And what happened to them?"

"I think you already know the answer to your first question, Shurwath. But as to what happened to the Gallgaliums...I can answer that for you. It was our very own Lysha, the priestess of Baas, who wiped them out in a single act of sacrifice...most of them anyway. And that was another thing we learned about the Gallgaliums on that day. Their powers were linked. The more they were in numbers, the more powerful they were. But when Lysha cut their numbers by more than half, the last few that remained had very little power to fight us.

"They were invading Hagaraak from both Gargaath and Mharadaath. At first, they seemed unstoppable, and many lives were being lost. So in order to stop their armies from taking over completely, Pagaroth had no other choice but to split the world on both sides and push the lands far apart.

"By this time, the Gallgaliums were destroying Mharadaath. The lykes and rykes, for all their might and strength, were defenseless against them. Millions of trees were set on fire, and the goddess, Morgah, was in danger of being destroyed as well. She cried out to Baas, begged the Eternal to send his armies. But Baas was no longer in existance, so her cries went unheard.

"But no...the priestess, Lysha, heard them. She went into the Sea of Baas, commanding the waters to raise the tides, and she hurled them west——all the way to the land of Mharadaath. And it might have been the entire Sea of Baas that had risen up, for the tidal wave had covered that whole land....Aye...the whole of Mharadaath had once been dipped under water for only Pagaroth knows how long. But when the water finally receded, the Gallgaliums were no more. The goddess, Morgah, had been washed from her temple, and she was carried by the water into the lake. And when she finally emerged, she said the priestess still lay at the bottom of what you now know as Morgah's Lake. To this very day, Lysha's body still rests beneath those waters."

CHAPTER
TWENTY-FOUR

IN ANOTHER REALM, a lone figure had been sitting (in the same position) for countless eons, as if frozen in time.

His white robe had all but rotted into fine dust. The nails on his toes and fingers had grown and buried themselves deep into the ground, like a treeling's roots.

He didn't appear to be any more alive than the rocks that surrounded him. In fact, they appeared to be one and the same, as they both shared the hot windy world. His eyes remained open (and hadn't blinked since the day of his arrival), despite the strong winds that whipped up sand and dust in the air.

For the millionth time perhaps, the sun would cast his shadow on the sand, then slowly spin it around his own body as the day wore on. The yellow horizon dwindled, then blushed into a dark orange. There came a sudden disturbance in the wind's pattern...like a foot, stepping into a stream of running water to disrupt the flow.

For the first time in many millennia, his eyes shifted to the left. He didn't move or become startled as a tall shadow eased up beside him. "The universe must be as vast they say," he suddenly said. His voice was clear, and as deep as e crashing wave.

"It is," Ragath replied. "But it's not infinite."

"And now I know...."

The two didn't say anything else for a while, but watched the horizon as the sun set then rise again. With two suns on either side of the planet, night never fell on the bright world, save for the darkening of the yellow sky. It was impossible for any mortal man to survive on the hot surface with no breathable air.

"Things still remain as they are," he said.

"They do," Ragath replied. "And opposition still remain."

"Opposition comes naturally enough with all things."

"That they do." Ragath looked down at the figure sitting on the ground beside him. His head was baked brown. The face had grown hard, and chiselled like that of a statue. His eyes were all white, and shone fiercely, but Ragath knew nothing escaped them.

"Our purpose still remain intact," Ragath said, staring into the white eyes. He saw power there. A deep, hidden power.

"Only as long as you exist."

"I'm bringing you back," Ragath said.

"There's nothing else left."

"There is," Ragath said, reassuringly. "A boy. The only one of his kind on my world. You'll find him a perfect fit. Even better than what you have now." It was hard to tell what he was looking at, but Ragath sensed that he was secretly regarding his present form. To live in such a prison for such a long time, was indescribable.

———•———

When they broke camp the next day, both Ahnon and Morlah were unable to be roused from sleep. The first assumption had been that the two had fallen under the Mhog's curse again. However, Rahjule assured them that this wasn't the case. He ordered that two cots be made for the sorceress and the mute, which were then used to carry them out of the cave.

"There's a much easier way of doing this," Julie told Syme, as she struggled with her end of the cot from behind. The loose rocks made it difficult for them to keep their footing, and it slowed their pace.

Shurwath and Ermma, hauled Morlah in the first cot up ahead. Rahjule and the trunket still rode on horseback. Phallock still took the lead up front.

"Why waste time then?" Syme said, without looking back at Julie. "It would save me some blisters."

"I'm not sure how the old man would––"

"No need to explain," said Syme. "Just do it, then we'll see what he has to say about it."

They stopped and lowered Ahnon to the ground. Julie pointed her spirit stick at the cot, causing the gem to glow to a soft pink as the mute's body levitated in the air.

"Come," Julie said, mounting her horse that had been walking beside her. "Ermma!" she called to the siren up front.

Both Ermma and Shurwath turned around. Upon seeing Ahnon's floating body, the idea immediately flashed in their minds.

"Why didn't I think of that?" Shurwath asked, lowering Morlah's cot.

With the slow wave of her spirit stick, Julie raised Morlah's cot and caused it to float back to her side, next to Ahnon.

"As long as you have the strength for it," Rahjule said from up front. He kicked the spotted gray into its normal trot, and Phallock was only too grateful to pick up the pace.

The clouds became brighter as the day wore on, though the clustering hills blocked off the sun's light in the horizon. It was the first sign that they were coming out of Pagaroth.

"Mhogs," Rahjule said, pointing to a nearby hill.

On the rocky crags, they stood by the dozens, and watched the travelers go by. Their black robes flapped in the wind and betrayed the sharp dimensions of their gaunt bodies. Large hoods buried their bland faces deep inside, so not even Phallock (with the eyes of a hawk) could see them.

"Great illusionists, they are," Phallock said, stopping just so he could make the comment. "How many do you see on those rocks?"

Jhavon made a quick scan of their numbers.

"I see fifteen," Shurwath said, beating him to the count.

"No, no," said Jhavon. "There's only twelve."

"And I count seventeen," Julie said.

"But you're all wrong," Phallock said. "There's only one Mhog there. He's putting extra things into our heads."

Rahjule's spotted gray neighed frightfully, causing a wave of panic to sweep through all the other horses.

Ermma's reared up, and sent the startled siren sliding off its back. She landed on the rocks, but scrambled out of the way just in time to avoid the horse's hooves as it stumbled back.

The Mhogs suddenly vanished.

"Save the oracle!" Rahjule shouted, riding back towards Julia.

Confusion fell on their faces, for it was the first time they'd ever heard anyone called by that name. They didn't know who they should be saving. And from what? The Mhogs were gone. The horses remained a bit jumpy, but there was nothing that lived, or moved, anywhere around them!

Rahjule brought the spotted gray to a hard stop near Julie, and dismounted. He unwound the black cloak from around his shoulder's, and (all in one swift motion) draped it over Morlah's unconscious body. "We have to protect the girl!" His voice seemed to bounce off the rocks and vibrate the air around them. "By all means!"

The others quickly moved into action, huddling around the old man and the blind sorceress. The armored trunket kept close to Syme as he morphed into the giant ryke. Phallock had already mounted the crag where the Mhogs once stood, but found no one there.

All sound, save for the howling winds, had ceased, and not even a nervous snort could be heard coming from the horses.

All that was left to do now, was wait for the unexpected to happen....

It soon came in the form of hideous growl that made the shying horses cling to the sides of the rocky walls. The fanged jaws of some unknown beast suddenly appeared before the trunket, causing him to stumble back with a loud gasp. He swung the mighty axe at its head, but then it slipped right through (as if through thin air) and chopped the solid ground.

"For Pag's sake, boy!" Phallock said, from the ledge behind them. "It's just an illusion! The Mhogs aren't attacking us!"

"Not just the Mhogs," Rahjule said. "There's something else out there. Just one. It's hiding. I can feel its movements through the ground."

"Look!" said Shurwath, pointing to a single Mhog, coming slowly up the passage.

"A Mhog," Phallock said.

They all stood still as the Mhog approached, expecting another illusion to follow soon. But none came, and the Mhog drew closer till they could all see its blank face. Just a small snout of a nose sat between two pointy cheek bones. The rest of its features, save for its ears, were gone. It had a long egg-shaped head, and its skin was as white as snow.

Seeing such a creature for the first time, brought a revolting recoil from the students.

"What's the meaning of this," Rahjule demanded of the Mhog.

But the Mhog didn't reply. It took a few more steps toward them instead.

"Perhaps he can't see us," Shurwarth said, as the creature approached. The beginnings of a spell was already coming to his lips.

"He sees," Phallock said. "All too perfect, I'm afraid."

The Mhog was now within arm's reach, and it didn't show any signs of stopping or slowing down. It was Syme, who was the first to lose his nerve, as he reached out with a mighty arm to stop the fragile creature. But his hand sunk right through its chest, coming out on the other side.

The Mhog walked right through the lykine's arm, then through his entire body.

"Another illusion then," an astonished Syme said.

They all watched with great curiosity as the apparition moved within their midst, knowing that any attempts of stopping it would be useless.

It went right to Julie's horse, where the two unconscious bodies floated.

Reaching down, the Mhog took the mute's body gently in its arms.

"Ahnon!" Jhavon cried out. He made a move for the Mhog, but the lykine grabbed him by the arm.

"Be still, trunket," Syme said.

Phallock leaped from his spot on the crag's ledge and landed directly behind the Mhog. He tried to pull the mute from the Mhog's grasp, but to everyone's surprise, his hands went right through Ahnon's body!

"All's not what they seem here," Syme told Jhavon. "Look," he said, motioning toward Rahjule.

The old man eyed the Mhog as it held the mute, but he didn't make any further moves. The two faced each other for an intense moment.

"Rahjule don't look concerned in the least," Syme said, close to Jhavon's ear. "Something's going on here, trunket. The old man only care about Morlah at this particular moment."

Just then, the Mhog seemed to regard Rahjule one final time, before vanishing in a shower of white, glimmering lights. The howling winds appeared as if to moan in its wake.

They ryke slowly dissolved into the tall lykine, freeing the trunket from his grasp.

Jhavon hurried over to Rahjule, as the old man was beginning to remove his black cloak from Morlah's body. "You allowed that to happen!" he shouted, angrily. The usual timidity in his tone was now gone.

Rahjule didn't reply, though he regarded the trunket in silence.

"You could've protected them both, but you didn't. Why?! You could've saved him, the same way you saved... Morlah...." He paused when the sudden thought occurred to him. "But you didn't actually save her, did you?"

"What's with all the sacrifices, old man?" Syme asked, coming up beside Jhavon.

Shurwath, Julie, and Ermma, appeared to be asking the same question with their silent, accusing looks.

Phallock avoided their eyes.

"Sacrifice?" Rahjule asked, with a hint of amusement still lingering in his voice. "Sacrifice...? And what do you know of sacrifices, boy?" he spat out the last word at Syme. "Those who have lived for eons, sacrificed themselves for you all...and when Ragath returned, they sacrificed their very souls for you. Those who didn't need lift a finger, have toiled over the centuries to ensure your survival today. Don't speak to me of sacrifices. We're dealing with GODS!!!" Rahjule's mighty voice echoed all throughout the hills in a great tremor, stirring the night-creatures in their caves. "There're rules you don't understand. And if you truly want to live, you will cease acting like little children from now on. Ahnon lives. You need not concern yourselves with him any longer. And trust me, we haven't seen the last of him." With that, Rahjule threw his cloak back on, then mounted the spotted gray and continued down the passage.

Phallock turned to the students with a face that seemed to apologize for the old man's rashness. "These things are never easy," he said. "But Rahjule's right. You have to stop being children. The worst is yet to come." He spun back around and jogged down the narrow passage, quickly catching up to the spotted gray....

Dinner was eaten in silence that night. There weren't any ancient tales being told, and Rahjule had reclined into his usual meditative state on the ground, staring up at the cave's ceiling.

When the sun rose the next day, the sky was brighter than any of them could ever remember, though the shadows of the looming hills became darker. The sulleness that plagued the prior day's mood had remained over their heads like the cursed clouds above. The blind sorceress was still unconscious, floating along beside Julie's horse....

It was just after midday when the narrow passage opened up and the hills became less clustered. They came to a slight incline that grew steeper as they went. Soon, they found themselves climbing up a grassy hill where the thick churning clouds that once covered the entire land of Pagaroth were beginning to thin. And as they came over the hill's crest, the first blue patch appeared in the sky.

———◆———

The howling winds were at least a quarter of a league behind them when they came down the hill.

Looking back, the clustered Hills of Pagaroth appeared like so many tips of carrots bunched together. The dark clouds above the jagged peaks churned slowly, with brief flashes of lightning that sent thunder rolling through the air.

It seemed like they'd spent their entire lives beneath those clouds. So much so, that the thin white sheets that barely covered the blue sky above them appeared unnatural. Even the warmth from the partially hidden sun felt strange, and its light gave the green grass an uncanny hue they weren't used to seeing. Or maybe they'd forgotten that such variety in one color existed.

"That must be Vlak's Forest," Shurwath said to the others.

Rahjule and Phallock were engaged in a deep private conversation up front. Phallock pointed toward the great forest that laid no more than a league from where they stood. Rahjule nodded, as though receiving grave instructions.

"It's apparently so, Shurwath," Ermma said. "For what else lays south, beyond the Hills of Pagaroth?"

"Treelings," Shurwath replied.

"And groths," Jhavon added, with a wry grin.

"Phmp!" Ermma scoffed, while adjusting the bridle on her brown horse. "I'm not concerned with either one."

"Maybe you should," Shurwath said. "From what Mr. Laash had taught us, the groths could be very disagreeable creatures when they want to."

"They'll have no other choice, but to be agreeable with me then," Ermma said. "Lest they want their insides cooked."

Phallock offered a reverent bow to Rahjule (for the last time). "May the Eternals guide you all."

Rahjule returned the sentiment to his old friend. "And may you reside in comfort for the rest of your days." A thin smile deepened all the wrinkles in his face.

"Pagaroth will always be my home," Phallock said. "No matter the outcome."

"Aye.... But there'll only be one outcome I'm afraid. One in which we don't exist."

"Oh...? And what could bring about such outcome? Other than the one in which Ragath destroys the world, of course. But according to prophecy, this isn't so."

Rahjule gave the creature an expectant look. "You don't know this, Phallock?"

"No.... And if I did, it probably slipped my wandering mind a very long time ago."

Rahjule shrugged, then kicked the spotted gray into a light trot. "I suppose the answer might come back to you one of these days," he said over his shoulder.

"Aye," Phallock said. "The answers always do." He chuckled to himself and walked back to the students. "You better hurry on, before the Master leave without you."

"But aren't you coming along?" the trunket asked in a worried tone.

"No," Phallock replied. "My part in this scheme of things has run its course. Maybe when he's up to it, Rahjule might tell you a tale of the once young Phallock, when the Eternals and the Gallgaliums had their little squabble."

CHAPTER
TWENTY-FIVE

VLAK'S FOREST WAS the most enchanting land in all of Hagaraak (aye...even more so than the Red Forest), where hundreds of thousands of creatures made their homes. Where the oldest trees grew watchful eyes that peeped through the rough bark in their trunks to spy on the strangers who rode by.

Life teemed and flourished, and gave the place a unique sound. There were plants that cured, and brought life from death. And plants that killed, and brought death from life; such as the poisonous nettles that guarded all the fruits that were sacred to the Eternal, Vlak. The wary traveler knew to stay clear of any small plants, whose black leaves are lined with orange stripes, where the slightest brush against bare skin can bring a man to his death!

Here, the black wolves are found, with their fluffy black coats and pointy ears. Their yellow eyes are sunk deep into their skulls, and their hungry snarls reveal sharp fangs that drip with slimy drool. However, unlike their cousins who dwell in Lagophar's Wolf Mountains, the black wolves are much smaller in size, standing just 1½ feet tall on all fours. But what they lack in size, they make up in sheer numbers, running with no less than thirty in a pack.

Here resides a wide variety of bears, more than anywhere else in all of Hagaraak. Here be the black bears, the gray bears, the brown bears, and the mightiest of them all: the giant rock bears!

Here be the borrowing fox. A sly creature with pointy ears and thick red fur, that live in holes and hunt below the ground.

Here be the swift-footed lynx, the white deer, the moose, the weasles, and the whispering plants––just to name a few.

Here be the home of the treelings––the remnants of Vlak––guardians of the forest. Then there are the infamous groths: creatures made from vines. In many ways, they can be more powerful than the treelings, for they're incredibly strong, and can coil themselves into shape they like. A chop from the sharpest blade would barely nick the surface on their thick skin. However, unlike the treelings, the groths are mortal creatures, whose life-span stretch no further than two years. At such a time (when death is near) they'll simply hang themselves upon a branch, or wrap themselves around a trunk, where they'll become dry and brittle, eventually crumbling into dust.

There're many groth plants in Vlak's Forest. Little slimy trees, with short vines that squirm like eels on the ground. It's also where the groths are first birthed, breaking themselves away from their parent plant when they grow to be at least twenty feet long.... On nearly all the trees in Vlak's Forest, the brittle remains of these special creatures can be found, hanging along the branches and tree trunks.

Here be the shepherds, the most mysterious of all creatures that live in Vlak's Forest. They were once cause for much debate between the most ancient of elders whenever the topic fell on the shepherds' true origin. With the legs of a man, and torso of a treeling, it was difficult to decide whether the shepherds were the remnants of Vlak, or Llok... or whether they were simply abominations.

But abominations were able to have offspring, whereas the shepherds could not, because their species only consisted of males. Not to mention that the shepherds were immortal creatures, so the question always reverted back to: Who made them...? And why...?

Very few of these shepherds remain in the world today. And they can only be found Vlak's Forest. They were the first creatures to live amongst the trees. The manifestation of a devine pact perhaps, formed by Vlak and Llok––that they may protect the beasts and the trees that live in the woods. Even the ancient Lhonaan, the first remnant of Vlak, and the oldest of all the treelings, cannot remember a time before the shepherds.

Another enchanting creature, though not as mysterious with their magic, are the fairies. Little green things that flutter about on dragonflies' wings––said to be a gift from the goddess, Laap. No taller than a man's hand, and no fatter than a finger, they too are an immortal species that consists of the female sex only....

Jhavon and the others' pleasant ride under the clear blue sky would come to an abrupt end as they were plunged back into the dark shade of the shadowy forest. Only here and there, in tiny little pockets, did the sun's light manage to slip through the dense canopy of the forest to form broad glares and long rays of hazy light.... The sounds of life could be heard everywhere in a wild symphony of chirps, squawks, and whistles....

A wide variety of trees stood all around. But very few were like the ones with the watchful eyes. Nor did they act shy, or pretend to be blind. As the travelers went by, a yellow, reddish eyeball would suddenly open up on a tree trunk and follow them as far as its sockets would allow.

The first tree to ever do this, had started Ermma so much that she nearly jumped from her saddle. The faintest peep of a gasp that slipped through her lips was dangerously unbearable to the rest of her company (any living creature within earshot for that matter), who plugged their ears from the sheer pain of it all.

But as grotesque and evil in appearance these eyes seemed to be, the trees were in fact the most gentle of all the creatures in Vlak's Forest. The main reason being, they were just trees, and nothing more. There couldn't possibly be any real harm beyond the eyes' disturbing gaze. However, this fact did very little to prevent the eeriest sense from being evoked into one's being....

The sudden sound of Rahjule's name being called, didn't stir as much excitement as the watchful trees had once done——for since after her first incident, Ermma had become very alert and expectant of the strangeness around her. The voices however, were tiny, like the squeaks of a dozen mice.

There...swaying from side to side in the soft wind, stood the "plantings" upon their roots. Small plant-like creatures with a single stem for bodies, and two green (or yellow) leaves for arms. Four yellow petals surrounded their white, fluffy faces. Their little beady eyes were barely visible, and only their animated mouths could be seen moving as they gazed up in wonderment at the travelers and shouted. They seemed delighted...almost ecstatic.

"Rahjule!" They shouted in unison. "Rahjule has returned....! The King of the Woods! The King of the Woods! All hail the King of the Woods...! The Queen of the Night. The Queen of the Night. All hail the Queen of the Night....! The Master of the Clouds! All hail the Master of the Clouds...! The Whisperer of heath——" They said the latter in hushed, whispering tones, lest they rouse the wrath of the dreaded whisperer. "All hail the Whisperer of death...shhh...!"

"The Oracle...look!!!" one plantling yelped, pointing with a leafy hand. "She's injured. The Oracle's injured! The Oracle's injured!"

The little creatures had gathered by the hundreds on both sides of the trail by now. Standing merely six inches tall, they followed the travelers on their frail roots, repeating the same chants.

Staring down at Morlah's limp body as it floated along beside Julie's horse, there weren't any doubts in the students' minds as to who this so-called "Oracle" was.

"You ever heard of such things?" Shurwath asked Jhavon.

"No," Jhavon replied, shaking his head. He'd been busy staring at the plantlings all around them. Every few minutes, their numbers seemed to double. "I can't say that I have. I think we were taught more about Mharadaath, than Vlak's Forest.... Never heard of such creatures. Nor did I know that trees can grow eyes."

"Not those I'm talking about," said Shurwath. Though he was curious about the watchful trees, he had more pressing matters on his mind. "I meant, the way these plants called Morlah the Oracle. Rahjule had called her by that exact name, and he was much eager to protect her against that Mhog. And not only that——but what about all those other names: kings, queens, and whisperers...? It's obvious that they were talking about us."

"Aye," the trunket said. "Rahjule had said the same thing to me a while ago. He know what the names mean, and who's to be called what."

"And what about these little plants here? I doubt they have any brains. But it's obvious they know of things that we don't. How could this be?"

Jhavon shrugged, though the answer wasn't too far beyond him. "There are many things of this world we don't know about."

"Aye.... I'm beginning to realize this myself."

"There's one other name I heard from Rahjule, that these little plants didn't say."

"Oh...? And which name is that?"

"The Soul Demon."

"Soul Demon?"

"Aye...."

"One of us?" Shurwath looked surprised.

"Aye," Jhavon replied. "But he isn't here. I'm guessing that's why the plants didn't say his name."

"Ahnon..." The revelation sent chills down the wizard's spine.

"Aye...."

"Is that a good, or a bad thing?"

The trunket shook his head with a doleful sigh. "I'm afraid that only Rahjule knows the answer to that question."

"And I have a strong feeling that he isn't going to tell us before we find out for ourselves...."

The day drew on until the dusk crept in and darkened the sky. Tall lamps, made from stout joints of bamboo, stood in the midst of the trees all around to light their path in the encroaching darkness. The sounds of the day were beginning to die down, just as the creatures of the night were coming awake.

They rode on for another league, before recognizing the vague shapes of huts slowly going by. The night had totally set in by then, and the milky moon glowed bright amongst the stars. The bamboo lamps became more dense, and when looking behind, one could see the difference between their sparsity and the darkness beyond.

"I wonder who lit all these lamps?" Ermma asked.

"There must be thousands of them," Shurwath said.

"It must be the fairies," said Julie.

"Bah!" Shurwath said in a dismissive tone. "You don't really believe in that jest, after all we have seen and been through. Almost nothing is as we were taught."

"Not at all true," said Syme.

"He's right, Shurwath," Ermma said. "According to Phallock, it's not what we have been told that's the problem. It's what we haven't been told."

"And there's more we need to learn," Jhavon added.

"But I haven't seen a single fairy since we entered this forest. Not even one groth...and they were said to be more than ants."

"But what about all the vines we see hanging from nearly every tree?" Julie asked. "And some didn't look too dead to me, either. I even thought I saw one move."

"It still looks like a regular old forest to me," Shurwath said. "Except for the trees with the eyes...and even they appear to be no more different from any other wood."

—————●—————

The first treeling appeared beside a tall (bamboo) hut, standing under the brightness of two lamps, with a dark cloak hiding its face. Then more came into view—most having at least one lamp that shone above their gabled roofs, where entire families of treelings had gathered outside.... None followed. Nor did they cheer the travelers on, as the jovial plantlings had once done. They all just stood by silently...and watched....

Similar to the elders of Pagaroth's castle, the treelings wore different colored robes—though not as bland, or formal. Their colorful attire seemed to be more of a personal preference than out of any custom or rule. And they all appeared to be of fairly modest height (except for the much smaller children of course); the average standing about six feet tall, though it's widely known that a treeling can stretch themselves much taller.

As the trees became less clustered, a clearing soon opened up to reveal an infinite pool of stars in the sky above.

There were seven giant statues standing in the middle of the clearing, to represent the likeness of the seven Eternals (even Ragath) that once walked the earth. They were surrounded by dozens of tall lamps that provided a circle of light at least eighty yards in diameter. Thin streams of water arched from the hands and mouths of each Eternal, to splash into the small pool with loud gurgling sounds....

Rahjule brought the spotted gray to a halt as two treelings appeared from the clearing to meet them. And just as Phallock had once done, they both offered their reverent bows to the old man before they addressed him.

"As always, Rahjule," the treeling, dressed in a black robe began. "Your timing is well perfected. And the stars have predicted as much."

"Things are bound to unfold upon us all, Lhonaan," Rahjule said.

"I hope all was well with your travels through the Hills of Pagaroth," the treeling in the blue robe said. There was a hint of concern in his voice. "I see that two horses are missing their riders." His big eyes shifted over to the sorceress's body that was floating beside Julie's horse. "And one's barely breathing."

"The Oracle lives," Rahjule replied.

"Then the other has already gone to fulfill his destiny?" Lhonaan asked.

"Aye," Rahjule said. "That he has."

The treeling looked past Rahjule, and noticed the weary look on the students' faces. "The others must be tired from their journey," he said. "Come with us, Rahjule." He reached out to grab the spotted gray by its reins, but then brought his hand back as the horse gave a violent snort. "I see the old beast hasn't lost her temper."

"No," said Rahjule. "She hasn't. The lykine boy back there can attest to that."

The two treelings looked over at the hideous scar that ran back along the side of Syme's face.

"Very well then," said Lhonaan, with as much of a smile as his wooden face would allow. "We'll see how she takes to her brother back in the stables. I'm sure they'll be happy to be united after all these eons."

CHAPTER
TWENTY-SIX

JHAVON WAS AWOKEN to the sound of snapping twigs. Through the fogginess of a groggy mind, he could barely make out the beams of hazy light that slipped through the narrow creases in the hut. He could smell the faint aromas of cooked vegetables and incense. Then he heard the vague sound of voices, and laughter....

He sat up with a stiff yawn and scratched at his tangled mass of black hair. His mouth felt hot and sticky, but at least his body was refreshed. Nearby, both Syme and Shurwath still snored by their own corners of the hut. Julie and Ermma slept elsewhere––while Morlah, accompanied by Rahjule and Lhonaan, had been taken to some other place with extreme care.

It was the first time being separated since their journey began. He remembered the tall treeling in the blue robe was very stern about women sleeping in different huts. He thought they were perculiar creatures. However...he did admit to himself that they had all slept in different dorms when they were still at the castle.

A sudden pounding rattled the hut's door. Both Syme and Shurwath jumped out of their sleep.

"Is anyone in there?" someone asked, before pounding on the door again.

"If Lhonaan says they're in there," he heard another voice (from outside) say. "Then they must be in there."

"Then why aren't they answering?"

"I don't know...."

"Maybe we have the wrong hut, Ghalum."

"Nonsense, Rhaal. We prepared these huts ourselves. The witches slept in the other one.... Strange creatures, these outsiders are. Things of the night. I'm willing to wager."

"Aye. Things of the night, they must be then. They look pale in the light. And did you see those two witches? All puffy-eyed and haggard-faced, as if they hadn't seen the sun in all their young lives."

"Aye...I saw them.... Ghaslty looking little creatures."

Jhavon, listening quietly inside, heard the one named Ghalum, reply.

"I can't begin to imagine what these ones, in here, might look like."

"Wizards, they say," Rhaal, said.

It seemed the two treelings had forgotten all about their assigned tasks, to pick up on some other chore of idle gossip. Jhavon, Syme, and Shurwath, all exchanged amused looks with each other, while listening to the conversation outside. But eventually (and very soon) they grew bored and impatient.

Syme found a small rock and threw it at the door.

Outside, the busy chattering stopped.

"We were sent to see if all is well," the one named Ghalum said. "The midday meals are about to be served. And after that, you'll be needing to see Lhonaan."

As if by its own will, the door swung outward, and the very alert treeling caught it in his hand––feeling the power of Syme's magic fade in the process. "You'll have to be quicker than that, wizard," Ghalum said. His tall frame cast a long shadow between the light that spilled into the hut.

"He's no wizard," Shurwath said, looking up from his mattress on the ground. He was surprised to see that the treelings were wearing purple robes (same color as his own robe) but he didn't show it. "That was lykine's magic. They are good at making things move and flying all about. So it's him——" he jerked a thumb over at Syme. "Who you should be to talking to then. Wizards change things. And had it been wizard's magic, that door might not have been a door at all."

"Nor was I trying to be quick," Syme added. "I was merely opening it. Or don't they teach you these things in Vlak's School of Merit?"

The treelings shifted their gazed from Shurwath, to Syme. "We know more than you think, lykine," said Rhaal.

"And perhaps," Ghalum cut in. "More than you were taught as well."

"So the School of Vlak, create mostly actors then," said Syme, with a wry grin.

"Aye," added Shurwath. "In Pagaroth, we were taught no such things."

———◆———

In a more elaborately built structure, with furnished rooms (and windows), three tiny fairies hovered over an unconscious Morlah. So effortless was their flight, it seemed their transparent wings barely moved beyond the single flap that appeared so subtle, it looked more like a nervous twitch––or the bat of an eyelid––than a necessity of staying afloat.

Long fiery hair flowed down the small of the fairies' backs, and whipped ever so slowly as if submerged in water. Their green gowns also moved about with the same slow effect, that often caused one to wonder if the fairies existed within their own bubbles of altered time....

"She could die if she stays like that," Rahjule said to Lhonaan as they looked on, just beyond the threshold of the room. "The body cannot live too long without food. Not even one that's in as deep a sleep as she is."

No longer under Julie's levitating spell, Morlah was once again laying on her back. But this time, she rested on a soft mattress instead of a cot. The fairies, with their eyes closed and faces furrowed in deep concentration, whispered their soft incantations––with their tiny hands joined, while they rotated in slow circles over the sorceress.

"I find it hard to believe that the Mhogs would interfere in this business," Lhonaan said. "Even after hearing your account of what happened. I still can't see what role they played in all this. They're merely prankish tormentors. They have nothing at all to gain by helping Ragath. Or killing the girl for that matter."

"My thoughts were the same at first," Rahjule said. "And now...I'm not quite sure that it was a Mhog that took the boy, either."

"Aye..." said Lhonaan, after a moment's thought. "One disguised as a Mhog, most likely."

"A trick meant for the eye," Rahjule said. "The Mhogs are peaceful creatures. Harmless to those who are gifted in the mind. And we both know there aren't too many of those.

But this one had power, Lhonaan. Limitless amounts. I felt it. And so did Phallock. It was there one instant, and gone the next. No Mhog can do such a thing. And I know of only one creature that can. A creature not of this world."

"No." Lhonaan shook his head in doubt. His little twig-nose twitched on his wooden face. "Those beings had been wiped out eons ago. There's no more left. And even if there were, their numbers would barely be enough for just one to summon the kind of power that you're describing to me now. Or maybe your own senses betray you."

"And Phallock's as well?" Rahjule stared into the treeling's owlish eyes. "Very doubtful Lhonaan. We never knew the full extent of their power. There could be an entire new race of them on some other world.... Besides..." he said, after a moment's pause. "They have caused too much destruction in these lands for either one of us to ever forget. I know a Gallgalium when I see one."

———•———

The treelings didn't eat meat (or anything else for that matter). Like all trees and plants, they got their nutrients front the soil. And being such simple creatures, there wasn't much to be seen inside their villages that one would consider to be extraordinary, either. Just a cluster of huts, of various shapes and sizes, that served different functions. Even the famous School of Vlak, was nothing too special to look at (given the small population of the village), with just a few larger huts that made up the classes where the young treelings learned their lessons.

323

The forest, and all that dwell within it, were sacred. Only through the means of bare necessity did the treelings make their homes. Nothing was ever killed or slaughtered. Even the bamboo that was used to make their huts had been transplanted from one section of the forest to another. Thus, the bamboo still lived, and never dried or turned brittle––but retained its natural green for many centuries.... The treelings themselves lived a very long time, and even the youth among them (Ghalum and Rhaal, for example) might be no less than forty years old....

It would seem that the treelings had forgotten all their chores for the day and chose to follow behind their visitors around the village instead. For many, despite being familiar with all the different beasts that lived in Vlak's Forest, it was the first time that many of them had ever laid eyes on a trunket, even though their school taught them that such creatures (and many more, far stranger) existed in Hagaraak.

"'Tis true," Rhaal said, to Jhavon and the others. "The Martyr's Lake do feed the Ghi River. But it's the Whirling Pools that feed the entire Vlak's Forest."

They had all gathered near the huge marble statue of the Eternal, Vlak. The finely carved features of the Eternal's long narrow face, with its pointy chin, nose, and ears, resembled those of the treelings. His head was bowed as if looking down. A thick jet of water gushed from his mouth and open palms, pouring into the swirling pool below that spun like a small maelstrom.

"We have no rivers here," Rhaal went on. "No streams, no creeks, no fish. Below these lands, churn the largest of all Hagaraak's lakes. And all throughout the forest, you'll see pools such as these. They provide all the forest's creatures with their drink."

"Isn't it all so strange, Jhavon?" Ermma said, close to the trunket's ear. "Like another world. So different from Pagaroth and Danwhar. And I'm guessing you don't see these things in Ragath, either."

"Aye..." Jhavon replied. "You've guessed right."

They all found Vlak's Forest to be the strangest land they ever saw. And more stranger, were the treelings themselves. The females looked no different from the males of their species. They could only be distinguished from the lighter color robes they wore (yellow, green, and orange), while the males wore the darker colors (black, red, and blue).

The School of Pagaroth had never portrayed the likeness of any of the Eternals––carved, painted, sculpted, or otherwise. Only the different attributes of the Eternals were taught, such as various symbols, words, and signs. All other perceptions and ideas were attained through myth and legend. So even though the students did retain some general idea of what the Eternals might've looked like, they didn't know for sure how they looked.

The treelings at the School of Vlak, however...did!

Forming a large circle around the whirling pool, were the statues of all the Eternals in their exact shape and form when they once walked the earth. From the statue of Vlak, the treelings led them clockwise to the frozen image of Llok.

Despite the accuracy of the folklore that was told by the descendants of Llok throughout the generations, the description of the Eternal had somehow waned from its original version over the countless centuries. Where the short horns and pointed ears remained, the Eternal's fox-like face had never been. Here, stood a statue with surprisingly humanoid features. The wrinkles in his robe captured perfectly by a sculptor's chisel. Long slender hands struck out from the sleeves, where water gushed from the open palms into the pool below.

They then came to the Eternal, Baas, who appeared just as normal, but without the horns and pointy ears. His forehead looked flat as he bent over the whirling pool to expel water from his mouth.

Pagaroth looked like an old man, instead of some dirt-rock creature as he was often painted on canvas.

The Eternal Laap, looked as beautiful as any woman. A seren expression was frozen on here face, while the water that spilled from her mouth had sort of ruined the image. Instead, she appeared to be disgusted, as if vomiting....

No one knew for sure how the trunkets came to be such small creatures. According to legend, the Eternal Ragath was just as small. However, the statue that confronted them now, appeared to be equal in size with the other Eternals.

Not even the Eternal Mox, for all his diversity of character and virtue, had lived up to the expectations of those who often painted his image as a cloud, in the shape of a man. For there stood a solid, though unique creature from all the rest. His face was that of a bull, with two thick horns curling out the sides of his head. Two great wings stretched out from his back. Only his feet appeared to be that of a man's, as the tips of his toes jotted out from under the hem of his robe.

Streams of water flowed from the palms and mouths of all the Eternals. A symbol that signified their contribution to the continuous pool of life. Even Ragath had a place in the vital cycle, and played a critical role in life's continuum....

The day ran its course...and as night pulled its blanket of stars across the heavens, the treelings were beginning to settle themselves back into the comfort of their own homes.

Elsewhere, more dire matters were being tended to, for Ragath still had his plans sat upon the world, and Morlah still remained unconscious.

In an adjacent room, from where the sorceress slept, Jhavon and the others were gathered around Rahjule, Ghaan, and Lhonaan. The latter was holding a small golden box in his hand. The same one that he received from Shurlan on his last visit to Pagaroth four years ago.

It had long been decided by Shurlan, that as the time of Ragath's return drew near, the golden box should be removed. And where should such a sacred thing be kept safely hidden, other than in Vlak's Forest...?

The treeling handed the box over to Rahjule, who didn't waste any time in opening it up. A large chunk of Ragath's sapphire sat inside while washing the old man's face in a soft, bluish light.

"Is that what I think it is?" A wonderous Ermma asked.

"It can only be that," an equally amazed Julie replied.

Rahjule dumped the sapphire in his palm, then held it up for all to see. Sharp, jagged edges remained where the countless tiny shards had pieced themselves back together.

"Pagaroth's stone....!" The words slipped through Shurwath's mouth without him even realizing it.

Even the trunket was at a lost for words, though for a different reason. Over the years, he'd forgotten all about the tiny jewel he'd given to Shurlan for his admittance into the school. It seemed he'd forgotten all about the gem as soon as it left his hand; mostly because he'd placed no special importance on the thing. He'd seen so many precious stones and jewels while he was an apprentice at Ghraan's shop, that he'd hardly thought anything of the stone at all.

But then another thought occurred to him. One that hadn't occurred to him before, not even after Ragath's return. He did remember holding the shard in those years past, and Shurlan must surely have known what it was—Rahjule as well. And no soul, other than the Eternals and their remnants, may touch the stone and live. Not even the tiniest of shards. Then surely, both Rahjule and Shurlan had been playing along, and there was more to the—

"Ragath has the rest of it," Rahjule said suddenly, breaking up the trunket's train of thought.

"Are you certain of it?" asked Ghaan.

"Aye," Rahjule replied. "I can't find any more of the remaining shards."

"But you could've easily—"

"I didn't," Rahjule shot back, cutting Lhonaan's words short. "I purposely left the other shards for Ragath to find. I rather deal with a hungry god, than a ravenous one."

"Then he'll come searching for them," Lhonaan said, not caring to hide his concern. "Now that the stone's out of the box, I'm certain he's had a whiff of it by now."

"Perhaps," Rahjule said, as he turned to face Jhavon. "But he won't come here." He motioned for the trunket to open, his hand, then sat the stone in his giant palm.

A chorus of astonished gasps filled the entire room as all those present watched the trunket take hold of the Eternal's stone! All (except Rahjule) had expected the poor trunket to drop to a lifeless corpse on the ground—–but when he didn't, they became confused, and fearful, because they weren't quite sure what it meant that a powerless trunket could do this....

Jhavon closed his palm while he held the stone, just as he'd done four years before. A strange feeling came over him, and he felt he knew exactly what he had to do.

"He certainly won't come here as long as the trunket has the stone." Rahjule was still looking down at Jhavon. A cunning smile nearly cracked his face, but then it was gone. "Pagaroth's stone now belong to you, boy," he said. "I don't think you'll ever have to worry about anyone trying to steal it. But losing it can be a much simpler matter. Do you think you can prevent that?"

There was a long pause before the trunket could finally gather his wits. He began to nod. "Aye, sir," he said. "I'll never lose sight of it."

"Hmph...!" Rahjule didn't seem convinced by the trunket's timid reply. But then he sighed, as if to say; what other choice did they all have? "For you sake, boy" he began. "And ours as well. I hope that you never do. Ragath's hands can be as quick as his thoughts. And at times, they can be even quicker. Especially in times like these."

"I won't lose it, sir," Jhavon said. "I'll keep it safe for the rest of my days."

A loud scream erupted in the adjoining room that startled them all. Then came the sounds of the fairies' frantic little voices. Their ancient language incoherent to all, except Rahjule and the two treelings. One of them zipped past the doorway in a hurry; her tiny body a red blurry streak.

"It appears that our Oracle has awaken from her long nap," said Rahjule, forgetting all about the trunket and the stone for the moment. "I wonder what lovely dreams she's been having?"

"Or nightmares, from the sounds of it," said Lhonaan.

"I see things are already setting themselves in motion," said Ghaan, eyeing the bright blue light that glowed between the creases of Jhavon's closed fist. "I really do pray that you don't lose that thing."

Two fairies came floating into the room just then. Tiny beads of sweat, like liquid crystals, sparkled on their foreheads as they bowed before the treelings. One of them addressed Ghaan in ancient tongue.

"All's well with the Oracle," Ghaan said. "She woke with quite a scare, and I think she might still be a little shaken."

"Do you suppose that it could've been the sight of the fairies that gave her such a fright?" asked Lhonaan.

"How could they?" asked Ghaan, with a shrug. "She's blind."

———•———

When they came into the room, Morlah was already sitting up on the edge of her cot. Her face looked calm; her head tilted up, as though trying to peer into the hollow of the bamboo in the ceiling. And though she didn't show any signs of acknowledging their presence, they all knew that she was well aware that they were standing nearby....

"Morlah," Julie decided to be the first one to address the sorceress. They all kept a safe enough distance from her, cautious of a sudden, panicked attack. However, long moments went by without Morlah saying anything. "Morlah," Julie repeated, stepping a bit closer this time. "It's——"

"I know who it is," Morlah suddenly said. Her voice was surprisingly clear, and sharp...unrestrained. "Has the stone found its carrier?" she asked. "Or am I too late?"

"You're just in time," Rahjule said, matter-of-factly. "The stone has found its carrier, and he's here with us now."

Oddly, Morlah appeared to give a sigh of relief. "Then it isn't too late," she said. "It hasn't occurred yet. The end can still be avoided."

"Ragath doesn't waste any time now, do he?" said Ghaan.

"And why should he?" Rahjule shot back. "By right, the stone do belong to him. He only wants it back. But tell us, Oracle..." he turned back towards Morlah. "Tell us about what's soon to happen."

She told them....

———•———

In the bleakest, darkest hour of the morning, a black hole swirled into existance amongst the jumbled mass of trees and bushes.... From out of this portal came a shadow's smoke, as thin as vapor, as it allowed itself to be taken by the gentle breeze. So subtle, so natural it seemed, that not even the vigilant trees with watchful eyes were able to detect the menace that slipped past their trunks. Nor could the plantlings feel the evil as it brushed up against their petals and leaves.

This would be his fifth——out of the nine treeling clans——having swept through the slumbering villages of the

Hytes, the Khollaphs, the Mauls, the Paaks, and finally...the Jhaabs. Aye! It was the Jhaab-clan's village that the portal had taken him to now. He could tell from the sound of the water splashing into the whirling pool; the light from the pole lamps surrounding the statues of the Eternals. And though all the treeling clans possessed whirling pools in their villages, only the Jhaabs possessed the statues of the Eternals––the largest and most dominant of all the clans.... He secretly wondered why he hadn't been sent there first....

The demon's mist spread itself thin, drifting beyond the pole lamps that lit the yards. He clung to the shadows, this misty haze, allowing not the faintest trail for the eye to see––whether it be treeling, man, or fairy. And soon, he spread himself so thin that he covered the entire village, settling between the short blades of grass so not even the flickering lights of the lamps could betray his location. A mere trick indeed, however, one in which very of his kind could repeat to such a fine degree.

He then lifted himself, coming through the narrow creases of a hut's bamboo floor, slowly, lest the sensitive fairies feel his presence.

Slowly...the fine sheet of mist retreated like warm steam on a cool glass. He squirmed his way through the floor, up into the dark room where he collected himself. All remained hidden in the dark, save for his glowing red eyes. He easily found what he sought. On smoky feet, he slid stealthly across the room and retrieved the small golden box with his only remaining hand. But then a bright light suddenly flashed, blinding the demon while the sharp blade of an axe bit into his arm at the elbow! The box fell through the severed limb and landed on the floor with a soft 'clunk.'

Ohlar howled in pain while he tried to puff himself back into his shadowy form. However, only a fraction, of his cloudy mist managed to squeeze through the hut outside, before he fell dead——floating down to the floor as fine specks of sparkling dust!

CHAPTER
TWENTY-SEVEN

THE NEXT DAY found the Jhaab-clan's village the same as it always had for thousands of years. The animals and the villagers would draw their daily water from the whirling pool. The young treelings would receive their schooling in their classrooms. And the elders would walk through the forest, conversing with both plant and beast about the wonders of life.

Long gone, was Ragath's portal, along with the dusty remains of the demon, once known as Ohlar. Life in Vlak's Forest carried on as usual, as if his death hadn't occurred there at all....

"I should think that Shurlan had raised himself quite a vicious lot," Lhonaan said, while riding through the forest on his black horse. "I almost fear for those who must face them."

"You shouldn't be that much afraid then," Rahjule said, riding close by on his spotted gray. "They'll have many who'll come up against them. And they have so much more to learn, in so little time."

"I don't think it matters," said Lhonaan. "They're only children. And yet, their talents have developed beyond most things of this world. Their training must've been very intense. Not even Shurlan and Morella could succeed in killing that shadow when he tried to steal Ragath's scrolls. Shurlan once told me that it was impossible to kill a shadow—especially the one who came for the stone this morning. But the trunket and the witch did it with much ease. How's this so, Rahjule?"

"Luck...! They had the advantage of surprise on their side. Shurlan and Morella did not. If it hadn't been for the Oracle, Ragath migth've had his stone by now...changing things, making things disappear."

"Aye..." Lhonaan shuddered at the thought. "The day belong to the Oracle then."

"Many days will belong to her...."

They rode mostly in silence for another league before the path began to veer to the east.

Lhonaan stopped, causing everyone else to do the same. "Best of luck, Rahjule," he said, staring deep into the man's ancient eyes. "Look after them; and yourself."

"Aye," Rahjule replied with a nod. "And may you continue to watch over the forest for many more eons to come."

"I don't think that's up to me now." Lhonaan's black horse leaned closer toward the spotted gray, then nozzled her affectionately with two quick licks on her nose. "Kiss and made up, have we?" Lhonaan observed. His black horse gave a bashful shake of its head.

"They are siblings after all," Rahjule rubbed the spotted gray gently along her neck. "I'm quite certain the witch back there could find a way to change them back, once all this is over with."

"Aye.... I think that might be something we all wish to see someday."

"Someday," Rahjule said in return. And with that, the two exchanged nods and parted ways.

On his way back, the treeling bid his farewells and best wishes to Jhavon and all the others who had been riding along closely behind. Then he was off at a canter back toward his village....

"So tell me, Morlah," Julie said, as they continued on their journey through the forest. "What do the end of the world look like?"

"The world never ends," Morlah said, looking well at ease as she rode along the path. "It only transcends."

"But didn't you say the end of the world could still be avoided if we stopped the shadow from stealing Pagaroth's stone?" asked Jhavon.

Morlah shook her head. "I didn't say the end of the world could be avoided. I only said 'the end', can be avoided. I wasn't talking about the world; but the end of things as we know it. All that the Eternals have created."

"Oh..." Jhavon said, then paused to rummage through the many questions that taxed his brain. "Then what will the world look like? A world where Ragath regains his power?"

Morlah shrugged. "I don't know."

"You don't know...?" asked Shurwath.

"No."

"But you said you saw it. The end of all the things the Eternals have created."

"I didn't see it," Morlah said to Shurwath. "I didn't see that far into the future. I only saw the shadow stealing the stone. The rest, I summed up for myself. As anyone would imagine how things might be if Ragath regains Pagaroth's stone."

A stunning, yet simple realization dawned in their minds as they considered this new revelation. The blind sorceress had obviously changed upon waking up from her long slumber.... Vlak's Forest was undoubtedly a very enchanted land that held many secrets, and yet, she hadn't voiced any warnings to some of the mysterious creatures that lurked amongst the trees as they rode by. Not even the unravelling vines that wrapped themselves up into two young ghroths, sitting atop a low-hanging branch. Normally, she would've alerted them from as far as one-hundred yards in advance; but all she did now, was smile and nod up at the curious creatures as they past by below them....

"Have you ever heard of a Mhog, Morlah?" Julie asked, after riding a quarter of a league in silence.

"Aye," Morlah replied. She then gave a melancholic sigh, as if remembering a pleasant thought. "The Mhogs are such wonderful and peaceful creatures. They taught me how to strengthen my power...how to enhance my sight."

"Bah...!" said Syme with a snort. "Wonderful, peaceful creatures, eh...? Is that why they stole Ahnon from us?"

Something in Morlah's face flashed––like surprise–– but then it was gone. She shook her head. "No, Syme," she said. "Whatever took Ahnon away from us, was no Mhog."

———◆———

Ahnon jumped out of his long sleep with a dreadful start. Horror, mixed with confusion, muddled his mind. Something had gone terribly wrong! His body tingled all over. He felt numb. The air was hot and stuffy, making it uncomfortable to breath.

The floating balls of glowing light seemed to pause momentarily in the air, as though becoming alarmed by the sudden noise below. Slowly, they floated down through the cavern, bumping into each other like blind fireflies. They reached the boy and clustered around him, moving in slow circles of blinding light while leaving the rest of the cavern in darkness.

Ahnon brought up a hand to shield his eyes.

"I see the stone is being donned once more," Ragath said. His deep, sonorous voice resonated throughout the entire cavern.

"Rahjule...?" asked Zhorghan. "Walking the land again, after all these years. It seems he's been planning a few things as well."

"Perhaps."

"And where's the stone now?"

"With the remnants of Vlak.... Other matters are secretly brewing. Quite naturally of course, but I'll tend to more immediate chores at hand..." Ragath paused to extend a motioning hand toward Ahnon, who was still encircled by the glowing balls of light. "Here's my gift to you. Though it may never amount to what you've lost––I must say that it comes close."

"Such a fragile thing," a third, raspy voice joined in.

Ahnon heard a shifting sound just beyond the light–– like dragging feet... but then it stopped. He felt the presence of three beings, watching him closely in the darkness; all ancient, all...very powerful....

"Why did you bring me here? Do you mean to do bring me harm?" Zhorghan suddenly found himself blurting. "Huh...?" the confused wizard faltered, feeling at his own mouth that seemed to have spoken on its own accord. He turned to Ragath. "I did not say that!"

The Eternal laughed. He had expected such a thing, however, he was still delightfully amused by Zhorghan's bewilderment. "Not such a fragile creature after all," he said. "This one's gifted in special ways. And yet, he's still very young in life. A remnant of Llok (much older than you) had found him. Molded him to become what he is now."

"Or rather..." the raspy voice began; the sound of hunger stifling his words. "What he's destined to become."

Ahnon could hear the shifting sounds starting up again, coming closer. Soon, the clustered balls of light parted, allowing a hideous creature to come crawling through. It was nothing but skin on bone, clothed with loose rags hanging from his gaunt body. And yet, a power beyond imagination radiated through the whites of his eyes. A mask of pure evil clung to his bony face.

Ahnon scrambled back! struggling to get on his feet, but only succeeded in stumbling and crashing back down on the glowing balls that were too slow to move out of his way.

"Don't hurt me!!!" Zhorghan blurted out again. And this time, a lethal bolt of lightning shot out from his hand, right into the back of Ahnon's pursuer.

But the creature seemed unphased by the wizard's attack (that would've surely blown a human being to pieces). It simply absorbed the bolt's energy.

"Don't let him control you, Zhorghan," Ragath said (out of sheer boredom). "He's only a boy. Hide your soul where he can't find it."

"Hmmm..." the creature said (in a thirsty way), while he gazed down at the cowering Ahnon. A new surge of hunger flashed in his eyes. "I think you've done well this time, Ragath. This boy, who can steer the soul, will do me just fine." The creature's skeletal body suddenly collapsed to the ground like a bunch of twigs––only the thin film of a bluish haze remained standing in its place. It took two more steps and grabbed the frightened boy by his curly hair. With its other ghost-like hand it punched right into Ahnon's mouth so that its arm was swallowed up, then the shoulder, the head, the torso...until the whole ghost stuffed itself inside the mute's body.

Now standing alone, and encircled within the cluster of lights, Ahnon's eyes flashed just as the skeletal creature's had once done. Then he flexed his arms and legs, examining the small hands and neat finger-nails in the light....

"I don't think you could've hid your soul from this boy, Zhorghan," Zhorghan heard himself say (again!). He looked over at the creature (now Ahnon) radiating with new power within the circle of light. "He's a great pretender, you know...."

END....

Printed in the United States
by Baker & Taylor Publisher Services